UNBREAKABLE

What Reviewers Say About Cari Hunter's Work

Breathe

"It's not always easy to explain why you like a book, what makes you give it five stars. Some books I love because they make me feel warm and cozy, others because they make me happy, others... because they bring this excited energy I associate with childhood, this feeling of sheer freedom. Others, and this one falls into this category, because they make me feel my brain working, the cogs turning. In other words, they make me feel alive."—*Jude in the Stars*

"Hunter carries on her tradition of writing great characters, heartfelt moments, and relevant thrillers. Her ability to write the medical stuff is great, as it feels real without being too technical."—Colleen Corgel, Librarian, Queens Public Library

"This book turned out to be an unexpected treasure...Jem and Rosie are both lovely, their relationship is precious and their conversations are so much fun. The book is as much relationship (not simply romance...it is a well developed relationship) as it is crime. The characterisations are excellent. ...Definitely recommended."
—*reviewer@large*

Alias

"The storyline, following the main character as she tries to work out who she is and why she came to in a crashed car on a mountain road, is incredibly engaging. ...As the main character is suffering from amnesia, she learns about herself at the same pace as the reader, which adds another interesting aspect to the story. ...This book has a great storyline with an excellent mystery to solve, and is well worth a read."—*Books at the End of the Alphabet*

"*Alias* is written in first person from the point of view of the amnesiac woman which gives us perfect access to her headspace. …Along with the characters, the reader slowly brings the pieces of the puzzle together. We suffer and get frustrated with the slow progress in reconstructing the events, the plot teasing us with incomplete memory flashbacks. Even though we know all that the character learns about herself, and without playing tricks on us, Ms. Hunter manages to deliver a twist at the end."—*Lez Review Books*

"[O]ne thing you can count on is that when you pick up a book by Hunter it is going to be awesome."—*Romantic Reader Blog*

"Cari Hunter's novels give you a kick as dependable as the sunrise and twice as exciting. Her latest, *Alias*, is no exception. Hunter's Dark Peak series is fast-paced and action-packed, and I wondered how she'd be away from those characters, and I can say she's still bloody marvelous. Hunter expertly ratchets up the tension, only deflating it long enough for the reader to breathe before another break-in or revelation happens. To say she has an aptitude for action scenes would be understating the case tremendously. *Alias* is one of Hunter's best rides—a rollercoaster with some mean peaks, some wicked drops, and left turns when you least expect them. Highly recommended, and I'm not just being nowty."—*Out in Print*

The Dark Peak Series

"Gruesome and compelling, mostly snowing and refreshingly English. They don't drink 'tea,' they 'make a brew' in this book. Sometimes they have 'a chippy' for supper. When it gets bad, they have a kebab. Use caution when reading the first 20% of any of the Dark Peak books right before bed, they start with a bang. Not a literal bang, but a pretty gruesome murder. You have been warned."—*She Sighed Blog*

A Quiet Death—*Lambda Literary Award Finalist*

"This cracking good mystery also has a thorough respect for the various ethnic subcultures it explores. I learned things, which is never bad for a reader. Moreover, it has a distinctly British flavour, not pandering to American tastes. Of the three of Hunter's books I've read and reviewed for this blog, this has got to be my favorite. Interesting plot, great characters, muscular prose—I'm more than chuffed. I'm potty about it. And that's no bollocks."—*Out in Print*

"[A]n awesome book, not to mention a kick butt thriller and mystery."—Danielle Kimerer, Librarian, Nevins Memorial Public Library (MA)

"Cari Hunter is a master of writing credible suspense laden crime detective stories that feel realistic. Sanne and Meg are extremely ordinary, two women trying to live quiet lives on their beloved Peaks, caught up in a dreadful ring of crime and, as always, doing their ordinary best to help those who need them. ...Once again I cannot recommend this series enough. If you like crime, thriller, and suspense with a cast of real life everyday folk and unassuming heroes, written with excellent if unpretentious style, you really cannot do any better than this."—*Lesbian Reading Room*

"Ms. Hunter is very skillful at building a fast paced thriller with unexpected twists and turns. ...Despite its level of violence, nothing seems gratuitous or unnecessary to the plot. As a matter of fact, I prefer that the author didn't decide to water down the cruelty of human trafficking for the sake of a lighter read."—*Lez Review Books*

Cold to the Touch

"Cari Hunter did a great job of keeping me 100% invested in the lives of Sanne, Meg and company. The mystery, (Sanne's current case), surrounding a rash of stabbing related deaths was intriguing,

and had me in suspense till the end. ...This book is intelligently written, and gives you an action packed adventure, with great characters. It is by far a fantastic way to spend your time."
—*Romantic Reader Blog*

"The mystery was well told and the gradual build up of tension was ideal. ...The romantic side story was subtle but just right. The murder case took precedence as it should in a police procedural."
—*Inked Rainbow Reads*

No Good Reason—*Lambda Literary Award Finalist*

"Cari Hunter is a master of crime suspense stories. *No Good Reason* brings tension and drama to strong medical and police procedural knowledge. The plot keeps us on the edge of our metaphorical seat, turning the pages long into the night. The setting of the English Peak District adds ambiance and a drama of its own without excluding anybody. And through it all a glimmer of humour and a large dose of humanity keep us engaged and enthralled."—*Curve*

"A new Cari Hunter novel? What mayhem will engulf her characters this time? The answer: Truly terrible things, as well as truly lovely things, abound in the mystery-thriller No Good Reason. "She hurt" are the opening words, and this is a bodily hurt. The plot takes off immediately as a captive woman makes her bloody escape and then—Well, this is not a romance, dear reader, so brace yourself. ...Our heroines are Detective Sanne Jensen and Dr. Meg Fielding, best mates forever and sometimes something more. Their relationship is indefinable and complicated, but not in a hot mess of drama way. Rather, they share unspoken depths, comfortably silly moments, rock-solid friendship, and an intimacy that will make your heart ache just a wee bit."—*C-Spot Reviews*

Tumbledown

"Once again Ms. Hunter outdoes herself in the tension and pace of the plot. We literally know from the first 2 pages that the evil is hunting them, but we are held on the edge of our seats for the whole book to see what will unfold, how they will cope, whether they will survive—and at what cost this time. I literally couldn't put it down. *Tumbledown* is a wonderful read."—*Lesbian Reading Room*

"Even though this is a continuation of the *Desolation Point* plot, this is an entirely different sort of thriller with elements of a police procedural. Other thriller authors (yes, I'm looking at you Patterson and Grisham) could take lessons from Hunter when it comes to writing these babies. Twists and turns and forgotten or unconventional weaponry along with pluck and spirit keep me breathless and reading way past my bedtime."—*Out In Print*

Desolation Point

"[*Desolation Point*] is the second of Cari Hunter's novels and is another great example of a romance action adventure. The story is fast paced and thrilling. A real page turner from beginning to end. Ms. Hunter is a master at an adventure plot and comes up with more twists and turns than the mountain trails they are hiking. Well written, edited and crafted this is an excellent book and I can't wait to read the sequel."—*Lesbian Reading Room*

"Cari Hunter provides thrills galore in her adventure/romance *Desolation Point*. In the hands of a lesser writer and scenarist, this could be pretty rote and by-the-book, but Cari Hunter breathes a great deal of life into the characters and the situation. Her descriptions of the scenery are sumptuous, and she has a keen sense of pacing. The action sequences never drag, and she takes full advantage of the valleys between the peaks by deepening her characters, working their relationship, and setting up the next hurdle."—*Out In Print*

Snowbound

"[*Snowbound*] grabbed me from the first page and kept me on the edge of my seat until nearly the end. I love the British feel of it and enjoyed the writer's style tremendously. So if you're looking for a very well written, fast paced, lesbian romance—heavy on the action and blood and light on the romance—this is one for your ereader or bookshelf."—*C-Spot Reviews*

By the Author

Snowbound

Desolation Point

Tumbledown

Alias

Breathe

Unbreakable

The Dark Peak Series:

No Good Reason

Cold to the Touch

A Quiet Death

UNBREAKABLE

by
Cari Hunter

2021

UNBREAKABLE

ISBN 13: 978-1-63555-961-3

This Trade Paperback Original Is Published By
Bold Strokes Books, Inc.
P.O. Box 249
Valley Falls, NY 12185

First Edition: October 2021

CREDITS
Editor: Cindy Cresap
Production Design: Susan Ramundo
Cover Design By Jeanine Henning

Acknowledgments

Thanks and a big fat bowl of jelly and custard to everyone at BSB, especially my editor, Cindy, for her feedback, veggie chat, and all the notes in the margins (we're going to have to agree to disagree on the salad cream thing, though). To Jeanine for another great cover. To Kel and Shireen for fielding random questions at odd times without batting an eyelid. To Julie S and Alena for the surprise sheep loot, sweets, and assorted goodies. To all the folks who read or listen to my books—many of you have become friends over the years and I couldn't be happier to have you around. And to Cat, who still rolls her eyes at the lamb wrangling but does it anyway.

Dedication

For Cat

Always

GRACE. SATURDAY, 6:05 A.M.

It was an easy mistake to make. Twelve hours and five minutes after starting her shift, Grace Kendal had replenished her kit, locked away her radio, and shut down the response car's data terminal. Beckoned home by the promise of a long weekend off, she was already planning her late, lazy morning, sitting up to her neck in a bubble bath, glass of wine in one hand, kebab in the other. She was so knackered she was tripping over her own feet, but still, when she heard the footsteps approaching, she shouldn't have assumed it would be Gav coming back for something he'd forgotten. She should have been more careful.

"Don't move. Don't make a sound." A woman's voice, low and rough. For a bewildered few seconds, Grace tried to place it, convinced it was one of her colleagues taking the piss, because the alternative was simply too ludicrous. But the command was underscored by a firm jab in the centre of her back, and she realised with a sickening lurch that the woman had a gun and that this wasn't a joke. The woman was close, her breath rasping on Grace's neck. She clamped her free hand onto Grace's shoulder, digging her fingers in around the bone. "Keep your hands where I can see them."

Grace splayed her palms on the ledge of the car's storage cage and then gripped the metal to keep herself upright. Her legs felt like jelly, and she thought she might vomit.

"Safe," she whispered. "They're in the safe. Key's in my pocket."

"What? What's in the safe?" The woman rocked back a step, and Grace had a fleeting impression of someone taller than her, but that was all. A dark hood concealed the woman's face, casting it into shadow.

"Morphine, diazepam, ketamine," Grace said, rattling off the drugs most likely to appeal. It was always the drugs, and nowhere—not the ambulances, nor the pharmacies, nor the hospitals—was out of bounds for the truly desperate addicts. "Just take them."

"That's not—" The woman broke off to snatch a ragged breath. "I'm not—I don't want them."

Grace took a deep breath of her own, forcing herself to stay calm. "Okay. That's okay. What *do* you want?" But even as she asked, she figured out the answer. The woman was shaking, not with the uncontrollable vigour of a delirious user, but with the insidious, subtle tremor that came from pain and shock. A metallic smell rolled off her, undercut by the sweetness of wet grass.

"You're hurt," Grace said. "Let me take you to the hospital."

The ambulance station was in the grounds of the Royal London Hospital, a ninety-second drive from the Accident and Emergency Department, where its trauma specialists could take care of the woman and its security team could call the police.

"No hospital," the woman said. Her voice was steadier, and she pushed the gun in harder. "You're a doctor, and I've been shot. Get what you'll need. My car's over there."

"No, I can't." Grace shook her head in a pathetic attempt to pacify the crazy, bleeding woman. It wasn't as if she could plead mistaken identity. Her high-vis jacket had DOCTOR emblazoned across its back, and she was standing by a fully kitted rapid response ambulance car. She tightened her hold on the cage, grinding the metal into her fingers. Everything was starting to feel off-kilter and surreal, and she wondered if she was about to faint. Cold sweat slapped her hair against her forehead, and the frost bit in, setting her shivering. Her words puffed out, white and rapid-fire. "I *can't*. It doesn't work like that. This isn't like you see on the telly."

"Shut up," the woman said, and for one stupid moment Grace thought: that accent's not from around here. Sounds like home. "Just shut the fuck up. Get your stuff. *Come on.*"

"Okay, oh God, okay, I'll do it. Give me a minute." Grace began to lower her kit to the ground: IV supplies, advanced life support, defib, oxygen, roadside surgical packs, trauma dressings, and frontline drugs. She dropped the last pouch and raised her hands. She still had her back to the woman. "I'm going to reach into my pocket for the safe key, all right?"

Cold fingers closed around hers. "I'll get it. Stay still."

Grace obediently spread her arms again. The hand the woman had touched had fresh blood smeared across it. As the woman patted Grace's pockets, Grace scanned the car park for CCTV. In all her years of working here, she'd never given security a second thought. The car park had a keypad-operated gate and a few lights on sensors, and those had always been enough of a deterrent. This particular morning, Gav had chosen the charging bay in the farthest corner before she'd sent him home early to see his new baby, and despite a full moon dodging a smattering of clouds, she and the woman were almost concealed in the shadows.

"Here." The woman dropped the key into Grace's palm and allowed her to open the car's rear door. The controlled drugs safe was fixed to the floor behind the driver's seat, and Grace shoved herself into the footwell, protected by the darkness for the few seconds it took her to retrieve the drugs. What would the woman do if Grace simply refused to move again?

"Don't touch anything else," the woman warned her, and Grace decided not to chance it, crawling back out of the door and leaving the car's mobile phone and the emergency button on the radio well beyond her reach. The woman had managed to pick up two of the bags. Grace collected the remainder and for the first time turned to face her. The moon chose that moment to break free, pouring silver light onto the car park. The woman winced, instinctively shielding her eyes with her gun hand.

"Jesus," Grace hissed. "Who did this?"

One side of the woman's face was a swollen mess of older bruising, her left eye almost closed and her jaw purple and green. An oozing laceration on her forehead that should have been stitched was instead pulled together by a haphazard application of Steri-Strips.

Tangled strands of dark hair stuck to her cheeks, and she was so pale she looked ethereal in the moonlight.

"Doesn't matter," she said. She gestured with the gun toward the pedestrian gate that no one ever used. "Go."

Grace set off, staggering beneath the weight of the bags. How long had it been? Five minutes? Ten? Too early for the seven o'clock day crew to be coming in for the start of their shift or for the night crew to be coming back. None of the station lights were on. Gav was long gone, and there would be no last-minute reprieve as a manager suddenly showed up or a crew limped back early with a broken bus. At the gate, she entered the key code without hesitating, resigned to her fate for now. She pushed the heavy metal door as the light blinked green, and held it open for the woman.

"Thank you," the woman said, and she sounded so weary that Grace almost smiled to try to reassure her. She didn't, though. She walked on in silence toward a black Audi parked by one of the maintenance buildings. She stopped when she heard the jangle of keys. The woman was holding a set out to her.

"You're driving," the woman said, and clicked the central locking.

Grace wasn't sure what the woman had been expecting. A swift getaway, wheels spinning and engine revving as they tore onto the nearest main road? In reality, none of that happened. Grace opened the car boot, shoved half her kit between two cases and a rucksack, and launched the rest onto the back seat. Leaning heavily against the bonnet, the woman waited until Grace had got into the driver's side and fastened her seat belt before easing herself into the passenger seat.

"How do I...?" Using both hands, Grace fumbled for the levers to adjust the seat. The car was some sort of sports model, its seat low and bucket-like, and the woman's legs were longer than hers. At full stretch, Grace could tap the pedals with her toes, but she couldn't press them.

"Left-hand side," the woman said. She still had the gun clasped in her fist, but it wasn't pointed at Grace. Her head fell back, her eyes half-lidded as she panted for air. There had been blood on the driver's seat, a large tacky stain coating the leather. It was little wonder she looked like shit.

The lever slid the seat into a more comfortable position, and Grace started the engine, setting off a deep, powerful burr that became an uncooperative snarl when she tried to drive forward.

"One foot," the woman said. "It's automatic."

"Oh. Of course." Grace had put the car into drive and then immediately forgotten that it didn't have a clutch. "Sorry. I'm not used to—I drive a manual." She tried to switch the windscreen wipers on to shift a thin film of frost and indicated left instead. "God, sorry," she said again. At this rate, the woman might decide to cut her losses and simply shoot Grace for sheer incompetence.

"Take your time," the woman said. "The windscreen needs a minute to clear, anyway."

Grace nodded and methodically worked her way through the car's controls, chanting the list to herself: headlights, heated windscreen, sidelights, wipers, no clutch, remember there is no clutch, handbrake…

The tension that had all but paralysed her abated as she settled into the car. She could do this. She had always thrived under pressure, returning to emergency medicine time and again during her years as a junior doctor, because no other element of her training gave her the same kind of pure adrenaline rush. She had snapped up overtime shifts, shadowed the trauma specialists, and sacrificed a summer she could have spent on the beach to work in the A&E of Groote Schuur in Cape Town, where the local gangs' fondness for machetes had given her more hands-on experience in six weeks than she'd had in six years of rotating placements. She was used to dealing with violent people and the aftermath of violence, and while this scenario was extreme, all she needed to do was keep her head down, do as she was told, and bide her time. The woman was clearly exhausted and clinically unwell; sooner or later she would either collapse or make a mistake. Had Grace been a betting woman, her money would have gone on the former.

"Give me your phone." The woman, apparently not as addled as Grace had hoped, gestured with the gun to emphasise the instruction.

Grace shook her head, tears prickling in her eyes. She had been dreading this. If her phone was destroyed, she would lose everything on it. All the photos she had meant to back up but never had, the messages she'd never been able to delete, that one voicemail asking which groceries were on a mislaid shopping list.

"What are you going to do with it?" A tremor ran through the question, despite her best efforts to sound reasonable. "Please don't wreck it. There's stuff—" She broke off, the explanation catching in her throat. "Stuff" was such a trivial fucking irrelevant word. For the first time since the woman had taken her, she resorted to begging. "Take the SIM out, that's fine. I'm not bothered. Just let me keep the rest of it. Please, let me keep it." She put the phone in the woman's outstretched palm, smothering a sob of gratitude as the woman removed the battery and SIM and gave the phone back to her. "Thank you. I really appreciate that," she said, shoving it out of sight before the woman changed her mind.

"Is anyone going to be missing you?" the woman asked. "Anyone at home?"

"No." Grace laid her hand across the phone in her pocket. "There's no one."

Something in her tone must have given her away, because rather than probing for more details, the woman bowed her head as if in apology. "When are you next in work?"

"Tuesday night." Grace didn't want to think that far ahead, to consider what might have happened to her by then. "But that HEMS car will be manned again at six tonight."

Let the woman sweat over that detail. At best, she had about twelve hours before someone realised the car had been ransacked and raised the alarm, and the HEMS management would undoubtedly attempt to contact Grace.

The woman checked the clock on the dash. "I won't have that long," she muttered.

Puzzled, Grace was on the verge of questioning why, when the woman cut off the exchange by switching the heater on full blast.

The demisting windscreen revealed little except the deserted road and the buildings around the rear of the hospital. Grace's pulse sped up as a man strode past, but his head was bowed against the cold, his collar raised to shield his face, and he didn't so much as glance at the car.

"Where are we going to go?" she asked. On some level, she was piecing this ordeal together as if already preparing the statement she would provide for the police. She had noted the top-of-the-range Audi interior and the woman's name brand clothes. There had been two matching Antler bags in the boot, and a nondescript rucksack. The woman was approximately five foot seven, and the few wisps of hair that Grace could see were chestnut brown and matched her eyes. She wore no makeup, but her fingernails were manicured beneath the flecks of blood and dirt, and her accent held more than a hint of northern English, possibly from around Manchester, though that detail meant little in a city as diverse as London. She didn't look like a stereotypical Category A criminal, but someone had recently beaten her to a pulp and shot her, and she seemed proficient with a handgun.

Oblivious to Grace's oblique scrutiny, she pressed a series of options on the built-in satnav and allowed a route to calculate. "Turn right out of here, then left at the main road," she said, muting the directions as a pink arrow appeared on the screen.

Grace accelerated smoothly, feeling the subtle shifts as the car changed gears. She braked in good time for a speed bump on the hospital access road but still heard the groan that the woman failed to muffle behind her hand.

"There's another one around the next bend," Grace said. She didn't know why she was warning her. Any sensible person would aim to incapacitate her captor by slamming the car into the bump, and then do a runner whilst screaming blue murder. Without assessing the woman's injuries, however, Grace couldn't tell whether such an impact would actually kill her, so she erred on the side of not committing premeditated murder and slowed the car to a crawl for the second bump. An ambulance approached from the opposite direction, its blue lights bouncing around the car's interior. The woman shrank back in her seat, tucking her face into her hood as if the driver might be able to identify her through the tinted windows.

"Fuck," she whispered. She wiped her face on her sleeve. Her arm was trembling. "Fuck."

Grace turned onto the main road without comment, picking up her speed to keep pace with the taxis and pre-dawn delivery men. London roads were never quiet, and there were enough Saturday morning commuters driving like hooligans to divert her attention from the woman and whatever might happen whenever they got wherever they were going.

The single carriageway merged onto the A13 trunk road, with the additional lanes thinning the traffic to give Grace more time and space to manoeuvre. She found herself refocusing on the woman, who had curled onto her right side, one knee drawn up as she clung to the dash with her left hand.

"How badly are you bleeding?" Grace asked. Unable to look away from the road for long, she was relying on other cues to gauge the woman's condition: her rapid respiration rate, her restlessness, and the inarticulate sounds of pain.

"It's fine. *I'm* fine," the woman said, through clenched teeth.

"Don't talk crap," Grace snapped. She might have been kidnapped, but she wasn't going to take shit from a patient. "It smells like an abattoir in here. If you can get to your wound, try putting direct pressure on it."

The woman grunted, a noncommittal noise that might have been disdain or outright defiance for all Grace could tell, but she took her hand off the dash, and another softer grunt of discomfort told Grace she was complying with the order.

"Good." Grace returned her attention to the road for a count of ten and then decided to push her luck while the going was reasonable. "What's your name? I'm Grace. Grace Kendal." Humanising herself seemed like a sensible tactic. Didn't that make her harder to kill? She was sure she'd read that in a book once. But the woman glared at her in lieu of answering, and Grace lowered one hand at a time to dry her palms. So much for that bollocks theory.

She checked the satnav. It gave no indication where they were heading, but a distance countdown displayed an ETA of ten minutes and forty-two seconds. "We'll be there soon," she said.

They were loosely tracking the path of the Thames, but the road had been designed for expedience, not aesthetics, and it cut out the river's deeper loops to blast ahead in a straight line bordered by litter-strewn verges. Grace knew the area well, knew which junction would take her to the Tobacco Dock or the Cutty Sark or the restaurant where that old boy had choked on his pie and liquor. The skyscrapers of Canary Wharf, home to most of London's financial powerhouses, formed an incongruous backdrop, as if someone had scooped up a random selection of New York's swankiest buildings and dumped them on the Isle of Dogs.

"Take the slip road," the woman told her as they approached a three-hundred-yard marker. Grace found the indicator at the first attempt, exiting toward Lewisham and the Blackwall Tunnel. A small flag appeared on the satnav, and she tapped the plus sign on the screen, zooming in.

"Is this where we're heading?" she asked. The screen identified it as a Radisson Hotel, which certainly hadn't been on her destination guess-list of abandoned warehouse, seedy motel, or wasteland.

The woman used her gun hand to open the glove box and fished out a key. "I have a suite there." She displayed a tag engraved with 63. "Underground parking is on the left, just after the main building."

The main building was an ugly piece of architecture shaped like the prow of a ship, with rust-orange blocks dividing the windows, the design reminiscent of a 1980s school brought in under budget but forming a permanent blot on the landscape. Grace drove past an entrance in night mode: no lights, no doorman, and an empty taxi rank. She turned onto the car park ramp, her spirits rising as she saw an automated barrier, but it opened as she approached, removing any opportunity for her to press its buzzer and summon a posse of burly security guards.

"Number plate recognition," the woman told her. She had probably noticed Grace taking an interest. "You register your car when you pick up your key."

"Clever." Grace searched for the camera. Would it spot an extra person in the car? Might that be enough to set all the bells and whistles off? Probably not, given that the woman had booked a suite. It wasn't as if she was attempting to smuggle Grace into a single room at a bargain-basement Travelodge.

"Bay forty-three," the woman said as the alarms failed to sound and security failed to materialise. "It's two levels down."

The car park was almost full but devoid of any actual people. The woman ordered Grace to reverse into the bay, ensuring the rear of the car was as far from view as possible.

"You need to get changed," she said, once Grace had switched off the engine. "You're too conspicuous."

Grace almost laughed at the understatement. Surely that was the least of their problems. "How the hell do you propose getting all my stuff up to your suite? What are you planning to do, ring for a porter and ask him to carry it for you, no questions asked? You're covered in blood and muck, and you can barely keep your eyes open. Someone is going to *see* you." She turned to face her, damping down the frustration that had caused her voice to rise. "Let me take you to a hospital. We can end this right now, and I'll walk away. I won't press charges. *Please* listen to me. Listen to me, this is ridiculous."

"I can't," the woman said. "I can't. I can't." She was sweating, her nostrils flaring as she fought for breath. She would probably faint as soon as she tried to stand. When she looked at Grace, Grace was shocked to see tears filling her eyes. "Please help me."

"God," Grace whispered. She had heard that plea countless times before, terrified and frantic from the kid knifed and bleeding to death, or gasped out between the wheezes of a brittle asthmatic. No one had ever done this to her before, though. No one had ever taken away her free will and forced her hand. Did the oath she had sworn still apply if she was being held at gunpoint? She bit her lip, acknowledging the question as rhetorical, and then moved a hand to the zip of her jumpsuit, her other outstretched to show she meant no harm.

"I'll need a sweater or something. My T-shirt's a dead giveaway as well." She shrugged out of the suit's top half to reveal a shirt with

HEMS embroidered across its back. Thanks to numerous television documentaries, the acronym was readily associated with London's Helicopter Emergency Medical Service. Her thin under-trousers were black and unadorned, and her boots were heavy duty high-leg Magnums. If there was a Radisson dress code, she suspected she was going to fall foul of it.

"The cases are full of spare clothes," the woman said. "Empty them and put your gear in. There'll be a sweater you can use." She shifted the gun as if to remind Grace she was still capable of using it. "Don't touch the rucksack."

She got out of the car when Grace did, clawing herself upright by way of the passenger door. Her knuckles blanched as she rested her forehead on the car's roof, but she didn't drop the gun, and she straightened again within seconds to watch Grace cram the cases with medical kit. She took a bottle of water from the back seat, drank most of it, and used the dregs to clean her hands and face.

"Here." She passed Grace a hooded top and retrieved a long grey coat for herself, though she stopped short of putting it on. Grace donned the hoodie and then took the coat from her.

"Bad arm in first," she said. The woman was consistently favouring her right side, and Grace could see the gleam of fresh blood soaking her black sweater. She allowed Grace to work the coat over her arm and fasten the buttons for her.

"I'm almost done here," Grace told her, shoving her IV pouch into a side pocket of the largest case and inching the zip closed. She cast an eye over the clothing she had stacked in the boot. The woman had packed practical outfits: jeans, casual sweaters, T-shirts. Here and there, splashes of pastel were folded in amongst the monochrome, but Grace had no chance to root through everything and she didn't want to accidentally unwrap a pair of the woman's knickers. Nothing stood out as unusual. The clothes were typical for a city-break, if you were intending to stomp around the landmarks and go shopping. And the woman obviously had been shopping; Grace had removed numerous bags from big-name stores and tourist favourites jammed into the extra pockets on the cases.

The bags were heavy, thudding onto the concrete as Grace hauled them from the boot, but they had wheels at one end and extendable handles, so they were manageable. She stood them up, handles out and at the ready, and then folded her arms to see how the woman wanted to play this. While Grace was sure she could manage both bags, she was less certain the woman would be able to walk unaided, and there was the small matter of where the gun was going to go. The last thing she wanted was all hell breaking loose in a reception area full of hung-over guests heading for a fry-up.

The woman slung the rucksack over her left shoulder and eyed the bags, clearly aware that things weren't going to plan. Kidnapping an unwary and vulnerable doctor on impulse when armed and agitated was probably quite easy. It was the related logistics that quickly became a pain in the arse.

Mindful that the woman wasn't firing on all cylinders and that any further delays to her treatment would be detrimental, Grace took the larger of the bags and gave her the handle of the other.

"Put the gun in your pocket," she told her. "I know it's still there, and I'm not going to do anything daft. You can't walk through the hotel with it, anyway."

The woman considered that for a moment, as if the logic was taking her a while to process, and then nodded and slipped the gun away.

"Good." Grace stood close by her side. "Stick your bad arm around my shoulders."

The woman stiffened. "No. I can manage."

"No. You can't. I can tell just by looking at you that you've lost about a third of your blood volume. You're white as a sheet, clammy, hyperventilating, and thirsty. You should be in an operating theatre, and instead you're stonewalling me in the car park of a fucking hotel. Which floor is your suite on?"

The woman blinked, obviously trying to remember. "Sixth."

"And the lift is…?"

"Far end of the reception."

"Okay then," Grace said. "Lean on me, try to look drunk instead of peri-arrest, and pull that sodding case."

The woman acquiesced far sooner than Grace had expected, her expression softening into something that might have been relief, as if she had done everything she could to get herself to this point and now simply wanted someone else to take over. She put her arm around Grace and set off with her, their steps slow but steady. The woman had a slight limp, favouring her left leg, but Grace couldn't tell what was causing it.

A car engine revved as they neared the exit, the sound ricocheting off the concrete walls, and the woman stopped dead, her knees buckling and her head whipping around to isolate the noise. The gun was out again before Grace could say anything to calm her, and Grace reacted without thinking, slapping the woman's arm down as a souped-up Porsche passed by.

"It's all right," Grace said quickly, keen to stave off retaliation. "They've gone, you're all right."

The woman was shaking, her hand knocking the gun against her thigh. She gagged and then vomited onto the tarmac. Her thin cry of distress made the hairs stand up on the nape of Grace's neck.

"What the hell happened to you?" Grace whispered.

The woman didn't reply—Grace hadn't thought she would—but she let Grace wipe her mouth with a tissue and help her back to her feet, and she put the gun away again without needing to be told.

There was no one in the lift to the reception area, but they walked out into a hotel now wide awake for the weekend. A gang of lads wearing shorts and Hawaiian shirts stood by a mass of luggage, and a couple who clearly hadn't yet been to bed tottered past, the woman barefoot, high heels in hand, and the bloke red-eyed and stinking of booze and cigarettes.

"Keep walking," Grace murmured, afraid of what might happen if the crowd became overwhelming. "We're fitting right in."

A smartly dressed man in a three-piece suit complete with bowtie hailed them as they neared the reception desk. His bright smile wavered a fraction as he took in their appearance, but, consummate professional that he evidently was, he plastered it back on.

"Good morning, Ms. Breckenridge. It's lovely to see you again. I noted you'd extended your stay. May we be of assistance with your bags?"

"No, thank you," the woman said. Her smile was more of a rictus, and he did well not to recoil.

"Long night and new painkillers," Grace said brightly. If the bruising hadn't been present the first time the woman checked in here, then that explanation wasn't going to suffice, and they were, to all intents, fucked.

"Ah yes. Well, we've all been there, Ms…?"

"Kendal." Grace frowned at the woman. "Sweetheart, didn't you register me as a guest?"

The woman gawped at Grace and then shook her head in apparent remorse. "Slipped my mind."

"Little wonder." Grace directed her next comment to the receptionist, engaging his sympathy. "She's had a rough few days." As luck would have it, Grace tended to carry her wallet in her trouser pocket for safekeeping. She passed him her driving licence, taking more and more of the woman's weight as he entered the details on the computer. At least he would have Grace's name on record for whenever the shit finally hit the fan.

"That's all done for you," he said. "Breakfast is seven till ten thirty. Will you be needing anything else?"

Police, ambulance, and a hostage negotiator, Grace thought. "A note that we're not to be disturbed," she said, and steered the woman toward the lift.

Floor to ceiling neon-lit glass panels greeted them as the lift doors opened. The woman let the doors close before she slumped against the closest wall. Her laboured breaths misted the glass, and she grappled at the strips between the panels as if fighting for purchase. Her complexion was the bloodless yellow Grace tended to associate with hypovolaemic corpses. Grace watched the floors tick by and practically dragged her out as the lift settled on the sixth. Room 63 was at the far end of the corridor, separated from the regular rooms by three small stairs.

"Use the handrail," Grace said. "I've got the bags."

Even with the awkward weight of the holdalls, she made it to the top before the woman did.

"Stop," the woman said. "Stay there." She had put her hand in her pocket, the threat clearly defined by the shape of the gun pressed against the material.

Grace widened her stance, both hands in view, still balancing the bags.

"If I was going to try anything, I'd have tried it by now." She took the key from the woman and unlocked the door, toeing it open and then shoving it wider as she took stock of the layout. "Bloody hell. If you can't make it to the bed, get on the sofa."

The suite came with a separate living room, river view, wall-mounted television, colour-coordinated soft furnishings, and approximately eight further metres of floor space she was going to have to get the woman across.

"I can make it," the woman muttered. She stayed where she was, just over the threshold, swaying on the spot as Grace shut and locked the door.

Grace didn't waste time arguing. She lugged both cases into the bedroom, grabbing all the towels from the bathroom on her way back and launching them onto the bed. In Grace's absence, the woman had taken off her coat and what looked like a bulletproof vest. After dumping them with her rucksack, she had managed a few steps, running out of steam close enough to a high-backed chair to hang on to its frame. Without waiting for permission, Grace half-dragged her into the bedroom.

"Lie down before you fall down," she told her, none-too-gently parking her at the edge of the bed. The woman capitulated the instant her legs touched the mattress and sat hunched over with the gun resting in her lap.

Grace stepped back, restoring the distance between them, but the reappearance of the gun didn't intimidate her, just pissed her off.

"I'm not doing anything if you're going to wave that in my face," she said. "If you're going to shoot me, get it over with and we can bleed out together."

The woman tilted her head and squinted at Grace, as if taking advantage of the improved lighting to really study her for the first time. Grace folded her arms and returned the stare, anger and defiance heating her cheeks and snapping everything into stark focus. It was the physiological details she noticed first, as she would with any patient: the tug in the centre of the woman's throat as she drew on her accessory muscles to keep herself breathing, the blood speckling her cracked lips, and the deep shadows encircling the eye that wasn't swollen. Had her hair not been matted and soaked with sweat, its style—a bob just long enough to tuck behind her ears—would have suited her. Grace could easily picture her in a high-end career, something in the private sector that came with excellent benefits and paid enough to finance her sports car and her designer clothing. What Grace found impossible to imagine were the circumstances that had brought the woman to this point, beaten and bleeding and deliberately setting a gun onto a hotel mattress.

"Hey." Grace relaxed her stance as the woman pushed the gun a symbolic distance away, though not quite beyond her reach.

The woman's raised eyebrow covered a multitude of responses: Are you happy now? What do you want? What next?

Grace went to crouch in front of her. Although she was accustomed to dealing with people in crisis, it was the utter hopelessness in the woman's expression that she was struggling to cope with. She placed a tentative hand on the woman's knee.

"What's your name?" she asked again.

The woman shuddered beneath her touch, a single tremor that became a violent series of shivers, rattling her frame. "It's Elin," she said between clattering teeth, as if giving the right answer might be the key to getting herself fixed. "God, what's happening to me?"

"You're in shock." Grace was so worried she hardly registered the progress she had just made. "I need you to lie down. You'll feel better when you do, I promise." Mindful of Elin's laboured breathing, she stacked the bed's pillows and guided her against them. Elin hadn't been able to take off her boots, and they smeared mud and grass onto the quilt as she dug in with her heels. The gun went with her, but she no longer seemed capable of gripping it, let alone aiming and firing it. Grace didn't care. She had more pressing concerns. She would phone 999 as soon as she had Elin stabilised.

With her kit spread out on the double bed, she pulled on a pair of nitrile gloves and began to work through her priorities, chief of which was figuring out where the hell Elin had been shot and what, if anything, she could do with the wound. As the defib confirmed Elin's blood pressure was dangerously low and returned oxygen saturations of eighty-six percent, Grace cut along the seam of Elin's sweater and peeled the sodden material from her torso.

"It's in my back," Elin said. "The entrance wound. Small calibre." She paused to catch her breath and then coughed, coating her lips with fresh blood. "No exit."

"Okay, enough talking. Here." Grace secured a high-concentration oxygen mask over Elin's nose and mouth, ignoring Elin's feeble protest. "Leave it on, your oxygen levels are shit. Can you roll on your side?"

Elin didn't so much roll as lurch and then flop, her arms bouncing off the mattress and her head lolling. Grace crooked Elin's uppermost leg for her, steadying her position, and then used one of the towels to wipe the blood from her back. The first thing she uncovered was more bruising: large, discoloured blotches that were yellowing at the edges. Some still bore the imprint of a boot's tread. They almost buried a silver-white twist of old scarring at the base of her ribcage, and a neater scar from a surgical repair. She didn't go looking for the corresponding scar on Elin's abdomen, but she had no doubt it would be there. Larger calibre that time, but the same messy aftermath. In a country with such strict gun laws, getting shot once in a lifetime might be considered unfortunate; getting shot on two separate occasions was something else entirely. Military, Grace concluded. That might explain the first wound, possibly inflicted in combat, though it did nothing to explain how Elin had been shot whilst dressed as a civvy in the city of London.

The fresh entrance wound was easy to locate: a small, frothing hole beneath Elin's scapula that sent out bubbles of blood in synch with her breathing. Grace pressed her stethoscope to Elin's chest, but the diagnosis was a foregone conclusion: the lung had collapsed, and Elin needed a chest drain. If there was a bright side, her heart sounds were perfect, or they would be once her pulse rate returned to its normal range. The ribs above and below the wound grated when Grace palpated the area, and Elin cried out, drawing her knees up as her fists knotted the sheets.

"Sorry," Grace said. "I'm done. I'm finished." She eased Elin onto her back and sat on the bed next to her.

Elin pulled her oxygen mask off. "Can you sort it?" she asked, and Grace realised she had known the outcome all along.

"Not your first rodeo, eh?"

"No." Elin didn't elaborate. "I was…last night, I was wearing a vest." She coughed so hard it brought tears to her eyes. "Bought it online, though. Got proper fucking eBayed."

Despite everything, that surprised a laugh out of Grace. "Well, you're still alive, so it did half its job."

"Mm." Elin watched Grace tighten a tourniquet around her arm. "He's getting shitty feedback when all this is over."

Grace slapped at Elin's wrist, encouraging a vein to fill, and pulled a large-bore cannula from her IV pouch. "'Looks the part, but I got fucked up anyway.' That kind of thing?"

"Yeah, I'm one-starring his arse." Elin caught hold of Grace's arm, almost sending the cannula flying. "No drugs."

"Do blood and plasma count?" Grace snapped, tired of being second-guessed. "Because you need both, and they're far more effective through a vein. If you want me to be your doctor, let me be your damn doctor, and stop pissing around."

Elin released her, allowing her to slide the cannula into place. "No morphine. No ket."

"Fine by me," Grace said, halfway to the wardrobe for a coat hanger. "I recommend a local for the chest drain, unless you've got a masochistic streak."

"No, I haven't." Elin coughed an abstract pattern of blood onto a pristine white towel.

"Any allergies?" Grace asked, as if this was just another day in the A&E. She could get through this if she kept to the agreed script.

"Hay fever. No drug allergies. Do you yell at all your patients?"

"Only the ones behaving like idiots." Grace connected a bag of plasma to Elin's IV and used the coat hanger to hook it onto the bathroom door. She put Elin's mask back on and showed her a vial of local anaesthetic. "I'm going to inject this into your side. It'll sting like hell, but it won't knock you out, okay?"

Elin didn't reply but merely raised her arm above her head without needing to be told and closed her eyes, steeling herself for what came next. Her stoicism tweaked Grace's conscience. In the years she had been a doctor, she had tried not to harbour any prejudices. She dealt with patients from all walks of life, and they each deserved fair and equal treatment.

"I shouldn't have shouted at you," she said quietly.

Elin tugged her mask aside again. "I don't think I get to claim the moral high ground here."

"Perhaps not. But I'm sorry all the same." Grace adjusted the angle of Elin's arm. It didn't make much of a difference, but the contact was a comfort somehow. "Try to stay still for me, and keep that bloody mask on."

Elin did as she was told, burying her face in the pillows, as Grace set out the equipment she would need and did her best to create a sterile field using the surgical drapes in her kit. HEMS had developed in leaps and bounds since its inception, with its doctors regularly performing life-saving interventions, diagnostics, and surgeries at the roadside. As a consequence, inserting a chest drain was a bread-and-butter procedure for Grace, though not one she had ever had to do solo.

"Bear with me, I usually have someone to assist me with these," she said, missing that extra pair of hands keenly as she sliced into Elin's chest and dissected a path through the intercostal muscle. It wasn't that she didn't know what she was doing. Everything just happened far more slowly when she had to do each element of the task herself. Besides which, Gav always took the piss out of her, and she missed that most of all.

"Bit of pressure and pushing now," she warned her, passing the tube though the space she had made. She had seen grown men cry at this point, but Elin never made a sound as frank blood and air sputtered into the plastic, the output sluggish and then a continuous heavy stream. By the time Grace had secured the tubing with sutures and dressed the site, the drain had collected over half a litre, and the flow was beginning to taper off. She noted the volume on her glove. If it continued to increase, she would know Elin was still haemorrhaging.

"Better?" she asked. She could already see an improvement in Elin's complexion, and her sats had climbed to ninety-four percent.

"Yes." There was so much contained within that one choked word: relief, gratitude, and sorrow. Grace wanted nothing more than to squeeze Elin's hand as she would any other patient, and to tell her she had done really well and that the best thing she could do now was sleep.

"I'm going to swap this plasma for a unit of blood," Grace said, sticking with the technicalities. "You might end up needing type-specific, but it'll tide you over for now. I'll start a broad-spectrum antibiotic, and you're getting a dose of tranexamic acid as well, to help you clot."

Elin frowned. "Side effects?"

"Nothing serious, if I give it slowly enough. It might upset your stomach a little, but it won't make you drowsy." Grace drew the drug into a syringe and resumed her seat at Elin's side. "You know I could make a run for the door before you manage to grab that gun, don't you?"

"Yes. Why haven't you?"

Grace sighed. It was an excellent question. "Because you'd have hold of it by the time the police arrived, and I don't want anyone else to get hurt."

Elin nodded and took a cautious breath. It was hard to be sure when most of her face was hidden by the mask, but she seemed satisfied with the impasse.

"How's the pain?" Grace asked, also keen to return to more familiar ground.

"Bearable. I think it's the local. Everything feels blanked out."

Grace connected the syringe to Elin's IV line and started to administer the TXA. The first tenth took a full minute; she hadn't been kidding about a gradual titration. She concentrated on the syringe. If she hit the plunger and gave the drug as a job lot, would Elin be one of those patients whose blood pressure dropped catastrophically? Best-case scenario, it knocked her unconscious. Worst-case, the hypotension proved irreversible. Grace adjusted her grip on the plastic and looked at Elin. Elin's good eye was half-closed, and she seemed comfortable. This must be the first respite she'd had in hours, her bullet wound numbed and her lung able to fully expand.

As Grace watched, Elin tried to scratch her nose with her free hand, forgetting that the mask was in the way. Her nails hit the plastic, and her eyes crossed in an effort to identify the problem. Taking pity on her, Grace adjusted the mask, and Elin murmured her gratitude in a senseless series of contented sounds that were interrupted by the whir of the defib cycling through another blood pressure check. Seventy-two over fifty flashed up in red, the alarm Grace had silenced still displaying an insistent warning bell in the corner of the screen. A bolus of TXA wouldn't just knock Elin out right now; it would probably kill her.

"How is it?" Elin asked.

Grace checked the drain: 650 ml at a persistent trickle. "Not the best." She depressed the plunger another fraction. "But this should help."

Elin shifted restlessly. Sweat was beading on her brow again as the local began to wear off. "Jesus, that's—" She clamped a hand to the right side of her chest. "Will you be able to get the bullet out?"

"What?" Grace was so shocked she almost dropped the syringe. "I don't bloody think so, no. A chest drain is one thing, Elin. I'm not performing major surgery in a hotel suite. That bullet could be anywhere."

Elin lifted a tattered flap of her sweater and reached for Grace's hand. Grace let her take it, and Elin pressed it to a livid purple bruise covering a third of her ribcage.

"I'm pretty sure it's here," she said.

❖

"I can't believe I'm doing this." Grace adjusted the angle of the ultrasound wand. The gel she was smearing across Elin's chest spread an uprising of goosebumps in its wake. "I shouldn't be doing this. It's stupid, really fucking stupid."

Elin's attention was glued to the small screen. She probably had no idea what she was looking at in terms of anatomy, but even a layperson would be able to spot a bullet amongst the blur of soft tissue. "Tell them I forced you to," she said. "If it's going to get you into trouble."

Ethics and the misuse of equipment were the least of Grace's concerns, and she had stopped considering Elin a serious threat as soon as she'd tethered her to a chest drain and an IV. She dug the wand in harder than was strictly necessary and then eased off when Elin moaned. "I'm not bothered about a slapped wrist. I'm bothered about you being hell-bent on killing yourself and using me as an accessory. What have you done that's so terrible you'd rather do this than go to a hospital and get treated properly? What on earth could be worth putting yourself through this?"

Elin refused to be drawn. "The less you know, the better," she said, and then writhed and arched her back. "*Oh God!* Please don't push there!"

Grace didn't need to ask why. She could see the bullet on the screen, embedded in the intercostal muscle. "What happens if I take this out?" she said, once she had assessed its position from every possible angle. Removing it did seem feasible, given a fair wind, a confident hand, and something for Elin to bite down on if she continued to forgo pain relief. "What's your plan? Do you even *have* one?"

"He'll tell me," Elin mumbled. Still transfixed by the ultrasound image, she barely seemed aware of having spoken. "He said he's thinking about it."

Grace cupped Elin's chin, forcing Elin to look at her. She was now more scared *for* her than *of* her. "Who said that, Elin? Who's thinking about what?"

Elin shook her head free and grabbed Grace's wrist, her grip surprisingly fierce. "You don't need to know. Don't ask me again."

Grace wrenched her arm away and rubbed at the reddened lines encircling the skin. Elin was panting into her mask. Had she not looked so stricken, Grace would have blamed the exertion.

"I might be able to get the bullet out." Grace kept her tone formal, unwilling to risk further provocation. "But I won't know what damage it's done, what structures it's hit, or whether you'll stop bleeding. If I take the drain out too soon, your lung might collapse again, and without surgery to clean debris from the bullet's cavity, you're more than likely to get an infection despite the antibiotics. Do you understand what I'm telling you?"

In the absence of a permission proforma or anyone to bear witness, informed consent was all Grace could rely on. Doctors would often gabble through the risks associated with a procedure, so certain of its necessity that the patient's opinion was little more than an afterthought, a tick in the right box for an audit. She couldn't ever remember wanting a patient to change their mind before, to refuse to sign, shake their head, or indicate in whichever way possible that they weren't happy to put their life in her hands, and she had never seen anyone so clearly determined to disappoint her.

"Yes." There was no hint of Elin wavering, and she looked Grace in the eye as she answered.

"Right, then." Grace set the ultrasound aside and opened another surgical kit. "I will do my best with this, but I can't make you any promises, okay?"

Elin nodded, and her breathing calmed as she tracked the equipment Grace was preparing. She didn't seem scared so much as contented by the way things were turning out. She didn't flinch at the first sting of local anaesthetic, or make a sound as Grace used a small pair of forceps to delve into the incision she had made between Elin's ribs.

Guided by the ultrasound, Grace located the bullet without difficulty, the sensation of metal hitting metal unmistakable even when distorted by bone and blood. She saw Elin's jaw clench, and the defib belied her apparent composure by displaying a pulse rate of a hundred and forty.

"Easy," Grace said. "Easy. We'll take a minute, all right?" It was too late to suggest stronger pain relief. Both her hands were occupied, and she knew Elin would rebuff the offer regardless.

"I'm fine," Elin said. "I don't want to take a minute."

"Yeah?" Grace flexed her fingers. They were cramping and slippery with perspiration inside her gloves. "Well, maybe I do."

The image on the screen was too opaque to be useful, so Grace continued to work blind, opening the forceps against the crush of surrounding muscle and attempting to manoeuvre them around the bullet. "I almost…God damn it," she whispered. She could hear an occasional gasp and the grind of Elin's teeth, and she knew the pain must be excruciating, because there was no way the local had reached this deep. The metal jarred again and again, striking bone, getting caught, twisting and sticking, until eventually she snagged a solid hold and, with no other options available, pulled hard.

"*Fuck.*" She had no idea what damage she was causing. Blood welled and then dripped from her incision, and the uppermost rib moved far more freely than it should have, but she could see the bullet now, and a final tug sent it tumbling onto the bedding. Elin retched, spitting bile and saliva into her mask, and Grace threw down the forceps and the ultrasound wand. Clamping a wad of gauze across the wound with one hand, she pulled the mask away with the other. Elin's face was grey and creased with misery, and she didn't resist when Grace wiped her chin and the mask clean. She started to cry as Grace repositioned the mask.

"I can't do this anymore," she said. "I can't—I can't do this."

Grace knelt by the side of the bed and put her hand on Elin's forehead. The hotel room and the gun, the fear and the exhaustion, the smell of blood and vomit faded to leave nothing except a woman in obvious agony.

"Let me give you something for the pain," she said.

"No," Elin said, though her refusal lacked emphasis. "It'll knock me out, and you'll leave me. You'll phone the police."

Grace couldn't lie. She couldn't pretend she would continue to sit and watch this absurd, suicidal scenario play out. She would phone for the police and an ambulance and whoever else it might take to get Elin out of the hotel.

"This has gone on for long enough," she said. She reached across Elin and picked up the gun. She had never touched one before, and she held it as if it were a wild animal, liable to bite her without reason or warning. "You need to be in a hospital. Everything else is secondary."

Elin shook her head, her words strangled and broken by sobs. "It isn't. It isn't. You don't understand."

"Explain it to me, then." Grace kept her voice level. No matter what Elin told her, it wouldn't change anything, but she still wanted to know why this had happened.

Elin shuddered. "Get my phone," she whispered. "It's in my coat pocket."

Grace went into the living room, put the gun on the table, and stopped by the chair Elin had flung her coat over. The door was right there. Four or five more steps and she would be in the corridor, free to run down to the reception desk and sound the alarm. Instead, she crouched by the chair and patted the coat until she found Elin's phone in an inner pocket. Then she took it into the bedroom.

"Here," she said. Already planning ahead, she snapped open a vial of morphine and drew up a dose. The layout of the suite would make for an awkward evacuation, and Elin would need to sit on a wheelchair until the ambulance crew could transfer her onto a stretcher. If the morphine wasn't enough, Grace could always give her the ket as well.

Grace's legs trembled as the adrenaline that had kept her going for the last couple of hours began to fade. She sat back on the bed, too weary to be relieved by the imminent end to the crisis. She couldn't remember when she had last slept or eaten or had anything to drink. A stifled whimper made her glance up. Elin was clasping the phone in both hands as if in prayer, her eyes squeezed shut. She didn't try to stop Grace when Grace took the phone from her, and the motion reawakened the screen. For a moment, Grace couldn't really fathom what was on there. A photograph. A line of text. And then she could.

"Fucking hell," she said. "What the fuck? *Elin?*"

Safia. Saturday, 7:05 a.m.

"Hmm."

The forensics stepping plate wobbled as Detective Sergeant Safia Faris crouched by the upturned boots. It was still dark, and the beam from Suds's torch flashed over Safia's white Tyvek suit, then tracked the man's length from his feet to what remained of his head. The small-calibre bullet responsible for the carnage had been retrieved from the trunk of a nearby tree by an eagle-eyed CSI.

"Hmm indeed," Suds said. He was standing on the plate behind hers, his lips smacking furiously around yet another piece of gum. Sometimes she wished he would go back to smoking.

She touched one of the muddied soles, rubbing the dried earth between her gloved fingers. "Do we have an estimate for time of death?"

"Miller wasn't keen to commit."

"When is he ever?" she muttered.

Suds blew and popped a bubble, no mean feat behind his mask. "He relented when I promised not to put it in a preliminary report, and said sometime between midnight and four a.m., which narrows things down slightly."

Safia stood and turned in a halting circle, trying not to fall off the plate as she took stock of the area. Although no attempt had been made to conceal the man's body, it lay in a small clearing surrounded by dense woodland on Hampstead Heath, and had it not been for the curiosity of a runaway beagle it would probably have remained undiscovered for days. She could hear the murmur of voices and the occasional crunch of the undergrowth as CSI techs continued to comb the area, but there was only one vague path to access the body, and that was overgrown and snarled with vegetation.

"It's not just me, is it?" she said, and Suds shook his head. They had been working together on the Murder Investigation Team for three years, and they tended to be on the same wavelength for these things.

"No, it's not. I don't think he was here on a date."

"He's incognito enough for cruising," she countered, playing devil's advocate. The Heath was infamous for its cruising areas, and the police tended to turn a blind eye as long as the men remained discreet. She kicked at the plate instead of disturbing the thick layer of leaf litter. "But he's way off the beaten path."

"And he's…I mean, I'm no expert, but—" Suds used his torch to highlight the man's black combat trousers, military-style boots, black gloves, and the black polo neck beneath the dark camo jacket. "Is this style a thing these days?"

Safia huffed a laugh. "Hey, each to their own, right?" She wasn't convinced, though. The man was dressed for a mission, not a fetish, and she didn't for a minute think he had come here for sex. She took out her notebook and aimed her own torch on its current page. "So, just to recap. We have a body with no ID, no keys, and no wallet, and no one reported a gunshot. He wasn't armed, or he isn't now, at least, and someone blew the top of his head off within the last seven hours."

"CSI are still searching for footprints," Suds added. "But the frozen ground is an issue."

She started to jot bullet points. "We'll need to request CCTV from the surrounding area, check whether there are any local ANPR cameras, door-to-door all the houses in the vicinity." She blew on her fingers. Her toes were numb, and her nose was running like a tap. "And find somewhere we can get a bloody cuppa."

"I'm prioritising that one," Suds said. "It's not supposed to get this cold below the Watford Gap. I'm not dressed for it."

She eyeballed his suit. Every time he moved, it rode a little further up his arse crack. "You're not dressed for anything in that, pal."

The sound of hurried footsteps made them turn in unison. Miller, the lead CSI, stopped two plates away from them, but even in the torchlight they could see the gleam of excitement in his eyes.

"Development?" Safia asked.

"Indeed, Sergeant," he said. He was in his late fifties and had the formal diction of an elderly professor. "We've found a second, primary area of blood splatter close to the scene, and further traces moving away from it."

She looked at the body. "The traces aren't from him, then." It wasn't a question. The man had died instantly from a single wound, and his body lay where it had fallen. He certainly hadn't been running anywhere.

"Not a chance," Miller said.

"How much blood are we talking about?" Suds asked.

Miller's frown was his usual response to being put on the spot. "Hard to say. We're getting the blood dog out here. Initial spray is indicative of another bullet wound, and the victim was still bleeding as they left the scene."

"Victim or perp?" Safia said, mostly to herself. She thumbed toward the body. "We need to screen him for gunshot residue. It's likely he got a shot off and the perp took his gun after the fact."

Suds was smiling at her when she turned back, his eyes aglow above his mask. "This just got very interesting."

"Indeed," she said, mimicking Miller's intonation. He was already striding away and well out of earshot. "Injured perps are the best kind of perps."

"Nice cup of coffee while you rally the troops, then take a look at the overnight reports and ring around the local hospitals?" Suds said.

"That sounds like an excellent idea." She gestured for him to lead the way. "And if I'm going to be behind you for the next ten minutes, can you please fix your wedgie?"

❖

"Well, I appreciate you taking the time to check. I know how busy you are." Safia scrubbed "Barts" off her list and stirred her coffee with the Chupa Chups lolly Suds had given her. He had found her favourite chocolate and vanilla flavour, and as his reward he was now munching his way through a bag of Hula Hoops from the stash at the bottom of her desk drawer. "I wish you could appreciate how perfect these are," she said, twirling the lolly in the light whilst googling another phone number.

Suds held up a finger. It had two Hula Hoops stuck on it. At some point unwitnessed by Safia, he'd apparently run his hands through his mop of hair to fix the mess the Tyvek had made of it, and it was now streaked with salt. "Could you put me through to A&E, please? Thank you." He crunched the uppermost crisp. "I am the savoury yin to your sweet-toothed yang, DS Faris. This is why we get on so well together. Well, that and I kinda like it when you boss me around. Ah, hello. I wonder if you can help me..."

Leaving him to deliver his introductory spiel, she resumed her own search, keying in the number for the Royal London Hospital switchboard and listening to it ring out. When nothing obvious had flagged in the crime reports from the previous night, they had started their enquiries at the most logical place, the Royal Free Hospital on the doorstep of Hampstead Heath, but neither had expected their injured perp to make things so straightforward, and they were now working on the assumption that any London hospital with an Accident and Emergency department was fair game.

"A&E, please," she said when yet another apathetic operator answered her call. She didn't blame the lad for sounding fed up. Prior to joining the London Met, to win a bet with her youngest brother, she had spent eighteen soul-destroying, energy-sapping months working for customer services at British Gas. Even now, some ten years later, the sound of certain ringtones set her teeth on edge. Her mother had never forgiven Qaadir for making that bet, but he had sat in the front row at her passing out parade, and both his young daughters wanted to follow in their auntie's footsteps.

"Hello," she said to the nurse who picked up the transferred call. "My name is Safia Faris, and I'm a detective sergeant with the London Metropolitan Police."

"Oh, okay." The nurse's tone instantly switched from "this better not be about that old bloke in cubicle five" to animated and engaged.

Safia stirred her coffee again. It had gone cold, but it complemented her lolly. "I'm investigating a murder from early this morning, where blood found at the scene suggests a second victim sustained a gunshot wound."

"And you think they might have come here?" the nurse asked, as Safia paused to draw breath.

Safia smiled at her enthusiasm. "We're asking all the nearby hospitals to check their records for anyone who may have self-presented or even come in by ambulance, though the latter is unlikely."

Any ambulance crew worth their salt would have alerted the police to the victim of a shooting, and most London crews would be able to identify a bullet wound even if their patient wasn't for telling.

"Yeah." The nurse dragged the word out as the rapid clicking of computer keys transmitted over the line. "I've got one, two—no, crikey, four stabbings. Two minor, two in surgery. No shootings. Are you sure it was a shooting?"

Safia hated to disappoint her, but the blood splatter analysis had been conclusive on that point. "Absolutely."

"They haven't come here, then, Detective. Sorry I couldn't help."

"Not at all." Safia struck a line through the hospital. "It was very good of you to check." She hung up, her attention drawn back to Suds, who was scribbling big untidy notes on his A4 pad. Even upside down, she could read: *M: 24 years, right upper chest, SP approx 2 a.m. Small cal. Stable HDU.*

"Guy's," he mouthed, still on the phone.

She entered the hospital into a new search, where Google Maps insisted on clocking the route from the wrong end of the park to give her a road distance of 5.7 miles. Grumbling at its ineptitude, she re-entered her parameters, choosing the street closest to the murder scene: 8.1 miles from Guy's Hospital, or twenty-six minutes in a car.

"Plausible," she said, once he'd hung up. "Not so close as to be obvious, but not so far that he'd bleed to death en route."

Suds screwed up his crisp packet and made a doomed attempt to throw it in the bin. "We're assuming he's not expired at a mate's house, or at his own house, or at any point between our scene and an A&E."

"Well, yes we are, because we work for the Met, which makes us super-optimistic about absolutely everything." She snorted at his expression. "Is Mr. Self-presented-with-a-GSW up for visitors?"

"Not sure." Suds consulted the latter section of his notes. "Staff informed the Met shortly after he was triaged. Wood Street CID attended, but the nurse wasn't sure who they'd sent. Whoever it was, they need a kick up the arse about updating their logs."

"Yes, they do," Safia said, rather looking forward to administering that arse kicking. She brought up a new directory. "Who do we know at Wood Street?"

Suds thought for a moment, clearly discounting a number of possibilities. "Big Al?" he offered at length.

She lowered her head to the desk. "No no no no. There has to be someone else." Big Al was five foot two, with a terminal case of Small Man Syndrome. He had taken a shine to Safia because she was one of the few detectives he could easily make eye contact with.

"He speaks very highly of you," Suds said, and laughed at his unintentional pun.

"Sod off. Just sod off," she said into the grainy wood, patting her hand around until she hit his phone and then tossing the receiver toward him. "Okay, I'm pulling rank. You're calling him, and you're doing all the talking if we have to meet him." She rolled her head when her phone pinged with a message. "Uh-oh. Summons from the boss," she said, showing Suds the WhatsApp.

He crossed himself and looked heavenward. "What's she doing in today?"

"Overtime. Just my luck." Safia sat up and straightened her shirt. "Do I look presentable?"

"You look marvellous, darling."

"Yeah?" She ruffled his hair, showering his desk with salt. "Don't go telling Big Al that."

She left the MIT office and headed for the stairs, skipping down four flights and following a dubious chemical odour to the third door on the left.

"Safe to come in?" she shouted from behind the glass panel.

"Course it is, idiot," came the immediate reply.

She entered the lab to find Kamila in her usual spot, poised at a scope and surrounded by samples. Peeling off her mask, Kamila came around to the front of her work station to meet Safia halfway. The overhead lights caught her emerald nose stud, making it sparkle. Forest green headscarf today, to complement the stud. That meant she was in a mellow mood, despite her permanently overwhelming caseload.

"Morning." Kamila's smile lit her dark eyes and showed most of her teeth. It also weakened Safia's knees, but she hoped she hid that reasonably well.

"Got a present for you," Kamila said.

"Have you now?" Safia licked her dry lips. She wasn't sure if it was the air con or Kamila's proximity that had stolen all the moisture from her mouth.

Kamila tugged her to one side, further away from a lad with an unfortunate bald spot and a habitual sniff, and pulled a sheet of paper from the pocket of her lab coat. "I think you'll like it," she said, presenting the typed data to Safia.

Safia skimmed the array of numbers. They might as well have been written in Cyrillic. "Come on, Kami, you know I don't read geek."

Kami laughed and plucked the sheet from Safia's fingers. "It's really not very complicated." She indicated a line midway through the report. "This is from the blood sample taken at your Hampstead scene. Your AWOL perp?"

Safia nodded, reading the line and then rereading it as the penny dropped. "Bloody hell. Are you sure?"

"Yep," Kami said.

Safia whooped and kissed her full on the lips. A sudden tinkle of glass from the lad's desk suggested he'd dropped a test tube.

"I love you," Safia said. "Please continue to prioritise my cases in a manner that's borderline unprofessional."

Kami kissed her again, quick and sweet. "Any time. You can walk Bolly tonight."

"Deal. I'll see you later." Safia hit the door at a run and jogged back up the stairs to the first place where her phone showed any sign of a signal. "Suds?" she said, still puffing for breath. "You can cancel our trip to Wood Street."

"Oh? Why's that?" He sounded intrigued rather than pissed off.

She rechecked the report. She'd been gripping it so tightly that it was crumpled into a ball. "Because our perp's a woman."

ELIN. SATURDAY, 10:32 A.M.

It was dark when Elin opened her eyes, and for a few disorientating seconds she knew nothing beside a blind panic that crushed the air from her damaged lung and made the walls close in on her.

"*No!*" She bolted upright, whining as pain shot through her torso like an arrow, striking her back and then her chest.

"Hey. Hey, Elin."

A scuffle of movement, a thud as someone collided with an unfamiliar piece of furniture, and then Grace was there, her hands warm and firm on Elin's shoulders, urging her to lie back.

"What time is it?" Elin couldn't see a clock or raise her wrist to check her watch. A grey suggestion of daylight outlined the blackout blind at the window. She was still in the hotel room. More to the point, Grace was still in the hotel room. What the fuck was going on?

Grace flicked on a bedside lamp. "It's only half-ten. You've been asleep for about an hour, that's all."

"Oh." Elin sagged onto the pillows. "Did anyone—"

"No." Without needing to be asked, Grace gave her the phone she was searching for. "I kept it with me, and it hasn't buzzed."

Elin closed her eyes, willing the room to stop spinning. How the hell could she do this if she could barely sit up?

"God," she whispered.

The mattress dipped as Grace sat on the bed. She held out a glass of water with a straw in it. "Here. Just sip it, okay? You brought half of it back up last time."

"I don't—" Elin was struggling to put the pieces together. She remembered showing Grace the photo, the stark horror of Grace's reaction, her own reaction slow to build but instantly debilitating, and then a sensation like sinking into warm velvet. For the first time in three days, she had slept without nightmares. "What did you give me?" she asked.

Grace was still holding the glass for Elin. She used two fingers to pinch the straw, keeping it in place as Elin sucked up another cautious mouthful. "Morphine." She didn't sound apologetic. She sounded like a doctor who had done what needed to be done. "And something for the nausea, though that wasn't quite so effective. How are you feeling?"

Elin took a moment to consider. "Better, I think." The giddiness had finally eased, leaving her thoughts clearer, and she could draw a breath without wanting to scream. She touched her forehead again, finding a fresh piece of gauze where Grace had cleaned and dressed the wound. The oxygen mask had been exchanged for a nasal cannula, and the defib showed an improvement in all of her numbers. She couldn't see the drain, but a regular bag of saline had replaced the transfusion. "Am I still bleeding?"

Grace set the glass down. "Elin," she said in the tone Elin had come to recognise as her "don't ask me stupid questions" tone.

Elin held up a conciliatory hand and added a qualifier. "Into the drain. Am I still bleeding into the drain?"

"No."

The sigh that followed this admission seemed to start at Grace's boots and rattle her entire body. Even in the flattering glow of the lamp, she looked worn out. Her face was drawn, her fair hair was straggling loose from its once tidy knot, and her expression had lost the blaze of anger and indignation that had carried her through the last few hours. She seemed more lost and unsure of herself now than she had when Elin had first encountered her in the car park. Understandable, Elin supposed, given what she had put Grace through and what she had recently shown her, but enough was enough. She was now almost certain that Grace wouldn't contact the police, and "almost certain" was probably as good as things were going to get. It wasn't as if Elin had any other options open to her.

"Grace?" She kept her voice low, ensuring that Grace focused on her. "You've done everything you can. Take the drain out and go."

Grace shook her head. "No. It's too soon. I'll stay for a while." She sat straighter, all the authority returning to her posture, as if she had spent time coming to a decision and wouldn't be swayed. "I can stay for a while longer."

Elin wasn't used to having her orders so comprehensively undermined, but there was a familiar glint of determination in Grace's eyes, and Elin knew she wasn't going to sway her. "Have you slept?" she asked.

"I had a nap." Grace thumbed toward a chair by the window that had a couple of blankets strewn across it. "I do well off naps."

Elin could relate to that. Back in her old life, she had regularly gone forty-eight hours or more without proper sleep, surviving on a snatched twenty minutes here and there. Her new life wasn't quite so gruelling, though it had its moments. She put a hand on her phone, assailed by her usual terror that she might somehow have missed a text, but there was no telltale vibration, nothing but cool, inert plastic and a rusty stain on one corner that was probably blood.

"Tea or coffee?" Grace asked. Elin hadn't noticed her move, but she had gone to stand by the chest of drawers, and the room's small kettle was in her hands.

"Coffee," Elin said, beset by a sudden craving. She hoped this was another sign of her recovery: a need for caffeine and sugar and something solid to eat. "Is there a room service menu?"

Grace gave her a packet of stem ginger biscuits. "How about we see if these stay down first, eh?"

The kettle came to a stuttering boil, clouding the mirror above the drawers and adding a touch of pink to Grace's cheeks. Still half-doped and kitten-weak, Elin watched the morning ritual play out, wondering how many other guests were performing their own version of it, and how many times she had enacted it herself. Numerous times, with numerous different women, was the easy answer, in those strange, wild, in-between years after her resignation and before Amelia.

"Sugar?" Grace held up a small packet.

"Two, please." The words choked out, and Elin covered her mouth and then her face with her hands. She could feel her fingers starting to tingle, and an alarm sounded on the monitor as she hyperventilated. These attacks were another unwelcome blast from her past, hitting her at the slightest provocation, and they were ramping up in intensity. She'd had coping techniques once, distractions and breathing exercises, but she had never had to do them with a hole ripped in her lung. The attacks had come later, when everything physical had been fixed.

"Elin. Look at me." Grace underscored her command by taking hold of Elin's hands and lowering them. "Slow it down. That's it, slow it down. You are buggering up all my hard work."

"Sorry," Elin managed. She was. For everything. "Shit. I'm so sorry, Grace."

"It's all right," Grace said, and she sounded as though she meant it. "That's good, nice and steady. In through your nose and out through your mouth." She waited until Elin had better control of her breathing and then went back to the brews, giving Elin the chance to compose herself. A subtle tinkle of spoon on porcelain announced her imminent return. "Here."

She made sure Elin had a firm hold on the mug before collecting her own. They sipped their drinks in silence for a couple of minutes, Elin nibbling on a biscuit but not really tasting it. She sensed the question that was coming, and she knew she would answer it. She owed Grace that much. Grace pulled the chair closer to the bed and then leaned forward, cupping her mug with both hands.

"Will you tell me what happened?" she said.

Elin. Wednesday, three days previously. 6:55 p.m.

No, that's great. I heard from Wickham about an hour ago, and he seemed happy with the new set. I told him to give it a couple of days for us to work through any snags and I'd follow up with him on Monday. Oh, hang on a tick." Elin held her phone to her chest, listening to the muted rustles and bangs coming from the kitchen. "Did you find it, sweetheart?" she called.

"I found it!" Amelia shouted back. More banging and a clatter of cutlery. "Then I dropped all the spoons."

Smiling, Elin shook her head and toed off her trainers. The soles of her feet felt as if someone had taken a tyre iron to them. "Sorry about that," she told Neil Lowry.

"She up to mischief again?" Lowry asked.

"Always," Elin said, hanging her coat over the banister and stepping around the bags Amelia had abandoned at the bottom of the stairs. "We did the tourist thing today: Natural History Museum, shops, screamed ourselves silly in the Dungeon, more shops, and rounded it all off by watching the sunset from the top of the Eye."

"Bloody hell." Lowry was laughing. He had been born near Charing Cross and had been back in London for the last five years. Like most of the natives, he gave the main hotspots a very wide berth. "How are your poor feet?"

"Throbbing and about three sizes bigger than they should be." She paused at the kitchen door, watching Amelia set out mismatched plates and bowls. "Tonight will be pizza and ice cream on the sofa, with a terrible film."

"Sounds like fun." There was a wistful note to his voice. She knew his evening would likely involve paperwork, chain smoking, and a ready meal for one.

"It does, doesn't it?" She would have invited him for supper had she not detected the slight blur of drunkenness in his speech. "Thanks for all your help the last couple of days. You know I appreciate it, don't you?"

"Of course. Thanks for coming down to smooth things over."

"Any time. We make a good team." The overstated pendulum wall clock let out a bong as it hit the hour. She had intended to take the batteries out of the damn thing last night, and would probably forget again before bedtime. "I'd better run. We ordered the pizza on the way home, so it'll be here any minute."

"No worries, El. Goodnight."

He hung up, and she stuck the phone in her pocket. Then she took it out again and tossed it onto the shopping bags. She had come to London to appease a high-profile client whose newly installed security system wasn't allowing him to keep tabs on his neighbour's dodgy builders in the high definition promised by her sales team. Although Lowry was excellent at procurement, project management, and the technical side of things, the finer points of dealing with actual people, particularly moneyed people, were often lost on him. It was one reason he and Elin worked so well together; their skill sets were contrasting enough that they rarely trod on each other's toes.

With the client happy and the tech behaving itself, tonight and the long weekend to come were going to be for her and Amelia: no work, no conference calls, no ditching Amelia with friends. If Amelia wanted to go and see the ravens at the Tower, or head to Buckingham Palace to wave at the Queen, then that was what they would do.

"Are you getting your jammies on?" Elin asked as Amelia set a bottle of salad cream by the plates. She ate the stuff with everything.

Fortunately, their Airbnb was close to a supermarket, and the taxi driver hadn't minded a short detour.

"Yep." Amelia blew her nose on one of the napkins she had put with the cutlery, and then shoved it back beneath a knife. "Are you?"

"Amelia Breckenridge, you're a grim little imp!" Elin retrieved the napkin and threw it in the bin. "I don't know who dragged you up."

"You did!" Amelia said, and screeched as Elin made to chase her from the kitchen. She was quick off the mark for a four-year-old, evading Elin's attempt to tackle her, and leap-frogging the shopping to hurtle upstairs.

"Saved by the bell!" Elin shouted as the door chimed. She found her wallet, surprised to see there was still cash in it after the day they'd had, and opened the door to the delivery lad.

"Ms. Breckenridge and…Mouse?" he read from the receipt.

"That would be my daughter. The one you can hear quietly getting ready for bed up there."

"Ah." The lad raised an eyebrow as a series of thumps above them made the hallway light sway. "I can see where she gets the nickname."

Elin fished out the last twenty-pound note in her wallet. "You might not believe this, but I hardly heard a peep from her when she was a baby."

"Making up for lost time, is she?"

"With a vengeance." She smiled with genuine delight—the one thing she would never tell Amelia off for was being too noisy—and waved away his offer of change. "Have a safe night."

"You too," he replied automatically, and then corrected himself. "I mean, enjoy your supper."

"Thank you. We will." She carried the pizza into the kitchen, calling "Ready in two" as she went. A garbled response implied Amelia was inbound, so she opened the box to cool its contents slightly and poured glasses of juice.

The doorbell went again, and she swore beneath her breath, not in the mood to deal with impromptu guests. A glance at the receipt stuck to the box lid set her mind at rest, however. The order was missing the complimentary dough balls and dips that Amelia would no doubt spend all night dropping onto the sofa.

"Good thing it's wipe-clean leather," Elin muttered, and opened the door. "Hey, thanks for coming back." She spoke without really looking, distracted by a burst of song upstairs that might have been in Spanish: *Dora the Explorer,* busy raising bilingual children all over the UK.

"Hey," a man said.

Her head shot up at the unfamiliar voice. There were two men on the doorstep, both tall and broad, both wearing balaclavas, and they were inside before she realised what was happening, a sharp shove in the centre of her chest propelling her backward. She stumbled on one of the bags, losing her balance and colliding with the wall.

"Okay, okay. Easy." Righting herself, she put her hands up: immediate and complete surrender, the first tactic in damage limitation. "All my cards are in my wallet—credit, debit—I can give you the pin numbers." She heard the door shut and shook her head convulsively as one of the men pushed past her, his boots thumping on the wooden stairs. "My car keys are in my bag," she told the man who had stayed in front of her, but even as she spoke, she could tell by the way the men moved—fast, no discussion, no hesitation—that they weren't here for any of that. This was no random opportunistic burglary.

"Please don't hurt her," she said. And then she kicked out, barefoot and reeling but absolutely ready to fight. She aimed for the man's leg, her heel hitting his kneecap hard enough to make him grunt and rock sideward. Upstairs, Amelia's scream was abruptly cut off by the sharp sound of a slap, and Elin screamed for her, throwing her entire weight into a punch that split the man's chin and took him to the floor.

"You *fucker!*" She kicked him again, right in the balls. "You fucking bastard!"

Barely reacting to the impact, he whipped his legs around to catch and twist hers. Unable to brace herself, she fell hard, her forehead bouncing against the parquet flooring, and all the light flickered and disappeared for a second.

The man didn't say a word. He got to his feet and stood over her until he was sure she was recovered enough to pay attention. Then he dropped a phone and a charger by her hand.

"You'll need these." He nodded to his accomplice as he came to stand beside them, Amelia blanket-wrapped and limp in his arms. "If you go to the police, we'll start posting bits of her back to you."

"I'll kill you." Elin spat blood onto the floor. "I swear, I'll kill you both."

The man ignored her. "Give me two minutes," he told his accomplice, who gave a short nod and walked out, closing the front door behind him.

Elin pushed her hands beneath her. It took far longer than it should have; nothing was working properly, but she had to keep trying.

"Won't stay down, will you?" the man said. He grabbed her shirt, hauling her to her feet and shoving her against the wall. She stared at him: dark eyes, white skin, dark eyebrows, a crack in one of his teeth, but the details wouldn't stick.

He put his mouth close to her ear. He smelled like bubblegum. "I'll make you fucking stay down," he said.

Elin heard the noise as if from a distance. A hollow note, recognisable but almost overwhelmed by the ringing in her ears.

"Oh God." It was the clock marking the hour, she realised as the tinnitus ebbed away. Was it eight now, or even later? "*Shit.*"

Her left eye wouldn't open, her right showing her a blurry stretch of white skirting board and radiator piping. She was still in the hallway, curled into a ball, her arms wrapped around her head in an effort to protect it, and she was alone. There was no sound other than the tick of the clock and the boom of her pulse in her ears. The men had gone, and they had taken Amelia. Anger and terror hit Elin like a wave, dragging her under and then just as suddenly throwing her back to the surface. She couldn't stay here. She had to get up, but every tiny experimental movement made her whimper like an abandoned pup. She touched her face with numb fingers, tracing tender lumps and a deep laceration that her fingertips slid into. She remembered the man punching her, the way his lips had rippled almost into a smile, his broken tooth. Not satisfied with knocking her into a stupor, he had kicked her, his boot belting into her again and again, until she couldn't do anything but lie still and wait for it to be over. It had felt like a lot longer than two minutes.

The floor seemed to dip and ripple when she moved, and she retched, sending bolts of agony through her battered abdomen. She made it onto all fours, swaying with her head hanging low and bloody vomit streaming from her mouth. The phone the man had given her was under the radiator. She managed to get a hand on it and tug it from the pipe it had slid behind. The jolt activated its screen, where a lone WhatsApp icon bore an orange *1*, indicating a new message.

She sobbed, her hands shaking so hard she couldn't hit the icon until she put the phone back on the floor. The three-word message was punctuated by a smiley face: *Wait for it...*

There was nothing else. Nothing to indicate Amelia was still alive, no instructions, no demands, and the message was fifty minutes old.

At a complete loss, she collapsed against the banister, her knees drawn to her chest and her face throbbing. She should be doing something, she *needed* to be doing something, but the man's threat was playing on a loop in her head. Though her memory was hazy on most of the things he had said and done, it was crystal clear on that. She couldn't go to the police, nor could she go to the hospital, because someone there would feel obliged to report her injuries, which left her the option of sorting herself out so she was ready for the next message. It wasn't as if she had never been hurt before, but that had been then, before Amelia. Amelia had smoothed most of her sharp edges away.

"Get up," she muttered. "*Come on.*"

Gritting her teeth, she took hold of the closest baluster and hauled herself to her feet. Her nails dug into the wood and she went up the first step without thinking about it, her desperation and sheer bloody-mindedness getting her to the top of the flight. She was back on her knees before she reached the landing, crawling into the bathroom and falling to pieces the instant she saw the blood splashed across Amelia's dungarees. She hugged the clothing to her chest, breathing in the scent of Amelia's soap, and underneath that the smell that was simply her, sticky and mucky after a day eating sweets and dancing around dinosaurs in the museum.

Elin felt calmer once she had stopped crying, as if she had hit a limit and had now to simply carry on. She could compartmentalise trauma with the best of them. She'd had years of experience doing that.

The water steamed hot and murky as she ran the tap. She cleaned her face with a damp flannel, turning the water pink and then red, and leaving a rusty stain around the bowl when she had finished. Accustomed to patching up the wounds of a rambunctious four-year-old, she used a crisscross of Steri-Strips to close the laceration on her forehead and taped a dressing over it. She hadn't thought to pack pain-killers stronger than ibuprofen, so she took a double dose, keeping her hands cupped beneath the cold tap afterward until the chill helped to mask the discomfort that the pills probably wouldn't touch.

She stayed in the bathroom, bent double and pissing streaks of blood, as the hallway clock marked another hour. The phone marked it as well, buzzing with a message.

One million cash. Have it ready by Friday. We'll tell you where and when.

The text ran across the base of an image: Amelia wide-eyed with bewilderment, standing in the middle of a bare room. Her lip was cut and swollen, and a deep purple bruise covered most of her right cheek. Thick grey tape bound her wrists in front of her.

Elin shut the message down, washed her hands, and walked out of the bathroom to find her laptop.

❖

The money was there, Elin was confident of that if nothing else. In its infancy, Bridge Securities had been a small firm employing three ex-military Close Protection specialists, but under Elin's guidance it had grown into a multimillion-pound company with an enviable reputation, and offices in London, Manchester, and the UAE. In an average month, she could spend the ransom demand on personnel and overheads and earn it back twice over. Her only problem was going to be accessing the cash by the deadline without questions being asked, and the only person likely to ask those questions was Lowry.

With three online bank transfers and a share sale pending, subject to business hours, Elin signed out of her personal and trading accounts and minimised the windows. The revolving Bridge screensaver demanded that she re-enter her password and took her directly to the Central London CCTV file, once it had verified her credentials. A quick search on postcode and distance parameters brought up two nearby installations: a private residence and a local prep school. Disregarding the residence, where she knew the cameras would be narrowly focused, she downloaded the most recent feeds for the school and opened the file with a view of the main road.

Her vision blurred as the video loaded. She closed her eyes, waiting out the barrage of iridescent shapes and black floaters. Despite the central heating, she was freezing cold, and she was still vomiting at regular intervals. Concussion, internal bleeding, probable rib fractures. Recognising the injuries from experience, she hadn't needed to google any of them. All she could do was manage the worst of the pain and hope the symptoms abated of their own accord. She could just about walk, and she could talk, and that was good enough at the moment.

An online route planner put the school within a five-minute drive of her rental house. Leaving a company stock inventory running in one window, she skipped the first forty minutes of the video and set it to play at half-speed from 6:20 p.m. The slow-motion passage of traffic on the screen had a calming effect on her nerves, giving her a task to concentrate on and taking her mind off everything else. It didn't matter that she had no idea what she was looking for, nor that several other main roads led to this address. She made a note of any cars with two front seat passengers, zoomed in on the registration plates, and compiled a list of eight promising vehicles, three of which she highlighted as vans or SUVs with tinted rear windows. Cursing the inventory for confirming the purchase of body armour in her size but only showing available stock in the Abu Dhabi warehouse, she abandoned the video and started an online search for suitable substitutes.

"Jesus, really?" she said as eBay and Amazon adverts filled the screen. Entering her size, gender, and a narrow timescale limited her options to the one UK seller offering next-day delivery. She clicked on the "buy it now" tab, organising a pickup from a local drop box and completing the purchase through a PayPal account connected to an anonymous Yahoo email.

Even in her current state she knew she had to be careful. Only a handful of people had been aware of her impromptu trip to London, and she had thought them all trusted colleagues. If none of them were involved in what had just happened, then the kidnappers had tracked her by some other means, and the obvious one these days was technology. Had the circumstances not been so dire, she might have appreciated the irony of her chosen speciality being utilised so effectively against her.

She continued to record everything, writing in precise all caps, because things kept slipping away from her and she wasn't sure whether she would remember what she had done five minutes hence. At one point she dozed, the pen falling from her grip and her head drooping. She woke an indeterminate amount of time later, vomiting into the bowl she had set by the desk, and terrified all over again. Somewhere nearby a phone was ringing. She stumbled to her feet, following the sound to her own phone, not the one the man had given her. Lowry's name was on the display, his call expected but sooner than she would have liked. As someone with a thirty percent share in the company, he was automatically notified of any significant financial transactions, and the transfer of £800,000 into accessible accounts had obviously set all the bells and whistles off.

The call went through to voicemail, but Lowry phoned again without leaving a message. She watched the screen flash, her finger hovering above "accept." She couldn't do this on her own, and there was no one else she trusted enough to confide in. It was almost a relief to have her hand forced; perhaps that was why she hadn't tried to hide the transactions.

"Hey," she said, answering the call. She heard the tremor in her voice but couldn't do a thing about it.

"Hey. You working late?" A clink of glass in the background and an audible swallow punctuated the question.

"No." Her head and stomach reacted in perfect synchrony, one pummelling behind her left eye, the other making her reach again for the bowl. "Something's happened."

"What?" His tone changed, and she pictured him setting the beer down, instinctively on the alert. "El, what's happened? Are you okay?"

"No," she said again, not recognising the voice as her own. "No. I'm not okay."

"Shit." Something banged, and cloth rustled as he moved. "Are you still at the house?"

"Yes."

"Okay, okay. Stay there. Is Mouse with you?"

She sobbed, unable to answer.

"El." He spoke with enough authority to snap her to attention. "I'm getting a taxi. I'll be there in twenty."

It was more like half an hour before he hammered on the front door, but she had taken advantage of the extra time to shower and clean her teeth. She folded her bloodied clothes and wrapped them in plastic bags, sealing the edges with tape. She might not be able to go to the police right now, but it seemed sensible to preserve evidence for that eventuality.

Lowry took one look at her, swore, and spat out the peppermint he'd been sucking. He still smelled vaguely of booze, but his hold on her was firm as he ushered her back inside, and he'd had the presence of mind to bring a heavily laden rucksack. Knowing him, it would be stuffed with enough supplies to put a Boy Scout to shame, and ale to wash it all down with.

"Jesus, El." He guided her around the blood in the hallway and brought her to a stop in the kitchen, where he turned her into the light and examined the injuries on her face. "When—fuck." His keen eyes surveyed the room, missing nothing, his analysis of the scene complete within seconds. "Did they take her?"

"Yes," Elin said. There was no point lying to him. Even an idiot would have been able to guess what had happened, and Lowry was no idiot. "Two men. Just after seven p.m. They were quick, organised. They knew what they were doing."

He touched her swollen cheek with the pad of his thumb. "And yet they did this."

"I know. It doesn't make any sense." Professionals would have efficiently incapacitated her before taking Amelia. They wouldn't have wasted time and risked exposure beating the living daylights out of her. She paced across the kitchen, too strung out to stay still. Every time she stopped moving or thinking or hurting, Amelia was there, alone and scared to death, her face cut and bruised. "They left me a phone. They're demanding a million in cash, by Friday."

Lowry had moved the uneaten pizza out of sight. In its place, he set a first aid kit and flipped open its lid, then steered Elin onto one of the breakfast bar stools. "They send proof of life?" he asked.

"Yes." She didn't show him the picture. She couldn't. "I can't go to the police."

"I know." He peeled the dressing away from the laceration on her forehead and frowned at her attempt to close it. "This needs stitches."

"It's fine," she said, though the amount of blood on the dressing suggested otherwise. "I can't go to A&E either, and I've seen what happens when you darn socks. Stick on a few more strips, if you've got any."

He set to work, his brow creased with concentration. "If this was planned, why do it here? How many days a month do you spend in London? Two? Three at the most?"

"And I don't usually have Amelia with me." She had already considered this, and it was reassuring to have him notice the inconsistencies as well. "I think they must have followed us down here—the one who spoke had a northern accent—but I can't work out why. Why not wait until we were at home? They can't have had the time to do a proper recon on this place, and if they're not based locally, it just adds complication on top of complication for them."

He was nodding along, making little "hmph" noises whenever she hit a salient point. "Did you recognise either of them?"

"No." She looked beyond him to the kitchen tiles, staring until her eyes unfocused and two dark, balaclava-clad forms loomed over her. She clapped a hand over her mouth as it began to water, and Lowry must have recognised the warning signs because he put a clean bowl in front of her and went to fetch a glass of crushed ice and a teaspoon. She fished out a couple of chunks of ice, crunching the first and letting the second melt gradually to numb her sore tongue. She couldn't remember biting it, but one edge was raw and stinging.

"We need to start looking at our own personnel," he said, lifting a laptop from his bag. "Have you pissed anyone off recently? Fired anyone? Noticed someone taking an interest in you, asking about Amelia, that sort of thing?"

She did her damnedest to think, to picture each of her employees present and past and compare them to the two men, but the images kept fading to nothing, and she was finding it difficult to balance on the stool. She heard Lowry swear, felt him wrap an arm around her and sling one of hers over his shoulders. He half-carried her into the bedroom and poured her onto the bed.

"I'll sort everything," he said, pulling the quilt over her and dimming the light. "You just sleep now."

Elin spent Thursday wrapped in the protective fog of a concussion and the prescription-strength painkillers Lowry doled out. She tried to keep track of the hours as they slid by, but the pills were strong and the blackout curtains gave little away. Twice she woke screaming and kicking at the sheets, until the pain kicked back and threw her from her nightmare. Lowry came in with regular updates for her to nod at: there had been no further messages, the cash would be ready but the largest withdrawal required both of their signatures first thing in the morning, and he had made a list of any employees sacked for disciplinary reasons or currently serving a caution. There were only two people on that list, he warned her, one of whom was black and the other a five-foot-three, fifty-year-old administrator.

As the light behind the curtains darkened and the hum of traffic on the adjacent main road grew louder, he brought her coffee and toast and a laptop. Nibbling a corner of the toast, she scrolled through the security-pass mug shots of all their active employees, concentrating on those working within the Close Protection sector, who were the most likely to possess the skills to kidnap and conceal a child. Out of two hundred-plus personnel, almost a third worked on an ad hoc basis, meaning their whereabouts couldn't be ascertained unless they were active on an assignment, and ninety percent were ex-service personnel.

"It'd be quicker to list those who *don't* have the background to pull this off," she said. She hovered the mouse over the taskbar, checking the clock for the umpteenth time. "Why haven't they been in touch?" A plaintive note rang through her voice. She sounded like a child asking an impossible question. Lowry shook his head, and she pushed her plate away, the rich smell of butter making her feel sick again.

"How many people knew you were coming to London?" he asked, for want of a better distraction.

She swapped her coffee for iced water, hoping she might keep that down. "I'm not sure, but it wasn't a secret. I'd asked my PA for ideas to keep Mouse entertained, and half the damn office heard her FaceTime me on Tuesday night. She was so excited she was bouncing off the walls." Elin tapped the burner phone, willing it to show something other than its factory-set wallpaper. "God, why haven't they messaged me?"

"They will. They said tomorrow, right? So they'll need to send you instructions and further proof of life before then. Have you taken the SIM out of your own phone?"

"No." She caught his gist at once and shook her head, despite the nausea. "They can track me with it, I don't care. I'm not going to risk their phone failing and them not being able to contact me."

"Elin…"

"*No.*" She was aware of the consequences, of the likelihood the kidnappers could pinpoint her whereabouts with a simple hack, but she wanted them to know where she was. It was the easiest way to prove she was following their instructions to the letter. She laid her hand over Lowry's to soften her rebuttal. "I'm not making this a mission. I just want her back."

His face fell in a subtle sequence of tells. He was older than her, and the booze had folded even more lines into his forehead. A spider's web of tiny blood vessels speckled his cheeks, and his nose was swollen and overly pink. He had gained weight and wore glasses for reading, but he was still up for this; he had been bristling with tension and excitement all day.

"I can help you," he said.

"You *are* helping me, and I can't tell you how much I appreciate what you've done, but whatever they want me to do with the money tomorrow, I have to do it on my own."

"We're not insured for this, El."

The blunt reminder felt like another punch to her gut. The money wasn't hers to give away. She had scraped together two hundred thousand from her own savings, but the remainder belonged to the company. It would have paid wages and bills and been reinvested, and she was essentially stealing it.

"I don't know what else I can do. I'll pay it back from my wages and any bonuses, or get a loan once I have more time to arrange—" The buzz of the burner cut her off. "Fuck." She grabbed the phone and opened WhatsApp. A video file sat waiting for her, its preview screen blank aside from the white "Play" arrow.

"Let me watch it first," Lowry said, but she couldn't let go of the phone.

An establishing shot of the same windowless room, thin overhead light, a small mat and a blanket on grey carpet. Then Amelia was there, blinking and shielding her eyes with her bound hands.

"Mummy, I want to come home," she whispered. "I'll be good forever, I pinky promise."

"Show your mummy the paper," a man's voice told her, and she stooped to obey, holding a copy of the *Evening Standard* newspaper in front of her. The camera zoomed in, focusing on the day's date, and the video snapped to black. A two-word message followed: *Tomorrow night.*

"Bastards," Lowry spat. "The longer they leave us hanging, the less chance we have to get anything prepped."

"We've never had a chance," Elin said. She was scared to take her eyes off the WhatsApp thread in case something else appeared. "I'm going wherever they tell me, and I'm going alone."

❖

The Radisson Hotel receptionist was the archetype of deferential civility, pretending not to notice Elin's patchwork of bruises as he smiled and registered her details and then offered his assistance with her bags.

"It's fine. I only have this," she said, gesturing to the rucksack Lowry had given her. It was packed full of banknotes, the majority sorted and sealed into blocks of thousands, and the rest folded into envelopes.

The receptionist beamed at her without comment. She wondered what he was thinking, what he imagined her story to be: battered trophy wife in hiding from her rich husband? Tourist involved in an accident, newly discharged from hospital and on her way home? She didn't care, so long as he came nowhere near the truth of it.

"Thank you." She wasn't sure whether she had spoken in the right place—his puzzlement suggested not—but she took the key and went to the lift.

The text had arrived at twelve p.m., dropping another single breadcrumb onto the trail: "Hampstead Heath." There had been no photo, no video, no hint as to when she needed to be there. According to Wikipedia, the Heath was three hundred and twenty acres of wild, public space, sitting on one of the highest points in London and miles away from the house she had been renting. It made sense to her to find a new base closer to the rendezvous point, so she wasn't forced to drive across the city on a deadline. Lowry hadn't been happy about it, but by then there was little left for him to do, and he had reluctantly agreed to go home. She would tell him where she was later. That way he wouldn't show up in the hotel's lobby, unannounced and armed to the teeth.

Although the hotel's exterior was as ugly as sin, her suite was well-appointed and comfortable, boasting a view across the Thames. The sun was beginning to set, dimpling the river's ripples with pink and orange, and on any other evening she might have sat on the balcony with a glass of wine whilst Amelia slurped juice and dropped crisps willy-nilly. Instead, she slumped onto the chair by the small dining table and released the straps on her new body armour. She had collected the vest en route to the hotel and decided that wearing it beneath her coat would be less conspicuous than carrying it, but its chest and back plates were heavy against her broken ribs, and she'd had to fasten it tightly to make it fit. She set the burner and her own phone on the table and dry-swallowed a couple of Brufen. "Try to eat something" had become a mantra for Lowry over the past fifteen hours or so, but the nausea came in waves whenever she thought of food, and she couldn't tell whether her head injury or her nerves were to blame.

"Probably both," she murmured, and drank more water to placate her absent friend.

The text arrived hours later, just as she was beginning to quiver with stress and the terror that no one was going to contact her after all.

3:00 a.m., plus a set of coordinates to enter into a web link. She loaded up the link on the burner and watched a tiny red arrow plot a route across the Heath and into woodland.

Come alone, a second message reminded her. They didn't bother to send a photo of Amelia. At this stage, Elin was obviously going to have to trust them.

By London standards, traffic was light when she set off, and she shaved ten minutes from an estimated travel time of thirty-five. She parked on an anonymous leafy side street, tucked in amongst the cars of local residents and close to the section of the Heath she needed. Slinging the rucksack across both shoulders made its weight easier to bear and kept her hands free, giving her the illusion of readiness, even though she'd refused Lowry's advice to come armed.

"Stop being so pig-headed," he had snapped, slamming blocks of money into the bag. "I could have a gun in your hand by this afternoon."

She had no doubt of that. In accordance with UK law, their Close Protection specialists operated unarmed, but Lowry had contacts in all the right places, and what he couldn't procure in person, he could obtain through alternative channels. However tempting his offer, though, the kidnappers would be sure to search her, and a concealed weapon was not going to convince them she was trustworthy. Her sole aim was to get Amelia out safely, not to risk her being caught in the middle of a fire fight.

The cold needled the tender skin on Elin's face as she set off walking, and she thought of the way Amelia thrilled at every change of season—bottle-feeding lambs at the petting farm in spring, picnicking barefoot in summer, and then swapping into wellies perfect for stomping through puddles and snow. Give her any extreme of weather and she was as happy as a lark. It was one reason Elin had moved them away from Manchester's perpetually mild and wet climate. They hadn't gone far, but they had gained height enough to give Amelia the seasons she craved.

Elin wiped her cheeks dry and kept her pace brisk, pushing through the stiffness of her limbs and the vertigo that threatened to upend her. The hike was reminiscent of a forced march, her team thrown into the middle of nowhere with weighted packs and a deadline to meet, and that was how she continued to see it, because it was safer that way. She could keep going, keep doing this, keep heading toward who the fuck knew what, if only she didn't stop to think about it.

Brittle grass crackled beneath her boots as she left one of the official footpaths and paused to get her bearings. The arrow on the phone's mapping directed her away from the sporadic flashes of torchlight and flares of cigarettes, and into rougher terrain where the paths became indistinct and she had to switch on her own torch to navigate a route through thickening undergrowth. Bare branches twisted overhead, the trees crowded closely enough to block out the sky, and every step she took sounded a warning of crunching leaves and twigs. She listened as she walked, straining to hear movement, but the noise she was making drowned everything else out. Besides which, whoever awaited her was probably in position already.

The arrow she was following began to flash, and a countdown appeared on the screen, drawing her in like a moth to lamplight: ten yards, five yards, stop. She stood in a tiny clearing, rigid with expectation, puffing out dense white clouds. She was early, but not by much, and a nearby rustle of leaf litter told her she wasn't alone. A sudden glare of well-aimed torchlight blinded her. She blinked, raising her hands, not to cover her eyes but to prove she intended to cooperate fully.

"Drop the bag," a man's voice told her. She didn't recognise it, and she couldn't see where he was.

She didn't move. "Where's Amelia?"

"Drop. The. Bag." He banged emphasis onto each word, and twigs cracked as he stepped into view. Everything he wore was black, and his hood dropped his face into shadow. His hands were crossed at the wrists, aiming the torch and a gun at her head. "I won't fucking tell you again."

She wrestled free of the straps and held the rucksack in front of her as if that would somehow keep her safe. "Please just let her go," she whispered, but she was hardly able to shape the entreaty, because Amelia wasn't there. They had never intended to bring her, and this wasn't going to get her back.

"Put it down and take four steps to your left." The man moved forward as he spoke, and Elin did as he ordered, keeping the distance between them. He crouched, using his torch hand to unzip the top of the bag, his gun still pointed toward her. "Kneel," he said.

She shook her head, too frantic now to be scared. "Where's Amelia? I've done everything you asked."

He was halfway to his feet, his face flushed and furious, when a sharp crack sounded and the top of his head disappeared. She froze, struggling to understand what had just happened, even when the man's body fell as if poleaxed and she realised that the fine mist coating her face was his blood.

Another crack. Oh *fuck*. Small calibre, suppressed, behind her and to the right. All of this as she dived to grab the man's gun and the rucksack, her momentum propelled by a dull thud just below her shoulder blade. She staggered, thrown off balance, but managed to hook the arm that still worked through one of the straps. She darted for cover, aiming for a darker area of the forest, her strategy narrowed to getting out of sight and keeping on her feet.

A shout, the words garbled but rising into a question, and the crash of someone chasing her. She kept going, kicking free of brambles and bouncing off trees like a pinball, her breath wheezing out as blood soaked her shirt. Unable to grip the torch properly, she ran almost blind but more slowly now, searching for somewhere to hide. A fallen tree loomed in front of her, its branches arching like monstrous claws, its trunk massive and stretching for what seemed like miles. Instead of trying to climb it, she slid beneath it, pushing into soft fungus and leaves, and tucking into a ball.

She didn't know how long she lay there. Long enough for the cold and the damp to seep into her and set her shivering, and for the noises of pursuit to grow distant and then disappear. When she finally moved, pain almost choked her, and blood fired into her throat, making her gag and heave onto the forest floor. She coughed, clammy and still nauseous, and hobbled by the burning in her back. She couldn't reach the wound without removing her vest, but the vest felt as if it was the only thing holding her together, and she was afraid to loosen it even by a fraction. She shoved the gun into the waistband of her trousers and then stood in agonised stages, resting both hands on the trunk until the dizziness passed. The burner phone buzzed as she began to pick her way through the trees. It wasn't a text but an incoming call. She knelt, one arm wrapped around an oak tree, to answer it.

"Hello?" Talking made her cough again, and no one replied until she had stopped.

"That was stupid," a man said. She thought it was the same man who had beaten her, but she couldn't be sure. "Which part of your kid do you want first?"

"No! Listen to me, *please* listen." She was gabbling, afraid she wouldn't get her chance to explain. "I don't know who that was, I *don't*. They weren't with me, and they shot me too."

"You told someone."

"Yes," she gasped, because she had nothing left to lose. "My business partner. I couldn't get the money otherwise, but he wouldn't—it *can't* have been him."

The man gave a short, disbelieving laugh, as unconvinced by her protests as she was. If the shooter wasn't one of his men, that left a very short suspect list.

"You need better friends."

She ignored the taunt. She couldn't process Lowry's probable involvement at all, let alone accept he might be the culprit. "I still have the money," she said. "Give me another chance to get it to you."

"I'll think about it," he said, and the line went dead.

She leaned her cheek against the tree trunk. Getting to her feet seemed insurmountable, when all she wanted to do was go to sleep and have Mouse run in to wake her when this was over. She wouldn't even tell her off for yanking the quilt back or shoving her cold feet against Elin's warm tummy. Christ, the asinine fucking things she used to get cross with her over.

"Come on," she muttered. "*Move.*"

She was standing before the pain registered, and she kept to the shadows as she took a roundabout route to her car. She worried that someone—*Lowry?*—might be waiting there to finish the job, but the street was silent, and she drove away from it with no sign that anyone was tailing her. She set off toward the Radisson, confusing the satnav by weaving through the back streets, avoiding the number plate recognition cameras on the bypasses and the CCTV on the busier roads. She wasn't sure why at first, but the reason finally slinked in under her guard, and she slammed her fists against the steering wheel. Lowry had always been an excellent hacker. It was one of the skills that had made him such a valuable asset.

Ninety minutes later, with black splotches spiralling across her vision and blood dripping onto her seat, she realised that she was lost, and that nothing the satnav was telling her was making sense. She pulled over and muted the voice, widening the screen to search for a landmark. A red cross on a white background showed the closest hospital: The Royal London, ETA six minutes.

She didn't remember getting there. One minute she was leaving the electric-blue light of the fish and chip shop she had stopped in front of, and the next she was skulking along one of the hospital's feeder roads, her headlights dimmed and her speed slowed to a crawl. Signs tempted her toward the main body of the hospital, to Outpatients, All Other Departments, and, most seductive of all, Accident & Emergency.

A flash of motion caught her eye as she approached the last in a line of maintenance buildings, and she stopped as if hypnotised, watching light bounce off reflective strips, the bright lines moving to and fro, their progress unhurried but efficient. A slight irregularity in step, and she saw one of the strips in full, its lettering bold and designed to be conspicuous: DOCTOR. Other details filtered in then: the ambulance response car with its HEMS insignia, the supplies being toted to restock the car's equipment cages, and a gap in the wire fencing that she thought she might be able to squeeze through.

She was standing by the corner of the ambulance garage, the gun held loosely at her side, by the time the figure wearing the reflective jacket came into focus. It was a woman, smaller and slighter than her, and completely oblivious of her presence. Must be at the end of a nightshift, Elin thought, well acquainted with the blank expression and automatic tread of the bone-weary.

Elin slumped against the cold brickwork, overwhelmed by waves of guilt and shame. What the hell was she thinking? How on earth could she justify doing this? She dragged a breath into her sodden lungs. She could taste fresh blood in her mouth again, feel its stickiness coating her lips, and it pared things down to the absolute basics: if she died, Amelia would die. It was that simple.

"Shit," she whispered. "*Shit.*"

It took her three attempts, but she managed to unload the gun and drop its magazine into her pocket. The woman was still standing by the car, her back to Elin as she restocked a kit bag. Elin took a proper hold of the gun and set off toward her.

Grace. Saturday, 12:17 p.m.

You were there for the rest of it," Elin said quietly. She wasn't being flippant, she had simply run out of steam. Her complexion was ghastly, and the muscles at the side of her neck corded as she struggled to moderate her breathing. She cradled her coffee with both hands, her knuckles blanching. Had she been able to lift it without spilling it, it might have eased the hoarseness from her voice.

They defaulted to sitting in silence, Grace cross-legged on the sofa and Elin in one of the armchairs. At Elin's insistence, Grace had helped her limp into the living room, and she had told most of her story watching the boats pass by on the Thames, as if the distraction made the details easier to recount. A thin mist drifted across the water, the winter sunshine working hard to burn it away, and life below the window was carrying on as normal. No matter how hard Grace tried, she couldn't get the images of Elin's daughter out of her head. She was so envious of the people sauntering along the riverside footpaths that she felt like screaming.

"Do you believe me?" Elin asked at length. There was no challenge in her question; she sounded wretched and desperate for reassurance.

"Yes," Grace said. She wasn't naive enough to have accepted Elin's version of events at face value, and the cynic in her had considered Elin might be telling her what she wanted to hear, or even using her to establish an alibi, but those initial suspicions had long since faded. Elin reminded her of the victims of random terrible violence she treated at the hospital. Like them, Elin had narrated her account in a disconnected monotone, her gaze downcast or flitting around the room, checking for the exits. At no point had she tried to play on Grace's sympathy, or embellished for added impact, or betrayed the emotions she must have been feeling, and there was no doubt in Grace's mind that she had told the truth.

Elin's lips pursed as she exhaled a prolonged, shuddering breath. "I try not to think about what they might—" She put her mug on the table, spilling coffee everywhere. "She's only four years old. She's a baby, and I can't—Oh God, Grace, I think they've probably killed her already."

The plea brought Grace off the sofa to crouch by Elin's chair. When she put a tentative hand on Elin's leg, Elin tensed as if scalded, and then crumpled, her entire body collapsing into Grace's arms. Grace held her tightly, letting her sob out three days of misery and the horror to which she had just succumbed.

"Shh," Grace murmured over and over. She wanted to tell her that everything would be okay, but she couldn't bring herself to lie.

"I'm sorry," Elin said. "I'm sorry for what I did to you. I'm sorry."

"Don't." Grace brushed damp hair from Elin's face. "You don't need to get upset about any of that." She wasn't saying it to placate her. She couldn't imagine what she might have done, had she been in Elin's place. Exactly the same, perhaps, if she could have found the courage from somewhere. She squeezed Elin's hand, keeping hold of it in a loose grip when Elin didn't pull away. "I can't believe the bloody gun wasn't loaded."

Her indignation succeeded in surprising a smile from Elin. Grace gave her a tissue, and Elin blew her nose and then wiped her eyes.

"It was the only sensible thing I did," she said, scrunching the tissue into a ball. "I wanted to be sure I couldn't accidentally hurt you. I know I scared the shit out of you, I know I did, and if there had been any other way, I would have taken it. That last hour, when I was driving and I couldn't find the hotel and I couldn't stop the bleeding, I don't remember it too well. I think I was on the verge of giving up and going to A&E, but then you were there, so I...I..." She left the thought hanging and lowered her head.

Grace put a hand on Elin's chin and gently raised it. "Stop it. We have bigger things to worry about, okay?"

"There is no *'we,'*" Elin said at once. "You need to go home, and I can't stay here." She checked the time on her phone, hitting the button twice as panic ruined her dexterity. "Lowry will find me. He can get into the CCTV. He could be here any minute, and he'll—I don't even...God, I still can't believe he'd do this."

"Elin," Grace snapped, bringing her to immediate attention. "I'm not going to leave you."

"No, no, you have to." Elin got up but immediately overbalanced, bashing her thigh on the chair and jolting the chest drain. Grace scrambled to help her, stabilising the tube and manhandling her onto the sofa. It wasn't dignified, but it worked, and her colour improved once her legs were elevated.

"You with me?" Grace asked. She had her fingers on the pulse at Elin's wrist, feeling it slow as Elin's blood pressure increased.

"Yeah."

"Good."

Elin was staring past her, fixated on a blank part of the wall. "Lowry never misses a single one of Amelia's birthdays," she said. "He sends her these little bears, all different colours, all getting a bit bigger each year. She still sleeps with them, even the one she's chewed half to bits. And I keep trying to come up with a different explanation for what happened on the Heath, but every time it brings me back to him, because there's no one else it could have been. And if I'm being rational about it, it does make sense."

It wasn't making much sense to Grace. "If he wanted the money, why didn't he just take it from you?" she asked. "It's not like you were in any state to stop him."

"I think that would've been too obvious," Elin said. "But if he'd killed me during the exchange, he could have retrieved the cash for himself, landed the blame on the kidnappers, and assumed control of the company. Amelia stands to inherit my share, but without the ransom being paid, she wouldn't be a problem for him, would she?" Her voice was raw with anger, and Grace didn't like to think what fate might befall Lowry, should Elin get her hands on him. She might be too weak to stand right now, but Grace was sure she'd rise to the occasion, given the opportunity.

"So now he's out to finish what he started," Grace said. "That's all we need."

"He's in too deep to risk leaving this undone," Elin said. "We have to move." She had clearly regained her equilibrium; her expression was steadfast, and she swung her legs off the sofa to sit herself up.

Grace wasn't going to argue. She handed her the burner and a glass of water. "Put it on charge, and drink that. I'm going to have a quick shower, and then we'll see about getting you on your feet. How does that sound?"

"Like a plan," Elin conceded. There was little point her arguing the toss when she'd just keeled over. Besides which, Grace had folded her arms and set her face, and Elin seemed to realise she wouldn't win against that.

"You stand up without me, you're going to fall on your arse again," Grace said, in case Elin had any lingering intentions to go solo. "So stay put."

Elin nodded. "Thank you."

Grace relaxed her stance. There had been a lot loaded onto those two words, and she understood everything Elin hadn't been able to say. "Don't mention it. I'll be back in ten."

She walked through the bedroom, preoccupied with practicalities: how could she best conceal what had happened here? Would it be possible to bag up the bloodied towels and bedding and take them, or would they have to be left behind for someone to find? She had been tidying the medical waste as she went along, but it was in a bright yellow incinerator bag, not something she could sneak out unnoticed. Would simply keeping the "Do Not Disturb" sign on the door and not booking out of the suite buy them enough time? How much time was enough time? How the hell was she going to manage Elin's chest drain, when it wasn't yet safe to remove it?

They had to get rid of Elin's car, ditch it, and hire a new one. And how long did they have before someone discovered the HEMS car, if they hadn't already?

It was only in the shower, with hot water peppering her scalp and the fresh scent of citrus washing away that of blood, that she wobbled. Figuratively at first, and then literally, her legs trembling so hard that she had to sit on the cubicle's floor. Delayed reaction, she told herself, as her skin crawled with goosebumps.

"We should go to the police," she said between chattering teeth, practising the line in readiness for repeating it to Elin. "We should go to the police."

It was too easy for her to say that, though, to wash her hands of the whole business and walk away from the promise she had just made. She thought of the video, heard Amelia say "I pinky promise," and bit her lip, ashamed all over again.

"Right, then." She stood and turned off the water, feeling better just for being clean. She found Elin sitting on the bed, surveying the mess they had made. Elin had the bullet Grace had taken from her chest nestled in the palm of her hand.

"The police are going to have a field day in here," she said.

SAFIA. SATURDAY, **10:32** A.M.

"Toblerone," Safia said, and looked aghast when Suds pulled his face. "What the hell is wrong with Toblerone? They're Swiss, so the chocolate is delicious. They're crunchy *and* chewy, and they're triangular. You cannot find fault with triangular chocolate."

Suds inched the car forward, switching off the heater when it began to suck in the fumes of the bus in front. "They stick in my teeth, and I never know which bit I'm supposed to bite first."

"Wha—the top! You bite the top first. Where else would you bite?" She threw up her hands. "So what would *you* take?"

"How hot is it on my desert island?" he asked. He had an annoying habit of putting far too much logic into their games.

"It's temperate. Warm days, cool nights. Stop beating around the bush and name your chocolate."

He slowed for a junction, hedging his bets by straddling two lanes. "Is it left here?"

"Yes. Then you need the right-hand lane for the roundabout."

"Biscuit and raisin Yorkie," he said, adjusting his position and making the turn just ahead of a learner driver. "Proper man's chocolate."

"Biscuit and raisin is the girl's version." She shrugged as his mouth dropped open. "Everyone knows that. Third left onto Honeysuckle Ave, and you should see the CSI van."

The avenue was well-heeled, tree-lined suburbia, and the curtain twitchers were out in force. Some of the residents were more subtle about it than others, washing their cars or mowing lawns that should have been left dormant till spring, but most were standing at their front windows, fingers pointing and chins wagging. They would find out the basic details soon enough when the door-to-door officers came knocking.

Safia fidgeted in her seat, thrilled to have made so much progress in such a short time. While she had never been the type of detective who obsessed about her solve and conviction rate, the constant pressures of working in the capital often meant that speed was of the essence, and, like all departments at the London Met, the MIT were chronically understaffed, under-resourced, and overburdened.

"Who's walking through with us?" Suds asked, as he pulled in a couple of spaces behind the CSI van. "Miller?"

"Harry Ascot, I think. Miller's still at the scene."

He gave her a thumbs up. If Miller was the aged, tweed-wearing, technophobic professor type, Harry was his young, unconventional, whizz-kid protégé who always had snacks.

They heard Harry before they saw him, his bellowing laugh carrying across the street and through the closed car windows. Thanks to a youth misspent at raves, he was hearing-impaired and never knew at what volume to pitch his voice.

"Ear defenders at the ready," Safia said, and clicked off her seat belt.

"DS Faris!" Harry yelled, as he saw her getting out of the car. He strode over to greet them, pumping Suds's hand and offering them both a bag of pretzels. Safia pocketed hers, while Suds tipped half of his into his mouth.

"Morning," she said. "You've been busy, haven't you?"

Harry beamed at her. "Oscar did most of it. You've just missed him."

"Damn." She loved the CSI blood dog. Her family had never had a pet, and her parents considered dogs unclean and only good for guarding properties. One of the first things she and Kami had done on moving in together was head to the local shelter for a rescue mutt.

She scanned the pavement as Suds and Harry caught up on the recent footy results. A cluster of individually numbered forensic markers indicated a particular area of interest, and crime scene tape sealed off a car's length section of the road and pavement. At the top of the street, officers were starting their enquiries. She craned her neck, checking lampposts and nearby houses for CCTV, but she couldn't see anything obvious.

"Number twelve," Harry said, pre-empting her question. "The white house there. It has one camera above the front door and another facing the street."

She considered the placement in relation to the CSI markers. "I'm assuming those are for blood."

"Indeed." Harry hit Miller's pompous intonation right on the nail. "We might get lucky with the street camera, given the direction of the trail we've picked up."

She gestured for him to lead the way, Suds licking his fingers clean prior to squeezing into yet another ill-fitting Tyvek.

"Shall we start at the end?" Harry asked, once they were suitably attired. He walked them over to the markers, letting them squat to examine a small cluster of droplets. There were nine in all, tiny, deep red in colour, and long since dried. A sharp shower of rain would have disposed of them instantly, and they would probably never have been found without Oscar's expertise. Further markers highlighted a route that continued across the street toward the Heath.

"This is where she was parked," Safia said. "She pauses here to unlock her door. Bleeds on the spot for a few seconds."

"Yep. Those are the last droplets found." Harry waited until Safia and Suds were standing again and then set off walking. "She was bleeding steadily, left us a proper little breadcrumb trail all the way back to the scene." He continued at a decent clip, past evenly spaced spray-paint circles, each demarcating another bloodstain. "There's nothing really of note for a while."

Safia nodded, using the circles to plot the perp's wavering egress. She could imagine the woman staggering off the Heath, bleeding and in pain, all of her adrenaline expended in getting back to the relative safety of her car. And then what? Where had she gone from here? Safia walked without speaking for a few minutes, listening to the bark of distant dogs and the shouted commands of their owners. The ground was rough underfoot, and the CSI markers were solid plastic again, weaving between the trees.

"Hmm," she said, and Suds stopped at the same time she did, his forehead crinkling.

"Something wrong?" Harry asked, crunching pretzels behind his mask.

"She zigzagged." Suds turned, re-evaluating the route. "Why would she do that?"

Harry consulted a timer he'd set on his watch. "Oh, you two are good. Fastest yet."

"What?" Safia started to laugh as she realised what he'd been doing. "You little sod. Was this a test?"

He coughed on an inhaled pretzel crumb. "More of a private bet. It took Matt ages, and I had to drop a lot of hints in the end. As the crow flies, our perp's shortest route is directly across there." He pointed to the wide expanse of grass beyond the tree line. "Instead, she came through here and even doubled back at one point."

"She might just have been lost," Safia said.

He set off again, his tread eager, as if he had saved the best till last. The exertion was making him puff a little, but he was still managing to shout. "That's certainly one acceptable theory. No footprints. The ground was too hard. There are plenty of places where the leaf litter has been disturbed, but there's nothing we can cast. However…" He left his sentence hanging as they approached a large, fallen beech tree with a CSI crouching at the midpoint of its trunk. "This is very interesting and might put paid to your 'she was lost' hypothesis." He ushered them to the side of the CSI. "We think she spent some time sheltering here. There's a pronounced area of disturbance just under this hollow, and we've found a substantial quantity of fresh blood."

Safia knelt and studied the small space. It was an ideal hidey-hole, with an obvious patch of flattened leaves and moss at its base where the woman had been lying. Unless someone had stumbled on that exact spot, she would have been all but invisible in the darkness.

"How much blood are we talking?" Safia asked.

Harry squatted by her side, his knees cracking. "Our best estimate is in excess of half a litre, and that over there is a puddle of bloody vomit."

She followed his pointed finger to a white marker. It was close by, as if the woman had finally crawled out and chucked her guts up. Or perhaps she had vomited, then collapsed and rolled under the tree, or perhaps... Safia knocked on the trunk, the scrape of her knuckles on the rough bark helping to clear her head.

"Are we assuming that someone was chasing her?" she asked, just as Suds said, "So who was she hiding from?"

"Jinx," Harry said.

Safia paced a couple of metres there and back, her boots sinking into newly defrosted mud. "It's hard to work out, isn't it? We know for certain that two people were involved, our perp and our vic. And they were both shot in, or near, that clearing. But did he shoot her first? Was there a chase then? She hides, he finds her, and they end up back in the clearing where she blows his head off?"

"Sounds pretty unlikely," Suds said.

Safia took no offence. She had decided against the theory even as she was voicing it, but talking these ideas through, no matter how ludicrous they were, usually steered her toward the right answer.

"There must have been a third perp," Suds said with the certainty of hitting an open goal. "At the very least. Our injured perp manages to get away, but there's someone else there to hunt her down."

"I wonder if they've caught her." Safia shivered at the possibility, picturing the scenario as he'd described it: the woman's pitch-black dash through the trees, hampered by a bullet wound, with footsteps pounding after her, gaining on her. She must have got back to her car in one piece, but what then? Was that why they hadn't been able to find her? Safia cut off that train of thought and gave herself a mental slap. The woman was just as likely to have been the hunter as the prey. She was probably involved in something illegal, and happened to come off worst.

"We need the gunshot residue results back from our vic ASAP," Safia said. Focusing on the science was far easier than trying to work through the messy human side of things. "If he's clean, that'll confirm a third party, unless the woman went and shot her bloody self, which at this moment I wouldn't rule out. I'll give Kami a call and see what she can do for us."

"We need that CCTV as well." Suds was already retracing the route to the street, his sense of urgency mirroring Safia's. She jogged after him, and he slowed until she fell in step.

"What the hell happened out here?" she said. She had hoped this would be a straightforward investigation where they could make a quick arrest and move on to the next, but they had suddenly gone from a clear-cut case of one murder with one suspect to one murder with two suspects—or was it one murder, one attempted murder, and multiple suspects?

Suds stopped, his expression uneasy as he looked back toward the fallen tree. "Your guess is as good as mine, Saf."

Mr. Grimshaw—"call me Howard, please"—at number twelve Honeysuckle Avenue insisted on serving tea from a proper teapot, with biscuits on matching china saucers. Grateful for the warmth of his living room, if impatient to get on with things, Safia sipped her tea whilst repressing the impulse to snatch the remote control from him and sort the damn DVD out herself. They could have taken the CCTV disc back to the office, but Howard was determined to host the premiere, and without a warrant they were dependent on his goodwill.

"Sorry, oops. I've not done this before. Ah, got it now," he said as he ejected the disc and had to start all over again.

"No problem, Mr. Grim—Howard," Suds said with enviable restraint. "You just take your time." He slurped a mouthful of tea and then seemed to remember his manners and stuck his pinky up. Safia stifled a laugh in her own cup. Suds had a far better poker face than she did, and he never failed to use it to his advantage.

"I've not had the cameras for long," Howard said. "There was a lot of antisocial behaviour on the avenue. Men coming and going at all hours, loitering, canoodling. You know the type."

Safia made a sympathetic noise, searching for some kind of distraction, because she really couldn't be arsed logging an official complaint. The DVD from the porch-mounted camera was on the coffee table. She reached for it just as Howard got the other disc running, which saved her from having to make polite conversation about the intricacies of CCTV installation.

"So, we can skip all of this bit, can't we?" Having found his mojo with the remote, Howard was fast-forwarding through the early evening hours. Safia watched the quick-fire images, the sky darkening in triple time, and the quality of the recording deteriorating to a grainy monochrome as night fell completely.

"Okay, slow it down from here," she said. The timestamp read *00:12 hrs*, and the parking space in front of the house was still empty. She held out her hand for the remote. "Howard, would you mind?"

He acquiesced, relinquishing the remote with a dignity more befitting the Olympic torch, and poured himself a cup of tea. He might not be wielding the control anymore, but they weren't getting rid of him.

Suds hunched forward, his tea forgotten, as Safia ran the DVD through at double speed. An hour ticked by on the time stamp, then two, then two and a quarter.

"Bingo," she said as a dark, sporty-looking car pulled into the parking space and the driver extinguished its lights.

"Audi TTS, very nice." Suds was an unashamed petrol-head. Fortunately, he had plenty of other colleagues who shared his enthusiasm, so Safia, who considered her car a necessary evil, was never called on to feign an interest. "Going rate for a new one would be about forty-five grand."

"Blimey," Howard spluttered. His modest Mondeo was front and centre in the CCTV image, its value a fraction of the Audi's, and Safia suspected the camera was there to satisfy Howard's prurience rather than safeguard his car.

"Is that an M on the reg?" She leaned closer to the screen, but the image remained unclear, the car parked at an angle too oblique for its registration plate to be visible. "M or an N, maybe. It's not a vanity plate."

"No, that would make our job far too easy." Suds squinted at the freeze-framed footage. "An M, I think. And that might be a two there. A tech may be able to clean the image up, but I bet there weren't too many of these driving around at this hour, so it should be distinctive when we get cracking on the local CCTV."

"Excellent." She set the DVD running again. After a five-minute gap where nothing happened, the Audi's driver door opened and a tall, slim figure got out, wearing a sweater with its hood raised. The figure hesitated by the car, studying a phone and allowing a brief flash of their ungloved hands. Then they slung a rucksack across both shoulders and, phone still in hand and head still bowed, strode out of view.

"Damn it." Suds rapped the arm of his chair, rattling his cup and plate. "They didn't look up once."

"She's white and taller than our vic." Safia skipped the DVD back and replayed the thirty-six seconds. "What's in the bag, missus?"

"Are we even sure that's a her?" Suds asked. "It could be a bloke."

"Not with that arse," Safia murmured, and shot Suds a mortified "Oh shit, we have to behave ourselves!" look when he sniggered. She paused a rear-end view and outlined the woman's body shape, trying to think of something suitably scientific to say. She floundered; the woman didn't even have child-bearing hips, just a figure that was distinctly feminine to someone who'd spent many enjoyable years admiring them.

"Okay, I see your point," Suds admitted in an undertone, and Safia touched a hand to her hot cheek, hoping she didn't look as pink as she felt.

"Is it just me or does she look like she's following something on her phone?" she asked.

Suds nodded. "Mapping, probably. Coordinates or a grid reference. Unless she met our vic and walked to the scene with him, there's no way she'd have got there without some kind of an assist."

"Did you find the bag?" Howard asked. He was so enthralled by the proceedings that Safia half expected him to whip out a notepad and pen.

"Sadly not." Suds capped his own pen in an unsubtle signal that it was time to make an exit. "Howard, would you mind us taking the DVD for further analysis?"

He clearly did mind—they hadn't even got to the good bit yet—but he complied without protest and ejected the disc.

"Many thanks." Safia slipped the DVD into an evidence bag, confirming Howard's fears that he would never find out how the saga ended. "We very much appreciate your help," she said, laying it on thick to ease their escape.

Suds didn't waste time heading back to the office, but drove their car around the corner and found a shaded spot to park in. "Okay, then." He dragged his laptop from its case and fired it up. "Mystery Woman Gets Shot, Part Deux."

Almost ninety minutes elapsed on the recording before Safia spotted a flicker of movement to the left of the screen and slowed the playback to normal speed.

"Christ." Suds winced, and Safia felt a similar pang of almost-sympathy.

The woman, approaching her car from a different direction, was stumbling over her own feet, her arms clutched across her midriff. The torch in her right hand bounced its beam off the cars and pavement, but she didn't seem aware of its light. Stopping at the driver's side, she cast a furtive glance around the empty street, but she had remembered to keep her hood up, and no matter how many times Safia clicked the disc forward frame by frame, she couldn't find a clear shot of the woman's face.

"No gun." Suds was tilting his head as if that would make a difference.

"Not that we can see, at any rate." Safia tapped the screen. "She still has the bag, and it still looks full."

The rucksack was bulky, its canvas sides pushed outward by the contents, as they had been in the initial footage. The woman took the bag from her shoulders prior to getting in the car, her movements stilted and evidently hampered by her injury. She drove off almost at once, the street darkening in the absence of her headlights. Safia skipped the disc through to the end of the recording, but the only other notable movement in the street was a pre-dawn milkman doing his rounds.

"Deal gone bad," Suds said. "That's my best guess. The vic wanted whatever was in the rucksack, they arranged an exchange of some sort, and she double-crossed him."

Safia was rewatching the woman drag the bag from her back. There was so much pain in the movements that Safia felt like grabbing one of the straps and taking the weight for her. "Or our mystery third party interfered." She pushed up in her seat. "Shit, Suds. If whatever's in that bag is the key to this, then she still has it, and someone else has already died for it."

Suds restarted the engine as Safia closed the laptop. "This kind of thinking isn't good for my blood pressure, Saf. My doctor won't be impressed."

"Yeah, yeah," she said. "Cry me a river and put your foot down."

GRACE. SATURDAY, 12:45 P.M.

G race had always considered herself fit. Gym three times a week: swimming, cross training, weights, and the occasional spinning class if the shouty woman in the yellow Lycra wasn't taking it. Five flights of stairs down, with another three to go, she propped the suitcase against the wall and bent double with her hands on her knees.

"Bloody hell." She mouthed the curse, though she might just as well have yelled it aloud, because no one in their right mind would use this staircase when there was a perfectly good lift at their disposal. No one, that is, except a sort-of-kidnapped doctor attempting to load a car without the hotel staff noticing her preparations for a stealthy getaway. The back staircase was ideal, bypassing the hotel lobby and heading directly to the underground car park, but it also meant lugging her kit down eight floors when she'd been awake almost twenty-four hours, on shift for half that time, and then held at gunpoint and stressed to fuck.

She picked up the case again. It was best not to think too much right now. Best just to keep going, keep moving, and get Elin out of the hotel as soon as she could. That would be her next trick, after stashing this final bag, and if the staircase was a struggle for her, she could only imagine how Elin was going to cope.

The car's indicators flashed when she unlocked it, the boot opening automatically at the push of a second button. As she had on her first trip, she kept her hood up and her head down, just another anonymous guest whom no one needed to take any notice of. She opened the boot fully, stopping short of lifting the case when she saw how little space remained. When she had initially emptied Elin's luggage, she had crammed the shopping bags—a couple of them sealed with tape, she now realised—into the gaps around Elin's clothing. Intending to amalgamate everything, she froze as a pile toppled over and Elin's neatly folded sweaters and jeans parted to reveal, not underwear as she had originally thought, but Amelia's pastel-coloured dresses, denim dungarees, and Dora the Explorer T-shirts.

She ran the thin cotton between her fingers. Amelia had been wearing pyjamas in the video, their bright blue and green stripes splattered with blood, one sleeve torn at the elbow as if someone had wrenched her arm. She wondered how many times Elin had rewatched the short clip, searching it for clues that weren't there. Would those be the last words Elin ever heard her daughter say? Would she cling onto the video no matter how much it broke her heart? Grace, of all people, could appreciate the need to do that.

She counted to twenty, concentrating on the individual numbers and blanking out the thoughts and memories until nothing remained but a weird sense of purpose. She took a moment to find all of Amelia's clothing, slipping it into a separate bag so Elin wouldn't have to see it every time she got changed. The case fitted into the gap she had made. She packed the bags in around it and shut the boot.

It was quicker to return to the room via the lobby, so she took a chance and headed in that direction. The receptionist spotted her at once, hailing her by name and asking her to come to the desk.

"Hey." She gave him her best disarming smile, prepared to lie through her teeth if he'd caught her on the car park cameras. "Lovely day out there, isn't it?"

"Gorgeous!" he said. If she'd told him it was blowing a gale and snowing, he would probably have agreed with her. He held up one finger as he flicked through an assortment of notes. "A man was here asking for Ms. Breckenridge."

Grace snapped her head around, searching the empty lobby. "When was this? Did he leave his name?"

"About twenty minutes ago." The receptionist consulted a slip of paper. "He said he was a friend but declined to give me his name and asked for Ms. Breckenridge's room number. Obviously, our security policy prevents us from providing that information."

"What did he look like?" Grace had no idea how she'd managed to sound so casual. She'd been rubbish at drama in school. "El—Ms. Breckenridge might be able to recognise him from a description."

"He was about, oh, six foot perhaps, early fifties, slight paunch. He was wearing a cap, so I couldn't see his hair." The receptionist leaned closer to the desk's dividing shelf. "He seemed a little, well, a little too intense, if you know what I mean, and I was concerned about Ms. Breckenridge's…" He was too polite to accuse the man of assaulting Elin, but his hand fluttered about his face, intimating the point. "He was becoming quite insistent, so I asked Security to escort him from the premises."

"Thank you," Grace said. "I'll let Ms. Breckenridge know."

Although clearly miffed that Grace wasn't going to confide in him, he relinquished the note without protest and excused himself to answer a phone call. She could feel him tracking her as she walked to the lift, but she gave nothing away until the doors had closed, when she slapped an open hand on the wall.

"*Fuck!*" She hit the button for the sixth floor, her damp palm smearing a print across the glass panels as she moved. "Come on. Come on!" The lift was crawling, not stopping for anyone else but not going fast enough. When the doors finally opened, she sprinted down the corridor toward the suite, the key readied in her hand. She called out to Elin as she entered, and found her sitting at the table in the living room. Elin took one look at Grace's expression and scrambled to stand.

"Careful." Grace went over to her, but she was already up, her fists clenched on the tabletop.

"What is it? What's happened?"

"A man." Grace licked her lips and tried again. There was no chance of her faking cool, calm collectedness in front of Elin. "A man has been at the desk, asking for you. Six foot, fifties, with a gut. Is it Lowry?"

The colour of Elin's face was answer enough, the description providing unequivocal confirmation of Lowry's betrayal. "When?"

"Within the last half hour. The receptionist had him kicked off the grounds, but that lad couldn't lie for toffee, so Lowry will know you're here. Why the hell didn't you register under a false name?"

"Because I don't have any fake ID, and the hotel demands a credit card as insurance," Elin said, and the explanation was so sensible that Grace felt bad for even asking the question. Sometimes, especially when she caught sight of the gun, it was easy to forget that Elin wasn't a career criminal.

"Do you think he'll try to get in again?"

"Yes, if he gets tired of waiting for me to go out."

The blunt response sent a chill through Grace. Common sense told her to shut the blinds, tell Elin to stay away from the windows, and persuade her to sit tight in this relative safe haven. But sooner or later another WhatsApp message would force them to make a move, and Lowry would be hunkered down somewhere, biding his time.

"I have one advantage, though," Elin continued. Her eyes met and held Grace's. "I have you."

"I think I'm more of a liability," Grace said, but she knew what Elin was getting at. Thanks to her, Elin wasn't septic or bleeding out, she was back on her feet, and she wasn't alone.

"You don't give yourself enough credit," Elin said. "I am very glad to have you on my side."

Grace's face went hot, but it wasn't the praise making her blush, more the intensity of Elin's gaze. She bit the inside of her cheek, suddenly shy for no apparent reason, and decided it would be safer to return to the business at hand.

"I need to sort that drain out. Where's the shoulder bag I brought up?"

"Bedroom," Elin said.

The bedroom still resembled a CSI's Shangri-la. Elin had managed to strip the bed and pile the sheets with the towels, but the mattress bore a deep red stain, and she hadn't been able to flip it.

"Shit." Grace ran her hands through her damp hair. She wasn't used to feeling this unsure of herself. She liked proven strategies and peer-reviewed techniques, not flying by the seat of her pants. "Should we take them with us?" she asked. "We've got maybe five hours or so before anyone will use the HEMS car. We could be well out of London by then. I'll be able to carry them if I put—"

"Grace." Elin lowered Grace's hands, keeping them in a loose grip. "We'll leave the sign on the door. I've booked this suite until Tuesday. If no one has noticed you packing the car, then no one will come in."

"Okay." The tight, panicky feeling in Grace's chest was starting to abate. "Okay. Let's do something with this drain. Here, put your coat on first."

Elin stood patiently as Grace fitted the plastic container into the shoulder bag and looped the bag into position. With a slight adjustment, it sat lower than Elin's hip, allowing the drain to function and Elin to carry it comfortably.

"Man on a galloping horse wouldn't spot it." Grace closed Elin's coat around the tubing and then picked up the rucksack and car keys. "Where's the gun?"

Elin patted her coat pocket. "Here. Now with added bullets."

Grace was glad she'd missed that part. The gun still gave her the collywobbles, even though it was no longer aimed at her. "Got both phones?"

"Yes." Elin toyed with her own phone. "I should turn this one off. I haven't because I needed a spare in case they couldn't get me on theirs, but Lowry could be using mine to track us, and if he is, we'll never get away from him no matter what we do."

"Elin." Grace held out her defunct phone. "Next time they contact you, give them my number."

Elin hesitated, the significance of the gesture clearly not lost on her. This was Grace committing to being involved for the long run. "Are you sure?"

"I'm sure. Turn yours off."

Elin used the confiscated SIM to resurrect Grace's phone and then disabled hers. In a sign of how far they had come, she immediately returned the phone to Grace, allowing her to unlock it and check it for messages and missed calls. A lack of either suggested the HEMS car had yet to be found.

"Right, then," Grace said, keen to make the most of the time they had. She gave Elin a brief once-over. Elin was still pale, and her respiratory rate was higher than Grace would have liked, but she had been up and about for half an hour now, and she seemed relatively stable. "It's eight flights of stairs. Do you want me to dose you up first?"

Elin gave her a look. "Only if you want to give me a piggyback."

Grace laughed. It was a fair point. "Ready to make a stagger for it?"

"As I'll ever be."

The corridor beyond the suite was empty, the occasional low rumble of conversation or burst of television the only signs that other rooms were occupied. Elin reached the staircase without incident, walking at a good clip and getting five floors down before she called for a break. Grace stood close by, one hand on Elin's pulse: rapid and thready, but palpable for now.

"Okay." Elin's nod was almost convincing. "I'm okay."

In contrast to her earlier luggage-toting tactic, Grace walked through the car park with her head held high, her stride unfaltering. It might be too little too late, but she wanted the CCTV to see her acting of her own volition, to convince the police—when they finally requested the recording—that, whatever happened next, no one had forced her to be a part of it. Meanwhile, to anyone watching live, they were simply a couple of tourists off to see the sights.

They were almost at the car when Elin stopped, clutching at her chest. Grace swore, wrenching Elin's coat open in time to see a flash of fresh blood coursing into the drain.

"It's all right," Grace said, lying through her teeth even as her heart sank. "These things happen. It'll sort itself out, don't worry." She activated the car's central locking, giving Elin something to aim toward as she shuffled the last few yards. Elin sank into the passenger seat, turning onto her good side as Grace pulled the seat belt around her and rechecked the drain.

"How bad?" Elin whispered.

"About two hundred mils and slowing." Grace couldn't take her eyes off the flow of blood. Was it really stopping, or was she seeing what she wanted to see? "How's the pain?"

"Fine."

Grace covered her incredulity by starting the engine. "Will you tell me when it's not 'fine'?"

"Yep."

Remembering the one-foot rule this time, Grace drove slowly toward the car park exit. Nothing to see here, she told herself. Just two women off on a day trip, who would definitely be back in their suite later that evening. She stopped short of the barrier to widen the screen on the satnav.

"Left or right at the end? Left takes us to the Poplar Interchange, right goes to the Blackwall Tunnel. The interchange is messy, which might be a good thing if Lowry is trying to follow us."

"Left, then," Elin said. "He won't have gone far, and he'll be keeping this junction in sight, so don't hang around once you've made the turn."

The Audi had no intention of hanging around, Grace realised as she sped away from the junction. Her own car was utilitarian, designed for short commutes and often abandoned in favour of the Tube, as it had been last night. She couldn't remember the last time she'd hit fifty miles an hour, let alone seventy. When she checked the rearview mirror, the hotel facade was nothing more than a distant ochre smear. There were other cars on the road, but nothing was obviously tailing them, and most of the traffic seemed typical of family outings: kids in the back seat, harried parents up front.

"What does Lowry drive?" she asked.

"Range Rover, navy blue." Elin's attention was glued to her wing mirror. "I can't see him." The skin above her top lip gleamed wet in the sunlight. Grace wasn't sure if it was anxiety, pain, or shock causing it, and guessed at a combination of the three.

"God, this car can't half shift," she said, attempting to distract them both.

"Amelia loves it." Elin spoke without turning, but her voice had softened. "She'll sit behind me in her booster seat, smacking the door and demanding I go faster. Her idea of a good night out is a razz around the country lanes as the sun's setting, and fish and chips eaten straight from the wrapping."

"That sounds splendid." Grace switched lanes, tiny needles of apprehension growing more insistent as a dark car a hundred yards behind them immediately followed suit. She pushed through an amber light and kept accelerating as the dark car barrelled through a blatant red. "Do you see him?" she asked.

"Yes."

"Shit. Okay. So we knew this would probably happen." She wasn't sure whom she was trying to reassure. "He can't just run us off the road, can he? Everyone will see him."

"He can force us onto a quieter road," Elin said. "This car's fast, but it only does thirty miles to the gallon."

"Oh." Grace hadn't even thought of that. The fuel gauge was on half. "Fuck."

The dual carriageway widened into three lanes, more traffic joining from a slip road, the cars hurtling past and changing lanes without warning, like a Saturday afternoon Formula One where the prize was pole position at Nando's. Grace weaved amongst the chaos, a kick of unalloyed terror somehow allowing her to manoeuvre an unfamiliar car, monitor Lowry's progress, and simultaneously swear a blue streak. The navy Range Rover gained on them and then dropped back, as if verifying their identity before continuing the chase.

"Definitely him?" Grace asked. She hadn't got a good look at the driver: a middle-aged man, a hint of a bald head, a reddened face.

"Definitely."

"He needs to watch his blood pressure," she said, adding a few digits to his systolic by cutting up a van and making him swerve to avoid it. She watched the junctions fly by, counting them down, biding her time. Three lanes narrowed to two again, the hard central reservation becoming an optimistic set of painted chevrons that did little to prevent the numerous head-on collisions she had dealt with along this stretch. Apologising to all her traffic police friends, she undertook a lorry and pulled out in front of it, using its bulk as a shield.

"Brace yourself," she said, and saw Elin double-check where they were, saw the start of a head shake, a warning half-voiced on Elin's lips, as Grace wrenched the car to the right and executed the most perfectly illegal U-turn across two lanes of seventy-mile-an-hour bypass. Multiple horns blared, their outrage rendered impotent by the Audi's blistering acceleration.

"I think it worked," Grace said as the dust settled. "I can't see him." Her knees were knocking, her redundant left foot hammering a beat on the leather car mat. She felt like laughing hysterically or vomiting, and thought she might end up doing both.

Elin was still unwinding herself, dropping her legs and loosening her hold on the chest drain. "Jesus wept," she said. "Amelia is going to fucking love you."

ELIN. SATURDAY, 1:52 P.M.

No matter which way Elin turned, she couldn't get comfortable. Stretching her legs pulled at the drain, while bending them put pressure on her ribs and her malfunctioning lung. Outside the car window, the streets were starting to blur, the passers-by merging into murky, amorphous masses as the drone of the traffic made her ears burn. Everything was too much, and she was too hot, too hemmed in. She batted at the air con, twitching the dial down a notch, and felt Grace catch her hand.

"Two minutes," Grace mouthed to her. Then, into the hands-free, "That's great. Yes, I'll be there in about half an hour. Thank you." She ended the call and pulled into the closest side street. It was a dead end and there was nowhere to park, but she stopped anyway, one eye on the road behind her. They hadn't spotted Lowry's car for over an hour now.

"Here." Grace lowered both front windows, creating a through-draught, and gave Elin a bottle of orange Lucozade she'd bought at a corner shop. "This stuff has remarkable restorative properties, and it's got me through many a night shift, though it may make you burp."

The drink was ice cold and just the right side of fizzy. Elin took a cautious sip, then a proper mouthful. On occasion, she had to admit, she almost welcomed that fading-away feeling—it was the only thing that stopped her from thinking about Amelia—but this wasn't the time to be mucking about fainting, so she drank her Lucozade and let the fresh air chill her face.

"Nice, anonymous Vauxhall Astra waiting for us at Easy Rent in Brockley," Grace said. As usual, she had moved her hand to rest her fingers on Elin's wrist, counting the pulse there. There was a self-assurance to her actions now, a growing fortitude that had by degree transformed her from browbeaten hostage to uncertain accomplice to active partner. "Will you be able to drive this for twenty minutes or so?"

"Yes." The idea of doing anything besides curling back in the seat filled Elin with dread, but they had already discussed and agreed to a loose strategy, and she had her part to play.

"Good." Grace restarted the engine. "Remind me where reverse is on this thing."

The administrative process at Easy Rent was a swift one, unsurprising when all of the rental plus a sizable deposit was demanded up front, and when none of their cars were less than five years old. Waiting in the Audi a few streets away, Elin slid the burner back into her pocket as Grace pulled the Astra alongside her. They departed again in convoy, Elin concentrating so hard on keeping the Astra in sight that she was able to tune out the spasm from the chest tube shifting every time she hit the brakes. Grace obviously knew this area well; she changed lanes in good time, allowing Elin to keep up with her, and she cut through the quieter side streets instead of queuing in the traffic around a retail park.

"New Cross," she had said, when Elin asked where they were going. "Southeast London, just off the A2."

They were just off the A2 now, exchanging the smog on the main road for terraced residential streets. A couple of dog-legs later, Grace stopped by a row of small garages and indicated that Elin do likewise.

"I rent the middle one," she said before Elin could ask. "Come on, let's get things swapped over."

She seemed edgy in a way unrelated to Elin, so Elin kept her counsel and did her best to unload and reload some of the lighter bags. With their kit, a bag of groceries, and a selection of spare clothes packed into the Astra, and Elin installed in the passenger seat, Grace reversed the Audi into the garage, avoiding an expensive-looking push bike, and locked the garage up again. And that, apparently, was that. Without offering further explanation, she retraced their route and parked in front of a mid-terrace house with a large bay window and a pale blue door. Overgrown pots of herbs and alpines sat on the gravel of its walled front garden, and there was junk mail wedged in its letterbox. The house had been loved once, but there was no sign of it currently being lived in.

"Grace?" Elin said, when Grace had turned the engine off but shown no inclination to get out of the car.

"I need a minute." Grace looked at the house, clucking her tongue at the junk mail. "I haven't been here for a while."

"Whose is it?" Elin asked, though she was starting to draw clues together. There had been something about Grace's phone, in the car, in those first few awful minutes. She had begged. Had she cried? Jesus, Elin felt as if she were snatching at fog, the strands vanishing as soon as she grasped at them.

"It's mine." Grace seemed to have got a grip on herself, and she answered with more confidence. She hauled the groceries from the back seat. "Come on. I'll put the kettle on."

Inside, the house streamed with light, despite the dust-streaked windows and the whiff of musty air. A stained-glass panel above the first-floor landing sent rainbows tumbling down the stairs, while the bay overlooking the main reception room made the space seem three times bigger.

"It's lovely in here," Elin said, sinking onto the sofa Grace had ushered her to. An open fireplace smelled faintly of coal and creosote, and the furnishings were a mismatched collection of antiques and upcycling. Medical texts were mixed with pot-boiler thrillers on the floor-to-ceiling bookshelves, though a fine layer of dust suggested nothing had been read recently. Beyond a set of patio doors, a lawn desperately needed a cut, and the plants that hadn't been felled by neglect had succumbed to the frosts. Elin listened to Grace filling the kettle and setting out mugs, but her attention was divided, and the framed photographs on the mantelpiece easily won out. She walked across for a closer look and was still there when Grace returned with the brews.

"What's her name?" Elin asked quietly. There was no point pretending she hadn't noticed the photo in the centre of all the others.

"Charlotte." Grace put the mugs down and came to stand by Elin. "That was the most perfect day." She took the photo from the mantelpiece and used her sleeve to wipe a smudge from the glass. The photographer had had a good eye, capturing Grace and Charlotte in an unguarded moment with their arms around each other. The white of their wedding dresses was dazzling against a cloudless sky.

Elin waited to see whether Grace would say more without a prompt, but Grace couldn't seem to do anything now that she had hold of the photo, and Elin, recognising the awful numbness of grief, understood why Grace no longer lived here. She gently prised the frame from Grace's fingers and led her back to the sofa, giving her one of the mugs and stirring sugar into her own.

"What happened to her?" she said as Grace tucked her legs beneath her and let the steam from her brew eddy around her face.

"She had a bleed." Grace spoke without inflection, and sipped tea hot enough to scald. "A cerebral aneurysm. They go suddenly, and she collapsed in the street while I was at work. She was already unconscious when the paramedics brought her in. I think Neuro took her to theatre as a kindness to me, to show they'd done everything they possibly could, but she never woke up. She died that same day. We'd been married for eleven months."

"She was beautiful."

"She was." Grace was crying, her words fractured and barely formed. "She was a nurse at the Royal. We'd been together for nine years before we married, and I loved her more than anything."

Elin took the mug from her and passed her a tissue from a box on the coffee table. Grace blew her nose and then sneezed.

"Think those are a bit dusty," she said as a cloud of motes erupted into the sunshine. "They've been there since...Well, it's two years, and I keep meaning to make a decision, you know? Move back in or move on, but it's easier said than done."

"Where do you live now?" Elin asked, shaking off another tissue. Grace had stopped crying, but her nose was still streaming.

"I rent a flat near the hospital. I do a lot of shifts, so it's just somewhere to rest my head."

It wasn't difficult for Elin to read between the lines, to imagine Grace's life revolving around work and excessive overtime, and coming back to a flat devoid of anything that might connect her to her wife. Elin had taken a different but just as destructive path to deal with her own PTSD. By the sound of it, her months of sleeping around and day-drinking had been as effective a therapy as Grace's avoidance tactics, and here she was rubbing salt into all of Grace's wounds.

"We don't have to stay here," she said. Up until this moment, she hadn't thought she could feel any worse for what she'd done to Grace, but she just kept digging a deeper hole for herself.

"I know we don't." Grace took the wedding photo from the coffee table and restored it to its original place above the fireplace. "But we'll be safe here until we hear anything, and I don't want to keep moving you if I don't have to."

Elin had to admit Grace made a good point. Now that she was sitting down, the prospect of getting up again wasn't a pleasant one, and the Artex on the ceiling was starting to do weird things when she stared at it. She felt Grace unfasten her coat and managed to get her arms out of it before her head hit the back of the sofa again.

"That good, eh?" Grace said, lifting the drain clear of the shoulder bag and checking the IV cannula in Elin's wrist. "Soup, fluids, and pain relief for you. Not necessarily in that order."

"The phone." Elin scrabbled for her coat, but it seemed to be miles away, and even when she got a hand on it, she couldn't lift it.

"I'll watch it, I promise." Grace showed her its empty screen. "There's nothing yet. What sort of soup do you like?"

"Tomato." Elin's bottom lip quivered. She had answered without thinking, and it was Amelia who always asked for tomato soup when she was poorly. Tomato soup, a warm knee, and a story. Grace pulled a tartan blanket from an armchair and tucked it around Elin in a gesture so sweetly familiar that it almost tipped Elin over the edge.

"Have a nap. I'll wake you if anything happens," Grace said, and a stinging sensation in Elin's wrist was the last thing she knew for a while.

Grace. Saturday, 3:17 p.m.

The house—*her* house, Grace reminded herself—was quiet, with the fitful tick of a clock with a fading battery the only sound beside the occasional car passing on the street. On her previous visits to collect clothes or check the post she'd forgotten to redirect, she had felt like an intruder, a stranger invading a space that no longer belonged to her, and she had left again within minutes, locking the door and retreating to a place Charlotte had never set foot in. Today, though, the house seemed like a sanctuary, and after that first inevitable sucker punch of sorrow, she found she could sit on the sofa beside Elin, look at the photos in front of her, and wonder what the hell Charlotte would have said about all of this. "You're a bloody idiot," was the first thing that sprang to mind, but Charlotte had been far more impetuous than Grace, and she would have said that a beat before offering to roll up her sleeves and dig out the bullet.

"I dug the bullet out on my own, Lotty," Grace whispered. She connected the IV tubing she'd been unravelling and set the transfusion to a steady rate. Elin had lost a further three hundred millilitres into the drain, and her most recent obs had been a blatant cry for help.

Elin twitched, murmuring something incomprehensible, and then woke all at once, her body jerking and her eyes flying open. She didn't seem to have a clue where she was, but she relaxed upon seeing Grace, and then frowned at the blood bag hanging from a lampshade. "How bad?" She made a token effort to lift the drain into view but capitulated as soon as Grace intervened.

"It's stopped. I'm just topping you up. That wall has more colour than you."

"Ha." Elin stuck two lazy fingers up at her. The wall in question was a subtle off-white.

"No news," Grace said, before Elin could ask. "Unless you count me putting the soup on and changing into clothes that fit."

"I like your T-shirt. It's very nice." Drowsing again, Elin sounded drunk, her words mashing together and her sentiment unguarded.

Grace tugged at the hem of the shirt, conscious that its fit was a little too snug, but all that did was tauten the cotton. Grateful that Elin was off her face on opiates and unlikely to remember a thing, she fussed with the transfusion until Elin slipped back into a doze. Most of her casual clothes—the stuff she could throw on at the end of a shift, the shapeless sweaters and jogging bottoms, and the T-shirts she'd almost worn the patterns off—were at her flat, where there was never anyone to see her and she was usually too tired to care about looking like something the cat had dragged in. As a consequence, the clothes still stored here had mostly been chosen by Charlotte, who would march her to Oxford Street for her yearly stock-up and refuse to go home unless Grace bought at least three different outfits. One of Charlotte's favourite hobbies had been ogling Grace in dressing room mirrors, and she'd had excellent taste where fashion was concerned. The T-shirt in question, baby blue and flattering in all the right places, had definitely been one of her recommendations.

The scent of ersatz tomato sent Grace into the kitchen, where she lowered the heat on the hob and rummaged for a couple of bowls. As she stood there, a patch of sunlight passed over the garden, highlighting the swing bench she used to spend hours reading on in summer, and the raised bed Charlotte had never completed. She turned away from the window, directing all her attention to the soup, adding a drop of milk it didn't need and putting a couple of slices of bread into the toaster. It was surreal to be doing this, preparing lunch for the near-stranger hooked up to the IV on her sofa, yet she couldn't deny that part of her was glad to be hauled along, busily figuring out their next move and how she was going to keep Elin stable enough to make it.

By the time Grace had loaded a tray and returned to the living room, Elin was awake. Sitting up properly took her a while, but she managed without Grace's assistance and then let Grace place the tray on her lap.

"Voila." Grace settled on the adjacent armchair. "It shouldn't be too hot."

"Thanks." Elin stirred the soup in slow circles, and Grace concentrated on her own bowl, inwardly wincing as Elin missed her mouth with the spoon. Elin swapped hands, trying again with her left, but she clearly wasn't ambidextrous, and her second attempt was even worse, spilling the entire spoonful. The spoon clattered against the bowl as she lost her grip on it, and she immediately grabbed it again. "Why can't I do this?" She looked at Grace, frustration and confusion rolling off her.

"Because you lost a hell of a lot of blood last night." Grace slid the spoon from Elin's fingers and set it aside. "And you may have nerve damage on that right side. You definitely have muscle damage. Here…"

Abandoning her lunch, she sat on the edge of the sofa and lifted the bowl to Elin's lips. There was only the slightest delay before Elin relented and swallowed a couple of mouthfuls. She shook her head to let Grace know she was finished, and she was still shaking it as Grace lowered the bowl.

"I run an international company." She sounded more bemused than anything. "I raised Amelia on my own, spent twelve years in the armed forces, and I can't even hold a spoon."

Grace parsed the information Elin had casually tossed into the mix and chose the least incendiary topic of the three. "Your company, you said it had offices in London and the UAE. How come you based yourself in Manchester?"

Elin shrugged. "I was born and bred there, I like it up there, and it's my company. Lowry was happy to run the London office, and I'd come down every few weeks, unless there were any major problems."

"Have you known him for long?" Grace asked, sensing there was more to their history than a mere business arrangement.

"He's been my best friend for eighteen years. We were in Special Recon together." Elin gave a sudden sharp laugh. "He's not Amelia's dad, if that's what you were thinking."

It wasn't. It hadn't even occurred to Grace. She had a pretty accurate gaydar, and it had been twitching for a while now. She could imagine Elin selecting the father of her child from a line-up of suitable donors and getting herself pregnant when she was good and ready.

"More soup?" she said.

Elin chuckled at the non-sequitur, and her fingers tangled with Grace's as she helped Grace tilt the bowl.

"I should have got some cheese to melt into it," Grace said. "That's the best thing ever when you're not well." She had gone into the shop for essentials, rushing around the aisles and out again in record time. When one of the store assistants had said good morning to her, she had been so flummoxed by the sheer normality that she had almost fluffed her response.

"I prefer it without," Elin said. "Mouse is the cheese freak in our house."

"Amelia?" Grace vaguely recalled her using the name for Amelia earlier that morning, when she had been talking about the pizza delivery lad. "Is that where she gets the nickname, then?"

"No." Elin pushed at the bowl, and Grace took the hint, moving it right away from her. "That's not where it comes from."

"Oh." Grace faltered, curious but reluctant to pry. She wasn't sure whether that was a full stop or an ellipsis at the end of Elin's comment. "You don't have to talk about her, Elin. Not unless you want to."

"I adopted her." Elin said it quickly, as if any pause would collapse the conversation. "I'd been thinking about it for a long time before I applied. I'd always wanted a child but never wanted to be pregnant. Does that sound weird?"

"Not especially. Lotty, Charlotte, was similar. She loved kids and she wanted to be a mum, but we'd already decided I'd be the one to carry them."

"I had no one to make that decision with." Elin stated it as a matter of fact, rather than something she was upset about. "I'd had relationships here and there but nothing I'd have wanted to bring a child into. I was newly single on the eve of my thirty-fifth birthday, and it seemed like a sign."

A vehicle began to reverse slowly down the street, its engine audible before it came into view. They both turned to peer through the slatted window blinds, but it was a white van with a black woman at the wheel, and she drove right past the house. Though no one had been able to see in, Grace got up to close the blinds fully, which left them in semi-darkness even when she turned on a small side lamp.

Elin leaned forward, one hand supporting her bad side, and her face slipping further into shadow. The facade of anonymity seemed to help her pick up the thread. "Amelia was sixteen weeks old when I brought her home. And for the first month, I wondered what the hell I'd done. I'd fought so hard for her during the adoption process, and I'd been so sure I wanted her and so confident I could cope, but it went to shit almost at once."

"Why?" Grace said, genuinely intrigued.

"I knew she'd been neglected by her birth parents, but I didn't realise how badly until that first night I was alone with her." Elin touched the burner phone Grace had left on the arm of the sofa. It was a habit she'd developed whenever she was most distressed, though she didn't seem aware of it. The phone's screen lit up, illuminating her haggard face, and then sent her back into the darkness.

"Social Services had told me she was an absolute angel," she continued. "Quiet, slept through the night. It sounded too good to be true, and it was. She didn't cry for weeks, Grace. No one had ever come to her when she cried, so she'd just given up. She was like a shell of a kid. It was as if she'd learned to be invisible, unless she heard a loud noise or a raised voice, and then she'd freeze, her eyes as wide as dinner plates, every bit of her tensed, waiting for the punch."

"Poor little mite." Grace was no stranger to dealing with abused children, and that thousand-yard stare was unmistakeable. "What on earth did you do?"

"Honestly? I spent the first couple of weeks wondering whether I could take her back." Elin shook her head. "As if she was something I'd bought that didn't fit right, but it was okay because I still had the receipt. And it would have been so simple to do that. I had all my excuses lined up and ready to go: it wasn't what I imagined it would be, and I wouldn't be able to change anything for the better, and she needed someone who was good at this, and that definitely wasn't me."

"But you didn't do that," Grace said. From the way Elin was speaking, she doubted Elin had ever admitted this to another soul.

"No, I didn't. I was in such a fucking state, it took me a while to realise I'd adopted a kindred spirit and she had a form of PTSD. It was easier after that. I got better at avoiding the things that might spark her off, and figuring out what she liked and what seemed to help her. There wasn't any major breakthrough, you know? One of those big moments you see on the telly, with the sun coming out of the clouds and the choir singing in the background? It was just a series of little things—she'd tug my hair, or her face would change when she saw me, not quite a smile but getting there, or she wouldn't stiffen so badly when I held her." Elin stopped. She had run out of air, and she was breathing hard. When she continued, her voice had dropped to a whisper. "The first time she cried, I felt like I'd won the lottery, and we never looked back. I told her once, when she was being naughty, 'you used to be as quiet as a mouse,' and she howled laughing at that and the name stuck." Elin tilted her head. "It's so quiet now without her. I can't bear it being this quiet. I feel like there's a piece of me missing."

Grace couldn't say anything in response. That feeling had been a constant for her over the past two years. She put her arm around Elin, felt Elin nestle against her shoulder, and sat with her in the silence.

ELIN. SATURDAY, 4:45 P.M.

Take a deep breath. And another. Okay, that's not too bad."
Elin used her free hand to tuck in her T-shirt as Grace
lowered it. Grace had done that thing where she'd rubbed the drum
of her stethoscope to warm it, but it had still felt like ice on Elin's
back, and goosebumps mottled her arms. She had been cold to the
bone for hours, and her jaw ached from clenching it to stop her teeth
rattling. She must be anaemic, probably still skirting shock. She
wasn't sure how many transfusions Grace had given her, but they
wouldn't be enough if she continued to bleed, and Grace's supply of
blood and plasma was finite. She wrapped her arms across her chest,
too overwhelmed to care that she was tangling the IV line. The last
time she had gone to the toilet, it had taken her twenty minutes to
get off it again.

"Here." By contrast, Grace's hands were deft and sure, unknot-
ting the tubing and draping a blanket around Elin's shoulders. She
had an expert poker face, but tight worry lines creased her forehead
and thinned her lips. "Do you want a hot drink?"

Elin did, but she was sure she would spill it. "No, thank you."

Grace folded her steth back into her obs pouch. She had packed
a small case for herself and propped it by the door, alongside any
kit she wasn't currently using and a bag of dried and tinned food
scavenged from the kitchen cupboards. Keeping busy was clearly
her way of coping, but there was nothing left for them to do now
except wait for all hell to break loose around 6 p.m., when the HEMS

car would be discovered. How long after that would the police start searching for Grace? They would no doubt go to the flat she rented first, but how long would it be before they came knocking on the door of this house?

Elin toyed with the burner phone. For her own sake, she was rationing the amount of times she refreshed its screen, and not being able to check it *just in case* was nagging at her like a toothache. "Maybe I should text *him*," she said. "Do you think that would help? At least it'll prove I'm still alive."

"You could try." Grace did a commendable job of hiding her scepticism. "But I'm sure they have a way to track this phone, so they'll know you've left the hotel."

"True." Elin leaned sideward, resting her head against the sofa back. She hated this inertia, sitting helpless, waiting for orders and unable to seize the initiative. She'd had enough of that during her early army days, and she'd sworn never to return to a role where the greatest asset she possessed was her compliance.

When the phone suddenly buzzed, she jumped so hard that she knocked it to the floor.

"*Fuck!*" Forgetting the drain, she dived toward the carpet, but Grace met her halfway, one hand planted on her sternum to keep her still.

"I've got it," Grace said, immediately proffering the phone to her. "Here."

Elin shook her head. For all the hours of longing and wordless bargaining, she couldn't bear to look at it now that it had something to say.

"Do you want me to?" Grace was holding the phone at arm's length, as if it might go for her throat if she brought it any closer. When Elin made a faint noise of assent, Grace tapped the screen and opened the new WhatsApp message. "What the—" She cut herself off and read it again to be sure. "Fucking hell."

"What? What is it?" Elin took the phone from her, reading and rereading the text. "Why?" she whispered. "Why are they doing this?"

A second message arrived, a video downloading in painstaking increments. Huddled together, they waited for it to complete. Elin pressed the play arrow as soon as it appeared. A different bare room this time, the camera panning a little to establish the change in location. There wasn't much to distinguish it from the last, but there was wallpaper in place of paint, and the carpet was beige not grey. A rustle as the person holding the phone shifted, then footsteps, the camera unfocusing and refocusing to show Amelia curled on a small nest of blankets. Still bound, she was sleeping, her chest rising and falling at a slow but steady rate, her eyelashes flickering as she dreamed. There was a cup of water by her side, and a plate of untouched beans on toast.

The phone buzzed again. Another text: *Ready. Steady. Go!*

Elin tried to stand, failed, and hit the sofa hard. Her elation at seeing Amelia alive had been annihilated by the deadline they'd been set. "Will we make it?"

Grace was on her own phone, consulting their instructions and entering them into a route planner. "We should. Just about." She surveyed the room, gauging how soon they could leave. "Right, then. Do you need the loo?"

Elin almost laughed, hysteria sending her thoughts haywire. "Yes." She read the first message again as Grace disconnected her IV.

B19 2EP. Number 3. 8:00 pm.

"The postcode matches a residential street in Birmingham," Grace said. "Travel estimate is two and three-quarter hours, which doesn't give us much leeway if the traffic is bad. What do we do when we get there?"

"I have no idea."

"Do you think that's where Amelia is?"

"No." Elin got to her feet this time, and her fury kept her there. "I think they're just messing with me now, and it's another hoop for me to jump through."

Grace's rapid winding of the IV tubing slowed and then came to a halt. Saline dripped onto the sofa cushion, but she didn't seem to notice. "Elin, do you still think this is about the money?" She asked the question carefully, as if afraid of tipping her over a cliff edge, but Elin had reached the same conclusion four and a half minutes ago.

"No, I don't. If all they wanted was the money, they could have had it by now."

"And you're still going to go it alone?"

"I can't phone the police," Elin whispered. "I *can't*. Please don't make me."

Grace touched the back of Elin's hand. "I won't. You go to the loo. I'll get everything sorted."

Grace was still in the living room when Elin came back down. She had her coat on, but she hadn't packed the last of her kit. As Elin walked closer, the lamplight caught the phone in Grace's hand. It was her own phone, its screen flashing up as it vibrated insistently.

"They found the HEMS car," she said.

Safia. Saturday, 1:35 p.m.

S af? Suds? Five minutes. Make mine a coffee with two. Easy on the milk."

Post-It in hand, Safia rocked back in her chair and made an exaggerated note of the request. She licked the nib of her pencil. "Want a KitKat with that, boss? Suds can nibble all the chocolate from its edges if you like. Then you won't even need to chew it."

Detective Inspector Chevington, head of the MIT, pulled his glasses down his nose and peered at Safia over their rims. His eyesight was so poor, she knew all she would be was a fuzzy brown smudge, but he showed no inclination to find a new quirk.

"Two sugars, DS Faris. And now you mention it, a KitKat would definitely hit the spot, thank you."

He re-sited his glasses before striding away, which bettered the last time, when he'd forgotten and walked into Safia's desk.

"They cancelled his bowling tournament." Suds clicked his mouse, logging off his computer. "That's why he's in today. One of the old boys had a heart attack slap bang in the middle of the green, and the paramedics made a terrible mess when they came to revive him."

"The audacity!" Safia said.

"I know. Lazarus is over in Coronary Care, wide awake and raising hell, but the grass may never recover."

Safia chuckled, collecting their mugs and locking her screen. "Poor Chevs. Do we actually have any KitKats? I was taking the piss, but I feel bad now on account of the grass."

Compared to the other DIs she had worked under, Alan Chevington was a dream, and one of the main reasons she had applied for a sergeant's post. Thanks to a chronic aversion to overtaxing himself, he left his team alone for the most part, trusting his sergeants to run the show. He signed any requisitions they submitted and only bugged them for updates when the detective chief inspector was pecking his head. It wasn't that often he put in a weekend appearance, but he was probably grabbing some easy overtime and fancied a cuppa he hadn't had to make.

"Here you go." Suds threw her a couple of KitKats from a tub marked "Safia's Solace." She had an identical one for him, dipped into whenever the Crown Prosecution Service knocked back a case file. "Get a wriggle on and grab those photocopies."

The briefing room only had eight chairs in it, and seven were occupied. Forensics and CSI were both represented, with the remainder those MIT members not currently out on assignments.

"Age before beauty," Safia told Suds. She perched on a desk behind Kami, who waited until Chevs was engrossed with unwrapping his KitKat and then blew a kiss at her.

"Lunch?" Kami whispered.

Safia gave her a double thumbs up. "Have to be a quickie," she said, and then mouthed "What?" when Kami blushed and threw a paperclip at her.

At the head of the table, Chevs dunked his KitKat and relinquished the floor to Safia. "In a nutshell, Sergeant, if you please," he said. "The DCI has requested an emailed progress report, and the rugby's on at three."

"Wow," Suds muttered, loudly enough for Safia to hear him as she walked past. She suppressed a giggle by staring at her boots. Chevs's average typing speed was six words per minute on a good day. Once, on a very bad day, a now legendary attempt to insert bullet points had lasted for over an hour.

She waited until Suds had handed around a summary she'd compiled and photocopied. She'd used a variety of bullet points all the way down it. "Okay, cutting a long story short," she began, as the bum and paper shuffling settled. "We still have no identity for the body found on Hampstead Heath early this morning. The vic had nothing of note on his person, and he was unarmed. His fingerprints and distinguishing features haven't matched anyone on the national database. A single gunshot wound to the head has been confirmed as cause of death, with the time of death narrowed to between two and four a.m. That would tally with the CCTV footage of our main suspect, who arrived back at her car, obviously injured, at three fifty-three a.m. The blood trail indicates she spent time sheltering beneath a fallen tree before making an evasive egress from the murder scene."

Chevs licked melted chocolate from his fingers. "Any idea whom she may have been evading?"

"Not yet, sir. No one else featured on the CCTV, but within the last hour Ms. Rasul has confirmed there was no gunshot residue on our victim, so we're working on the assumption that a third party is involved and may still be a threat to this woman."

"How exciting." Chevs beamed at Safia and then turned his attention to Kami. "And excellent work getting the samples processed so efficiently."

"Thank you, sir," Kami said, smiling innocently back at him.

Safia chugged her tea, nearly taking a layer off her tongue. While she was by no means closeted at work, Chevs never had fathomed how she got most of her lab results back days before anyone else on the team.

"The woman's car is a navy blue or black Audi TTS," she continued. "Further CCTV analysis has given us a partial plate of MA20 F. We're continuing to requisition local cameras, and we're hoping such a distinctive car will be easy to pick out, given the early hour. Door-to-door is ongoing, and we've an alert out at the hospitals for anyone matching the woman's description and potential injuries."

"Media?" Chevs asked.

She gestured to Daniel Marks, a junior DC she had assigned to that task. He shuffled his papers, bringing his own to the top of the pile. "We've secured a bulletin on tonight's local news, with an appeal for information via a dedicated phone number. It's already up on our Facebook page and Twitter feed, the BBC has it on their rolling news, and we expect it to be covered in most of the national papers."

Chevs slurped the last of his coffee. "Well, chaps and chapesses, clearly you don't need me." He lowered his mug, frowning. "But on the off chance that you do, I'll be available on my mobile all afternoon." He said the last as if reciting it at gunpoint, adjusted his glasses, and hotfooted it from the room.

Kami watched the door swing shut behind him and then sidled onto the desk with Safia. "So, lunch?"

They carried an assortment of Tupperware into the small MIT kitchen and piled them into the microwave. Last night had been their monthly trip across London to visit Kami's gran, and the leftovers had almost filled a freezer drawer, even after they'd taken out enough to see them through the weekend. Like Kami, her gran spoke Bengali rather than Urdu, and though she'd not picked up much English, she certainly understood the joy of a good meal and a full stomach.

Safia tore off a piece of paratha and dipped it into her spicy lentil curry. Kami's gran was a traditionalist, and she had made the haleem with mutton, giving it a depth of flavour the more modern versions weren't getting with chicken.

"This is a bad idea when I'm going to be staring at CCTV all afternoon," she said. "It'll make me full and sleepy, and that Audi will drive past my nose and I'll miss it."

"Maybe set an alarm to go off every ten minutes." Kami squeezed fresh lemon onto her portion. "I've got a three-week backlog of fingernail scrapings and semen samples to process."

Safia chewed, contemplating the two options. "Not sure who has the better deal here."

"Me neither, but I'll get to go home at six, and I'm guessing you won't."

"It's unlikely," Safia conceded, conscious of the time, just five minutes into the fifteen she'd allowed herself for lunch. "I can't stop thinking about her, the woman from the Heath. She must have lost so much blood. I was going to google to see what she'd be able to lose without collapsing, but I didn't know where to start."

"If memory serves, about one and a half litres." Kami had done her degree in biological sciences and toyed with segueing into medicine before opting for forensics. "That's the upper limit of stage two shock, where your lady would still be compensating for the loss and still be able to function. Stage three is where it all starts to go to shit: low blood pressure, racing pulse. She'd be clammy, agitated, confused. Stage four is pre-terminal. If she's reached that stage outside a hospital then the chances are you'll be finding her body."

"Shit, Kami." Safia played her fork through the thick paste of lentils and meat. It was delicious, like everything Kami's gran cooked, but the ghee smelled too rich all of a sudden, and what Safia had already eaten was settling like a brick in her stomach.

"What?" Kami stopped eating as well. "Hey. You okay?"

"Yes. No," Safia said, genuinely undecided. "I'm not sure. It's just—on the CCTV, the one from the road near the Heath—Kami, you should've seen her."

"Do you feel sorry for her or something?" Kami sounded surprised, which was understandable given that Safia, like many experienced detectives, generally defaulted toward cynicism.

Safia was still messing with her haleem, trying to dissect the question. Some cases did hit her hard, that much was true—she wouldn't be human if she could let everything she dealt with wash over her—but she rarely took her worries home or allowed things to bother her for long.

"I suppose I do," she said at length. "She looked so beaten down. And don't give me that look, I'm not stupid. I know she's probably up to her neck in organised crime or whatever, but she doesn't deserve to bleed to death holed up on her own somewhere, and I don't think we're going to find her in time."

"She may well have blown that bloke's head off," Kami said, ever the pragmatist. "If she was innocent, she'd have gone for help, wouldn't she?"

Safia carried her plate to the sink. "So you think justice has been served?"

"No, love. I'm trying to make you feel better. If you're scraping my granny's haleem into the bin, then I know something's really bothering you."

Safia tugged Kami's sleeve, bringing her close enough to kiss the tip of her nose. "Don't worry about me, I'm fine. And I should get back. Suds gets this nervous little rash if I'm away from him for too long."

"Text me if you need me." Kami tweaked Safia's shirt collar, arranging it just so over her jacket lapels. She was a stickler for neat and tidy in the office. At home, however, all bets were off, and she'd spend every day in her pyjamas if she could.

"I will, I promise. Let me know when you're home safe, and give Bolly-pup a big smooch."

In the MIT office, Safia found Suds at his desk, typing an email with two fingers, which made him twice as fast as Chevs.

"CCTV requisition," he said. "Honestly, the palaver we have to go through." He stopped typing and sniffed the air. "Is that what I think it is?"

She put a tub of still-warm haleem, a fork, and a tinfoil-wrapped paratha in front of him. "Granny sends her love."

He let out a whoop, spat out his nicotine gum, and attacked the food as if he'd not eaten for weeks. When they'd first been partnered, he'd been a staunch pie-and-mash man who considered a splash of HP sauce exotic. While he'd never said anything offensive, he'd pulled his face at everything she brought to eat and declined every offered sample, until one bank holiday night shift when he'd forgotten his supper and not been able to find an open shop. She'd halved her chicken karahi, given him a couple of Kami's homemade singaras, and, as he so often reminded her, "opened him up to a world of possibilities." Granted, that was an exaggeration, given that she and Kami tended to stick to Pakistani or Bengali dishes, but he had been quite excited at the time.

"Which are you taking?" she asked, scrolling through the CCTV files on her desktop. There were seventeen when she counted them, and the process of acquiring more was ongoing. Another pinged into the file as she sat there. Ordinarily, she would have batted the job off to one of the less experienced detective constables, but they were out supervising the door-to-doors, which was just as onerous a task, if not more so.

"Top half, down to the…oh, the ninth one now. They're quite quick to go through, because there's not much happening on the roads."

She opened a screen grab of the Audi TTS, reminding herself of its shape and shade. If she'd had to stereotype the driver, she would have said divorced male, company exec, skirting a midlife crisis. He would drive the car to the golf course and charity functions, and feel daring if he exceeded sixty-five miles an hour. But she supposed underworld criminal would fit just as well.

The first file she loaded was a gantry camera located above the main road closest to the avenue where the woman had parked. With the photo of the Audi in one corner of the screen, she skipped through the recording until the time stamp read 3:45 a.m. and then let it play out, her finger poised on the mouse, ready to pause the footage if necessary. Suds had been right: the Audi was easy to spot, and it drove east five minutes after the woman had left the avenue.

"Do we have a map of these cameras?" she asked Suds, who was cleaning his Tupperware with his index finger.

"What?" he said as she gaped at him. "At least I'm not using my tongue this time."

"Let us be grateful for small mercies. Map?"

"In the main case folder. I called it 'Map.'" He pondered that one for the space of a finger-lick. "With hindsight, I could have been more specific."

"Well, I'm here now." Safia added "of CCTV locations" to the file name, then opened the map and pinpointed her specific cameras, altering the order of her files to keep them in accord with the woman's possible routes, though there was no guarantee she had taken any of them.

In between fielding enquiries and chasing updates from the door-to-door teams, it took Safia almost four hours of widening and narrowing her search and second-guessing the timeframe to find the Audi again, being driven slowly down an arbitrary main road. The car stopped at a kerbside for a few minutes and then pulled out, overcorrecting its position as a car approached from the opposite direction. The time stamp on the recording read 5:52 a.m., which meant the woman had been driving around for over an hour but travelled less than six miles. It was little wonder Safia hadn't been able to find her sooner, when her route made absolutely no sense.

"Where's that?" Suds asked, watching the footage over Safia's shoulder.

"Hanbury Street, Spitalfields. The camera belongs to a chippy. I have no idea what she's doing there, aside from being a danger to herself and others."

Suds twiddled Safia's mouse, replaying the Audi swerving for no apparent reason. "What kind of state might she have been in by this point? She probably hasn't a clue where she is or where she's going."

"True." Safia glowered at her desk phone as it began to ring. Everyone useful knew her work mobile number, which meant this person would not be useful and might further delay her eventual escape from the office.

"Might be a wrong number," Suds said, and quickly collected her mug when she gave him the evil eye. "I'll make you a nice cuppa."

"DS Faris, MIT," she said into the receiver.

"Hi—uh, sorry to disturb you, Sergeant." It was a youngish-sounding lad, a slight stutter betraying his nerves. "My name's Pete Wiley. I'm a police constable at Bethnall Green."

"Hey, Pete. How can I help you?" she said, brightening her tone. It wasn't so long ago that she'd been on the other side of this call, tasked to contact one of the lead detectives with a tip or an update, and never knowing whether they'd thank her or laugh her off the phone. The deference she received as a sergeant was still something she was getting used to.

"Okay, well, this is sort of odd, but my sarge said I should definitely give you a call." He paused to swallow audibly, and there was a crinkling sound as if he was finding the right place in his pocketbook. "I responded to a 999 call just before half past five. The caller was a paramedic based at the ambulance station in the grounds of the Royal London Hospital. They run that doctor car from there—you know, HEMS? It's linked to the helicopter?"

"Yep." Safia was all ears now. "I know it."

"Okay, well, this chap got in early for his shift, he should've started at six, and he went to check the response car. He found that most of its kit and drugs were missing, and there were spots of blood nearby. He was worried about the crew who'd worked on the car last night, so he tried to phone them. The paramedic, a lad called Gavin Cason, answered and said it had been fine when he left it, but the doctor, Grace Kendal, lives on her own and isn't answering her phone. She didn't come to the door when the sector manager went round to her flat."

"What did you find at the scene?" Safia had pulled up Suds's CCTV map, widening it to show the hospital's location. It was 0.7 miles from Hanbury Street, where the Audi had been seen driving erratically.

"Nothing much," Wiley said. "It was like the paramedic described. The car's equipment cage is mostly empty, and the drugs are gone. It hasn't been trashed, though, not like you'd expect it to be after a smack-rat raid. Oh, and they took the blood as well."

Safia stopped note-scribbling mid-bullet point. "The blood as in blood transfusions?" she asked, beckoning Suds over with such vigour that he broke into a trot and spilled their brews everywhere.

"Yes, exactly. And when I told my sarge that, he said I should call you."

"Tell him I owe him one." If she could have hugged the lad down the phone, she would have. "Did you request CSI for the scene?"

"Not yet. I taped everything off, though, and I'm still here taking a statement."

"Good stuff. I'll liaise with CSI and see you in about twenty."

Suds raised an expectant eyebrow at her as she hung up.

"The plot has just thickened, mate," she said. "I think our mystery woman might have bagged herself a doctor."

Frost was beginning to form on the ambulance station car park, a delicate white layer glistening in the beam of Safia's torch as she accompanied Wiley and Gav Cason, the paramedic who had worked the previous night with Grace Kendal, across to the HEMS car. Every so often, Wiley stopped to indicate a splash of blood he'd marked. Whilst waiting for Safia and Suds to arrive, he had used his initiative and searched the perimeter fence until he'd found a gap large enough for a person to climb through. The wire around the breach was also bloodied.

"Which is the normal way in?" Safia asked Gav.

He pointed to a solid metal automated gate. "Crews drive in through there, but to leave on foot you'd need to use the pedestrian entrance." He used his torch to pick out a smaller gate. "They both have key codes on them, but the fence is always getting wrecked. We've all had our cars broken into while we've been on shift." He checked his phone's messages for the umpteenth time, his eyes wide and wet in the moonlight. "Still nothing. Do you think she's all right?"

"I hope so," Safia said. It wasn't the reassurance he needed, but she didn't want to feed him false promises. Suds was in the ambulance station, using one of the managers' offices to request a tactical team and arrange a warrant for a search of Grace Kendal's flat. If the suspect had forced Kendal to take her there, Gav might have his answer soon enough. "I'll need a list of everything that's missing from the car," she told him. "Can you do that for me?"

"Yeah." He nodded, pivoting toward the station and then back to her. "Now?"

"Yes, please."

He hurried away, passing Suds, who met Safia in the middle of the car park.

"Half an hour, tops," Suds said. "Paperwork is sorted and the team are in prep. We're going to have to assume she's armed, Saf."

"I know." She looked beyond the wire to an access road fronted by tall maintenance buildings. "Gav said that Kendal told him to go home just before six and that she would have been restocking the car. If our woman parked around this point, maybe she acted on impulse after seeing Kendal."

"Hell of an impulse."

"It is, but what's the chance she had this in mind? I wouldn't even have known the station was here. Most likely she was on her way to A&E and changed her plan when a better one presented itself."

Suds let out his breath in a thin whistle. "Kidnapping your own personal physician. That's a pretty desperate move. Even if there was a third party involved, I'm liking our woman for the murder more and more."

"Me too." Safia couldn't ascribe another motive, and if the woman had already killed once then Kendal's chances were poor. "Did hospital security get back to you about CCTV?"

"Yes. There's a camera on that access road and this main road, and they're pulling the footage together. Wiley is going to collect it for us, and CSI are en route. I've updated Chevs, and he said to let him know how we get on."

Safia took his arm. "Just the two of us, then, is it?"

"You, me, and a load of hairy arses on the Armed Response Team," Suds said as a CSI van pulled in through the gate. "Come on, time's a-wastin'. Let's show this bunch where we need them and crack on."

❖

The apartment block where Grace Kendal rented a one-bedroom, second-floor flat had a palpable air of convenience over aesthetics, a perfunctory lump of concrete and glass the architects had stuck on the street corner, whose sole selling point was the nearby tube station.

The Armed Response Team had arranged access to the block's main entrance, and Safia stood in the lobby, breathing in the scent of weed and fresh laundry, and watching six heavily armed men run up the stairs. Discreet enquiries with neighbours, since evacuated, had yielded no recent sightings of Kendal or the woman, and there was no sign of life in Kendal's flat. With no suggestion of a hostage crisis in the making, the team had been given the green light to force entrance.

"Three, two, one…" Suds whispered as the boots fell silent above them, but his countdown was premature, and all Safia could hear was the boom of her own pulse and a child's toy singing a tinny nursery rhyme in the flat closest to her.

The team didn't give a warning. They battered the door to smithereens and piled in, their voices rising and fading as they scoured the flat. Safia counted to sixty, then again: one Mississippi, two Mississippi under her breath, her foot keeping the beat. The team leader was back in the lobby before she'd started her seventh count, his balaclava still in place and wet with perspiration.

"All clear," he told them. "Doesn't look like anyone's been there. No signs of disturbance, no blood."

"Thanks," Safia said, relief edging out her disappointment. Though she hadn't admitted it to Suds, she'd been expecting to find at least one body. "Are we okay to go up there?"

"Absolutely."

The last of the team left the flat as Safia and Suds entered a poky hallway lit by a low-energy bulb. There were four doors visible, all standard cheap plywood, and all wide open.

"Not what I'd imagined," Safia said with considerable understatement. A pair of trainers and a pair of low, simple black heels sat beneath a small telephone table, and two jackets—both Regatta raincoats—were hanging from wall hooks. There was a faint smell of damp and nondescript cooking, as if no one had ever bothered to prepare anything tasty or to open a window and air the place out. According to the doctor whom Suds had spoken to at Royal London's A&E, Grace Kendal had been a consultant there for twelve years. She clocked in excess of thirty-five hours' overtime a month and worked the HEMS car on a regular rotation. All told, she could definitely afford better than this flat.

"Bathroom, bedroom, living room, kitchen." Suds had reached the end of the corridor in eight long strides. "This place is depressing the hell out of me."

Safia clicked the bedroom light on. "It certainly lacks a personal touch. If you didn't know otherwise, you'd think no one lived here."

The bedroom was neat and tidy: bed made, brush and comb set just so on a chest of drawers. And that was all there was to see. There were no knickknacks, no photographs, no clothes chucked in a corner or books on the bedside table. The walls were white, the floor laminate wood unadorned by a rug or a runner. The clothes in the wardrobe that Safia opened were mostly T-shirts and sweaters and baggy jogging bottoms, with a few pairs of smarter trousers that Kendal probably kept for work. Everything was black or grey or mud brown, which suited the flat's dour ambience to a tee.

No one at the ambulance station had had a clear photograph of Kendal, and Safia needed one, so she started with the chest of drawers, found nothing of note, and moved on to the bedside table. Sitting cross-legged on the laminate, she laid out the cabinet's contents: two tangled pairs of headphones, lip salve, antihistamines, supermarket clubcard vouchers, and a wallet full of unspent euros. She found what she was looking for pressed between the pages of a two-year-old diary. Grace Kendal was an old-school organiser, and for the first nine months she had noted all of her educational courses, shifts, and appointments. The entries tapered off in mid-September, and when Safia turned to October, four photographs dropped onto her lap.

She recognised Kendal from the fuzzy team-building photos on the messroom wall of the ambulance station, but no one had mentioned her wife. They were together in all of the pictures: two printed selfies snapped on golden-sand beaches, and two lovely candid shots from their wedding day. Safia arranged the photos on the floor and picked up the small booklet that had fallen out with them: *Charlotte Kendal: A Celebration of Life*. Charlotte had died on 20th September. She had been thirty-six years old.

"So lose not heart nor fall into despair," Safia whispered, as all her snap judgements about Grace Kendal were thrown on their arse. She heard Suds come into the bedroom and patted his thigh as he sat on the floor beside her.

"Damn," he said as she passed him the photos and the funeral booklet. "This puts a whole new spin on things."

"She's pretty, isn't she?" Safia held up one of the beach selfies. Grace Kendal had a disarmingly sweet face that dimpled on the left when she smiled. She wore her sandy blond hair knotted back in all of the shots, and seemed just as comfortable in ragged shorts and T-shirts as she did in her wedding dress. "I bet she's lived here since her wife died, because this flat does not go with this woman."

"No, it doesn't," Suds said. "Keep that one and put everything else back. I feel like we shouldn't be in here."

The same sense of unease was creeping between Safia's shoulder blades and tensing the muscles there. What might have happened to Grace Kendal in the last fifteen hours was bad enough without an invasion of her privacy compounding the trauma.

"Time to phone the boss," she said. "Given that our nice simple murder is now a bloody kidnapping, we need the media involved sooner rather than later, and you know how much Chevs loves a good statement to the press."

"Sooner him than me."

"Yep." She slid the photo into her pocketbook for safekeeping. "I hope you weren't planning on getting home in time for supper, mate."

The skitter of paws across hardwood floor warned Safia that not only was Bolly the rescue pup awake, she was also being given free rein of the apartment.

"Incoming!" Kami yelled, seconds before a tornado of black-and-white idiot launched herself at Safia.

"Hey, pup." Safia knelt to unfasten her boots and scratch whichever body part Bolly presented. "You are a shameless hussy and a useless guard dog. Where's your other mother?"

Safia followed her nose instead of Bolly, who chose to wander into the bathroom for no discernible reason, and found Kami in the kitchen arranging slices of cheddar and tomato onto buttered toast.

"As ever, you have excellent timing," Kami said, kissing her and then shooing her off to get changed.

They ate supper in front of the television, washing down doorstep wedges of cheese on toast with mugs of homemade chai. For all that Safia adored cooking her family's recipes from scratch, there were times when simple bland English favourites really hit the spot. She'd never been quite sure whether Bolly had been named for Kami's love of Bollywood or her own love of spaghetti bolognaise, but suspected it was probably the latter.

"Shop talk or no shop talk?" Kami asked. She kept the question casual, dipping a piece of chocolate into her chai, but her eyes were bright with interest. If she hadn't eaten such a big supper, she would have been jumping up and down with impatience.

"No shop talk," Safia said, and laughed as a cushion hit her in the face.

"I saw you on the telly." Kami had changed the channel before Safia got home, but she was a big fan of the BBC's scrolling news. "Actually, I saw you twice. It's replaying every hour."

Safia hid her face in her hands. "I didn't have much time to prepare. Chevs was supposed to be coming in for it, but I think he might've been drunk when I phoned him. Did I sound nervous? Because I was shitting it."

Kami wound a long strand of Safia's hair around her finger. The motion tugged pleasantly at Safia's scalp, and she felt the stress of the day lift a fraction.

"You sounded every inch the professional. Suds, on the other hand, had spilled something on his tie."

Safia edged lower on the sofa and stuck her feet on the pouffe. "Haleem, most likely. Mm, keep doing that."

"Do you think you'll find them?"

"Yes, especially now the appeal has been made." Safia yawned. She was knackered, but her odds of getting to sleep were slim to none when her head was buzzing with things she needed to be doing. "What state they'll be in when we do, though…that's the million-quid question."

The televised appeal had been made directly to the woman seen on CCTV leaving the ambulance car park with Grace Kendal at gunpoint. Irrefutable confirmation of the kidnapping had spurred

Chevs into taking inebriated but effective action, resulting in the media briefing, and in additional personnel being transferred to Safia's team. She was on call through the night, should there be any developments, and was scheduled to meet her expanded team at 6:30 a.m.

"I'm not going to be seeing much of you for a while, am I?" Kami inched her free hand beneath Safia's T-shirt, her other cupping the back of Safia's head and pulling her into a kiss.

"No." Safia breathed the word against Kami's lips, tasting chocolate and cardamom when she touched them with her tongue.

"Are you very tired?" Kami ran a hand across Safia's nipple. "Do I need to stop this and let you go to bed?"

Safia managed a strangled noise of protest. "You stop now and I'll arrest you for something."

"*For something?*" Kami laughed. "You'll have to do better than that, DS Faris. And don't swear at me in Urdu. I know what all those naughty words mean."

Safia was only swearing because Kami had her fingers poised on the edge of Safia's underwear and was refusing to move them any lower.

"Okay, I won't arrest you," she said. She wasn't above begging if it came to that. "I promise."

"No?" Kami's hand dropped beneath the elastic. Smothering Safia's moan in a kiss, she slid her fingers lower still and found a rhythm that made Safia writhe. "All right, my darling," she said. "*Now* you can swear."

GRACE. SATURDAY, 7:48 P.M.

Half a mile, that's all. We'll make it in time. It'll be all right." Grace almost chanted the update, delivering it for her own benefit as much as Elin's. Her back and head ached, and her eyes were blurring from driving nonstop for just shy of three hours. There had been roadworks on the M25, slowing them to a crawl as Elin alternately dozed or twisted in pain or felt sick enough to travel with a plastic bag on her lap, but they had made up the time on the quieter stretches of motorway, and they were snaking through Birmingham's inner city now, the streets becoming increasingly destitute the closer they got to their destination.

"Next left," Elin said. She had been trying to help by keeping an eye on the satnav as the route became trickier, and this was her longest spell of staying awake. Grace focused on the road, refusing to consider how she would manage Elin's inevitable adrenaline crash or what might await them when they arrived at the address the man had sent them to.

"What number was it?" she asked. The satnav indicated they were on the right street, driving along a row of redbrick terraced houses, most of them boarded up and labelled for demolition. A scattered handful had lights on or televisions flickering behind curtains.

"Three. It'll be the far end. Odd numbers are on my side."

The far end was even worse, and the only house without an "everything of value has been removed" demolition plate across its doors and windows was the penultimate one in the row.

"What now? Do we go in? How would we even get in?" Grace said, constantly checking the street through her rearview and side mirrors. There were no other vehicles down that end, and theirs was standing out like a sore thumb.

As if on cue, the burner phone buzzed. Elin opened the message without wavering this time: *Try the back. Sleep tight. Speak to you tomorrow.* The man had signed off with the kiss-blowing emoji.

The phone skittered into the footwell as Elin let it go. She bent double, dry heaving into the bag, her eyes filling with tears. Grace handed her a wet wipe, but Elin dropped that as well. "Is he watching us? Is he here somewhere?"

"I doubt it," Grace said. There was nowhere to watch them from. She wiped Elin's face for her, skirting the bruises and the dressing on her forehead. "He'll be tracking the phone, like we thought. Do you want me to go in? You can stay here. I don't mind."

"No." The suggestion seemed to galvanise Elin. She pulled the gun from her pocket and screwed up the plastic bag. "Thank you, but no."

In the end, Grace moved the car around the corner, parking it by the entrance to the back alley, and they went together, one torch between them to pick a path through burned-out wheelie bins and rat-chewed sofas. The gate to number three hung on one hinge, allowing access to a typical terrace yard, strewn with litter blown in from the alley and thick with weeds where the concrete had cracked. The back door opened when Elin tried the handle, a stench of stale cigarettes and mould wafting over them as she led the way into the kitchen, with the gun clutched in both hands.

"I'm going to try the light," Grace said, unsure whether the house still had power until the neon strip half-blinded her. An empty tin of baked beans and half a white loaf were the first things she saw as the stars faded from her vision, and she made a grab for Elin as Elin worked it out too.

"Bastard," Elin spat. Where she got the energy from, Grace would never know, but she kicked the door leading into the living room and stormed through it. "*Amelia!*" she yelled, as she ran up the stairs with Grace right behind her. "*Amelia!*"

Two bedrooms, one a double, its sole furnishing a mattress in the middle of its floor, and the other a smaller box room with beige carpet and peeling wallpaper. In case they failed to join the dots, a blanket had been left beside the plate of beans on toast that Amelia hadn't eaten.

"She's not here," Elin said. "Grace, she's not here."

"I know." Grace had never expected her to be, and she couldn't imagine the terrible hope that must have flared in Elin. She saw the effect of that hope disintegrating, though. It took Elin to her knees, made her grab at the blanket and press it to her face. The scream she stifled in the cotton brought Grace across to her.

"This is cruel," Elin whispered. "It's cruel, and I don't know why he's doing it."

Grace knelt beside her. "Elin…"

Elin shook her head, negating anything Grace might have said, so Grace did the only thing she could think of: she put her arms around Elin and pulled her close, holding onto her until her sobs turned into ragged hiccups and the tension ebbed from her. Elin didn't move even when she had quietened, and Grace stayed there as well, stroking absent patterns through the tangled mess of Elin's hair. Elin's grip on the blanket eased, and she opened it out as if checking it for damage.

"I can smell her shampoo on this," she said. "She hates the baby stuff. She threw a tantrum in the toiletries aisle until I bought her some peach and mango crap that made her smell like a smoothie. Every time I wash her hair, she tries to eat the bubbles."

Whenever she spoke about Amelia like this, her demeanour changed. It made Grace wish she had met her before, back in her other life where she was the long-suffering mum of a tearaway infant, dry-humoured and full of affection.

"Oh to be a fly on the wall," Grace said.

"You'll like her. You both have a stroppy streak."

Grace put her hand to her heart. "Me? Stroppy?"

"Back in the hotel. You gave me a proper bollocking."

"Well, you deserved it. You were behaving like a knob."

"Yeah, I was." Elin's fingers were cool where they touched Grace's cheek. "Should I apologise again?"

"No. Enough apologies," Grace said, leaning into that touch, just for a moment. "Come on downstairs and let me take a look at you."

Elin allowed Grace to help her up. "We'll have to stay here tonight, won't we?"

"If he's tracking the phone, then he'll know if we move too far," Grace said. "He obviously knew the minute we arrived." She switched off the bedroom light and made no comment when Elin carried the blanket out with her. "We could sleep in the car, but we have electricity here, which means we can have a hot meal and perhaps put the heating on, and I'll be able to see what I'm doing."

Elin was struggling on the stairs, the drain knocking against her thigh as she stumbled. "I don't mind. It's fine," she said. She didn't seem to know what she was offering an opinion on, as the crash Grace had feared came on hard and knocked her for six.

"Here, sit down." Grace led her to the sofa that took up most of the living room. Its only companion was a lopsided wooden unit that sported an antiquated television. "I bet he rented this house," she said, trying to work it through. "The owner probably snapped his hand off, no questions asked."

"Probably." Elin curled onto her side, not caring about the filthy cushion she rested her head against. Her face was overly pink, and when Grace put a hand to her forehead, the skin was warm and damp.

"Will you be okay here while I go and fetch some more stuff?" Grace asked.

"Yep."

Thick purple curtains were already drawn at the front window, so Grace left a lamp on and took the torch back to the car. She carried as much as she could, remembering the damn rucksack at the last minute. Leaving a million in cash unattended in this neighbourhood was probably not a good idea.

There was no key to lock the back door of the house, but the top and bottom security bolts were hefty enough, settling into place with a satisfying clunk when she closed them. Wearing a pair of nitrile gloves, she moved the tin of beans and the bread into a cupboard, out of sight but preserved as evidence for whenever Elin agreed to contact the police.

Still in the kitchen, she froze at the sound of voices, straining to listen, to establish whether someone was in one of the neighbouring houses after all, watching them and waiting for the right moment. Could Lowry have—

"For goodness' sake," she muttered, as a familiar piece of music started. It was the BBC news. Elin must have switched the television on.

"Hey." Elin was hunched on the edge of the sofa, breathing as if she'd run a marathon. "The police know you're missing, and they've linked it to the murder on the Heath."

"Christ. That was fast." Grace had anticipated this. They both had. It was inevitable after the discovery of the HEMS car, but she hadn't thought the police would be so adept at pulling two apparently unrelated crimes together. "How the hell have they managed that? Was it the hotel?"

"They've not said yet. The report will be on in a few minutes. It was the second headline."

It was a long few minutes, but the bulletin eventually switched from politics to a photograph of Grace.

"They've been in my flat," Grace said. She'd kept that photo in her diary. It was a holiday selfie from Skiathos that the BBC had cropped Charlotte out of. While she understood that the police had her best interests at heart, the thought of strangers rooting through her belongings made her skin crawl, as did the casual excision of Charlotte.

"Police in East London are increasingly concerned for the welfare of an Accident and Emergency doctor apparently kidnapped at gunpoint from the grounds of the Royal London Hospital at six o'clock this morning," the newscaster said. "Paramedics raised the alarm when an ambulance the doctor had been working on was found to be missing most of its drugs and equipment. Jabal Nasir has this report from the scene."

Nasir was standing by the HEMS car with a thirty-something Pakistani woman and a taller white man. They both looked weary, and wary of their moment in the limelight.

"CID," Grace said. "Detectives. We see them in A&E all the time, and you can spot them a mile off. They must teach that stance at training school."

After the brief establishing shot, Nasir launched his piece to camera.

"CCTV from the hospital grounds shows forty-one-year-old Grace Kendal, an experienced A&E consultant, being taken from the ambulance station car park by a woman whom police suspect of being involved in an earlier crime. The body of an unidentified man was found in remote woodland on Hampstead Heath this morning, and police believe the incidents are connected. Detective Sergeant Faris from the East London Murder Investigation Team is leading the enquiry. What can you tell us, Detective?"

Faris stepped closer to the camera, edging out her colleague. After what must have been a long day, she was still smartly presented in a grey trouser suit, and a neat knot held her hair in place at the nape of her neck. She wasn't wearing much makeup, but it flattered her despite the garish television lights. By that stage of a shift, Grace's hair usually resembled a bird's nest, and she would be on her umpteenth pair of ill-fitting scrubs. She'd given up on makeup entirely after Covid-19 had made surgical masks the hottest fashion accessory in the department.

"Thank you, Jabal," Faris said. "Obviously, we are very keen to get in touch with both of these women. There is strong evidence to suggest the suspect sustained an injury during the incident on the Heath, and although we can place her at the crime scene, we have reason to believe a third party may also have been involved." She looked directly into the camera, personalising her appeal. "Contact the police and tell us your side of the story. Your safety and welfare, and that of Dr. Kendal, are our paramount concerns. If you are in danger, let us help you. That's what we're here for."

"And what can the public do to help, DS Faris?"

"We have a dedicated phone line for any information the public may have. This is the woman we wish to speak to." Faris held up a grainy black and white still of Elin. Little could be seen of her face beneath the hood of her jacket, and the image was no clearer when the broadcast pinned its own version to the upper right of the screen. "You can find this photograph on our Facebook page and Twitter feed. We believe she is driving a black or navy Audi TTS with an MA20 plate. You can report information anonymously if you wish. It is important that you do not approach this woman if you happen to see her in public."

"Thank you, DS Faris," Nasir said. "That phone number is 0207—"

Elin muted the television and placed the remote on the sofa. "We need to get rid of the car. If someone at the rental agency sees that report and remembers your face, the police will know we've ditched my Audi, and they'll know what we're driving now, and they—"

"Elin, we can't," Grace said, cutting across her. "We need it, and we can't risk renting another. Not now. If the chap at the rental agency does phone in, it might keep the police focused on London."

"Fucking cameras are everywhere," Elin said. "And we probably installed most of them. No doubt the police will appreciate the irony when they trace me to my company. That photo they had of me was from the street I parked on near the Heath."

"Ah, I did wonder." Grace turned the television off properly. She didn't want to see the piece repeated every thirty minutes. "That detective seemed fair," she ventured, but Elin was already shaking her head.

"I know what you're going to say, but no. Not now. You won't phone her, will you? Is your phone still off?"

Grace showed Elin her phone. She had turned it off and removed its SIM again as soon as the messages had started to flood in from her colleagues and friends. "I won't phone anyone."

"Thank you. When the man holding Amelia sees the news, I'm going to be in enough shit as it is." Elin flattened her palm on her cheek. "Why do I feel so hot?"

Grace swore beneath her breath, cross with herself for being so distracted that she'd neglected to monitor Elin's condition. "I think you're running a temperature. Lean back for me." She fished the thermometer from her bag and angled it into Elin's ear. Its beeps heralded a reading of 37.9°C. "It's up a little. How are you feeling?"

Elin took stock for a couple of seconds. "Tired. Thirsty but a bit sick. Sore. The usual."

"Okay, let's see what we can do about that."

A top-to-toe assessment found no further haemorrhage into the drain, and obs consistent with a brewing infection. Grace inserted a new cannula and hung another bag of antibiotics.

"This is the last of these," she warned Elin. "So you need to behave yourself from now on. You hear me?"

"I hear you." Elin stiffened as Grace peeled the dressing from her entrance wound. "How's it looking?"

"Slightly inflamed but nothing too drastic. Your chest sounds clearer than I'd expected. I might be able to take the drain out in the morning."

"Oh God, yes please," Elin said, and then whipped around as the burner phone buzzed, not with a text but an incoming call. "Shit, it's him." She answered the call before Grace could react. "Hello?"

"You really are determined to fuck this up, aren't you?" The man was yelling loudly enough for Grace to hear him, and there was nothing but hatred in his voice. "I just saw the news. You kidnapped a doctor? You stupid fucking bitch."

"I was bleeding out, and you took my child." Elin spoke with measured calm, sounding as dangerous as the man, if not more so. "What exactly was I supposed to do? Do you think it's *easy* getting a million pounds together without anyone noticing? Don't you think I'd have followed your rules if I could? You have my *daughter*."

He laughed, dismissing her outrage. "Not really yours, is she, this scrawny little skank? I suppose she'll do for now, though."

"Fuck you. If you've got an axe to grind with me, you take it out on me, not on a child, you fucking coward."

"Oh, I intend to," he said, and the phone went dead.

"*Fuck!*" Elin bowed her head. Her entire body was reverberating with tension, and heat was rolling off her. "I'll kill him," she said, and Grace had no doubt she was telling the truth. "I'll fucking kill him when I find him."

ELIN. SUNDAY, 3:20 A.M.

Elin woke to the worst hangover she'd ever had, but one that came without a stale beer aftertaste or the urge to eat a fry-up and chase it down with a pint. She shivered, burrowing further beneath a thin sheet—where was her quilt?—and felt a trickle of cold water on her lips. When she licked them dry, the water came again, along with a quiet question.

"Can you hear me?"

She nodded, and something cool bathed her face, wiping the stickiness from her eyes so she could open them.

"Hiya," Grace said. Her smile dimpled her cheek, and her shoulders fell as she exhaled. Her reaction, and her rumpled hair and clothing, suggested she'd been even more stressed than Elin usually made her, though Elin wasn't sure why. "Here, have a drink." Grace brought Elin's head forward and held a mug to her lips. It was only tap water, but Elin was so thirsty that she guzzled and made herself cough. "Okay, easy. That's enough for now."

The mug disappeared, and Elin felt a pressure in her ear, then heard the thermometer give its series of beeps. It didn't take her long to put two and two together. *Shit.*

"What is it?" she asked.

"Thirty-eight point three."

"What was it?"

"Thirty-nine point six, at its worst. It spiked about ten minutes after the phone call. Do you remember that?"

"Yes. The phone call, not the rest of it."

"I'm not surprised. You were delirious by then, but you've had paracetamol and another bag of saline, and they seem to have done the trick."

"For now," Elin said. She was well versed in the risk of infections linked to bullet wounds. Her first had almost killed her.

"Yes, for now." Grace smoothed the sheet, moving a stained corner away from Elin's face. "On the bright side, I took the drain out while you were away with the fairies."

"You did?" Elin lifted the sheet and then her T-shirt, finding nothing attached to her side but a fresh dressing. How on earth had Grace tugged a plastic tube out of her without her feeling a thing? For how long had she been unconscious? "What time is it?"

"Twenty past three in the morning. You slept, I dozed. No one phoned, messaged, or came knocking. Are you hungry?"

"Not really."

Grace wasn't giving in that easily. "What about some jelly and custard?"

"Grace, I'm thirty-nine years old."

"I know, but it's good invalid food. Slips down, full of sugar, and as luck would have it I bought both from the shop."

Elin gave in graciously. "I will if you will."

"You're on."

It was more palatable than she had expected, and she polished off a second helping as Grace opened a packet of digestives.

Elin pointed at the biscuits with her spoon. "I bought those for Amelia once, and she thought I was trying to punish her for something. She kept checking them one by one, looking for the chocolate. She was convinced the first ones were faulty."

"Poor kid. I like them, but I wouldn't inflict them on a child." Grace proffered the packet. "Try one, they'll settle your stomach."

Elin accepted a biscuit but used it to scrape up the last of her custard, which was, she realised, exactly what Amelia would have done.

"I didn't even think to ask," she said as the guilt that was always there, nagging at her nerves in the background, swept right over her.

"I should have asked to speak to her, but I was so angry, all I did was antagonise him. What if he takes it out on her?"

"I can't answer that," Grace said. "I can't tell you he won't, because he might, and I can't tell you not to think like that or worry about the things you can't change, because that'd be stupid and I'm not going to insult you."

She must have had similar conversations with countless patients or relatives, and Elin, who preferred blunt talk to fanciful thinking, appreciated the lack of sugar-coating. It made her feel calmer, somehow.

"He wouldn't have let you speak to her anyway," Grace continued. "He knows that's the hold he has over you, and he only phoned to remind you of that and to scream at you. If you had asked to speak to her, he'd have said no just to torment you."

"You're probably right." Elin was exhausted but fizzing with energy from the late supper, a weird combination that gave her the clarity to replay her conversation with the man, word for word. "How badly do you think I've fucked up?" she asked, once she thought she could bear the answer.

"I'm not sure. But I was thinking about this while you were being terrible company."

"Oh." A different sort of regret hit Elin this time. It was the one reserved especially for Grace, that made her want to tell Grace to go home and not be involved in any more of this. "Sorry."

"It's okay. You're far easier to manage when you're insensible. Anyway, I came to the conclusion that if the money isn't the issue and he has a different end game in mind, then you'll have pissed him off but probably not deterred him, which means he'll carry on with whatever he's got planned." Grace grimaced, acknowledging that her bright side was actually loaded with awful.

"And this *has* been planned, hasn't it?" Elin said. "I thought at first that maybe he'd seen me in a magazine or something, some random connection, like he needs money and he picks up a copy of *Entrepreneur Monthly* or whatever in his local dentist and it's the issue with my profile in it. But that's bollocks. I know this bastard from somewhere, or he knows me, at the very least. That's why he battered me. He just couldn't help himself, could he?"

"You don't recognise him, though, do you?"

"No, I don't." No matter how many times she tried, she couldn't put a name or even a face to the man. With the exception of his skin, everything she'd been able to see of him had been dark—his hair and his eyes—and she couldn't fill in the blanks covered by his mask. "That's what I don't understand. If someone hates me enough to do this, why don't I know him? Shouldn't I know why he hates me? Otherwise, what's the point?"

Grace pulled her jacket more tightly around herself. She hadn't been able to switch the central heating on, and the house was cold. "I'm sure he'll tell you," she said. "When the time comes."

Grace. Sunday, 4:57 a.m.

It wasn't much: a flutter of movement where there shouldn't have been any, perhaps a scrape on the back door, but Grace was a light sleeper and it was enough to wake her. She sat on the very edge of the chair, hands on the armrests, poised for fight or flight. She had prepared for the latter half an hour ago, packing her kit and tidying their food away, but a fierce protective impulse told her she was up for a scrap if it came to that.

"Elin?" Grace knelt by the sofa, putting a hand over Elin's mouth as soon as she awoke. "Shh."

Another noise, unmistakeable this time: a rattle of the windowpane, as if someone was checking for a weak spot. Elin heard it as well. Her fists clenched, and her breath came fast and hot against Grace's palm.

"We need to go," Grace whispered. "Now. Leave the lamp off."

Elin nodded once. If the intruder realised they had heard him, he would abandon stealth and force his way in. "Where's the gun?" she asked.

"Top of the rucksack. Leave it. You're in no state to be firing it. Check for a front door key."

Elin didn't argue, which spoke volumes in itself. Grace helped her to stand, bracing her through the inevitable head rush and then shouldering the rucksack as Elin went into the hallway. She bent low and shoved at the sofa, shifting its bulk inch by squealing, protesting inch, until it was blocking the kitchen door. For a fleeting moment, she thought she might have got away with the noise, but she knocked the lamp when she turned, sending its stand clattering to the floor.

"*Shit.*" She jumped at a louder smash as the kitchen window suddenly imploded. "*Elin!*"

"I'm here." Elin was almost invisible in the dark. "There's no key."

Behind the barricaded door, more glass hit the tiles as their intruder climbed through into the kitchen.

Grace tried the front window. It was locked. "Fucking unbelievable. Get the bags." She yanked at the lamp stand, pulling it free from the socket and wielding it like a javelin. "Stay back."

The glass was shoddy single glazing, and it capitulated at the first strike, throwing fragments into the tiny front garden and leaving a vicious, jagged row around the edges. She started to knock out the worst of them as the living room door shook beneath a rapid volley of blows. Giving up on the glass, she hurled their bags through the gap.

"Go! Go!" She shoved Elin in front of her. The sofa jolted forward and then snagged on a rumple of carpet as Elin dropped clear of the frame. Grace tossed the car keys at her. "Run! I'm right behind you!"

Elin hesitated, clearly torn, before common sense kicked in and she set off toward the car, cradling one of the kit bags. The sofa jumped another few inches, and Grace saw a man's hand and half his face, a horror-film mask in the glare of his torch. Terrified, she grabbed the lamp stand and hurled it at him before hoisting herself onto the sill, but the rucksack snagged on something, dragging her back when she tried to jump down.

She reached upward, groping blindly until she found the splintered piece of wood the bag was fast on. Behind her, the hammering ramped up, and she gasped as part of the door caved in and the man boosted himself through. She gave one final desperate pull, pitching forward when the bag came loose, and tumbling onto the paving flags beneath the window. She landed badly, the impact knocking the breath from her and driving a shard of glass into her arm.

"God!"

She pulled the glass out, splashing blood across the concrete, and stumbled to her feet, one hand clawing at a drainpipe for leverage, the other hooking the strap of their last bag.

She ran without looking back, careering onto the street and aiming for the corner they'd parked around. Elin had just disappeared round it, when Grace heard a sharp bang that made chips of brick fly up from the wall on her left.

She staggered, her feet clipping each other as she half-turned to check whether that had really been a bullet and how close the man was. He was too close, close enough that she could see the gun in his hand and hear the rasp of his breaths as he chased her. She weaved into the road and then back onto the pavement, but there was nothing to shelter behind, and another shot flew just wide of her. She got to the corner as their car made a screeching U-turn, sped past her, and accelerated straight at the man. He fired, obliterating the driver's wing mirror, but that was all he managed before the car mounted the kerb, gathered him on the bonnet, and braked to send him flying over a garden wall.

Elin reversed the car back to Grace and flung open the passenger door. Grace dived in, huddling half on the seat, half in the footwell as the car picked up speed. She felt Elin reach over, patting her shoulders, her head, anything she could reach.

"Are you hurt? *Grace?* Are you *hurt?*"

"I don't think so." A thin line of pain and a trickle of heat from her left arm told her otherwise, but they had enough to deal with. "Are you?"

"No, I'm fine. Knackered, but fine. Jesus." Elin rested her hand against the back of Grace's head, and Grace leaned into it, craving the comfort.

"Was it Lowry?" she asked.

"Yes." Elin turned onto a main road, slowing the car to the speed limit. "I hope I broke the bastard's legs."

Grace shivered. She hoped so too, but she didn't think Elin had hit him hard enough. "How did he find us?"

"I haven't a clue. He could've killed you, the fucking arsehole."

"I had the money." Grace shrugged out of the tattered rucksack. "Do you think anyone will call the police?"

"Probably not, or not soon enough to catch him, unless I really did break his legs."

"You might've dented them a bit." Grace put the bag in the footwell and managed to get onto the passenger seat. Her body felt rubbery and sluggish, and nothing was moving quite how she wanted it to. Her left arm burned when she fastened her seat belt, and the fabric around it felt wet and heavy. A surreptitious exploration found a five-inch laceration that was bleeding freely.

"Elin?"

"What?"

"Can you find somewhere to stop?"

"Yes. Why?" Elin saw Grace's bloodied fingers and almost mounted the kerb again. "Did you get shot?"

Grace corrected the steering wheel for her. "No. I think…I think it was the window." Her recollection was hazy at best. All she could remember was a seemingly endless fight to free herself, and realising she was probably going to die. She had pulled glass out of her arm, hadn't she? She probably shouldn't have done that. "It's not too bad. I just need to get a dressing on it."

"Okay. I'll find somewhere." Elin adjusted the satnav screen. "Don't faint on me, will you?"

"I'm not going to faint. Keep your bloody eyes on the road." Taking her own advice, Grace watched the streetlights and shopfronts pass by in degrees of blurry colour, and tried her damnedest to keep her promise.

ELIN. SUNDAY, 5:44 A.M.

It was getting harder for Elin to drive. Her right leg, usually
her strongest, wasn't cooperating, and her foot repeatedly
slipped from the accelerator. Beside her, Grace was conscious but
subdued, and Elin had no way to tell how serious an injury her jacket
was concealing.

The Saturday night mayhem had yielded to a Sunday morning
lull, clearing the roads and pavements. Elin followed signs to an
industrial estate, circling the units until she found an unlit scrap of
land, attached to nothing and well beyond the main thoroughfare.
She switched off the engine and flicked the small overhead light on.

"Which bag am I looking in?" she said. There were two on the
back seat, upended and speckled with dirt.

Grace took her right arm out of her jacket and started to peel the
fabric from her left. It obviously hurt, and she paused to compose
herself before she answered. "Try the orange one. The end pocket
has dressings in it."

Elin wrestled the pouch free and found her torch, directing its
beam at Grace's arm, where a deep laceration split the underside of
her biceps. Removing the jacket had aggravated the wound, and it
was bleeding heavily.

"'Not too bad,' eh?" Elin said.

Grace shrugged. "Well, I can't really see it."

"Here." Elin took a photo on the burner phone and showed it
to her. "It needs stitches. How the hell did you cut yourself there?"

Grace raised an eyebrow at the extent of the damage but didn't seem keen to let Elin loose on it. "I did a swan dive out of the window." She sighed as Elin continued to stare at her. "And got a bit stabbed."

"*A bit stabbed?*" Elin made a show of enlarging the photo. "Is that like me getting *a bit shot?*"

"Yes, well, there's no real harm done." Grace passed her a padded bandage. "One of these and Steri-Strips will be fine. Just put them on good and tight."

"Don't trust me with a needle and thread, then?"

"Nope."

"To be honest, I wouldn't either. I once tried to sew the arm back onto Amelia's favourite teddy and accidentally grafted it to its ear." Elin opened a packet of gauze, cleaned away the worst of the blood, and set to work with the strips. It was difficult to be precise when her dexterity had been shot to hell, so she erred on the side of over-application instead. She took another photo. "Is that okay or does it need a few more?"

"Mm, it's fine," Grace said, but her eyes were half-lidded and she wasn't really monitoring what Elin was doing. More than anything, that latter fact told Elin how badly Lowry's assault had affected her.

Elin opened the bandage, fumbling with its strips and unravelling one length into the footwell. She swore beneath her breath, skirting her own private meltdown. For several interminable seconds after hearing the gunfire, she hadn't known what she would find when she drove around the corner. She hadn't planned to batter Lowry with the car. Now, seeing Grace so traumatised, she only wished she'd hit him harder.

She ducked down to retrieve the bandage, staying in the shadows until she was sure her expression wouldn't give her away. This was Grace's turn to fall apart if she wanted to. She didn't need Elin throwing a wobbler as well.

"Right, here we go," Elin said, forcing brightness into her voice. She wasn't squeamish, but blood was still oozing through the Steri-Strips, and the wound looked too sore for direct pressure.

"Good and tight," Grace reminded Elin as she heard the crinkle of the dressing.

"Yep. I've got it." Elin wrapped the wound as firmly as she dared and then stroked Grace's palm. "Still feel that?"

"Yes."

"Make a fist."

Grace closed her hand around Elin's finger. Her grip was reassuringly strong, and she didn't let go straight away.

"Do you want any painkillers?" Elin asked.

"No, I'm all right."

Elin used the lever to recline Grace's seat and covered her with her jacket. "Is that better?"

"Yes." Grace blinked when Elin shut off the overhead, but the moon was dominating the horizon and there was enough light to see by.

Elin set her own seat to the same level as Grace's. They could stay here for a while to recover, and then she was almost sure she would be able to carry on driving while Grace continued to rest. Behind the car, a pair of foxes growled and yapped at each other, and an early jet roared overhead, temporarily drowning them out. Grace shuffled to her right, keeping the jacket tucked in close.

"Were you a medic in the army?" she asked, as the rumble of the plane's engines faded. She kept the question low-key, as if she wouldn't push the point if Elin didn't want to answer.

"No, I wasn't a medic." Elin turned onto her good side, which left her facing Grace. This conversation was long overdue, she supposed, and she was grateful that Grace had left it alone until now, when she almost felt strong enough to have it. "I had basic field training. The rest comes from—well, I got shot before all this. You know I got shot. You can't really miss it, can you? Anyway, it…I…" She paused to get a grip on herself. A little over twenty-four hours ago, she had repeatedly stuck a gun in Grace's face. She hadn't earned the right to go to pieces over this. Still, she skipped the worst of it. "It made a real mess of me, and I ended up with sepsis."

"Don't do anything by halves, do you?" Grace said. She must have guessed that most of Elin's medical knowledge had come from first-hand experience. If nothing else, surviving catastrophic trauma had left Elin with a ridiculously high pain threshold. "How long were you in the hospital for?"

"Ten weeks, three days." Elin rolled her eyes. "Not that I was counting. I did another month in rehab, but they couldn't fix everything." She patted her recalcitrant left leg, assuming Grace had noticed her uneven gait. "It's no wonder Mouse runs rings around me."

"Kids will do that regardless," Grace said. "I have three nieces and two nephews, and I can't keep up with any of the little sods."

Elin huffed out a clouded breath. The car was cold without the engine on, and tiny crystals of frost had started to gather on the windscreen. She tugged her sweater sleeves over her hands and folded her arms. On the bright side, at least the frigid temperature would be keeping her fever at bay.

"It's weird." She ran her hand over the scarred section of her abdomen. "Because without this, I wouldn't have Mouse. I was in the Forces for life, Grace. I loved it, and I couldn't imagine myself ever doing anything else."

"Had you always wanted to sign up?"

"Not at all." Elin was fine with the scene setting; she could talk about her early army life all day. It was safer than bolting right to the blood and guts part, especially when it was her blood and guts. "I joined at eighteen, but it was more to piss off my dad than anything else. He'd assumed I would follow in my brother's footsteps and join the family company, and the last thing I ever wanted to do was sell double glazing in Ashton."

"Ashton?" Grace chuckled. "I thought your accent was familiar. I grew up in Heaton Chapel."

"Small world," Elin said. She had spent her formative years about six miles up the road from Grace. "Have you lived down south for long?"

"Since university. I studied medicine at King's, fell in love with London and then with Charlotte. I never thought I'd leave, but that was before." Grace licked her chapped lips. "It's been a lonely couple of years."

"I'll bet it has," Elin said gently. "I like visiting London, but I'd never move there. Back then, I just knew I didn't want to be stuck under my dad's thumb."

"Rebel without a clue, eh?" Grace said.

"Yes, something like that. My mate pierced my ears for me at thirteen and honestly my mum thought it was the end of the world."

"Here?" Grace touched her own earlobe, then the top of the ear. "Or here?"

"One of each," Elin said. "I've always preferred to keep my options open."

Grace laughed. She'd had no trouble reading between those lines, making this as easy a coming out as Elin had ever experienced.

"Hey, there's no point pigeonholing yourself. You never know who's around the corner."

"No, you don't." Elin coughed, resetting the subject. "Just out of interest, how old were you when you decided you wanted to be a doctor?"

"Five," Grace replied immediately. No deliberation, no counting on her fingers. "My gran bought me one of those plastic doctor's kits for Christmas, and I spent the day in my shiny white coat, listening to chests and knocking my dad's knees with a tendon hammer. I flirted with a few other options in my early teens—firefighter, professional footballer, pastry chef—but I always came back to medicine in the end."

"See, I never had an inkling," Elin said. Her own ambitions had been fickle and usually established in opposition to those of her parents. She was on far better terms with them now, and they adored Amelia, but she had spent years at loggerheads with them. "I bet you'd done all your research before you chose your university, but I joined the army without even realising that women weren't allowed in combat roles. I really wanted to raise hell with the blokes, though, so I knuckled down, got through my first few years and applied for the Special Reconnaissance Regiment, who did allow women. They armed us to the teeth and treated us like one of the lads. I'd still be on the unit now if things had turned out differently."

"What happened when you got hurt?" Grace asked the question quietly, but they were too deep into this to avoid the subject.

Elin unscrewed the cap from a bottle of water so cold that part of it had frozen solid. She drank it regardless and then offered it to Grace.

"We were doing the recon for a hostage retrieval in Syria," she said. "A couple of Brits and a French lad kidnapped by ISIS and on a tight execution deadline. I was the lead on a team of four, tasked to plan a route in, scope out any ordnance, and plot sniper positions. We tripped something and the shit hit the fan. It was so quick." She inhaled sharply, smelling smoke and cordite, and sumac from a cook pot. The lingering tang of blood from Grace's arm thickened and coated her throat. "Toller, our point man, died instantly," she continued, making an effort to lower her voice. She'd had chronic tinnitus since that night, and her ears were ringing. "The body armour was all geared for men back then, and it left gaps. The bastards hit me right through one as we retreated."

"What happened to the hostages?" Grace asked.

"They were moved and executed." Elin had never forgotten their names. Some of their families had released videos to the press, hoping to appeal to their kidnappers' better natures. They were everyday videos of them mucking around on the beach or cooking at a back-garden barbecue. Their faces, smiling and suntanned and rosy with drink, mixed into Elin's recurring nightmares of getting shot and falling into the dirt. "I would have been taken with them," she said, "had Lowry not dragged me out."

"Lowry? Jesus." Grace made a weak gesture toward Elin's chest, her own arm, all of it. "How the hell did we get to this?"

Elin took the water back from Grace and swallowed another series of sips. Her cheeks felt overly warm, but she couldn't tell if it was stress or fever.

"I accepted a disability payout and left the Forces," she said. "They'd offered me an administrative position, but I just couldn't bear the thought of a desk job with them. I blew through quite a lot of the money—PTSD doesn't half muck up your common sense—but I finally got a grip and decided to start my own company." She raised a hand to acknowledge the discrepancy. "Yes, it was essentially a desk job, but it was different by then. This was going to be my choice, something for me to build from nothing, and I wouldn't be working in my dad's or the army's shadow. Lowry came on board right from the outset, put some money in, brought in a load of contacts, and worked his arse off, which meant I overlooked all those meetings he'd show up for stinking of drink, and occasionally bailed him out of his gambling debts."

"That explains a lot," Grace said.

"I know." It explained but it didn't excuse Lowry's actions, and Elin was nowhere near coming to terms with what he had done. One day, she might understand his behaviour, but she would never be able to forgive it. "I tried to get him counselling and rehab, but nothing stuck for long. He didn't need to do this, though. I would never have thought him capable of this."

"Do you think he's using your security cameras to find us?" Grace said, but she was shaking her head, dismissing her theory as soon as she had posited it. "He can't be, can he? He doesn't know what car we're driving. Is it your phone? Or the burner? You were mostly out of it all day Thursday, so he could have put something on either of them."

Elin placed both phones on the storage compartment between their seats. She and Grace took one each, dismantling them quickly to check for signs of tampering or suspicious additions, and then, because Elin's phone had been switched off, examining all the settings and apps on the burner. That didn't take long. Its sole download was WhatsApp, and its settings were all factory standard.

"Not the phones, then," Elin said. "What else? I have my laptop in the boot. It was there in the house we'd rented." She coughed, splinting her chest against the force of it. The rattle of fluid sounded loud in the confined space, and she knew Grace would be able to hear it even without her steth.

"I'll check the laptop after I've checked you," Grace said. She found her obs kit and stuck its pulse oximeter on Elin's finger.

Elin turned her hand to read the numbers as Grace took her temperature. "Ninety-five's not that bad, is it?"

"No, it isn't, all things considered, and your temp is only up a notch."

Elin pulled another coat from the back seat and arranged it over herself. "How can my temperature be up when we're freezing?"

"Because the body is a mysterious and fickle beast." Grace leaned over to start the engine and turn the heater on. "Maybe we can find an all-night café and get a brew. Do you know where we are?"

"No. I just drove." Elin touched the burner. "This bastard's going to know we've moved."

"We can't go back," Grace said. "Someone might have phoned the police by now, or Lowry could still be at the house." She propped the burner on the dashboard where they could both see it. "We'll wait here. There's no one around, and it's Sunday so it'll probably stay that way."

"Okay." Elin tried not to calculate the time Amelia had been missing, but she couldn't stop herself. Three full days. Four full nights. Jesus. "Maybe today will be the end of it," she whispered. "Maybe he'll let me have her back."

She wasn't sure whom she was trying to convince, though, and Grace, watching the moon's sallow reflection on the corrugated roofs, said nothing.

SAFIA. SUNDAY, 5:00 A.M.

The predawn ring of the phone set everything off: Bolly barking and racing in a circle, Kami swearing a Bengali blue streak, and Safia slapping a hand around on the bedside table. Far better at being sensible at daft o'clock, Kami switched her lamp on, and Safia rolled onto her back, the phone pressed somewhere near her ear.

"DS Faris." It could only be work at this time, and she covered her naked chest with the sheet, feeling underdressed for official business.

"Morning, Sergeant Faris. Sorry to disturb you." The young woman sounded mortified but determined to press on. "I'm Police Constable Tina Riggs, and I've been working the tips line for your case overnight."

"Hey, Tina. What have you got?" Safia found the pen and writing pad she kept by her bed and tried in vain to stop Bolly from chewing a corner of the paper.

"A receptionist from the Radisson Hotel on Canary Wharf just phoned in. He saw the televised appeal when he arrived for work this morning, and he recognised Grace Kendal. He said she's staying in one of their suites with another woman."

"Bloody hell." Safia forgot all about her modesty and her moronic dog and kicked out of the bedding. "Is he sure they're still there?" she asked, throwing clean clothes onto the quilt.

"He seemed to be. I advised him not to go and check. They've had the 'Do Not Disturb' sign up since they arrived on Saturday morning, but he was very excited, so some of his information was a bit weird."

Safia ran into the bathroom, with Bolly hot on her heels. "Weird how?"

"Well, he reckoned Kendal had been down in the lobby on her own yesterday, but she wouldn't do that if she was being held hostage, would she?"

"No, she wouldn't." Safia frowned into the mirror. Seven hours of bedhead and pillow creases frowned back. "Get everything sent across to me, will you?"

"Of course."

Safia jabbed Suds's number as she started the shower. The scent of coffee and frying luchi drifted in through the steam, confirming once and for all that she had fallen for the right woman.

"'Lo," Suds mumbled. He coughed, improving his ability to form actual words. "This better be good, DS Faris."

"Oh hush, you'd have been up in half an hour anyway." She perched on the bath. "What would you say to a date? You, me, and Armed Response at a Radisson hotel overlooking the Thames."

"Sounds very romantic. Do I need to bring anything?"

"Just your good self. I'll meet you at the office in twenty."

Twenty minutes gave Safia a name for her suspect, Ms. Elin Breckenridge, and confirmation from the hotel receptionist that Breckenridge's Audi TTS was not currently in its allocated parking space.

Safia paced across the threadbare carpet tiles separating her desk from Suds's, one ear listening to a hold tone, the other to Suds theorising.

"Are they in cahoots now, then?" He was chewing gum as fast as he was coming up with new ideas. "Some sort of Stockholm Syndrome thing going on, where Kendal is actively helping this woman?"

Safia held up a finger as the Armed Response Team leader came back on the line. "Great. Yes, we've got access to the suite next door for visuals. Yes, okay, we'll see you there."

"How long?" Suds asked as she pocketed her phone.

"An hour, tops. We're to rendezvous at the far end of the ground-level car park. We've got officers there already, and they're working on an evacuation plan with the hotel staff."

Suds took his jacket from the back of his chair. "This would all be terrific if we actually believed our suspect was still there."

"I know." Safia dropped into her chair. This case was driving her mad. One step forward, three steps back, and every lead sending them in circles. "So we go and confirm that they've gone, and then we try to pull everything together and work out what the hell is going on."

Suds held out her coat. "Don't pout. We are awash with new leads."

She kicked his boot as she walked past him.

"That was assault, that was," he said, looking around for witnesses in the entirely empty office. "I'll have you for that."

"Whatever." She gave him the car keys as a peace offering. "Come on. I'll let you drive on blues, just this once."

The Radisson was an ugly building whose compensatory river views were currently illuminated by an almost full moon. Standing in the car park, Suds stomped his feet and blew on his gloved hands as Safia monitored a bewildered straggle of hung-over guests rousted from their beds and herded to a safe distance by the ART. She could see suite 63, four windows along on the sixth floor. Both its windows were dark, their curtains open, and surveillance from the neighbouring suite had all but confirmed 63 was unoccupied. A commotion in her earpiece signalled the start of the raid, and she tracked torch beams zigzagging from one room to the next, before someone felt confident enough to switch on the lights and the team leader announced an "all clear" across the comms for her benefit.

"Right, then," she said, glad about heading inside if nothing else. "Let's crack on."

The ART leader met them in the suite's main living room, where two mugs and a couple of side plates had been left on the table and the smell of clotted blood made Safia's nose twitch.

"No doubt they were here," he said. "They'd left the 'Do Not Disturb' sign out like the chap said, but that'll have been to stop anyone from going in. I reckon they're long gone."

"Thank you." She waited until he shut the suite's door behind him before she stepped cautiously over the bedroom threshold. "Wow."

Suds popped the bubble he'd just blown in his gum. "What the ever-loving fuck went on in here?"

She unknotted the top of a yellow clinical waste bag and took a wary peek inside. "Major surgery, at a guess." The bag was crammed with used medical paraphernalia—syringes, empty blood bags and drug vials, soiled dressings—and it had been placed almost apologetically beside a pile of bloodstained bedding and towels. A large, deep-red patch on the right side of the bare mattress completed the macabre picture.

"Let's get CSI in, for what it's worth." She was already itching to get out of there and pick up the threads of the chase. "We need to speak to the receptionist and grab the CCTV files."

The receptionist, Lewis Montgomery, was so eager to cooperate that he set Safia's teeth on edge. He escorted them to the security lodge, shooed the guards away, and sat at the desk they had vacated.

"I've made notes," he said, removing a crisply folded sheet of paper from his jacket pocket. "I knew you would want a sequence of events."

Safia sank into one of the empty chairs. The fake leather was still warm and smelled greasy. "Take us through it from the start."

"Well." He flapped open the paper and began to read down a timeline that started on Friday at sunset with Elin Breckenridge checking into the suite. "She was very badly bruised," he said. "Her eye was swollen, and there was a bandage here." He tapped the centre of his forehead. "But she declined my assistance."

Safia stopped writing. "This was definitely Friday evening?" If the receptionist had his timeline right, those injuries would predate whatever had happened on the Heath.

"Definitely. I remember because the sunset was just glorious."

"And the next time you saw her, she had Dr. Kendal with her?"

"About six forty, Saturday morning," he confirmed. "They had two pull-along bags with them, and Dr. Kendal registered with her driving licence. She made it sound"—he put a hand to his chest, obviously flustered—"she implied they were partners, and really, I had no reason to believe otherwise."

"That took some guts," Suds muttered.

"Yeah," Safia said. "I wonder whether Breckenridge forced her or whether she improvised. She did well either way, because she must have been scared to death."

"Did Dr. Kendal have any injuries?" Suds said.

Lewis gave a decisive shake of his head. "No, not that I could see."

"And how did Ms. Breckenridge seem?" Safia asked.

"Not very well. Dr. Kendal was sort of propping her up, but she said something about new meds, so I didn't think anything of it. Am I in trouble?"

Safia gave him her best reassuring smile. Despite his histrionics, he was proving to be an excellent witness. "No. Not at all. You're doing great. And you didn't see them leave yesterday, is that right?"

"That's right. I saw Dr. Kendal in the lobby on her own, and we had a bit of a chat because that man had just been asking for Ms. Breckenridge."

"What man?" Safia asked, managing not to snap, though she wanted to grab Lewis and shake all the information loose.

As if sensing her impatience, Lewis displayed his notes: *Man in cap. Saturday 12:20 p.m. Security called.*

"I don't know who he was. He was pushy and belligerent, and I thought he might've been the one who"—he rubbed his forehead—"well, someone had clearly beaten her. I've written a description of him for you."

She took the headed notepaper he held out. He had beautiful penmanship, his flowing script recording details of an overweight white male, approximately fifty years old, with a reddened face. "But he was annoyed," he had added as a qualifier.

"Does the reception area have CCTV?" Suds asked.

"No." Lewis turned a deep shade of crimson. "There should be a camera on the desk, but it's been faulty for over a week now and our management has done nothing to get it fixed. We have car park CCTV and the registration of Ms. Breckenridge's vehicle, if those are of any use to you."

"Certainly," Safia said. She reviewed her notes, spotting a discrepancy. "You seem very attentive, Lewis."

He nodded, his confidence restored. "I don't miss much."

"In which case, how might Ms. Breckenridge and Dr. Kendal have got by you with two large bags when they left yesterday afternoon? Is there an alternative route to the car park?"

"Yes, the back stairs. But no one uses them because we have the lift—Oh! They sneaked out!"

"I'm afraid so." She patted his arm. He was so outraged that he was almost purple. "Now, about that CCTV…"

Having plied Safia and Suds with coffee and pastries, Lewis reluctantly returned to his desk, ceding control of the CCTV files he had primed by date and time order.

"Elin Breckenridge." Suds was on his phone, googling away. "Is that Romeo Echo Charlie, or Romeo Alpha?"

"Echo, it's with an E." Safia had skipped ahead to Saturday afternoon and was watching a slight figure, her hood raised, skulk toward an Audi TTS with a wheeled suitcase in tow. Given her height and general agility, the woman had to be Grace Kendal, and this was the second trip she had made, alone and clearly not under duress. "What the hell are you playing at, Dr. Kendal?" Safia said. She fast-forwarded to the next time marker that Lewis had provided, pinpointed via the Automatic Number Plate Recognition on the car park barrier. Both women this time, walking slowly toward the car, Kendal making a blatant "I'm here under my own volition" statement, with her head uncovered and held high. They were almost to the car when Breckenridge suddenly stopped walking, her hands flying to her chest. Kendal stopped as well, opening Breckenridge's jacket to check something before they continued.

Safia rewound and replayed the footage as Suds swore at his phone, but she couldn't fine-tune the picture to provide anything beyond a grainy but positive identification of Grace Kendal and the woman caught on Howard Grimshaw's camera near the Heath.

"Here we go." Suds wheeled his chair closer. "Blimey. How the mighty have fallen."

He set his phone between them and used two fingers to home in on a photograph of a prim, dark-haired woman with a smart suit, snappy bob, and polite smile. Everything about her screamed successful entrepreneur.

"Is that her?" Safia scrolled to the photo's tagline: *Elin Breckenridge explains the winning formula behind Bridge Securities.* "Bloody hell, Suds."

He clicked to the company's home page. "They have offices here and in UAE, and a HQ in Manchester, where she's apparently based. Close security and CCTV installations for the private and business sector. They're certainly worth a few quid."

"Curiouser and curiouser. I am most intrigued," Safia said. "I wonder if security is all they're providing."

Suds had redirected his google rage toward its maps. "Only one way to find out. Or possibly three ways, according to this piece of crap."

She gave him a thumbs up as he showed her the route planner. "Excellent. Let's go pay them a visit."

❖

"This is all very nice." Safia lowered her window, letting cool air wash into the car and watching the rows of Georgian houses pass by. Sitting on the outskirts of London, Richmond-upon-Thames was the definition of well-heeled, with boutique shops and upscale restaurants lining its main street, and Kew Gardens luring in the tourists.

"I'm glad we phoned ahead." Suds whistled between his teeth at a grand three-storey pub fronting onto a cobbled terrace, where stallholders were setting up a farmers' market. "This whole place has an 'invite only' vibe."

"Yeah." She waggled her fingers at a labradoodle out for its morning constitutional. "Breckenridge certainly chose a prime spot for her business."

The London office of Bridge Securities was located in the heart of Richmond, close enough to the city to be convenient for its clientele, but favouring an area that wore its wealth on its sleeve whilst affording maximum discretion. Safia had been surprised when someone answered her call on a Sunday morning, but the office was apparently staffed around the clock, and an appointment with one of the personal assistants had been arranged for eight a.m.

"That's it, there." She pointed to an attractive brick building with sash windows and subtle signage. "The PA said to park around the back."

They were a few minutes early, but a middle-aged Pakistani woman in a smartly tailored salwar kameez and matching hijab was waiting for them in reception. She introduced herself as Ghadir Azam, greeting Safia in Urdu and smiling at Suds. If she disapproved of Safia's western dress, she hid it well. Even so, Safia endured her customary stab of guilt, ingrained by parents who had raised her in a traditional household. Out of respect to them, she wore a hijab when she visited, but those occasions were few and far between now, and they had never agreed to meet Kami.

She followed Ghadir into a generously appointed, sunlit office with two comfortable chairs arranged in front of a large desk. When she and Suds declined the offer of refreshments, Ghadir took the chair behind the desk, sitting formally with one hand atop the other.

"How may I help you, Detectives?" She seemed perturbed in a "what's going on?" way, rather than anything suggestive of a guilty conscience.

Safia slid a printed screen grab from the Radisson's CCTV across to her. "Do you recognise this woman?"

Ghadir put on a pair of glasses and took the photo. She didn't need to study it closely, and her shocked gasp was as good a confirmation as any. "It's Elin. Ms. Breckenridge. She owns the company. What happened to her? Is she all right?"

"We're not exactly sure." Safia accepted the photo back and placed it face down on the desk. With the likely outcome from this interview being a positive identification, Breckenridge's image and name hadn't yet been released to the press, and though she felt sorry for not having warned Ghadir, she'd wanted an unprejudiced reaction. "We think she's hurt and in trouble, and we were wondering whether anyone here might know something that would help us find her."

"Trouble?" Ghadir was shaking her head, incredulous. She obviously hadn't linked any of this to the Grace Kendal media appeal. "What kind of trouble? She was only here on Wednesday, and she was fine. Is she missing? I have her mobile number."

Suds cleared his throat to curtail the flurry of questions. "Can you tell us what she was doing here? She mainly works at your Manchester HQ, is that right?"

"Yes. She lives in Mottram, but she came down to meet with a client, and she was planning to make a long weekend of it." Ghadir touched the edge of the photo but didn't turn it over. "We were chatting only the other day. She was going to go to the museum to see the dinosaurs."

Hoping Ghadir wouldn't take offence, Safia assumed the role of hostess and poured her a glass of water from a jug set out in readiness. "I understand this is difficult for you," she said as Ghadir nodded her thanks. "We're trying to piece together a number of different elements in this case. To that end, would you have any access to the company's financial records? Or any insight into clients who may have caused problems for Ms. Breckenridge?"

"I'm afraid I don't. My role mainly involves administration and diary-keeping for Mr. Lowry, who would be a far better person for you to speak to. He part-owns the company with Ms. Breckenridge, and he's been a close friend of hers for many years. They were in the Forces together."

"Lowry." Safia scribbled a note, pointedly not writing "in the Forces" in all caps beside a ton of asterisks. "Could you give us his phone number and address, please? And the same for Ms. Breckenridge."

Ghadir acquiesced with some trepidation, as if mindful that she was overstepping her authority. She wrote Breckenridge's address on a clean sheet of paper, then found a business card for Lowry in the desk drawer and printed his details on the back.

"Mr. Lowry lives in Kingston," she said. "It's not far from here."

"Thank you." Safia held out her own card. "If you think of anything else that may be useful, please contact me at any time."

"Of course. Will someone let us know when you find her?" Ghadir stood when they did, but then leaned forward, supporting herself with both hands on the desk. "Allah! Amelia, who is taking care of her?"

Safia stopped by the door, as confused as Suds, by the look of him. "Amelia?"

"Amelia, Ms. Breckenridge's daughter. She was here in London to see the dinosaurs. She is only four years old."

Safia heard the tap of Suds's gum falling to the floor as his jaw dropped open.

"Oh shit," he said.

GRACE. SUNDAY, 9:40 A.M.

The motorway service station was far too busy for Grace's peace of mind, with families and daytrip coach loads piling in for overpriced coffee and breakfasts. Keeping her head down, she paid cash for the sandwiches and water she'd grabbed and thanked the cashier without making eye contact. Subtitled rolling news was playing on multiple televisions in the food court, but her kidnapping had been relegated to a footnote on the bulletin. As far as she could ascertain, tips were still being sought via a specially established hotline, but no new leads were being reported.

The lack of updates and urgency seemed sinister somehow, as if the investigation was developing so quickly behind the scenes that the need for public input had been superseded by a desire to keep things under wraps. Intent on the news report, she jumped as someone bumped into her, but it was a young lad who reeled away, laughing, and continued to chase after his mate. No one was paying her any attention, she told herself. Everyone was wrapped up in their own business, looking without really seeing, and preoccupied by the mundanity of finding the café with the shortest queue or the best offers on substandard meals. Unless she said or did something to make herself memorable, she could be invisible, for all the general public cared. Shielding her eyes against the low sunlight, she crossed the car park and rapped on the driver's window of their rental.

Elin clicked the central locking and smiled at her as she got into the car. "Is it as depressing in there as I remember?"

Grace dropped the food and drinks onto the back seat. Although they had managed to get her medical kit out of the house, their pre-packed provisions had been abandoned when Lowry came calling. "Probably worse," she said. "Are you going to the loo?"

"Yep." The certainty of Elin's answer was at odds with her physical condition. She had dozed for most of the journey up the M6, and Grace didn't need to check her obs to know she was deteriorating. She opened the car door, but getting out of it took a lot of effort. "I won't be long," she said, and then set off at a pace that would have shamed a geriatric.

Grace waited until she had disappeared amongst the throng before reopening their most recent WhatsApp message. They were chasing a new postcode, another random street, this one in Moorside, Greater Manchester. Elin knew the area in passing—her parents lived just outside it—but she had never been there, and she could think of nothing obvious to connect her to it. There was no deadline this time, as if the man responsible knew by now how well he had them trained. On street view, the address appeared to be a normal residential road, overlooking green space and a church. Grace opened the accompanying video and rewatched it twice over. It was a short clip of Amelia sleeping, and viewing it alone confirmed what Grace had originally feared. In the twenty seconds the video ran for, Amelia only took four shallow breaths, giving her a rate of twelve per minute, around half what it should have been for a child her age. She was pale and sweating, her lips chapped and her hair matted. She had almost certainly been drugged with an opiate or benzodiazepine, both of which were dangerous and potentially addictive in adults, and absolutely not something a layman should be administering to a child.

Grace returned the phone to the dashboard and scanned the entrance for Elin, seeing nothing except parents corralling their kids and a tribe of football fans sparking up cigarettes in unison. She switched the radio on, then switched it off again and sat on her hands. The man might not have set the clock going, but they were still running out of time. Elin had an infection and was probably bleeding again, and Amelia needed a hospital just as badly.

Meanwhile, the police were—where? Wandering around clueless, or right behind them, ready to swoop? Grace chewed her thumbnail, a habit that had always earned her a rapped knuckle from Charlotte. Not knowing how close the net was to snatching them up was definitely worse than seeing the damn thing coming. She was sure the hotel receptionist would have contacted the police by now—that man had eyes in the back of his head—which meant the police would know Elin's full name and personal information. Would they try to speak to Lowry, if they could actually find him? And at what point would someone realise that Elin had a young daughter?

A stooped, limping figure caught Grace's eye, and she watched Elin keep to the periphery of the main thoroughfare as she made her way back to the car. Grace had to admit that part of her hoped the police would connect the dots sooner rather than later, that they would stop thinking of Elin as a murder suspect and throw their resources where they would do the most good. She leaned over to open Elin's door for her. Elin looked as unwell as Amelia, and she shook her head, panting, when Grace offered her a bottle of water.

"Not right now," she managed, her head back against the seat and her eyes tightly closed.

Grace started the car. There was nothing more she could do here, and she resolved to keep going for a while and then pull in somewhere more secluded. She rejoined the motorway, accelerating to a reasonable speed and keeping a constant vigil on the cars around her. Beside her, Elin shuddered and tried to turn onto her side. They approached a sign that read simply "The North." Grace put her foot down and sped past it.

SAFIA. SUNDAY, 9:12 A.M.

Safia was distracted enough to open the email without checking its header. A photo filled her screen, an impish young girl with an ear-to-ear smile, pigtails held in place with rainbow ribbons, and a face full of naughtiness. She looked nothing like her mum, whose hand she was holding in the shot, but that was hardly surprising.

"Did you get this as well?" Safia asked Suds.

"Yeah." He sounded as troubled as she was. His mouse clicked a couple of times. "What the hell are we thinking here, Saf?"

She went round to sit on the corner of his desk. A frantic volley of phone calls to numbers gleaned from Ghadir had revealed that Breckenridge, while on good terms with her family, only saw them on a "Sunday lunch once a month" sort of basis. Her mum had confirmed that Amelia had accompanied Breckenridge to London, and she hadn't been able to think of anyone Amelia might have been left with. Meanwhile, Suds had listened to Chevs almost choke on his full English breakfast and then make an executive decision not to jump to conclusions until more digging had been done.

"You had one job," he'd spluttered. "Solve a very simple gunshot-to-the-head murder. Two days later, it's snowballed into a business exec kidnapping a doctor, and now you're telling me you might have a missing kid as well. I don't get this shit from Stokes and Muscar. They do as they're told, play nice with the CPS, and make all my stats look good." He'd lowered his voice then, no trace of false outrage remaining. "Stay away from the media for now. If this child is currently at risk, I'd rather we didn't push our perp or perps into making a hasty decision. I like happy endings, Suds. They're better for my digestion."

Safia pulled a pen from Suds's stationery pot. His daughter had given it to him for his birthday, and it had a neon pink, fluffy-feathered flamingo on it. He used it to sign all his official documents.

"I'm *hoping* Breckenridge stashed her daughter somewhere safe while she went out getting up to no good and getting shot," she said, twirling the pen to make its feathers bob. "But I'm probably *thinking* exactly what you're thinking."

"Someone took the child," he said, hitting the bullseye in one.

"It makes sense. And if you follow the logic through, it does explain a hell of a lot."

He pinched his pen back and used the feathered end to tap her on the nose. "We need to talk to this Lowry chap sooner rather than later. You never know, he might be babysitter-in-chief, if he's Breckenridge's best mate."

"And he's not answering his phone because he's too busy chasing around after a four-year-old."

"Exactly." He groaned as her phone rang. "Bloody hell, what now?"

She reached between their desks to snatch up the receiver. "DS Faris." She listened to an excitable young lad gabble on at her for five minutes as she took notes and used a series of imaginative and increasingly impolite hand gestures to persuade Suds to go and put the kettle on. "Change of plan, Lowry will have to wait," she told him, as he proffered her mug with a little bow.

"Do tell." He pulled his chair over.

"Well, it seems Dr. Kendal owns a house in New Cross, and her neighbour, a Mrs. Dixon, swears she heard noises coming from the property yesterday. It struck her as unusual because Kendal rarely visits and pops in to say hello whenever she does."

"But Dixon didn't actually *see* anyone?" Suds said, not seeming overly impressed by the new lead.

"No, and she said she's heard nothing since about five in the afternoon. She's recently had a hip replacement, so—despite being a card-carrying member of Neighbourhood Watch—she didn't go round to check things out. She does, however, have a key, due to a long-standing burglar alarm problem, which means Armed Response won't have to make a mess of the front door." Safia entered the postcode into a route planner. "They'll be there before us. I'm going to give the go-ahead, because I think we're probably about twenty-four hours too late again."

"Do the rest of our gang know what they're supposed to be doing?" Suds asked. He wasn't trying to catch her out. He knew she liked to go through things with him, to double-check she'd covered all her bases.

"Yes. The team at the hotel are almost done with the staff and guests, and CSI are still busy in the suite. Traffic are running the Audi reg through ANPR, and a DC currently on desk duties is calling local car rental firms, because we know damn well that Audi's been ditched by now. I've got Daniel double-checking the hotel CCTV, and a sketch artist is working with Lewis Montgomery."

Suds scratched the stubble on his chin. "Ah, for Breckenridge's mystery male caller."

"That's the one. Lewis gave us such a good description, I thought he might do well with an artist. And last but not least, we have a team of two chasing down Kendal's and Breckenridge's friends, family, business associates, and any other potential bolt-holes they might own, although Mrs. Dixon just stole their thunder on the latter there." She leaned back and sipped her tea. "How did I do?"

"Very impressive," he said. "This is why they pay you so extravagantly."

"Ha. It's true. I am filthy rich. Come on, let's get going." She put her mug down and then picked it up again to carry out with her. "What?" she said as he arched an eyebrow. "I'm not wasting it. You make a good cuppa."

This time around, the ART leader was waiting for them in the front garden of a mid-terrace. He was crouching by a terracotta pot, but he stood when he saw them approaching. "Lemon thyme," he said, handing Safia a small sprig. "Beautiful with chicken. If you ever do find this doc, ask her whether I can take a cutting."

She crushed the herb between her fingers, admiring its citrus scent. "They're not here, then."

"No. They were at some point. The detritus in the living room is similar to that left behind in the hotel, only there's less fresh blood. CSI are coming to do their thing, and Mrs. Dixon is making sandwiches for everyone, so my gang are happy."

"Is she at number five or nine?"

"Nine. Nice old dear, said the doc lived here with her wife until the wife died suddenly—brain haemorrhage, I think. She just dropped in the street. Kendal moved out soon afterward, but never sold up."

Safia didn't react to his casual summation. It was easier to let it roll over her, to not think of Kami simply dropping in the street or wonder what she might do in those circumstances. Experienced police tended to develop a variety of coping mechanisms: compartmentalising, dark humour, or bending a mate's ear when it all got too much. This case was starting to prickle at her, though, when she wasn't distracted enough; telling her to do things faster, to be better, to fill in the gaps and pull it all together, because there were at least three lives at stake now and one of them was a four-year-old.

"Cheers, mate," she said, jovial, casual, giving nothing away. "Are you sticking around for a while?"

"Well, she's making bacon sarnies," he said, grinning.

Safia clapped him on the shoulder. "Seeing as we're keeping you so busy today, you can have mine." Ignoring Suds's grumbling, she led the way to number nine, where one of the ART opened the front door before she could knock. The smell of fried bacon hung around him like a miasma, setting her stomach rumbling, but there were some rules she still held sacred, and she was happy to stay hungry.

Having given free rein of her kitchen to the ART lads, Mrs. Dixon was sitting on the sofa resting her new hip. She acknowledged

Safia's introductions and patted the empty cushion beside her. Safia took the spot, leaving the armchair for Suds.

"I wish I could be more helpful," Mrs. Dixon said without waiting for a prompt. "But all I heard was a few noises. You know, when people are moving around and whatnot."

"Any voices?" Safia asked.

"No. The walls are quite thick. I never heard a peep from Grace and Charlotte when they lived here."

Safia wrote a note, mainly for want of something to do, trying to make Mrs. Dixon feel useful. "This may be an odd question, but did you hear anything to suggest a child was in the house? Perhaps crying, or a loud toy or television programme?"

"Definitely not. I'd have remembered that. The girls always wanted children, but, well, poor Lotty. That was a terrible thing."

The carriage clock on the mantelpiece was keeping time like a metronome. Safia wanted to launch it out of the window.

"We very much appreciate you getting in touch with us," she said, preparing to make a quick exit now that an ART lad had presented Suds with a sandwich.

"Oh, there is one thing." Mrs. Dixon slapped the arm of the sofa, sending up a waft of lily of the valley. "Grace rented a garage on Harrier Street. I used to have one as well, before my glaucoma, and I still have the owner's number somewhere. Would you like me to find it for you?"

"Yes, please," Safia said as Suds remembered his manners and stopped gaping with his mouth full. "I'd like that very much."

Three of the ART lads came to Harrier Street with them, turning heads in the sedate neighbourhood as they paraded down the road in full tactical gear. The garage's owner met them outside Grace's rental, giving them permission for access and then retreating to a safe distance.

"Silly bugger," the ART leader said. "It's padlocked from the outside. They're not going to be in it." He cut through the lock and raised the door, revealing a black Audi TTS whose number plate matched the one registered at the hotel.

"Well, would you look at that," Suds said.

"Bloody hell." Safia stepped forward, turning to the ART leader. "Can you get in this as well?"

He could, and then cut a couple of wires to stop its alarm blaring. "Misspent youth," he said, clicking the boot open. He found the garage lights, their neon throwing everything into sharper focus: the blood smeared on the leather of both front seats, the tacky prints on the steering wheel, the child's booster seat in the rear footwell.

"Jackpot!" Suds called from the boot. He was lifting out a pair of plastic bags sealed at the edges with masking tape.

"Is there something we can lay these out on?" Safia asked, and the ART leader rummaged around until he found the groundsheet for a small tent stuffed in a corner.

Kneeling on the sheet, Safia carefully unpeeled the tape from one of the bags. Her initial guess of clothing turned out to be right on the money as she removed an adult-sized, short-sleeved blouse, torn in several places and covered in blood.

"Doesn't fit with a single gunshot wound," Suds said. The blood was cast liberally across the cotton, more concentrated toward the upper half.

"No, but it would fit with a woman having the crap kicked out of her before she got shot. She's bagged these as evidence, hasn't she?" Safia set a pair of jeans alongside the shirt. "Sizes are in line with Breckenridge rather than Kendal. She's a few inches taller."

"I'll defer to your judgement on that." Suds indicated a patch of blood on the left knee. "This is almost a handprint. As if she's touched an injury and then wiped her fingers."

"Mm." Safia wasn't looking. She had opened the second bag and pulled out its first item. The dungarees were a bright patchwork of clashing colours, the sort of thing a parent would buy a child because the child insisted and thought they looked brilliant. There was blood on those as well, the irregular dark red pattern standing out against the yellow and orange.

"Fucking hell," Suds said.

Safia put the dungarees next to the jeans. They barely reached the hip. "I think we need to call Chevs," she said.

❖

The desk chair squeaked as Chevs rocked it back and forth. The last time Safia and Suds had been in his office, they'd made a pact to oil the hinges on the damn thing, but an opportunity had never presented itself.

"Okay." Chevs sounded quite placid for a man dragged away from a golf game. "Lay it all out."

The first thing Safia laid out was a series of photographs: Elin Breckenridge with the rucksack, before and after her ill-fated trip to the Heath; the bloodstained clothing now in the CSI lab; the bloodstained hotel room and Audi interior; the dead man on the Heath; Grace Kendal walking through the hotel car park, furtive in one shot, her head high in the next; and finally, the picture of Amelia that her gran had emailed.

Safia gave Chevs a moment to take it all in. When he looked up at her, she considered that her cue.

"Given the current evidence, we think Elin Breckenridge was violently assaulted and her daughter, Amelia, was kidnapped. We don't yet have the date or the location for this, but the clothing and anecdotal reports of Breckenridge's injuries seem to support the theory. The incident on the Heath could have been a planned ransom exchange, which would explain the rucksack and Breckenridge appearing to follow mapping or coordinates on her phone. Something then went awry during the exchange, leading to the murder and Breckenridge getting shot."

"You think a third party intervened here?" Despite Chevs's tendency to feign indifference, he knew the ins and outs of each case his team were working on.

"Yes, sir," Suds said. "No ID on them at present, though. Breckenridge has no criminal record, but she spent twelve years in the Forces, so she'd know her way around a gun. It's the forensics and evidence that strongly suggest someone else's involvement."

Chevs picked up the photo of Grace Kendal. "So, desperate mum, still trying to safeguard her child, refuses to involve the police and kidnaps a doctor to patch her up. The doc doesn't look very kidnapped here, does she?"

"No, she doesn't," Safia conceded. "The only explanation we can come up with is Kendal continuing to help Breckenridge for the sake of her daughter."

"Which presumably means the kidnapper is still in contact with them."

"Yes. It would seem so."

"Leads?" Chevs said, and Safia gave silent thanks that they appeared to have passed the acid test.

"Neil Lowry, a close friend and colleague of Breckenridge, is probably our best bet at present," she said. She had plenty of other irons in the fire, but none of them were currently yielding anything useful. "He's second only to her in seniority, and if he gives us permission to access the company finances, they might confirm activity indicative of a ransom being prepared. We're still keeping an open mind about other possibilities, of course. Even if Amelia has been kidnapped, it doesn't mean it's unconnected to criminal activity involving her mother and the company. We're liaising with the local police to double-check she isn't simply with a babysitter, but the clothing suggests otherwise."

Chevs was making notes. "Sounds sensible," he said, his pen still moving rapidly. "In terms of the media, a direct appeal to Thelma and Louise here would not go amiss. Something couched in vague 'we think we know why you're doing this and really you'd be better not doing it alone' terms, before anyone else loses their head. I don't want the tabloids on a rampage, though, so keep it to the BBC and regional news broadcasts for now, and keep the child out of it."

"I'll speak to the media department," Safia said. "See whether they can script something."

Chevs chewed the top of his pen contemplatively. "You front it. You're already the face of the investigation."

"And it's a nice face," Suds murmured.

"Precisely," Chevs said as Safia's cheeks burned. "You're very empathetic, and, without sounding sexist, this whole thing needs a woman's touch."

"That *is* a bit sexist, boss," Safia said.

He shrugged. "Practical, though. Good work on this. Even if it turns out you're barking up the wrong tree, I can't fault your process."

"Thank you, sir," she said. He didn't give praise away easily, and she felt like bottling it for the next time she messed something up.

"Let me know how you get on with Lowry." He turned to the window behind him, taking in the blue skies and the sunshine. "If you need me, I'll be at the nineteenth hole."

❖

In a piece of fortuitous timing, the wrought iron gates to Mill Court, the complex where Lowry owned a flat, opened to let out a car as Suds approached them. The elderly driver gave Suds the evil eye, lowering her window as if about to challenge him, but she drove on without remonstration when he displayed his police warrant card.

"She was pleased to see us," he said.

"Well, we're always the bearers of such good news." Safia peered up at the grey-brick block. "This place should come with serotonin on tap." She had grown up in worse—social housing stuffed to the brim with people too downtrodden to make a fuss—and every penny she saved was going to go toward a house with a garden that Bolly could rampage through.

"Funny you should mention the news," Suds said. "How was your star appearance?"

Safia was amazed it had taken him so long to ask. No wonder he'd been fidgety on the drive over. "It was fine. Splendid. I loved every minute of it."

He laughed. "That good, eh?"

"It got the message across. If the kidnapper sees it, he might be able to read between the lines, but the script was as subtle as we could make it. It'll start airing later this afternoon, along with a reminder of the hotline number."

Suds pulled into a parking space. "At this point, we don't have an awful lot to lose. Shall we go and see what falls out when we shake this tree?"

The court had a single main entrance, and no one answered when she pressed Lowry's buzzer.

"At least it's not too early," Suds said, sticking his thumb on the numbers either side and thanking the obliging neighbour who let them in as soon as she heard the word "police."

Safia checked the floor plan by the mailboxes. "He's on the second floor, and there's no lift."

The enclosed staircase smelled faintly of urine and opened out onto a dour walkway that estate agents would no doubt describe as a balcony. A few residents had claimed patches as their own, dotting the concrete with potted plants and even the odd bench, but most of the space, including the section outside Lowry's, was unadorned and littered with cigarette ends and windblown rubbish.

A light was visible behind the closed blinds at Lowry's front window, and the briefest flicker of movement told them someone was home. Suds gave his best policeman's knock, and they took an habitual step back and to the side as they waited for an answer. None came, so Suds resorted to bellowing "Police! Sir, can you open the door, please?" through the letterbox, which was universal code for "open it or lose it."

Safia began to count. By fifteen, she heard a slow drag of footsteps, while eighteen brought the rattle of a key in the lock. The door opened a quarter of the way, and a middle-aged chap squinted out at them.

"Mr. Neil Lowry?" she said.

"Yes." The word carried a strong smell of alcohol with it, which was a good effort for the time of day. "Can I help you?"

She displayed her ID. "We hope so. I'm Detective Sergeant Faris, and this is Detective Constable Sudbury. We're working on an investigation that seems to involve a colleague of yours, a Ms. Elin Breckenridge, and your PA kindly gave us your address."

He was nodding slowly, still blinking as if the daylight hurt his eyes or, more likely, his hangover. It was difficult to see him properly, but Safia realised the spread of shadows that darkened his left cheek and his chin were actually bruises.

"Are you all right, Mr. Lowry?" She gestured at his face. "How did you hurt yourself?"

"I fell," he said. "Bit of a heavy one last night."

"Ah, gotcha," she said. The bruises looked fresh, and she could see grit embedded in a scrape on his nose. Given the fumes rolling off him, the explanation seemed plausible enough.

"Would you like to come in? What's happened to Elin? Is she okay?" He asked the questions without pausing for a response, limping heavily as he led them through a cigarette-hazy kitchen to a dimly lit living room. The rudiments of furniture—sofa, television on a stand, coffee table covered with ash and empty beer cans—were present, but the cardboard boxes by the radiator suggested he hadn't lived here long.

"Sorry about the mess." He swept the cans into a bin. "I only moved in a month ago."

"Not a problem." Safia declined to sit on the two-seater sofa with him and remained standing by the door. None of this felt quite right. This man in this state did not fit in with Bridge Securities' swanky office or the chic countenance of its managing director.

"Where is Elin?" he asked. "Have you spoken to her?"

"Could you tell me when *you* last spoke to her?" Safia said, deflecting his questions. He wasn't the one leading this interview.

"Uh." He put a hand on his knee, stilling the rapid tap of his foot. "Wednesday evening, I think. Yes, I'm sure it was Wednesday. She was getting dinner ready for Mouse."

Safia looked at Suds through the gloom. He answered her unspoken query with the slightest shake of his head. "Mouse?" she said.

"Amelia, her daughter, that's her nickname," Lowry said. "Calls me her 'grandpoppa,' the cheeky little thing. I'm only fifty-two." His chuckle turned into a hacking cough, and he grabbed his chest as the colour drained from his face.

"Do you need to see a doctor, sir?" Safia asked.

"No, no." He reached for the one can he hadn't put in the bin, and then changed direction for a mug of coffee that looked stone cold. "I'm fine. I pranged a rib when I fell."

"Okay, if you're sure." Thrown off her stride, Safia consulted her interview prep. "How did Ms. Breckenridge seem to you that evening?"

Lowry gulped his coffee and wiped his mouth with the back of his hand. His shirt sleeve was filthy. "Perfectly normal. She said pizza and a bad film were on the cards, and, knowing Mouse, it would've been a very bad film."

"Do you know where they were staying?"

"Sorry, I don't. It was one of those Airbnb things. She didn't give me the address." He folded his arms and then unfolded them and set his hands on his thighs. Surreptitious movements told Safia he was drying his palms. "Look, I'd like to know what's going on, please. Are Elin and Mouse—do you know where they are?"

Safia didn't reply, but she noted it was the second time he'd asked. "Do you have access to the company financial records?" she said.

"Yes, of course." Hubris made him answer without thinking, but he seemed less sure when he added, "But my laptop's been acting up all weekend, so I might not be able to log in from here. May I ask why you want them?"

"We'd like to check for any irregularities. Could you try your computer for us?"

"It's in my bedroom." He stood with some difficulty and pointed to the door. "Am I okay to go and get it?"

"Of course." She stepped aside. He had barely left the room when she caught Suds's eye. "Man from the hotel," she mouthed, and he nodded once.

They moved in tandem, Suds requesting backup in an urgent undertone as she pushed gently on the first door she came to.

"Mr. Lowry?" The curtains were drawn, a thin crack in their centre allowing her to distinguish an unmade bed and a desk with a laptop sitting open on it. There was another door. En suite? "Shit. *Suds?*"

She took a step back and heard Suds do likewise, just as that door flew open and Lowry barrelled out, glint of metal in one hand, his other raised like a club. He swung wildly, catching Safia hard in the face and propelling her into the door jamb. She saw stars, black and then silver sparking all over, but she managed to fling herself forward as he tried to step past her. He caught the door, half closing it and trapping Suds in the hallway. She could hear Suds banging and swearing but getting nowhere fast, so she grabbed Lowry's ankle and yanked it hard. Already off balance, he staggered against the wall, and Suds burst in to tackle him like a prop forward, bouncing to the floor on top of him and pinning him face down.

"Saf? *Saf,* you okay?" Suds yelled. He knocked Lowry's head again when Lowry started up a weak struggle. "Keep the fuck still. *Saf?*"

"I'm fine," she said. She spat a mouthful of blood onto the carpet. Her cheek was wet and burning, and the sound in that ear kept disappearing beneath a high-pitched scream. She crawled forward, following the path of whatever she had seen skitter away from Lowry as Suds had dropped him. She found it under the bed, hooked it with a pen, and drew it out. It was a small-calibre handgun.

"Allah," she whispered. Through the tumult in her ear, handcuffs ratcheted into place, Lowry moaned, and Suds's voice rose and fell in no discernible pattern: "You do not have to say—but it—your defence if you—mention when questioned—"

The shriek of approaching sirens overwhelmed him entirely. When she tried to get up, the room tilted on its axis, and Suds yelped a warning at her to stay put. She didn't want to stay put, there were things she needed to be doing, but she couldn't take her eyes off the gun, and she couldn't get her legs beneath her. The sirens were extinguished one by one, replaced by the slam of car doors and the thud of boots on the stairs.

"Hey." Suds was kneeling by her. He pressed a clean handkerchief to her cheek. She'd never seen him use a handkerchief in his life. "You with me?"

"Yeah. Help me up."

"No. You're very pale, and I don't want you puking on me." He settled beside her, pushing back against the wall and putting an arm around her. "That was a bit fucking close, Saf."

She leaned her head on his shoulder. He was shaking. Neither of them was wearing body armour, and she could still see the gun, a grey metal glint on the grimy carpet.

"I know," she said. She would move. Any minute now, she would move and get back to doing her job. "I think we just got lucky."

GRACE. SUNDAY, 11:33 A.M.

The peal of church bells welcomed Grace and Elin to their destination, the discordant clang signalling the end of the Sunday service as its attendees straggled out to shake the vicar's hand and dodder off for tea and biscuits and gossip at the church hall.

"I'd forgotten it was Sunday," Elin said. She was watching a group of Brownie Guides play tag on the front lawn, burning off the energy amassed during a long spell of sitting and behaving. It was the most coherent she had sounded since the motorway services, and she was holding on to the burner, waiting for its next instruction.

Grace drove on past the church, stopping in a small lay-by at the end of the street, where a path led onto a patch of common land. She could see dog walkers and the odd jogger in the distance, but theirs was the only car parked there.

She opened her baseline obs pouch and draped her steth around her neck. "Right, then. Let's get sorted." They had a routine now: observations, pain relief, Grace pushing fluids, and Elin trying not to throw up on anything vital. "I'm going to ditch the rucksack," Grace said as Elin gagged on a couple of paracetamol. "It was Lowry's, and it's torn to pieces anyway. I'll put the money in one of the kit bags."

"Okay." Elin eyed the back seat, obviously weighing her odds of getting around to it. "Do you want any help?"

"No." Grace did want her awake, though, and suspected she would do better with that if she felt useful. "You stay there and keep a lookout."

"Okay," Elin said again, more chipper this time. "I can do that."

Grace set to work, repacking the blocks of cash into the emptiest of her medical bags. There was a disconcerting amount of space to fill, reminding her that she had used most of her supplies and had no way of replenishing them. She rolled up the redundant rucksack, wrapped one of its straps around it, and went out to push it into the litter bin at the edge of the lay-by.

"Shall I have another look at the laptop, just in case?" she asked Elin as she got back into the car. Before leaving the industrial site earlier that morning, they had searched through every application and folder on the laptop and examined its shell for signs of Lowry having tampered with it. If Grace had her way, it would be in the bin with the rucksack, but Elin had refused to let it go, and Grace, remembering how many photos of Charlotte she had backed up on her own computer, hadn't pushed the point.

"I think it's clean," Elin said. She touched Grace's injured arm, careful to avoid the bandage. "And if Lowry comes anywhere near you again, I'll do more than hit him with the car."

When Grace took her hand, the ferocity of Elin's grip matched that of her threat, and her eyes, so often dulled by pain, were bright with resolve. Although Grace was spending most of her time worrying about Elin's physical condition, Elin's resilience never failed to astound her.

"Let's hope it doesn't come to that," she said.

"But if it does?"

Grace tapped a side pocket on her kit bag. She had zipped the gun firmly inside, in a futile attempt to diminish its threat. "If it does, it's in here."

"I can teach you how to fire it, if you want," Elin said.

"I don't—" Grace answered instinctively and then stopped to really think about the offer. She had felt utterly helpless when Lowry attacked them. With no means of defending herself, she had been reduced to running for her life, and she never wanted to be that vulnerable again. "Could you?" she said, because hers wasn't the only life at stake, and if Elin was incapacitated, Grace had accepted the responsibility of keeping her and her daughter safe.

"This is a terrible spot for a tutorial," Elin said, unzipping the bag. There was no one near the car, but she withdrew the gun warily and kept it below the level of the car windows. She tilted it into the light, letting the sun catch the etchings on its length. It was probably the first chance she'd had to examine it since taking it from the dead man. "Okay, so we have a Sig Sauer P229, nine millimetre. Typical bloke's gun. The Glocks are lighter but less flashy. It holds fifteen rounds, plus one in the chamber, and there's no external safety."

"That pull-back thing?" Grace said. Her firearms knowledge would fit on the back of a postage stamp, and most of it was gleaned from films and television. She could dig bullets out of people, but she'd never considered putting one in.

Elin smiled at her. "Yes, that pull-back thing. It's an inbuilt mechanism on this gun, so you release it with your first trigger pull. If you ever fire it, you'll feel a slight catch you need to go beyond, which means you have to be firm with the trigger, okay?"

"Yep, okay." A surgeon had once given Grace similar advice whilst showing her the best way to perform a traumatic thoracotomy: "Cut right through, firm pressure, and don't stop till you reach the other side." If she could hack through some poor lad's chest, she could pull the trigger of a gun.

"Sure about that?" Elin asked, and Grace briefly wondered whether she'd spoken the anecdote aloud. She hadn't, she realised, but she was staring at the gun as one might regard a venomous snake.

"Be firm," she said. "I can be firm."

"Of that I have no doubt. I can't really show you how to sight it properly, but you hold it like this"—Elin demonstrated a two-handed grip—"and aim it using these sights. Here, have a go."

For the first time, Grace took the gun without flinching, and mimicked Elin's grip. "How bad is the recoil?" she asked, and laughed at Elin's expression. "Come on, everyone knows about recoil."

"You'll feel it." Elin adjusted Grace's hold a fraction but then covered the muzzle and eased the gun from her hands. "Chances are you'll miss whatever you're aiming at, but it might make someone think twice about trying to hurt you."

"We only have one between us," Grace said. She had an inkling of what Elin was thinking, and she didn't like it.

Elin slid the gun back into its pocket, pulling the zip across in a slow, deliberate action. At least a minute passed before she looked at Grace again. "He won't let me go in with a gun," she said. "Whenever all this comes to a head, whatever he wants me to do, I won't be armed, and I don't think I'll—" She swallowed, and drew in a breath that made her bite her lip. "Grace, can you look after Amelia for me? Not forever, I don't mean that, but if he lets her go? Because I know he's been giving her something, and she's going to need help, and I don't want her to be with strangers."

"*You'll* be there with her," Grace said, but Elin was already shaking her head.

"Chances of that aren't too good, are they?"

"No, they're not," Grace admitted. The thought made her feel sick. She touched Elin's cheek, letting her thumb stroke the heated skin. "She won't be with strangers, Elin. I promise I'll stay with her."

"Thank you." Elin relaxed back into her seat. She didn't seem afraid so much as reconciled to her eventual fate, and she reached calmly for the burner as it buzzed. The message was a mapping link that provided coordinates and a walking route when she clicked on it. "He sent me one of these for the Heath." She widened the screen as Grace started the car. "This one ends in the churchyard."

The bells had long since fallen silent, and the yard stood empty, the church's arched wooden doors shut fast. There was nothing here but gravestones and frost-withered flowers, and unease swirled in Grace's belly as she watched the arrow blink on the map, urging them around the back of the building. Elin obeyed it without speaking, her limp more pronounced now, making her stumble against ancient headstones that had toppled into the unkempt grass. The graveyard stretched wide beyond the church, its outer edge given over to a thick copse of holm oak and yew. A few of the trees bore remembrance dedications, but most were large enough to have predated the custom.

Feeling far too conspicuous, Grace shifted the kit bag strapped across her shoulders, wishing that it wasn't bright red, that its fluorescent stripes weren't catching the sun, but it had the money and the gun in it, and she hadn't wanted to leave either behind. Although she couldn't see anyone at any of the graves, numerous vases of fresh flowers suggested weekend was a prime time for visiting.

"Almost there," Elin said, her attention narrowed to the phone and its arrow. She turned toward the treeline and walked along a row of headstones, stopping just shy of the end. "This is it." She toed through the grass, as if expecting some sort of sign—X marks the spot—but then slowly raised her head and studied the inscription on the gravestone. Grace had already read it, and though it meant nothing to her, it clearly meant something to Elin; her bad leg began to quiver at the knee, and she clutched the stone to stop herself falling. Grace darted to her and slung an arm around her waist.

"Who was he?" she asked, once she was sure Elin was steady. Thomas Elson, "Beloved father, son and brother," had been thirty-nine when he'd died, but the engraving gave nothing else away.

"I know who's doing this," Elin whispered, and even as she spoke, the burner buzzed with a new message: *Now do you understand?*

A rustle nearby made Grace whip around, her hand moving unbidden to the bag's closest pocket, but it was just a blackbird, scurrying from one pile of dead leaves to another. She turned back to the grave, to Elin, who seemed incapable of doing anything beyond remaining on her feet.

"Who was Thomas Elson?" Grace kept the question succinct, forcing Elin to focus.

"He was one of the hostages we lost in Syria." Elin showed her the phone, where a photo of a man with kind eyes and a toothy smile filled the body of another new message. "ISIS put his execution video on the internet. They didn't do it with any of the others, just his. He was from a large family. He had a teenage son and a younger daughter, and two, maybe three brothers."

"And this is what? Payback?" Grace struggled to keep her voice level. "None of that was your fault."

"I was the lead on the recon." The flatness in Elin's tone suggested she had always shouldered the blame for the deaths, no matter how misplaced, and if she blamed herself, it was easy to believe a bereaved relative might also hold her accountable.

"No, fuck that," Grace said. "I'm not having that. It's one thing for this bastard to decide you're responsible, but don't do that to yourself."

Elin gave her a weary smile. "It doesn't matter now, does it? Either way, the damage is done." She touched the dark grey etching on the headstone, drawing Grace's attention to the date of Thomas's death. "I guess this explains why he came all the way to London for us."

"Jesus," Grace said. "Was that last Wednesday?"

"Yes, he waited exactly ten years." Elin's hand moved to her scarred abdomen. "I should have made the connection sooner, but I stopped marking the date after I adopted Amelia. I couldn't go out and get absolutely wrecked with a toddler on my hip."

"I guess not." Grace was about to suggest going back to the car when the phone buzzed again, making them both jump.

"What the hell?" Elin was trying to orientate its screen, and Grace saw another arrow, another set of coordinates.

"It's in the trees," she said.

Elin didn't move, and her face, already wan, turned grey. "Grace, what has he done?" She set off without waiting for an answer, as close to a run as she could manage, holding the phone in front of her like a pitiful shield. Grace ran as well, ignoring the slip and scuff of her boots in the half-frozen mud and the thud of the bag against her back. She slowed as she crossed the tree line, allowing her vision to adjust to the sudden twilight. She could just about distinguish Elin's form a few yards ahead, but Elin abruptly dropped out of sight, and a thin, anguished cry made the hairs prick up on the nape of Grace's neck.

"Elin?" Grace sprinted forward, almost falling over Elin, who was kneeling beside a mound of freshly dug earth.

"Oh no." Grace shook her head. "No. Elin, *don't*." She threw off the bag and tried to pull Elin away, but Elin shoved at her, both fists striking her in the chest.

"Help me," she said. Her hands were already covered in dirt. "Please help me. I can't leave her here."

The entreaty sent Grace back to Saturday morning, to the underground car park with Elin holding a gun on her and bleeding everywhere. Grace hadn't been able to deny Elin then, and she certainly couldn't deny her now. They dug with their bare hands, scooping the loose earth away, throwing it behind them and pushing back in again and again. The mound collapsed, but they kept going, driving into a firmer layer, recently disturbed but packed harder.

The man hadn't bothered to go very deep. Less than a foot down, Grace's battered fingernails scraped against something solid.

"Elin…"

Elin had felt it as well. She drew her hands out as if burned, and Grace persevered in her stead, clearing the edges of a sealed wooden box.

"Don't look," she said. "Elin, don't look."

Elin turned away, her shoulders shaking as she started to cry. Functioning on autopilot, Grace took a pair of scissors from the bag and used them to prise the lid from the box. It came away without a protest, and she heard the rattle of stones and earth cascading into the cavity. She took a breath, smelling nothing but damp and dirt, and looked down. The box was completely empty.

"Fucking hell." Grace hugged her arms across her chest, welcoming the sting from the laceration. "Elin, it's okay," she said, but she couldn't stop shaking and she couldn't make her voice loud enough. She crawled over to Elin, unwound her from the tight little ball she'd wrapped herself in, and held her close. "It's empty, Elin. She's not here. It's not Amelia."

The phone buzzed. One message, three words: *NOW you understand.*

SAFIA. SUNDAY, 11:33 A.M.

"Give it another hour, Detective." The doctor checked his watch as if setting Safia a deadline, but his order and his manner lacked conviction, and he seemed relieved when she got off the A&E bed. Grace Kendal worked in this department, a fact that had seen Safia assessed, scanned, and sutured in record time.

"Thanks, but I need to get back to it," she said, her speech thickened by an anaesthetic-numbed cheek. "My partner has collected one of every advice leaflet, and he'll drag me back here if I do anything daft."

"Like collapse."

"Yes, that."

The doctor wasn't finished. "Or vomit, or become confused, or bleed from your ears, or lose your vision, or—"

"All of those as well." She put her jacket on and held out her hand. He took it in both of his and shook it firmly. "We'll find her," she told him.

"Inshallah," he said.

She nodded, though his faith was probably stronger than hers. "Yes, inshallah."

Suds met her outside the cubicle. Someone had supplied him with a brew, and he'd picked the polystyrene cup to pieces once he'd emptied it. Although not an overt worrier, he had a tendency to destroy whatever he had to hand whenever he was stressed, and Safia had lost countless pens to him over the years. He scooped the debris into a bin and gave her an ice pack.

"Obliging nurse," he said to her arched eyebrow. "Nice chap, but not really my type."

She laughed and instantly regretted it. Her cheek was ripped on the inside and held together by four stitches on the out, and she had a thumping headache. "Where are we up to?" she asked, gingerly pressing the pack into place and walking in step with him toward the exit.

"Techs are in the process of unlocking Lowry's laptop. I spoke to a very confident lad who said it shouldn't be too much longer. The ANPR desk are checking their cameras to see if they've caught Lowry's car out and about, and Ballistics are comparing his gun to the bullet found on the Heath. The medic who examined him in the custody suite reckons his injuries are inconsistent with a fall, unless a brick wall hit both his legs and then threw him over it."

"Hmm," Safia said, wondering what he'd done to deserve that. "If he was the man at the hotel yesterday, he can't have had those bruises, because Lewis Montgomery would have mentioned them, so he's been truthful about the timeline if nothing else. Was he assaulted?"

Suds waited until a paramedic had steered a wheelchair past them, its patient lolling over the edge whilst bleeding onto the floor and singing a hymn. "I put that to the medic," he said as the racket faded. "She thinks it's more likely a case of man versus car. One of Lowry's neighbours heard him stumble past her front window at about eight thirty this morning. The light wasn't great, but she swears she saw fresh blood on him. We've no idea where he's been or what he's been up to."

"He's not said anything, then." Safia raised her jacket collar as they went outside. The sun was just ducking behind murky clouds, and a recent rain shower made the tarmac shimmer. She usually kept an eye on the weather forecast for walking Bolly, but she hadn't seen it in days.

"Not a peep," Suds said. "He's requested a solicitor and hospital treatment, which he knows is going to delay his interview and eat into the custody clock, and that's all he's done."

"Balls to him," she said. "He'll 'no comment' the interview anyway. I'm more interested in his laptop. It'll probably tell us a lot more than he will."

Suds hit the central locking on the car and opened her door for her.

"I'm glad you're all right, Saf," he said quietly. As a rule, he avoided getting emotional, which gave her an idea how shaken he was.

She kissed his cheek. "Thank you for your impeccably timed intervention, and for being built like a brick shithouse."

Laughing, he stepped back and flexed for her. "I do have exquisite musculature."

She fake-swooned, grabbing the door for support. "Stop it, now, when I'm so vulnerable. You'll give me palpitations." It felt good to take the piss, to push aside the trauma of the morning and get on with things. Later, she would probably crawl into Kami's arms and have a proper meltdown, but for now the distraction of the case was exactly what she needed.

Her phone rang as she got into the car, an unknown number showing on the caller ID. "DS Faris," she said, fastening her seat belt as Suds left the bay he'd illegally parked in.

"Morning." The woman on the other end sounded cheery and very northern. "It's DC Shaw from Serious Crimes at Moorside Met. I've spoken to DC Sudbury a couple of times, and he passed me your number. I heard you ran into a spot of bother. Are you feeling better?"

"I am, thank you." Safia smiled at Shaw's genuine concern. It might sound like a cliché, but no matter where you worked or which department you worked out of, if you were police then you were family. "How have you been getting on?"

"I think we're about done, if I'm being honest," Shaw said. "We had a list of Breckenridge's family and friends to chase down, but we've worked our way through the lot and drawn a blank. None of them have seen her or her daughter for at least a week, and quite a few maintained that she rarely leaves Amelia with a babysitter. Her mum's beside herself and absolutely adamant that Breckenridge wouldn't have done anything to endanger Amelia. Did you get hold of the military records?"

Safia nudged Suds, who was the world's most unsubtle earwigger, and he shook his head. "Work in progress," he mouthed.

"No, not yet," she told Shaw, putting the call through to speakerphone so Suds could listen and still concentrate on his driving.

"Her mum was quite forthcoming," Shaw said, her tone implying she'd charmed a whole load of useful information from the woman. "Breckenridge was Special Recon alongside your Mr. Lowry. She got gut-shot out in Syria about ten years back when an assignment went to shit, pardon my French. It was touch-and-go for a few weeks— multiple surgeries, sepsis, it all sounded very unpleasant—and she ended up accepting a payout and walking away."

"That might explain her being able to kick-start a company," Suds said.

"Hey, Suds." Shaw sounded as if she'd known him for years. He shrugged when Safia poked him. "That's exactly what she did," Shaw continued. "Her mum confirmed as much. There was a brief spell of her going completely off the rails, and then she settled down, started the company, and adopted Amelia three years later." Shaw sighed, and her chair creaked. She was probably leaning back on it; Safia did that all the time when she was troubled.

"You think Amelia was kidnapped down here, don't you?" Safia said, making things easier for her.

"Yes, I do. And, having looked Breckenridge's mum in the eye, I don't think Breckenridge is caught up in anything other than her worst nightmare."

Safia could have played devil's advocate and argued the point, advising Shaw not to rely on sentiment or take a frightened grandmother at her word, but it was the same theory that Safia and Suds had been circling for a while now.

"We very much appreciate your help, DC Shaw," Safia said noncommittally.

"Any time," Shaw replied. "And it's Jo, please. I'm in on overtime today, and helping out with this has been far more interesting than my backlog of paperwork. If you need anything else, just give me a shout."

"They're nice up north," Suds said, when Safia had pocketed her phone. "She promised to buy me a pie and a pint."

Safia reapplied her ice pack. Her headache had almost gone, but the local had started to wear off and her cheek was on fire. "You're such a cheap date."

He chuckled, slowing for the turn into the police station. "That's not what my wife says."

To Safia's relief, the MIT office was empty, and she was able to catch up on her emails whilst Suds headed for the kitchen.

"Lewis Montgomery has positively ID-ed Lowry as the man who came to the Radisson," she said as Suds set a glass of chocolate milk on her desk. "I'd bet my next wage on him being the third party at the Heath."

"He's certainly up to his neck in something," Suds said.

"Might he be our kidnapper?" she asked. "He knows Breckenridge, knows what she and the company are worth, and he'll have contacts with the expertise to pull this off."

Suds shrugged. "Right at this moment, I'm open to any and all possibilities. At any rate, he's an arsehole who needs to pick on someone his own size." He stuck a straw into the glass and angled it toward her.

"You're too good to me," she said.

"I really am." He smiled, but he was chewing on his thumbnail, a sure sign he'd done something she would want to kill him for. Despite her fuzzy head, it didn't take long for her to work it out.

"Oh, bloody hell, Suds. When?"

"I couldn't help it. She rang me because she couldn't get hold of you. She's on her way over."

Safia touched her tangled hair, then her swollen cheek and the welt above her eye from hitting the door frame. "How bad is it?" She hadn't thought to check in a mirror. She'd planned to let Kami enjoy her day off and then break the news gently an hour or so before leaving for home.

"Scale of one to Mr. Potato Head, you're only about a four," he said.

"Great."

She was halfway through writing a plan for Lowry's first interview when Kami stuck her head around the office door. Kami didn't do histrionics—her mother had passed the Rasul neurotic genes exclusively to Kami's elder sister—but her reddened eyes and smudged mascara told Safia she'd been crying. She crossed the floor quickly and knelt by Safia's chair to pull her into a tentative hug. Safia rested her unsutured cheek against Kami's chest, breathing in her familiar scent and listening to the frantic boom of her heartbeat gradually quieten and slow. Kami was whispering something in Bengali; most of the words were unfamiliar to Safia, but their rhythm was soothing nonetheless.

"You should be at home, tucked up in bed where I can keep an eye on you and feed you ice cream," Kami said, switching effortlessly to English. She smoothed Safia's hair away from her face and kissed her forehead. "Are you sure you're okay to work?"

That was one of the things Safia loved most about her; she understood the job, and she knew exactly when a case had got under Safia's skin to the extent of this one. There would be no impassioned pleas to be sensible, no foot-stomping conniption fits if Safia spent very little of the next few days at their flat. Kami would do her own shifts, get on with her life, and make the most of whatever time they managed to snatch together.

"I'm sore," Safia said, because Kami wasn't stupid. "But I'm all right, and Suds is babysitting me, see?" She swirled the straw around her glass, drawing a spiral of chocolate through the milk.

"I have many advice leaflets," Suds said. "I know all the"— he double-checked the precise terminology—"red flag signs and symptoms."

"That's very reassuring." Kami stole a mouthful of milk. "By the by, my darling, if I remember correctly, Eddie Beresford is in charge of Ballistics today."

Safia pushed the glass closer to Kami and offered her the straw. "Do go on."

"Well, I could pop in and say hello."

Despite Safia's aches and pains, the gleeful twist to Kami's lips and the tickle of her little finger along Safia's forearm made her think thoughts that should absolutely not have been entertained in the office.

"I'm sure he would appreciate that," she said. "But aren't you encouraging him?"

"He slapped my arse the last time we met, Saf. And he's never had a conversation with anything but my breasts. I may as well make it count for something."

Safia kissed the back of Kami's hand. "When is he retiring?"

"Three weeks tomorrow. We're planning a party, and he won't be invited." Kami stood and rearranged her shirt. "How do I look?"

"Gorgeous," Safia said with feeling. "I'll probably be late tonight."

"I know, love." Kami waggled a stern finger at Suds. "No red flags, mister."

He held up his vast array of leaflets. "I will call you if she so much as sneezes funny."

"Excellent." Kami took a last look at Safia's face and clucked her tongue. "My gran will be feeding you mishti doi till it's coming out of your ears."

"Pretty sure that's a red flag," Suds muttered.

Safia shooed her away. "I love you. Behave yourself in Ballistics."

Kami pouted. "Where's the fun in that?"

Safia waited for her to leave before returning to her emails. A preliminary report from the Automatic Number Plate Recognition desk had placed Lowry's Range Rover on the M6 heading toward Birmingham at three a.m. and returning via the same route four hours later, which tied in with the neighbour who'd seen him arrive home with fresh injuries. "Why would Lowry be going to Birmingham?" Suds asked, apparently trawling through his emails as well.

"I haven't the foggiest. If he's in cahoots with the kidnapper, perhaps that's where they are." She answered her desk phone as it started to ring. "DS Faris."

The lad on the other end didn't muck about. "It's Wes from Tech. We got into the laptop, and you are definitely going to want to come down and see this."

Wes was as efficient in person as he'd been on the phone. He took one look at Safia and rolled a chair over for her, setting it in front of a bank of computer monitors that were somehow channelling Lowry's laptop.

"Company finances," he said, pointing to the left-hand screen. "Missing about eight hundred thousand since last Thursday. There was a series of significant transfers and withdrawals starting Wednesday night. Lowry was a co-signatory on the largest of them."

"Really?" Without thinking, Safia dabbed her finger on the mouse pad, and the middle monitor lost one of its windows. Suds snorted, and Wes intervened before she did any more damage, zooming in on a scan of the relevant proforma.

"That's his signature there."

"Unlikely to be the kidnapper, if he's co-signing probable ransom withdrawals," Suds said, and Safia shook her head, just as perplexed as he was.

Having served the appetiser, Wes seemed impatient to move on to the main course, and he rejigged the central monitor until it showed a set-up similar to Google Maps, except that this program came with a detailed side bar and appeared to be plotting in real time.

"What am I looking at?" Safia asked, though she was starting to make sense of it without his input. If she was right, the implications were staggering.

"It's a tracking program," he said, confirming her hunch. "Lowry activated it that same Thursday afternoon at an address just outside Richmond. And this is where it's been since."

Safia watched open-mouthed as a thin red line hit the Radisson Hotel on Canary Wharf, then Hampstead Heath, and then took a roundabout route back to the hotel, where it remained for about seven hours. Kendal's house in New Cross came next, after a short stopover at an address in Brockley. Safia scribbled that postcode in her notepad. Thanks to the internet, it would be easy to find out what the property was.

"Holy shit," Suds said as the line left the house and tore up the M6 toward Birmingham for an overnight stop in Solihull. "Where are they now?"

Another thirty seconds and he had his answer: a postcode in Moorside, Greater Manchester.

"They've been there a while," Wes said.

"Aren't Breckenridge's parents in that neck of the woods?" Safia flipped back through her pad, searching for the address. "Bloody hell, the postcodes don't match. This is brilliant, though, Wes."

"I don't think it's brilliant," Suds told him. "I get dizzy if I go past the Midlands."

"I'll update Chevs," Safia said. "Suds, get on to your new pal at Moorside and tell her she might be buying you that pint sooner rather than later."

Buoyed by "a superb birdie on the fifth," Chevs was in a benevolent mood, hardly raising an objection when Safia sought his permission to head north and shrugging off the expense of a hotel stay.

"Quite the saga this is turning out to be," he said as someone bellowed for a waitress in the background. He had always been fascinated by complex investigations, no matter how much they mucked up his solve rate. "I'll give Nige Ellard a bell—he's the Serious Crimes DI at Moorside—and touch base as a courtesy. He shouldn't be a problem for you, though. If you've already made contact with one of his team, he'll know exactly what's going on."

"Thanks, boss. I'll speak to you later." She ended the call and began to collect her case notes. To an observer, she would have appeared unflappable, but her mind was awhirl with prioritising tasks to delegate and fretting about cross-departmental cooperation. An email notification brought her back to her computer, and she opened the message from the custody suite sergeant without the faintest hope of it containing anything useful.

"It's official: Lowry's been deemed medically unfit for interview," she told Suds, whose expression of surprise—mouth agape, hand splayed across his heart—was so outrageous that she chucked a pencil at him.

"What a shocking twist," he said. "I honestly did not see that coming." He stuck the pencil in his brimming stationery pot. She should probably stop lobbing stuff at him; it cost her a fortune in supplies.

"On the bright side, it frees us up for our road trip." She checked her watch. She had texted Kami about the developments but hadn't yet received a reply. "I might nip down to the basement before we go."

"I'll attempt to requisition us a car with four wheels and functional seat belts," he said, grabbing his jacket.

She laughed. "Yeah, good luck with that."

The door hadn't finished closing behind him when Kami strode in, toting a carrier bag and looking smug.

"How much do you love me?" she asked, stopping a few feet shy of Safia.

"A very lot?" Safia took a step toward her. There was only one possible explanation for that smirk. "Kamila Rasul, you did it, didn't you?"

Kami nodded. "Ninety-eight-point-seven percent match, which is about as good as it gets. Eddie hasn't completed or submitted the paperwork yet, so this is all on the QT, but Lowry's gun is almost certainly the gun that killed the man on the Heath."

Safia whooped and threw her arms around Kami, and then put both hands on her shoulders and pushed her back a little. "Oh no. What the hell did that cost you?"

Kami kissed the knuckles on Safia's right hand. "Not much, really. He's a very cheap date. All I had to do was bend down a little lower and give him a bar of Dairy Milk Whole Nut."

"Really?"

"Really. He's quite forthcoming when you offer him your undivided attention and a hint of cleavage."

Safia hid her face in her hands. "You're setting the Women's Movement back an entire generation here."

Kami's shrug was the very definition of sanguine. "Or, I am playing the old bastard at his own game to achieve a desired result. I have no regrets, my honour is still intact, and you just solved a murder, so happy days."

"All my days with you are happy," Safia said, pulling her close again.

"I love you," Kami murmured against Safia's cheek. "You will be careful, won't you?"

"I will, I promise."

Kami rustled the bag. "I brought you snacks. And a toothbrush and toothpaste, and spare knickers."

"That's the essentials covered, then," Safia said. There were supplies in her locker for cases that ran into the early hours or kept her out overnight, but you could never have enough clean knickers.

Kami kissed her, lightly at first, and then with more intensity. "Come home safe," she said as they parted.

Safia swayed into her, reluctant to lose the contact. "I'll be home before you've missed me."

GRACE. SUNDAY, 2:00 P.M.

The key was where the man said it would be, sealed in cling film beneath the first step of the static caravan. Grace unwrapped it quickly and used it to open the filthy front door, although a stern talking-to would probably have been enough to make the fibreglass capitulate. A dank smell of wet dog and mildew rushed out to greet her, but she ushered Elin inside regardless and sat her on a recliner with a sagging base. Elin didn't seem to notice. She had barely spoken since the churchyard, and every time she breathed, her chest rattled like a fifty-a-day smoker with double pneumonia.

Tomorrow, the man had said in his final message. Grace had tried to reply, to tell him Elin might not have that long, but their number was blocked and her plea had gone nowhere.

She drew the living room curtains and switched on a lamp, whose deep red shade dulled the sight of peeling wallpaper and decades-old cobwebs. A glass cabinet in the corner of the room held shelves full of Tonka trucks and cars, but a television guide on top of the lopsided television was four years out of date, and it was clear no one had lived there in the interim. Situated on the edge of the Saddleworth moors, the caravan site had appeared deserted as she'd driven along its access road. A few of the static homes were secured for the winter, their windows covered with locked shutters, but most had been abandoned to the elements lashing across the hills. A fierce wind had smothered the blue sky with moody grey clouds, and intermittent showers of sleet and hail were battering the caravan's roof. Her hand poised to pull the cord on the kitchen blind, Grace stayed by the window to watch snow turn the high moors white, before more cloud rolled in to swallow them whole.

A quick check of the taps told her they had water, but nothing happened when she turned on the gas hob, and she didn't dare light the ancient gas heater in the living room. Giving the bathroom a wide berth—she would venture in there only when absolutely necessary—she went into the bedroom, whose sole positive aspect was a cupboard full of blankets that didn't stink to high heaven. She grabbed them all, and the least stained of the pillows, and took them back to Elin.

"Here. Let me try this." To her amazement, the recliner actually reclined, and she used the pillows to prop Elin in a position that wouldn't make her feel as though she was drowning. Elin's lips were tinged with purple, and the hand Grace took was tacky with blood Elin had coughed up and tried to hide. Grace felt her own chest tighten as she cleaned Elin's palm and fingers. Without oxygen or fluids or a fresh surgical kit, she could do little more to treat her, and short of raiding a hospital store the options to remedy that were very limited.

"I'm not going to sit here and watch you die," she said. "I can't. Not after all this."

Elin muttered something inaudible, responding more to the sound of Grace's voice than to anything Grace had said. She coughed again, too slow with her hand to prevent crimson froth sliding onto her chin and throat.

"Sorry," she whispered. Her eyes rolled, and then fixed on the far corner of the ceiling.

"So am I," Grace said, but Elin had just made her decision for her.

The television came on when she flicked its plug socket. She found the remote control and turned to BBC News.

SAFIA. SUNDAY, 3:30 P.M.

Sunday afternoon wasn't the best time to be hurtling up the motorway with blues on and siren blaring. Safia interrupted her phone call to brace herself as yet another useless driver of an oversized SUV dawdled, panicked, and then slammed on the anchors a few yards in front of the unmarked police car. Suds, whose general rule of thumb was always to expect the buggers to do the most ludicrous thing possible, had seen it coming, and he cut wide into a spare lane without breaking a sweat.

"Do carry on," he told her, gesturing at her phone. He loved driving response, and a mate on Traffic regularly took him out to maintain his skills, even if they were seldom tested.

"Sorry about that," she said to Daniel Marks. "Can you pass the reg on to the ANPR desk and let me know whether they get a hit?" She ended the call on his affirmative and rolled her neck to alleviate a crick.

"Car rental, then?" Suds said. Daniel had been tasked to trace the Brockley address from Lowry's tracker, and Safia's side of the phone conversation had obviously provided Suds with the salient points.

"Vauxhall Astra, on Saturday afternoon," she confirmed. "Kendal signed the agreement, and then I guess they must have driven in tandem to ditch the Audi, which is a good effort." She couldn't help but feel slightly inadequate. A couple of knocks to

CARI HUNTER

the face had made her unsteady enough to delegate driving duties, while the medical debris from the hotel room strongly implied Elin Breckenridge had taken a bullet in the chest.

Suds whizzed past a lorry, the M6 toll road making short work of the route around Birmingham. "What on earth would they be doing up here?" he asked. "They must be following some sort of demand from the kidnapper, but why would he risk moving a child all this way? Surely it'd be in his best interests to hunker down in London and rearrange a ransom drop."

"Without a doubt," she said. "But nothing about this case makes much sense, unless…"

The toll booth operator raised the barrier on their approach, and Suds flashed his headlights in appreciation. "Unless what?" he said, accelerating as soon as he'd cleared the gap.

She folded her arms, telling herself to get off the damn fence and commit. "Unless you take the ransom out of the equation. Things make far more sense if you do that." The drive up from London had given her plenty of time to think the idea through, although she had stopped short of discussing it with him. At first, she had dismissed it as the product of a fertile imagination and a knock to the head, but the more she mulled it over, the more convinced she became that the kidnapper had a motive other than financial gain. There was only eight hundred thousand pounds missing from the Bridge accounts. Even if Breckenridge had topped the total up to a million or a million and a half, that wasn't all that much money these days. Enough to pass under a bank's money-laundering radar, perhaps, and give the kidnapping an appearance of authenticity, but not enough to justify the associated risks and logistics. If Breckenridge herself was the target, however, the money would merely be a bonus, something to string her along with and make her believe there was a chance of getting her daughter back.

Suds cruised up the outside lane, the speedometer hitting ninety miles an hour and then creeping beyond. "It would explain a lot," he said at length. "It also makes me very antsy indeed."

"Yeah, you and me both. Hopefully, Jo Shaw—" She glanced down as her phone rang. "Oh, speak of the devil." She wasn't superstitious, but she felt a compulsion to cross her fingers as she answered. "Hey, Jo. Any progress?" She flicked the call onto speaker for Suds's benefit.

"Everything's sorted, and we're en route," Jo said. "It took a while to snag Armed Response and finalise a raid strategy, but it's all in hand now. Address looks to be waste ground, easy for Breckenridge and Kendal to park up on. Your tech bloke sent us the exact GPS coordinates, and we're about fifteen minutes out, with medics on standby."

Torn between envy and an eagerness to close the case, Safia defaulted to magnanimity. "We're just through Birmingham," she said. "Good luck, and keep us updated."

"Of course. I'll phone as soon as we're done."

It was a long and tetchy forty-five minutes of swearing at traffic and feeding Suds coffee and bite-size pieces of sandwiches. Drizzle turned to sleet at Stafford Services, where Suds nipped to the toilet, and the heavens opened properly on the link road past Tatton Park.

"It's just keeping things interesting," he said through gritted teeth. The windscreen wipers were going full pelt and barely clearing his field of vision. "No wonder they say it's grim up north."

"Maybe that's just in reference to the weather." Through the sheets of rain, Safia could see large detached houses with ornate gates and sweeping driveways. She had relatives who lived near Manchester, and their tiny boxed-in suburbs *were* grim, but plenty of London boroughs had nothing to shout about either. Her phone went again as Suds sped through a red light and joined the next motorway.

"Do you want the good news or the bad?" Jo asked her without preamble.

Safia went cold, but she preferred ripping the sticking plaster off the wound. "The bad."

Jo evidently subscribed to the same school of thought. "They're not here. Coordinates took us to a lay-by overlooking common ground. The good news is they've definitely been here. Armed Response fished a rucksack out of a litter bin. It was torn to shreds, and there's blood on one of its straps and a couple of loose fifty-pound notes in the bottom. We've dug a small device—we're assuming that's the tracker—from its lining, so we're back to square one."

"Anything of significance in the vicinity?" Safia asked.

"Not really." Jo's footsteps crunched as if she was turning to take stock. "It's a residential street on one side, with a church at its top end. We've started door-to-door, if that's all right with you."

"Absolutely." Safia managed to keep a lid on her temper. She didn't want Jo to know how close she was to a full-on tantrum. Every time she thought they were actually getting somewhere, they slammed into a dead end. She dug her nails into the palm of her hand and checked the satnav. "We're about an hour away. Our DI has been in touch with yours, and we're cleared to carry on up to you regardless. No point us being in London when all the evidence suggests they're halfway across the country."

"None at all," Jo said. "Drive safe. The roads are full of pillocks."

Seconds after Jo disconnected, Safia's phone rang again. The withheld number covered a multitude of possibilities, but at least it wouldn't be Chevs pecking her head for chasing two hundred and twenty miles after a rucksack.

"DS Faris," she said.

"Afternoon, Detective." The man on the other end cleared his throat awkwardly. "I'm really sorry to bother you, but I've got a call here that my supervisor has told me to put through to you, if that's okay."

She mouthed one of her dad's favourite swear words, one he'd started throwing in her direction after she'd told him about Kami. The last thing she wanted was half an hour listening to a crank. "Who is it?" she asked.

The man coughed again. "Well, she's claiming to be your missing doctor, Grace Kendal."

"Really?" Safia scratched her cheek where the stitches were irritating her. "Did she offer anything to substantiate that?"

"Not much. She's quite on edge. She said to tell you she's with Elin somewhere near the Saddleworth Moors, and that the ransom for Amelia is due tomorrow."

"Fucking hell." Safia signalled frantically for Suds to knock the sirens off. "Put her through *now*."

GRACE. SUNDAY, 3:40 P.M.

An automated message told Grace that her call was important as she started her fifth minute on hold. She was using her own phone, and paranoia nagged at her, urging her to hang up in case the police were tracing her location. She needed this to be on her terms. If the police turned up mob-handed, everything she and Elin had gone through to get this far would be for nothing. Six minutes. In the recliner, Elin was wheezing in a staggered, stertorous rhythm. Six and a half. Seven.

"Shit." Grace held the phone away from her ear, her finger poised to end the call.

"Hello?" A woman's voice, its authoritative tone undercut by a tremor of apprehension. "Dr. Kendal? Are you still there?"

"I'm still here," Grace said. Even that slight a connection robbed her of her composure. She closed her eyes so she wouldn't have to look at Elin while she did this. "Is that Detective Faris?"

"It is. Can you speak freely, Dr. Kendal?"

"It's Grace." There was no time to waste on formalities. "And yes, I can speak freely. Is anyone else listening to this call?"

To her credit, Faris answered without equivocating. "I'm with my partner, Suds, Detective Constable Sudbury. We're actually on the M56, near Manchester Airport. We arrested Neil Lowry this morning and found a program he'd been using to track you."

"Jesus," Grace whispered. They were only about an hour away from the caravan site. She hadn't expected that, hadn't thought they could be on the doorstep so soon. If she was honest with herself, she hadn't thought beyond bargaining for a delivery of supplies and playing the rest by ear, and if the kidnapper forced them to change locations before Faris arrived, then so be it.

"I know Ms. Breckenridge is familiar with this gentleman," Faris said, breaking into the long silence.

"We both are." Grace shuddered. The image of Lowry glowering at her through the smashed door was never far from her mind. "He was the man who shot Elin, and he attacked us again early this morning." She sank onto the sofa. She was so desperate for reassurance that she felt like curling into a ball and sobbing. Let them come and help to end this. She didn't care anymore. "Did you really get him?"

"We did," Faris said firmly. "And for some reason, his tracker was sending us to a patch of wasteland in Moorside."

Grace made the link in fits and starts. They had only left one thing behind at that location. "He'd put something in the rucksack, hadn't he?"

"Yes, it was in the lining. The local police found it about an hour ago."

"We moved," Grace said. She felt punch-drunk with information, unable to process much of anything. "I saw you on the news. You know someone kidnapped Elin's daughter, don't you? The man who took her, he's been moving us around. He sent us to that street in Moorside, and then he sent us here."

"Where are you now?" Faris asked.

"I can't—" Grace covered her mouth, fresh doubts and second thoughts piling up on top of each other. In the corner, Elin's cough sounded like a death rattle. "I can't tell you yet. Because I need you to promise you'll come alone, Detective Faris."

"Safia," Faris said. "Seeing as we're not standing on ceremony." She seemed to be playing for time, though a strident murmur in the background suggested her partner had plenty to say about Grace's request.

"Would it be possible for Suds, sorry, DC Sudbury to come with me?" Safia said as the other voice ceased. "He's harmless, and he makes a good cuppa, and I trust him implicitly."

Too jittery to keep still, Grace got up again and went to the window. She wanted to open the curtains and break the claustrophobia of the tiny room, but it was already getting dark outside, and she was scared of what might be lurking in the shadows. She knew she was demanding a lot from Safia, insisting she walk into what would ostensibly have been an armed standoff, had Elin been conscious and Grace not a complete novice with a gun. All things considered, Safia's request was far from unreasonable.

"Okay, just him," Grace said. "But you'll have to bring your own brew stuff."

"I think we can manage that," Safia said. She had looked young on the television, but her gentle confidence was like a balm on Grace's frayed nerves. "Do you need anything else?"

"Yes." That was an understatement. Grace had prepared a list. "Have you got a pen and paper handy?"

"Of course."

She read the list out, spelling some of the items using NATO phonetics and asking Safia to repeat it back to her once she was done.

"Any hospital with an A&E will have those in stock," she said. "Do you think you'll manage?"

"It's going to take some finagling," Safia admitted. "Fortunately, we've already made a friend up here, so she might be able to assist. I'm guessing Ms. Breckenridge isn't doing very well."

"No, she's not. She doesn't know I've phoned you, but the man said tomorrow, and she won't be able to—" Grace stopped dead and told herself to calm down. If she wanted Safia to take her seriously, she couldn't come across as a brainwashed hysteric. She planned her next sentence before she actually spoke it. "Unless I can stabilise her condition, she won't be able to follow his next set of instructions."

"I'll do my utmost to get you what you've requested," Safia assured her.

Grace wasn't finished. "You can't arrest her for this. She hasn't done anything wrong."

"Apart from kidnapping you," Safia said quietly.

Grace already had that one covered. "Shock does funny things to a person, Detective Faris. Elin didn't have a clue what she was doing at the time, and I'd be more than willing to attest to that in a court of law."

She heard Safia chuckle. "I'm not coming there to arrest her, Grace. We have ballistics evidence that makes Lowry our prime suspect for the murder on the Heath. I simply want to get to the bottom of all this and ensure that you, Ms. Breckenridge, and Amelia are safe."

"Thank you." Grace felt as though a tonne weight had just fallen from her shoulders. There was another one still there, but the load was definitely lighter to bear. "Have you got that pen handy? We're going to be quite difficult to find."

SAFIA. SUNDAY, 5:12 P.M.

The ambulance bay was busy, full of vehicles and dotted with crews hiding fags from the CCTV and shivering in wind that kept blasting wet snow under the canopy. Suds had parked at its top end, and he and Safia were standing by the car, stretching tired legs and aching backs after hours on the road.

"Is that her?" she asked. The short-haired woman at the A&E entrance had CID written all over her: sensible trouser suit, sensible boots, warm coat adorned with a lanyard. She was missing the ubiquitous file folder, but she clearly pegged Safia and Suds as kindred spirits, because she smiled and headed over to them. Behind her, an older chap in scrubs was towing a trolley stacked with bags and plastic crates.

"Jo Shaw," she said, shaking their hands in turn. "Is your boss having a meltdown as well, or is it just mine?"

"He's having a meltdown," Safia confirmed. Upon being informed of Grace's phone call and what Safia had subsequently agreed to, Chevs had read Safia the Riot Act, though it was difficult for him to bollock her effectively when he was in a crowded clubhouse and she was halfway across the country. After stomping his feet and getting it all out of his system, he had offered to continue liaising with Jo's DI and told Safia to keep him updated. As micromanaging went, that was about the best she could have hoped for. "Did you get everything?" she asked Jo.

"Yep. At least, I think so." Jo looked at the medic for assurance. Grace had given Safia her General Medical Council registration number, which had helped smooth the way with the hospital to some extent, but no one was entirely comfortable with the arrangement.

"It's all here," the medic said. He looked around, as if checking for witnesses. "She didn't request any controlled drugs, but I've prescribed IV morphine. I'd want something stronger than paracetamol if I'd been shot in the chest."

"Thank you," Safia said. "I'm sure they'll both appreciate that."

He left them to it, and Suds began to pile the kit into the car boot.

"Looks sore," Jo said to Safia, and Safia realised she had only just turned the bruised side of her face into the light. She touched her cheek. It was still swollen, but the cold was lessening its sting.

"It's not too bad," she said as Suds shoved the last bag into place. "Are you going to be around later?" It was always easier to have a contact, someone who didn't need briefing or permission to drop one case and assist on another.

"Definitely. I should finish at seven, but I'm not going anywhere." Jo's eager expression implied her overtime shift had been well worth coming in for. "I'll start putting into place whatever you might need, and I'll be on the end of the phone if you get any new leads to chase down." She rummaged in her pocket as Suds came to stand with them and handed him a small menu. "This is the best takeaway around here. If someone had held me hostage for two days and forced me to do emergency surgery, the least I'd want is a decent kebab."

Even with the high beams on, Suds was struggling to keep the car steady. The wind was conspiring with the dirt track to try to toss them into the bushes either side, and Safia had caught glimpses of waterlogged ditches beneath the hawthorn and brambles. If he spun a tyre into one of those, he wouldn't be getting it out again in a hurry.

"Perfect place for an ambush," he muttered. His furrowed brow gleamed in the dull light, and his gaze was flitting in all directions, as if the bogeyman might leap out at any moment. He hadn't spoken much about their close call at Lowry's that morning, but it had obviously rattled him.

"Not far now," she said, acutely aware that she had dragged him into this. He had insisted on accompanying her, of course, but she outranked him, and she could easily have refused him permission.

A ramshackle section of fencing bearing a weather-worn welcome sign refocused her attention. The tyres rumbled across a cattle grid, where the remnants of a wooden gate marked the start of the caravan site proper. Peering into the gloom, Safia could see the dark hulks of static homes, their pitches scattered at random, as if neighbours that might once have given the place order had long since upped sticks for more hospitable climes.

"Was that a light?" Suds was squinting against a sudden shower of snow. He slowed for the world's most unnecessary speed bump and pointed toward a flickering splotch of red a hundred or so yards ahead.

"It must be them," she said. Grace had repeatedly assured her there was no one else on the site. "What on earth are they doing in this shithole?"

"It's a great place to send them if he doesn't want them to be found."

"Yeah, I suppose so. How the hell did *he* find it?"

Suds jerked the steering wheel to avoid a rut. "Local knowledge? That might be something for Jo to look into."

She nodded. "Good thinking. Remind me when we're not knee-deep in mud and slush."

A Vauxhall Astra, slowly disappearing beneath a layer of white, confirmed they had the right caravan. Suds drove a distance past the rental car, parking out of sight by a shed with a listing roof. They got out of the car one at a time, their hands raised.

"What now?" he asked, when nothing happened. "Do we grab the stuff and knock on?"

She found her torch and aimed its beam at the front door of the caravan. It opened a crack, and she swiftly re-aimed the light at the floor.

"I think we've been spotted," she said. Neither of them moved any closer, and she felt pellets of snow pinging off her face and settling in her hair as Grace Kendal came out and hurried toward them.

"I'm not armed," Grace said quickly, displaying her empty hands. It was clear she wasn't going to waste time on introductions. "Did you get what I asked for?"

"Yes." Safia nodded to Suds, who opened the boot to reveal its contents. "How is she?"

The question seemed to wrong-foot Grace, as if she had steeled herself for a battle, only to be provided with succour. The rigidity left her posture, and she rubbed her eyes with the heel of her hand. "Not good," she said. She looked and sounded shattered, but she hauled one of the bags over her shoulder. "I need to get back to her."

She led the way up the caravan's front steps and into a dingy kitchen that smelled like Bolly after a romp in the rain. The wind was shaking the foundations, and the floor felt unstable underfoot, as if one decent gust would send the whole thing plummeting down the hillside. Safia panned her torch around, its light skimming off lopsided cupboards and shelves, and the handgun that was sitting in the middle of the kitchen table. Grace paid it no heed as she went into a narrow hallway, but Safia paused to kick the table leg.

"Suds," she said in a sharp undertone.

"Got it."

Leaving him to secure the gun, she followed Grace to a living room lit like a cheap bordello. She stopped in the doorway, letting her eyes adjust and frowning at a noise reminiscent of her nephew blowing bubbles into his lassi. It was only when she began to distinguish Elin in the far corner that she realised she was listening to her breathe.

"Fucking hell." She crossed the tattered carpet as Grace threw down her bag and yanked at its zip. Safia set her own box of supplies next to it, staying in a crouch by Grace. "Can you fix this?" she asked.

"I'm not sure." Grace was rummaging through the bag, sorting equipment and drugs into some semblance of order.

With one hand on the arm of a decrepit recliner, Safia played her torch over its occupant. Elin Breckenridge was unconscious, her head tilted back and supported by pillows. Every time she took a breath, she gasped like a fish out of water.

"Jesus Christ," Suds said from somewhere behind Safia. "She needs a fucking hospital, Doc."

"I *know* she needs a fucking hospital," Grace snapped. The glove she was pulling on tore at the thumb, and she ripped it off to start again with a fresh one. "She's needed a fucking hospital since Saturday morning, but instead she's got me and the both of you and whatever's in these bags." She passed Safia an oxygen mask. "Stick the tubing on the cylinder and crank up the dial."

"Okay." Safia did as she was told and placed the mask over Elin's nose and mouth, careful to avoid the dressing in the centre of her forehead. Plum-coloured bruising surrounded Elin's left eye, and Safia thought back to the ruined clothing in the Audi, and Amelia's tiny pair of dungarees. "Allah," she whispered, momentarily overwhelmed by the task facing them. She had persuaded Chevs to authorise her coming here, but she didn't have the faintest idea what to do next. In stark contrast, Grace couldn't seem to work fast enough, and Safia winced at the size of the needle she was digging into Elin's wrist.

"Pass me that bandage," she said to Safia. Safia popped it out of its wrapper for her, glad to feel useful. She hadn't heard Suds leave, but he came back looking puzzled, with a couple of coat hangers.

"Perfect," Grace told him. She appeared calmer now, her actions methodical and efficient as she hooked IV bags over the hangers to use them as improvised drip stands, and attached the leads from a monitor she'd slapped a new battery into. If this had been her life for the past couple of days, she had certainly adjusted to it. Without hesitating, she sliced through Elin's shirt, baring the right side of her chest, and then held Elin's arm up and out. "Safia, can you keep her like this for me?"

They swapped places, Safia putting one hand on Elin's elbow and the other around her slack wrist. She had left her torch on the coffee table, and it rolled back and forth, revealing flashes of silvery scar tissue, black bruising, and a white dressing with a bloody bullseye. She watched Grace lay out a surgical kit and peel off the dressing. As bad as things had evidently been for Elin, she knew they were about to get worse.

"Detective Sudbury, can you hold her if she tries to move? I don't"—Grace wavered, almost dropping the syringe she had filled—"I don't think she'll feel this, but be ready just in case." As if afraid of any further delay, she dug the needle into the blackened area of Elin's chest, injecting clear liquid around a small patch of stitches, and then snipped the stitches free.

Without being asked, Suds trained his own torch on the area as blood bubbled from the wound. Grace readied a length of plastic tubing.

"Bit of pressure now, Elin," she said. "You know how this goes."

There was no obvious reaction from Elin, but Safia felt a twitch in the hand she was holding. "It's all right," she murmured. "You're okay, you're safe." She wasn't sure any of it was true, though, and she had to look away as Grace inserted the tube.

"Holy shit," Suds said, and Safia dared a glance down to see blood sluicing into a large plastic container.

Grace was mumbling to herself, the same words over and over: "Please stop, please stop." She sagged onto her knees when the flow eventually stuttered and then slowed to a trickle. A check of the monitor brought the ghost of a smile.

"How's she doing?" Suds asked. Like Safia, he seemed afraid to speak too loudly or make any sudden movements.

"Better." Grace took off her gloves and adjusted the flow of an IV. "Her sats—the oxygen level in her blood—were seventy percent when I put the drain in." She tapped the monitor, where eighty-six flicked to eighty-eight, then eighty-nine. "If I can get her to ninety-three off the oxygen, I'll be happy. Her blood pressure is still crap, but that might take longer to improve."

"Will she wake up then?" Safia asked. Although Elin's breathing was less guttural and her overall colour had improved, the hand that Safia was still clasping was limp again. Were Safia in Elin's place, she'd prefer to be out for a while yet.

Grace used bottled water to wet a piece of gauze and bathed Elin's face. "Knowing her, she'll be awake in a few minutes." She swapped the gauze and dampened Elin's chapped lips. "And she won't be pleased to see you."

"No, I imagine not."

Grace dried her hands and pulled a blanket over Elin. "I didn't have a choice. I have to get her back on her feet by tomorrow."

Safia couldn't imagine Elin sitting up unaided by then, let alone walking around. "I think we might need a plan B," she said.

Grace gave a short, hopeless laugh. "We don't even have a plan A."

Grace. Sunday, 7:42 p.m.

A distinct white glow behind the curtains tempted Grace to reach over and open them a crack. Beyond the smeared glass, snow was falling, large flakes spiralling in the wind and massing in sheltered spots. She couldn't remember the last time she had seen proper snow—it rarely fell in London—and she watched until the wind nipped at her through the rotten window sealant and set her teeth chattering. The room was so cold that she could see her own breath, and frost was forming on the inside of the windowpane.

She arranged another blanket over Elin, who hadn't yet woken, thanks to a low dose of morphine. In truth, Grace wasn't sure whether she'd administered the drug for pain relief or to keep Elin under for another hour. From the kitchen, she could hear the low murmur of Safia's telephone conversation, the words inaudible beneath the hiss of oxygen. It seemed strange to have other people there after she and Elin had struggled for so long on their own, and while she was glad to have someone to share the burden, she knew their presence would bring its own stresses, particularly where Elin was concerned.

"Here, Doc," Suds said, coming into the room. "Get this into you." He set down a steaming polystyrene cup, rocking the coffee table and sending two empty syringes to the floor. He stooped to retrieve them, making sure to remain at a respectful distance. He'd been treating her with kid gloves ever since she'd finished recounting the events of the last two days, and he'd barely raised his voice above a whisper.

She smiled at him as he stood and retreated a few steps. She had been brave enough to look out the window only because he and Safia were there.

"Thanks, Suds. This smells really good." Cradling the cup with cold-stiffened hands, she took a sip. He'd made proper milky coffee in the microwave and piled the sugar in.

"Not too sweet, is it?"

"No, it's lovely."

"My dad always made it like this when he took me to the footy. I think it's colder in here than it was on the terraces, though. I wish I'd brought my woolly Gunners' hat." He sat on the far arm of the sofa. "How is she?"

Grace checked the monitor, but took her actual cues from Elin, who was now sleeping comfortably. "Stable-ish," she said. "None of her numbers are great, but everything's relative."

"Speaking of relatives…" Suds handed Safia a cup as she came back through. "Any joy?"

"Jo's on it," Safia said. "She actually remembers Thomas Elson's death. All the local papers covered it because he did a load of charity work around here. She's sure the reports would have mentioned family members, so she should be able to get their names."

Grace stroked the back of Elin's hand. It was bruised like the rest of her, but Grace had caused that by siting and resiting IV lines. "We don't know for sure that one of them is behind all this."

"Perhaps not," Safia said. "But it's the most logical place to start."

"Then what?" Grace asked, afraid all over again. "Will Detective Shaw start knocking on doors? If she does, he'll know we've told you."

Safia brought her cup to the sofa and sat beside Grace. "She won't be doing anything of the sort, you have my word. Once we have those names, we can check if any of them have a criminal record, and search for their addresses and any vehicles they own. We can build a picture of them as individuals and possibly narrow down the actual culprit. One of them might be the body on the Heath, if this was a family affair." She took a mouthful of her drink, giving that unconscious little sigh that signified a good brew. "Elin didn't see the face of the man who assaulted her, did she?"

"No." Grace thought back to Elin's description of him, such as it was. "Both men wore balaclavas. The one who stayed behind to beat her was tall, white with dark features. He had a broken tooth. I remember her saying that."

Safia's notepad was out, her pen moving briskly across the pages. "It may not seem like much, but these details can make the difference between a conviction and a perp walking away scot-free." She glanced at the burner phone, the third time she had done so in as many minutes. She and Suds had studied the videos and read each of the kidnapper's messages. Shortly afterward, she had excused herself to fetch something from the car, returning empty-handed a short time later. Cold air had rolled off her, and tiny crystals of snow had sparkled in her hairline, as if she had taken a handful and used it to clean her face. Grace, following Suds's lead, hadn't commented.

"Did he say when he would next be in touch?" Safia asked.

Grace shook her head. "He never does. There's no warning, no time for her to do anything except exactly what he tells her."

"I guess that's the point," Suds said. "Which will make things very tricky tomorrow. If he only discloses his location at the last minute, we're stuffed for any kind of prep or recon. We'll never be able to get Armed Response in position or scope the place out in advance. If he's good with tech, he might have eyes on any possible approach route."

"I know." Safia's foot beat a discordant rhythm on the leg of the table.

Grace rescued her obs kit before it hit the floor and distracted herself by taking Elin's temperature. She didn't want to think about tomorrow and the countless ways everything could go to hell. She had somehow convinced herself that involving the police would stack the odds in Elin's and Amelia's favour, but it was clear that Safia and Suds were equally helpless. Had she kept Elin alive just so Elin could die on the kidnapper's terms? She touched the curve of Elin's ear and the petal-soft skin of the lobe, one of the few unmarred areas on her face. It was hard to believe she had only known her for forty or so hours. So much had happened in the interim that it seemed as if several lifetimes had passed.

"Up or down?" Suds asked, and Grace remembered she still had the thermometer in her hand.

"Uh, down slightly, but still up, if that makes sense. She has an infection. I managed to get the bullet out—oh, you'll need that, won't you?" For want of a better idea, Grace had been keeping the bullet bagged and sealed in her trouser pocket. She fished it out and gave it to Safia. "It should be a match for Lowry's gun."

Safia held the bullet in the light. The plastic bag was streaked with blood. "I'm afraid to ask."

"Yeah. Probably best you don't." Grace turned sharply as Elin whined and tugged at the mask on her face. She took Elin's hand and lowered it, keeping her still. Elin's eyes flickered, half-open but unfocused.

"Grace?"

"I'm here, love." The endearment came naturally, a northerner falling back on her roots. "You're safe."

"I had a bad dream." Elin's voice was hoarse, as if she'd been screaming unheard. She groaned, her free hand pawing toward her side. "God, what's that?"

"I had to put the drain back in." Grace swallowed. Elin hadn't looked past her yet. "And I called—I had to call them, Elin, because I needed things I didn't have, and you were so poorly."

"What? Call who?" Elin frowned, trying to fathom what Grace wasn't telling her, and the confusion in her expression segued into comprehension as she finally noticed they weren't alone in the room. She pushed weakly at Grace, who stepped aside, letting her see.

"No," Elin said. "Oh fuck, *no*. Grace, what the fuck have you done?"

ELIN. SUNDAY, 7:52 P.M.

Elin wrenched the mask so hard that its elastic detached. Tubing and monitoring leads were tethering her in place, and she wanted it all off so she could shake an explanation out of Grace. She already had an answer to her question; the man and the young woman sitting on the sofa might as well have had "police" tattooed on their foreheads. She ripped the blood pressure cuff from her arm, taking an IV line with it, but that was as far as her anger let her get. She collapsed back against the rotten chair, blinded by tears and sucking at air that felt like wet cement going into her lungs.

"Why?" she asked. "Why did you tell them?"

Instead of replying, Grace opened a packet of gauze and pressed a wad against the leaking vein in Elin's wrist. Her hands were shaking, but she didn't let go. She glanced over her shoulder.

"Could you give us a few minutes?" she said, and the police officers immediately left the room, closing the door behind them. Grace taped the dressing in place and then sat on the arm of the sofa. She looked hollowed out, her eyes dull and her skin pale to the point of transparency. She didn't try to touch Elin again, to hold her hand or feel for the pulse point at her wrist, and Elin, realising how familiar that tactility had become, instantly missed it.

"Do you remember coming here?" Grace asked.

Elin didn't. She didn't even know where "here" was. The last thing she could recall with any clarity was the box that the man hadn't buried Amelia in. God, how long had it been?

"Has he tried to contact me?" she asked.

"No. Not since the churchyard."

"When did they get here?"

"A couple of hours ago."

"He'll kill her," Elin said, her fury getting a second wind. "No police, he told me *no police*. How could you do this without asking?"

Grace bore Elin's onslaught as if she deserved it. She didn't seem to have any fight left in her. "You were dying," she said quietly, as Elin ran out of breath again. "And I couldn't do anything to stop it. I didn't have anything to stop it with."

For the first time, Elin took note of the fresh equipment and replacement drugs. The oxygen had been replenished, and the monitor whose battery had run out late last night was complaining about her heart rate again. Some distant, sensible part of her registered those missing two hours and added several more. "Couldn't you have gone to a hospital?" she said. "You're a doctor, for fuck's sake. They gave all this to the police."

In other circumstances, Grace would probably have tried to calm her. Instead, she reached down and muted the monitor. "They wouldn't have let me walk away with it. They would have asked why I needed it and what I was doing up here, and when I gave my name so they could check I really was a doctor, someone might have recognised it from the news. Safia was discreet. She told one local detective, who told one local doctor, and they kept control of the information between them."

"Safia?" Elin tasted blood when she licked her lips. Her mouth was foul and coated with it. That, combined with the pull of a new drain, strongly suggested her lung had collapsed again.

"Detective Faris." Grace dropped a straw into a bottle of water and held it for Elin. "We saw her on the TV. She was leading the investigation in London, and she and Suds, Detective Sudbury, were most of the way up here when I spoke to her. Lowry's been arrested. He'd put a tracker in the rucksack I binned near the church."

With so much going on, Elin was finding it difficult to compartmentalise, and she barely acknowledged the news about Lowry. On a basic level, it was good to have him out of the way, but he wasn't the one drugging her daughter into a coma. "What if this bastard has seen their car?" she said. "We know he's tracking us as well. How do we know they've not been spotted?"

"I think we'd have heard about it by now. There's no one but us here. He might keep tabs on the burner, but he's never been close by with Amelia, and I can't see any reason for him to change that pattern now. Not when he's absolutely sure you're doing everything he's telling you to do." Grace used more gauze to wipe a dribble of water from Elin's chin. "I won't apologise for contacting Safia, Elin. You asked me to take care of Amelia, and the only way I can keep that promise is by taking care of you."

Her defiance punctured Elin's indignation, leaving nothing but the shame that had become a constant companion where her treatment of Grace was concerned. "You should have left me in that hotel room," she said.

Grace's smile brought life to her tired face. "I probably should've. You don't half cause me some grief."

"Why didn't you?" Elin whispered. She still couldn't fathom the risks Grace had taken for her. Elin had regularly put her own life on the line in the Forces, but the job came with that understanding.

"Honestly?"

Elin nodded. "Honestly."

"I swore an oath as a doctor," Grace said, but then she faltered and her eye contact slipped away. "Honestly," she repeated, as if reminding herself of a commitment. When she raised her head again, she'd obviously reached a decision, because her gaze was rock steady. "Yesterday morning, being so scared of you and then so scared *for* you—that was the first time I'd felt something, *anything* properly since Charlotte died. It hit me like a sledgehammer, and it's not stopped even when things have been awful. I hadn't realised until now how bad the last two years have been. I feel like I've sleepwalked through them."

"And I woke you up by waving a gun in your face?" Elin ventured.

Small splotches of pink fought off the chill to colour Grace's cheeks. "Yes, in a manner of speaking. As soon as you showed me that photograph of Amelia, I knew I'd be sticking with you no matter what. And no," she added before Elin could ask, "I don't have any regrets."

"You should have loads," Elin said. Had she not been effectively bound to the chair, she would have crawled onto the sofa and wrapped her arms around Grace. She made do by taking Grace's hand and interlacing their fingers. "I've been nothing but trouble."

"I'm not going to dispute that. To say you've been a challenge would be a slight understatement." Grace made a little "hmm" sound as a thought occurred to her. "On the plus side, you'll be a hell of a case study for a clinical paper. HEMS docs get up to quite a lot of mischief, medically speaking, but I doubt any of us have been tasked with bullet removal in a Radisson before."

"Well, that's something to look forward to." Feeling far more rational now, Elin took stock of herself, surprised to find that her bonds were all medical in origin. "Am I under arrest?"

"No." Grace chuckled at her raised eyebrow. "How about I sort this IV, and then we get Detectives Safia and Suds in for a chat?"

Elin compared her arms and held out the least contused one. "Do your worst," she said.

SAFIA. SUNDAY, 8:45 P.M.

The mingled scents of spices, garlic, and grease set Safia's stomach rumbling, and she dropped the parcels of reheated takeaway onto the plates Suds had scrubbed in microwave-warmed water and ancient washing-up liquid. This part—catering for people who clearly needed some TLC—she could manage; one of her mum's strictest rules involved hospitality and full bellies. The rest, the small matter of what the hell to do next, was very much up in the air.

"Come on, Saf. These won't stay hot in here for long," Suds said, and she realised she had frozen in the middle of the kitchen floor. Figuratively frozen, though damn near literally, given how cold it was in the caravan. It was still snowing, but the downturn in the weather was simply one problem too many, and she refused to add "What if we can't shift the cars tomorrow?" to her list of things to fret over.

She followed Suds into the living room, where he had wrapped his thick winter coat around Grace's shoulders and cleared space on the coffee table for the plates. Although Elin hadn't moved from the recliner, she was awake and seemed somewhat improved. Her oxygen mask had been downgraded to a nasal tube, and her lips had lost their bluish tinge. Safia had only been able to hear patchy fragments of her argument with Grace through the thin walls, but they must have reconciled, because their hands were clasped together and Elin made no attempt to launch anything in Safia's direction.

"Hey," Safia said. "I'm assuming Grace has told you who we are."

"She has," Elin said. "Sorry about before."

Safia began to arrange the food on the table. "It's okay. This isn't exactly how I thought your case would pan out either."

Elin coughed and shifted in discomfort. "Wish it'd been different."

"Yeah, you and me both. We're going to do everything we possibly can to get your daughter back safely."

"Thank you." Elin didn't seem to have the energy to dispute the point, to tell Safia that there was no "we" and the police had no part to play. Perhaps that would come later, when Safia had actually worked out a counterargument.

For the moment, Grace's priorities seemed far more mundane. She was eyeing the food as a desert wanderer might eye an oasis. "Have you been out?" she asked.

"No, we came prepared," Suds said. "Detective Shaw recommended a local place, and we weren't sure whether you'd have had any supper."

Grace took the plate and napkin Suds held out. "I don't think we had any lunch." She tilted her head, reconsidering. "Or breakfast, come to think of it. I bought sandwiches, but we never ate them."

Safia returned to the seat beside Grace and popped the lid off a tub of kheer. "My gran always made this when I was ill," she said to Elin. "It's basically a rice pud, but Pakistani-style, which involves slow cooking and cardamom, and a family battle over who gets the best bit on top."

Grace propped the tub in Elin's lap and gave her a plastic spoon. "There's lassi if you can't manage," she told her in an undertone.

"I'll manage," Elin said. She was obviously right-handed but gripped the spoon in her left hand and worked it into the tub. Safia added probable nerve damage to Elin's significant array of handicaps and shared a troubled glance with Suds that basically said "we're fucked."

They ate without speaking: no polite chitchat to break the ice, no mention of what might happen tomorrow, and if the silence wasn't quite comfortable, it was at least comradely. Suds brewed up again, and Safia huddled over her cup, letting the steam warm her face and listening to the soft skitter of snow on the windowpane. She had no idea what time it was; there was no traffic to tell her the footy had finished or the local church was emptying out after evening mass. Living in London, she wasn't accustomed to absolute stillness, and she couldn't decide whether the lack of light pollution and noise was eerie or tranquil. She pulled her coat tighter and sipped her tea. The meal had left her full and sleepy, and her face was reminding her she'd skipped her last dose of painkillers, but there was no chance of her getting any rest yet.

"Jo Shaw, the detective here in Moorside, phoned while you and Grace were talking," she told Elin. "You were right: Thomas Elson has three brothers, a twenty-six-year-old son, and a twenty-year-old daughter. One brother doesn't live local, one doesn't appear to be at home, and there's a surveillance team keeping a watch on the third."

Elin dropped the spoon she had been jabbing into her unfinished kheer. "Keeping a watch from where? Jesus, what if he sees them?"

"He won't, Jo assured me of that, and this lad's married with a couple of kids, so he's unlikely to be our suspect. By the sound of it, the sensible money is on the brother who's currently AWOL, or on Elson's son, Kieran, who's not at home either. Kieran has a string of convictions for public order offences but nothing amounting to jail time."

"He'd have been sixteen at the time of his dad's murder," Suds said. "That's the perfect age to have been completely fucked up by it." He cleared his throat. "If you'll excuse the language."

Grace smiled. "I couldn't have put it better myself. I wonder how old he was when he started getting into trouble."

Safia consulted her notes. "His juvenile record is sealed, but the fact that he has one speaks volumes. His early accessible offences were all alcohol or recreational drug related—skirmishes in the street, drunk and disorderly, that kind of thing. He was linked to a more serious assault, but the vic refused to cooperate, which meant there wasn't enough evidence for a prosecution. That was two years ago, and he's been oddly quiet since then."

Suds crunched a poppadom and chewed it thoughtfully. "Maybe he came up with a scheme that's been keeping him occupied. Unless he settled down, married, got a job, and opted to be a peaceable citizen."

Safia helped herself to half of his poppadom. It was his fault for leaving it unguarded. "This may come as a shock, but he was unemployed at the last count. No details on partners, children, or other lifestyle choices. His mum recently remarried and moved to Leeds, and his younger sister is a teacher in Manchester. Jo hasn't contacted them, of course; I think she Facebook-stalked them. She couldn't find any photos of Kieran, but she said she'll keep trawling."

"People make it so simple," Elin said. She had been following the discussion with interest, and Safia could easily picture her holding the floor in a boardroom, keeping her employees on their toes and taking no shit from any of them. "I haven't, though," she continued. "I only use social media for the business, and I never mention Amelia in interviews. There was an enquiry into the Syria deaths, but it was closed-door and the reporting was largely anonymous."

"Is anything truly anonymous these days?" Grace asked. "Your name was probably mentioned somewhere in relation to the enquiry. All it takes then is a phone call to a gullible employee."

"Grace is right," Safia said. She hunched forward. The sofa was more springs than padding, and the room, though marginally warmer with four people in it, was still Baltic. "Whoever is behind this, he's played the long game, and he's been meticulous in his planning, as well as absolutely single-minded. He wasn't deterred by your London trip throwing things out of synch or by the loss of his accomplice. Instead, he's been able to adapt, and he's no doubt drawn you back to wherever he'd intended this to come to a head."

"So what do we do now?" Grace said, voicing the question on everyone's lips.

"Besides wait for him to get in touch?" Safia rechecked her notepad, but she'd flipped it to a blank page that was no help at all. "What I should be doing is calling the National Crime Agency's Anti

Kidnap and Extortion Unit for their assistance, but I'm assuming that won't be an acceptable option."

"No, it's not," Elin said. "No one else can be involved in this. I'm not jeopardising everything at the last minute by bringing in a bunch of experts whose children are all safe and tucked up in bed."

Although she'd started out defiant, the latter part of her reply fell away as her head bobbed, and Safia, accustomed to reading the expressions and body language of countless guilty perps, saw a mum who'd pretty much reached the end of her endurance.

"In which case, you should get some sleep," Safia told her gently.

Elin turned to Grace, whispering, "I need the loo," and Grace began to unhook the IVs and the drain and disconnect the monitor.

"Slowly," Grace warned her, as she righted the recliner and prepared to help Elin stand.

Safia and Suds stood as well, sidelined but ready to step in if needed. Safia could almost hear the grind of Elin's teeth as she shuffled past.

"Christ on a crutch," Suds said, once they were alone in the room. "What the hell are we playing at here, Saf?"

"I don't know, but we need to have every man and his dog on standby tomorrow: ART, negotiator, medics, Tactical Aid. I'll put Jo on it, if she's not already got started. We might be able to get Elin wired if she'll give her consent. Beyond that"—Safia threw up her hands—"I think I'm just going to say a few prayers."

GRACE. SUNDAY, 9:52 P.M.

The snow had turned to rain, the change ushered in by a grey pall of cloud that smothered the caravan park and pockmarked the small drifts. Grace glared at it, furious that it was removing any excuse for Elin to be late the next day and reducing the likelihood that specialised teams could get into position beforehand.

"Why haven't the local police, detectives or whatever, stomped in here and taken over?" she asked Safia and Suds, who were huddled with her on the sofa, sharing a packet of biscuits. "This isn't your patch, so you don't have jurisdiction here, do you?"

Safia looked as guilty as a burglar caught toting a bag of swag. "I'm sure they would have, if they actually knew where we were."

Grace was so taken aback that she inhaled a crumb and set off coughing. "You haven't told them?" she spluttered.

"Would Elin still be here if I had?"

It was a good point. Elin was the kidnapper's sole contact. Without her cooperation, the case would crumple, and the mass invasion of a multi-agency task force would have ended that cooperation in a heartbeat.

"Our detective inspector, and Jo's, are on board with this," Safia continued. "I'm not going to lie and say they're over the moon about it, but they're supporting this approach for the moment."

Grace nibbled the edge of her chocolate digestive. Suds had been so pleased to find them at the bottom of his overnight bag that she hadn't had the heart to refuse one, but every bite reminded her of Amelia and the faulty biscuits, and she was glad Elin was fast asleep.

"Are we going to get you in trouble?" she asked.

Safia dunked her biscuit, the gesture far more relaxed than her expression. "That probably depends on the outcome of the case. We'll have a better chance of a positive one if Elin agrees to wear a wire and accepts the involvement of our teams."

"You want me to persuade her, don't you?" Grace knew the question was rhetorical. She also knew it would be a miracle if Elin was able to walk unaided tomorrow, let alone drive, though she didn't say so.

"She might listen to you," Suds said. "I'm sure she won't listen to us, despite our not inconsiderable charms."

If he'd aimed to make Grace smile, he succeeded. "I'd listen to you," she said, through a yawn.

He rooted in the holdall by his feet, pulled out a towel, and went into the hallway. She thought he'd gone to the bathroom, but he returned seconds later, wrapping the towel around a pillow.

"In which case, Doc, I reckon it's time for you to get some shut-eye." He plumped up the pillow and placed it at her end of the sofa. "I'm guessing you'd rather stay in here with Elin."

"Yes, thank you." Another yawn caught her off-guard, and before she knew anything about it, she was lying down, snuggled into his thick coat.

"We'll wake you if anything happens," Safia said, unintentionally echoing an assurance Grace had given Elin countless times over.

They left the red lamp on, its glow too subdued to be anything but soporific, and Grace closed her eyes, willing her brain to switch off and allow her to catnap. She pulled the coat closer, wrapping her arms across her torso. She could still feel a slight sting on her wrist where Elin had gripped her on the way to the toilet, her cold fingers digging in even harder as she staggered past Safia and Suds.

A snuffled cough made Grace's eyes fly open, but Elin slept on undisturbed and nothing was setting off alarm bells on the monitor. Reassured, Grace thumped her lumpy pillow and settled her head in a suitable hollow. She drifted, stirred, and drifted again, the same single thought chasing her into and out of sleep: she had stayed with Elin through all of this, and she wasn't going to let her down now.

ELIN. MONDAY, 4:02 A.M.

Elin woke in fits and starts, cold and thirsty and nagged by a constant low-level pain that reminded her not to do anything sudden, or at all if she could help it. The living room was dark, a check of her watch confirming that dawn was still three hours away. The only thing she could hear was Grace's soft, regular breathing.

"Grace?" Elin hardly made a sound, and Grace, more attuned to noises of distress or alerts on the monitor, didn't stir. Moving with the utmost caution, Elin studied the readings on the screen and then lifted the drain to gauge its contents. Grace had disconnected the IVs, leaving the access bandaged into place, and the oxygen was only running at a couple of litres. Taking courage from these small signs of improvement, Elin raised her voice.

"Grace?"

"Hmm?" Habit, no doubt ingrained by long hours on call and a body clock destroyed by shift work, simultaneously snapped Grace from sleep and brought her to a sitting position. "Are you okay? Did he call?" she asked.

"No, he didn't, and I'm fine." Elin spoke with certainty, bolstered by her clinical observations. "Sorry to wake you."

"It's all right. Do you need the loo?"

"Not right now." Bracing herself, Elin pushed down with her legs to force the chair upright. "I want you to take the drain out."

"What? Now? What time is it?"

"Four."

"Oh."

"I don't think he'll leave it too long," Elin said.

"We don't know that." Grace still looked worried. "What if he waits till tonight?"

"I think we'll have to risk it." Elin winced, acknowledging that that wasn't the best of endorsements. "He's likely to give me a tight window, and we can't be messing around with minor surgery while the damn clock is ticking. How long did I last without it the first time?"

"About sixteen hours."

Elin nodded. "Realistically, a knackered lung is going to be the least of my problems, isn't it?"

Grace didn't argue, instead getting up from the sofa to start sorting through her kit. She seemed different somehow, as if a few hours' rest had revitalised her, and she set out her equipment with confidence.

"Is that thunder or Suds snoring?" she asked, removing the drain's dressing as a low rumble Elin had assumed was a plane engine reverberated through the walls.

"Christ, his wife must really love him," Elin said. "I don't snore, do I?"

Grace snipped a suture free. "No. At the moment, you wheeze, cough, and occasionally sound like you're gargling with porridge, but you don't snore."

Elin felt heat rush to her cheeks, which was a novelty in the current climate. "How attractive."

Grace shrugged. "I wouldn't kick you out of bed for eating crackers." Distracted by the local anaesthetic she was injecting, she seemed to have spoken without really thinking, and her blush rivalled Elin's when she looked up. "Well, I wouldn't," she said, unapologetic, and Elin laughed right up until the moment Grace pulled the tube out.

"Bloody hell!"

"Sorry. You'd have tensed if I'd warned you."

Elin breathed through her nose, waiting out the discomfort. "I didn't know you had such a devious streak."

"I hide it well." Grace selected a curved needle and began to reclose the wound left by the drain. "Safia wanted me to talk to you."

Elin stiffened in the chair. It had felt good, just for a moment, to pretend things were normal. "What about?"

Grace continued to work, her face hidden in the shadows. "About today. About you possibly wearing a wire, and whether or not you'd allow some sort of backup to go with you."

Elin wasn't arrogant or suicidal. Whenever she had been lucid enough, she had tried to imagine how involving the police might work to her advantage—the only problem being that she couldn't.

"If their kit was to a high enough spec, I'd wear a wire," she said. "But it would be useless without an earpiece, and it runs the risk of bringing more personnel here to supply and fit it. It's the same with backup." She looked at Grace, wanting to convince her that she wasn't dismissing the options lightly. "If I had my team, we'd have a chance. This is what we did. We were trained for this kind of covert infiltration and surveillance. No disrespect to the police, but they aren't. We'll get no warning from this arsehole, no opportunity to prepare or strategise, and we already know he's savvy with tech, so he'll probably have a way to monitor my approach. All he'll need to do is get a drone up and he's got the surrounding area covered."

She stopped talking as her throat went into spasm, breaking her words apart. A few sips of water eased the choking sensation, but the terror that had caused it was still there.

"I don't want to die," she whispered. "I'd trade my life for Amelia's in a heartbeat, but I don't want to leave her on her own. I want to watch her grow up, Grace. Her birth mum didn't give a shit about her; I don't want her to think I abandoned her as well." She was crying, the tears streaking hot lines down her cheeks. Grace quickly tied off the last suture and passed her a tissue.

"Don't be getting upset," she said. "We'll sort something. It'll be all right." It would have been a trite sentiment, had her voice not sounded so odd and tight. She took the tissue back and caught a tear before it dripped off Elin's nose. "It'll be all right," she said again, firm and fearless, and for a blissful second or two, Elin actually believed her.

SAFIA. MONDAY, 5:28 A.M.

Safia caught hold of the quilt as Suds executed an impressive tuck-and-roll manoeuvre to drag it more firmly around him. She no longer cared that it was filthy and moth-eaten; it was warm, and she'd be damned if she was relinquishing her half of it.

"Oi!" She poked her toe into his midriff as he set off snoring again. He grunted but didn't wake, letting her return to her study of the ceiling's numerous mould stains. The buzz of her phone came as a welcome interruption, even more so when she saw it was Kami on a video call. Habit made her run a hand through her hair, before she acknowledged the futility of her efforts and accepted the call.

"Morning, sunshine," Kami said and then peered into the screen. "Where are you?"

"Right here." Safia switched on the bedside lamp and laughed as Kami recoiled. "Oh, sod off, I don't look that bad." She touched her hair again. Little was left of the knot she had tied it into. "Do I?"

Kami was ready for work: glowing from the shower and wearing one of Safia's favourite headscarves, with red swirling across a bright yellow base. When she smiled, all Safia's worries and aches seemed to melt away.

"You look beautiful," Kami said. "But also very tired and rather bruised. What the hell is that noise? Are you on a farm?"

Safia panned the phone around until Suds's face filled the screen. "We topped and tailed."

"And how did that work out for you?"

"Not brilliantly." Safia had marked the passing of almost every hour, and woken properly at four when she heard Grace and Elin talking and moving around. She had been so relieved to hear Elin's voice that she hadn't been able to settle again since.

"Mm-hm." Kami did a fine impersonation of her gran's sternest look. "I hope he's making the breakfast."

Safia grimaced, considering the state of the kitchen. "The facilities here are somewhat lacking. We might be safer sticking with jam sarnies." She turned away from Suds a little. She didn't want to waste the call talking nonsense, not when Kami was the only person she could have this conversation with. "Kami, I think I might be out of my depth here."

Kami nodded. She wasn't one to offer placation without cause. "How so?"

"Where do I start?" Safia wanted to get up and pace, but she was afraid of waking Suds. "We just don't do this kind of thing on the MIT. We solve murders, and interview grubby little scumbags, and argue with the CPS. We don't get involved with kidnappings, and we certainly don't let badly injured civilians walk into a hostage situation."

"Ah," Kami said. "Shit."

"Yeah. She's not going to let us interfere. I know that without even asking her, and if I press too hard, she'll probably cut us out of the loop altogether, unless I arrest her or something. Grace is playing go-between for me, but if push comes to shove, she'll side with Elin, and I can't even blame her for that."

"What's Chevs had to say?" Kami asked.

"Plenty." Safia had updated him just before going to bed, which was another reason she hadn't slept well. "He's pleased we're likely to get a good outcome on the murder, but he wanted to involve the National Crime Agency—with or without Elin's consent—and I had to tell him what I just told you. He was all for coming up here to rattle some sense into her, but I managed to talk him round."

Kami shook her head, her eyes glistening with tears. "You told him you'd take the blame, didn't you?"

"Yes," Safia whispered. "I said I'd accept full responsibility for all decisions made, and that he could say I'd stepped beyond my authority and acted outside of my remit if it all goes to shit."

"You're a bloody idiot," Kami said. "I love you to bits, but you're a bloody idiot."

"I know." Safia understood exactly what would happen to her if things ended badly. She only hoped she could protect Suds from the fallout. "I couldn't think of anything else, and I'm still not sure it worked. Chevs might be on his way up here with a whole brigade of reinforcements, and that'll be that. Elin's right about one thing: the more people involved in this, the more chance there is of this bloke cutting his losses and killing her little girl."

"If he hasn't done that already," Kami said.

Safia cupped the screen, as if she might be able to feel the warm skin of Kami's face if she tried hard enough. "I don't think he has. I've no doubt that he's planning to, but I think he'll be waiting for Elin. There's no point to all this otherwise."

"What a fucking psycho." Kami kept her voice low, but she was obviously livid. "How twisted in the head is he, if he thinks murdering a child will set any of this right?"

"Very, at a guess." The room seemed colder all of a sudden, and Safia inched closer to Suds's leg just to feel something solid and human. On the screen, apprehension was written all over Kami's face. "Will you still love me if I fuck this up?"

All the worry lines faded from Kami's face as she smiled and blew Safia a kiss. "I'll always love you," she said.

GRACE. MONDAY, 6:25 A.M.

"How's that? Any better?" Grace continued to play the warm flannel across Elin's face and neck, as Elin, her eyes half shut, murmured an affirmative. Trying to quell the thought of preparing a victim for their execution, Grace dipped the flannel again and dampened Elin's hair.

When Grace had gone to the car for clean clothes, she'd found Elin's wash-bag full of Amelia's shampoo and bubble bath. Not knowing whether emptying them out would be worse than bringing them into the caravan, she had erred on the side of caution and left the bag untouched in the boot. Safia, seeing her readying a towel and filling a bowl of water, had shared out her own stash of overnight toiletries, and the piquant scent of her apricot body scrub was a welcome change to that of blood and the caravan's general mucky miasma.

Elin blinked as water trickled onto her eyelashes. "It's getting light."

"Hard to tell, really," Grace said, but Elin was right. A pale grey line was edging into the darkness and swirling patterns through the mist cloaking the hillside. "It's still pouring down, though."

Elin inclined her head, listening to the ping of rain on the roof. "We always fall back on the weather, don't we? Brits, I mean. In times of crisis, we can always get by just talking about the weather."

"Mm." Grace combed Elin's hair, dividing the bedraggled strands into some semblance of a style. "Weather, or how to pronounce 'scone.'"

"It rhymes with 'gone,' you philistine," Elin said, but then caught Grace's wrist, stilling her hand. "I'm so scared, Grace."

"I know." Grace put the comb down and carefully pulled Elin into her arms. "I don't think I can say anything to make this right." She felt Elin's breath stutter out of her, felt the thump of her pulse and the fine tremors of fear and cold. Then the burner phone started to ring, its volume ramped up high so they wouldn't miss it, and they broke apart, Elin making a clumsy grab that knocked the phone to the floor.

"*Shit.*"

Grace stooped and returned it, but not before she'd seen the screen. "It's a video call!" she shouted, alerting Safia, who had rushed into the room, and sending her straight out again. As soon as the door clicked shut behind her, Elin accepted the call.

No one spoke. From Grace's position, she could still see the WhatsApp window, a dark blur coalescing into a man's shape, then a face abruptly coming into focus. No mask, no balaclava, just an unshaven white man with a mop of dark hair and bloodshot eyes full of spite. The family resemblance to Thomas Elson was unmistakeable, but he was too young to be Elson's brother. Behind him, a stone wall gave no clue as to his whereabouts, and there was no sign of Amelia. His smile bared his chipped tooth, confirming his identity as Elin's assailant.

"You know who I am, don't you?" he said at length.

"Yes. You're his son," Elin said, but she went no further, letting him control the conversation.

Kieran Elson nodded, seeming satisfied with her response. "Today's the day, then. You ready to come and get your kid?"

"Yes." Although she managed to keep her voice level, every part of her was rigid with tension. "I need to see her first."

Demand proof of life, Safia had told her last night. Don't agree to anything until he's given you that.

His jaw clenched, clacking his teeth together. Even on the poor-quality video, Grace could see he was flushed and sweating. Unless he was running a fever or had the central heating on full blast, cocaine or amphetamines were a likely cause. He was studying Elin as if she were an insect he had pinned.

"Do you, now?" he said.

"Yes." Elin was too breathless to sound imposing. "Or I don't go anywhere."

His laugh was harsh and humourless. "You don't look fucking *capable* of going anywhere, you stupid bitch." The screen shook as he began to pace, his face disappearing and reappearing at random. "I've given you every chance, and you look like you're going to drop at any fucking moment. Why the hell am I even bothering with this crap?"

Grace saw despair flit across Elin's face as she struggled for a response. Without saying anything, Grace calmly took the phone from her.

"No, don't," Elin said. She grasped at Grace's arm, but Grace easily moved beyond her reach.

"Kieran." She snapped his name, stopping him in his tracks, and he peered into the screen with fresh interest.

"I've seen you on the news," he said. "You're that doctor."

"I am." Unlike Elin, Grace was able to match the hardness of his tone. She had been dealing with cocky pieces of shit like him for years. All she had been waiting for was the opening he'd just handed her. "And I can make sure Elin gets to you."

"Yeah?"

"Yeah," Grace said. "You know damn well she's not going to get there on her own." She heard Elin say her name, begging for her to return the phone, and walked into the middle of the room, ignoring the increasing desperation of Elin's demands.

"You want to come with her," he said, incredulous.

"Yes. None of this is going to work otherwise." She knew he had a plan, a plan he could undoubtedly see unravelling before him, and she only had one card left to play. She swallowed, feeling sick. "I can wake her daughter up for you."

That got his attention. He stared at her, his nostrils flaring. Somewhere in her periphery, Elin covered her face with her hands and sobbed.

"How the fuck you gonna do that?" he asked, but he sounded more curious than sceptical.

"I can give her a drug to reverse the one you've been dosing her up with." Grace made it sound simple, and it was, in theory. In reality, there were far too many variables to guarantee success, but she wasn't going to tell him that. She just needed him to believe it was possible. Tuning out the sounds Elin was making, she went for broke. "What's the point of going to all this trouble if she's just going to sleep through it?"

She saw the instant he made his decision. Exhilaration lit up his face, and he squared his shoulders, broadening his chest.

"Okay, then, if you're stupid enough to want to do this, you can come with her. Forty-five minutes, with the money. I'll send the address. Park at the turn-off and walk the rest of the way."

"Right." There was no time for Grace to contest the specifics. "Show me Amelia."

He didn't argue. He took a couple of steps and then crouched and re-angled the phone until Amelia's profile filled the screen. Deeply unconscious, with vomit-stained lips, she looked worse than she had yesterday morning, but a twitch of her nose confirmed she was still alive.

"Jesus," Grace said, before she could stop herself.

Kieran turned the phone around. "See you in"—he tapped his watch—"forty-three minutes." He waved and cut off the call.

Still clutching the phone, Grace went back to kneel by Elin.

"What the hell have you done?" Elin said.

"Exactly what I needed to." Grace checked the phone as it vibrated. Two messages: a local address, and a stock photo of a drone, along with the warning: *I'll see you coming.* Mindful of the countdown he had started, she patted her jacket for the car key. She would need to organise her kit and the drugs, and tell Safia what had happened, and simply keep moving, because if she stopped to think then everything would fall apart.

"Grace." Elin's voice had lost its edge. She just sounded bewildered, thrown by a gambit Grace had fixed upon but never discussed. "Are you really going to come with me?"

"Yes, I am." Grace kissed her forehead. "Shall we let Safia in and break the news?"

SAFIA. MONDAY, 6:45 A.M.

The Ordnance Survey map rumpled and peaked as Safia threw it open. To her left, a double crack of cartilage told her Elin had managed to kneel with her. Working from the postcode on Kieran's message, Jo's breakneck internet search had identified an isolated rental cottage at the foot of the Saddleworth moors. Google Earth showed it surrounded by pastureland, approximately four hundred yards from the turn-off he had ordered Grace to park at. Safia slapped a hand on the worst of the map's creases, flicked her phone to speaker, and set it on the carpet.

"Suds found an OS map stuffed in a wardrobe. The area code is 277," she told Jo, as Elin cross-referenced the postcode's address with Jo's directions and the map covering half the living room floor. She shook her head when Elin stuck her thumb on a specific point. "Bloody hell, this place is not going to be easy to sneak up on."

"I'm guessing that's the idea," Jo said. "It's sixteen minutes' normal travel time from your current location. Twenty-three on blues from ours. Shit. How long do we have?"

"Thirty-four," Suds called on his way past with one of Grace's medical bags.

"Bollocks," Jo spat, and then yelled "Well, hurry the fuck up, then," to someone in the background. "Okay, we'll be leaving in the next five," she told Safia. "I've got Armed Response and Tactical Aid with me. The negotiator's running from home, so he'll be twenty minutes or so behind. North West Ambulance are sending a couple of buses to stand by with us, and their chopper and Yorkshire's have been given a heads-up as well. How close do you think we'll be able to get?"

Safia turned to Elin, who'd used a marker pen to plot the access route and highlight potential points of cover.

"The cottage is at a slightly higher elevation than we are here, so it should be thick with fog," Elin said. "He'll still be able to get a drone up, though, and we'll have to assume it's capable of infrared until proven otherwise, which means he'll be able to see the teams if they set out too soon." She circled a patch of woodland that crept alongside the fields for a distance. "Armed and Tactical could approach through the woods at grid 245673, but beyond its perimeter they'd be far too exposed. All he'd need to do is look out a window at the wrong moment." She didn't sound particularly unhappy about that. She seemed amenable to the police coming along, now that she was sure they couldn't actually intervene.

"I'll pass that on," Jo said. "We need to make a move. Good luck to you both. Safia, keep in touch." She hung up without waiting for an answer, her urgency making Safia antsy to leave as well. If they were really going to go through with this, she didn't want them to faceplant at the first hurdle.

The pen dropped from Elin's fist, and Safia picked it up and slid it back between her clawed fingers.

"Thanks." Elin's expression was strained, and she was shuffling constantly, unable to find a comfortable position. "I didn't mean for Grace to get involved," she said quietly. They hadn't spoken much about the deal Grace had made. Grace had presented it to Safia as a fait accompli and rushed outside with Suds to pack the ransom and sort her equipment.

"I know you didn't," Safia said. With hindsight, though, she should have seen it coming. Grace was as protective of Elin as a lioness with a new cub, and her offer to Kieran hadn't come out of nowhere; the baited hook she'd dropped had been prepared in advance, and he'd duly swallowed it whole. Had Safia not wanted to knock her and Elin's heads together, she would have been impressed.

She refolded the map and helped Elin to her feet, where gravity made her reel and pant for air. Safia took her arm, and Elin shook her head in dismay.

"I won't get there without her, will I?" The question dropped like a guilty verdict. She looked and sounded devastated.

"No." There was no reason for Safia to lie, when the damage was already done. "I don't think you will."

A sudden draught of cold air and the stomping of boots announced the return of Grace and Suds. Grace came over to Elin and ushered her onto the sofa, setting a holdall by her feet.

"I just need to draw these drugs up, then we're good to go." She snapped a glass vial and dipped a needle-topped syringe into it, eyeballing Elin as she did so. "What's your pain score?"

"Four," Elin said. "It's bearable."

"Why do I even ask?" Grace took Elin's bandaged wrist and uncapped its IV port. "Tell me when it's really bearable," she said, injecting a clear drug.

Elin let her get a couple of markers down on the syringe and then nodded.

"Honestly?" Grace was studying Elin's face as if searching for tells. Seeming satisfied, she broke into a new vial and began to repeat the process of drawing it up.

"What's that?" Elin said.

"Narcan." Grace didn't explain, but Safia recognised the drug from her time as a response officer.

"Will it work?" she asked.

"It should, but it all depends on what he's been giving her. Narcan will reverse the effects of opioids, and this"—she started on another vial—"will reverse benzos like diazepam." She topped both syringes with fresh, large needles and zipped up the bag. "Right, then. Let's go."

Grace. Monday, 7:04 a.m.

Grace hit the brakes for a bend that seemed to come out of nowhere, its warning chevrons lost in an opaque murk of early dawn and blanket fog. The road was empty, bar the odd long-distance commuter, and she was pushing the speed limit as hard as she dared, unsure whether the deadline they'd been set accounted for Elin hiking along a single-lane track. If it didn't, they were going to miss it.

"Why's he doing that, anyway?" she said, forgetting she'd been having this conversation with herself.

Elin, who was alternating between staring at the dashboard clock and following their progress on the satnav, tore her focus from the latter. "Doing what?"

"Making us walk."

"Because he's an arsehole." Elin's answer, fuelled by loathing, came quickly, but she tapped her foot on the car mat and gave the question more thought. "It'll give him plenty of time to ID us. If we got out of a car by his front door, he'd have a few seconds to decide whether it was us or an armed unit ready to batter their way in. It'll also allow him to monitor any potential backup. The longer his drone is up, the less chance there is of anyone getting close to the house before we go in." She checked the satnav again. They were three-quarters of a mile from the turn-off. "Grace…"

"What?"

Elin was back to watching the clock. "Please don't wake her up," she whispered. "I don't want her to know what's happening."

For the first time, Grace was grateful for the adverse conditions, because the corner she was spinning the car around stopped her having to face Elin. At some barely remembered point in the night, she had committed to the plan she was now neck-deep in, and its success had been contingent on not warning Elin beforehand. The video call had made it even easier, with Elin's revulsion captured live and in colour, all the better to convince Kieran that this would be the cherry on top of whatever else he had in mind for her. One of the hardest things Grace had ever done was hide the filthy sensation crawling across her skin as she used Amelia as a bargaining chip.

"Let's see what happens," she said, unable to make any guarantees. If treating Amelia was her only way to buy Elin more time, she knew she would do it.

She slowed the car as the satnav began a fifty-yard countdown to a left-hand turn, where a wooden sign above a tarnished mailbox read "Honeysuckle Cottage." She parked on the verge of a rough lane, its pothole-ridden tarmac patchy with puddles and flanked by tall hedges of holly and hawthorn. The text she sent Safia from her own phone was a pre-written "On foot," and she tossed her phone onto the back seat without waiting for a reply.

The first thing she heard as she got out of the car was a waspish buzz, the noise encroaching but impossible to pin down, until she opened Elin's door for her and the drone swooped over the hedge. They stood obediently, letting it zoom in on them. Then Grace collected her holdall and went back to loop Elin's good arm around her.

"I don't think we need to rush now, do we?" she said as they set off at a reasonable but unsustainable pace.

"Probably not. He's confirmed we're here and on our own."

Elin's answer puffed warm across Grace's cheek, and Grace found herself trying to memorise everything: the delicate feel of the mist on her lashes, the deep green spikes of the holly leaves, and the roll of loose stones beneath her boots. She hugged Elin close, listening to her breathe, to the hitch at the end of every exhalation that told Grace how much this was taking out of her. The drone flitted above them like a curious insect, monitoring their every step, and Grace gradually slowed, letting Elin lean more comfortably upon her.

"I've got you," she murmured. "Keep going. I've got you."

SAFIA. MONDAY, 7:11 A.M.

The National Trust car park, hidden amidst trees a mile from the cottage turn-off, was the perfect place for an emergency rendezvous, and the weather seemed to have deterred even the hardiest of hikers, because every space was empty.

"They've just left the car," Safia told Suds as he reversed into the first bay. "Jo's ETA is two. I'm not going to ask what speed they've been doing."

"Might be for the best." Suds took the key from the ignition, but rather than pocketing it, he began to pick at the fake leather on the fob. "This is crazy, Saf. We're going to get them all killed."

She didn't bite his head off or ask whether he had any brighter ideas. If he'd had an alternative strategy, he would have told her. Sometimes he needed to state the obvious before he could get on with things.

A flash of headlights behind them stopped her from having to answer, but she prised the fob from his hand and gave his fingers a squeeze. "Come on," she said. "Grab that map just in case."

As they got out of the car, Jo ran around to the rear of the police van she'd arrived in and flung open its doors. "You're up, Ben," she said to the lad in the back, and he swapped places with her, carrying a small drone. "It's got great range and thermal vision capability," she told Safia. "And he swears Kieran won't see it coming."

Safia watched Ben tinker with the drone's settings. "Elin and Grace are on the lane. Can you get this in behind the cottage and confirm occupancy before they arrive?"

"Yep," he said, confidence personified. "I can take it out so wide, he'll never suspect a thing, especially if he's focused his own on them."

"Excellent. Do we have an ETA on Armed Response?"

Jo distributed handsets and earpieces for the comms. "Five."

"Okay." Safia settled her earpiece into place, automatically tuning out the chatter on the channel. "If we can say for sure there are only two people in the cottage, I'm happy for Armed Response and the TAU to approach through the woods once Elin and Grace are inside. If Kieran is on his own with Amelia, we're going to have to take a leap and assume he won't be able to deal with them and keep an eye on the exterior at the same time. If we see three heat signatures, suggesting an accomplice, then we're fucked."

"Should have an answer for you in approximately"—Ben sent the drone zipping into the air—"ninety seconds."

The ART and TAU vans careered into the car park as the drone swooped above the trees and vanished into the mist.

"If anyone needs a fag, they have it now," Safia said. "I want them ready to go the second we get feedback from Ben."

Jo gave her a curt nod. She'd probably had as little sleep as Safia, but she was bouncing with adrenaline. "They'll be ready, and the paramedics are en route. Negotiator's somewhere on the outskirts of central Manchester, the useless shite."

Safia thought of Grace and Elin making their way up the lane, trusting her to have the rest of this sorted just in case, but willing to go in alone regardless. All things considered, a missing negotiator was the least of their problems.

"I've got the cottage in sight," Ben yelled from the back of the van. "Two heat signatures still on the lane, closing at around fifty yards."

Safia clambered in beside him and peered at a laptop monitor showing indistinct outlines of black and grey.

"That's the cottage," he said. "I'm high behind it, and if he has a drone capable of catching this one, I'll show my arse." He tapped a button that probably didn't need tapping. "Sorry, Sarge."

"Not a problem. Carry on."

He pushed his glasses higher on his nose and twiddled one of the drone's controls. "Single heat signature in the first ground-floor room." He marked a splash of colour on the laptop screen. "Smaller signature toward the rear, probably in a different room."

"Smaller as in child-sized?" she asked.

"Most likely. Two confirmed, Sarge. There's no one else there."

She looked at Suds, who opened his hand to show the car key. "Ready when you are," he said.

Grace. Monday, 7:27 a.m.

Grace could see the cottage now: a pleasant stone building with curtains drawn at its sash windows. Beyond the garden gate, a stepped path wound between well-tended flower beds and lawns. Whoever owned this cottage, they'd certainly never intended it to be used for this purpose.

The drone overtook them to hover above the front door like a benevolent host. At one point, she could have sworn she heard a second, more muted whine, but she hadn't been able to identify its source.

"Almost there," she said to Elin. She didn't know how Elin had managed those final few yards; she was limping so badly that her foot was carving a trail through the mud, but the sight of the cottage door opening rammed steel into her spine, and she walked up the steps almost unaided.

"Put your hands out in front of you and get inside." The order came from beyond the darkened doorway, a shift in the light and shadows revealing Kieran's form in irregular bursts. He was tall and well built, with tattooed sleeves on thickly muscled biceps, and Grace didn't want to go anywhere near him. She raised her hands when Elin did, holding them outstretched before her and willing them not to tremble. The smell of coffee and fried bacon hit her as she crossed the threshold into a traditional country kitchen— range cooker, Belfast sink crammed with dirty pots. She couldn't see Amelia anywhere, and the thought of Kieran preparing a hearty breakfast that morning made her want to take her chances and go for his throat.

He took a step toward them, staying well clear of the window above the sink, and shifted his right hand to show the gun in it.

"Close and bolt the door, Doc. Then put the bag down."

He didn't bother to point the gun at her, and she didn't attempt to defy him. The bolts slid easily into place, and she stayed crouching by the lower one for a moment, gathering her courage.

"Bag," he warned her.

"It's the money and my medical kit." She lowered the strap from her shoulder and put the bag on a well-trodden hearth rug. "For Amelia."

"Kick it over to me."

She did as he instructed, mesmerised by the weak stream of daylight playing off the gun as he opened each of the bag's pockets in turn. Satisfied with its contents, he tossed a length of electrical cord into the no-man's land between them.

"Use that to tie her hands," he told Grace. "Behind her back. Tight. No fucking around."

"Where's my daughter?" Elin said, apparently tired of being an observer. "You have the money, and we've done everything you've asked, so where is she?"

He ignored her and aimed the gun at the centre of Grace's chest. "Tie her hands. Now."

"I will," Grace said. "I will, I'll do it. Just stay calm." She bent to retrieve the cord, but before she could straighten, Elin had barrelled past her, shoving her out of the line of fire with one hand as she threw herself at Kieran. He batted her away as if swatting a fly, stepping into her double-fisted blow and slamming the gun into her face. Propelled back against the wall, she hit the stone hard and crumpled in a heap.

"Elin!" Forgetting everything else, Grace knelt and grabbed at Elin's shoulders, rolling her onto her side. She was conscious but bleeding heavily from a gash on her cheek.

"Sorry," Elin whispered. "Had to try."

"Shh." Grace leaned over her, trying to shield her, but Kieran kicked her onto her front and pressed her down with his boot.

"Tie her fucking hands." He was quivering with rage, and he emphasised every word with a jerk of the gun.

Still on her knees, Grace brought Elin's hands together and wrapped the cord around her wrists, pulling it taut enough to whiten the skin and then double-knotting it. "Is that all right?" she asked him, keen to delay any further escalation.

"Yeah." He shoved his boot under Elin's chest, lifting her a fraction. "Get her up."

Grace scrambled to comply, lugging Elin onto her feet and keeping her there by leaning her against the wall. Kieran spat onto the rug between her boots, then fisted the back of her jacket and shoved her in front of him.

"Get your bag and go first, Doc." He gestured to the adjoining door, and Grace walked ahead of them, collecting her bag and entering a cosy, fire-lit living room. He switched on an Anglepoise lamp, its bulb perfectly positioned to spotlight the child lying prostrate on the sofa. Behind her, Grace heard Elin gasp, and then a scuffle that ended with a sharp slap and a thud. When she dared to turn around, Elin was on her knees, facing Amelia, with Kieran holding the gun to her head.

"I wasn't sure which would work best," he said to Elin. "I thought killing you in front of your kid would do it, but she's too young to be really fucked over by that, so I think I'll switch it around."

With an obvious effort, Elin tore her gaze from Amelia to look at him. "Do you think this is what your dad would have wanted?" she said quietly. She didn't sound afraid, she sounded heartbroken. "He went to Syria to help children. That was the sole reason he was there. How will any of this put right what happened to him?"

"Maybe I'll get the chance to ask him," Kieran said. "You're going to be the only one left standing, Elin. You get to carry this now, like I've carried it." He went to a bookcase and took a machete off the top shelf, angling it toward Amelia as if pondering the correct technique. Frowning, he swapped it for a knife with a broad, serrated blade. "They used one like this on my dad. Did you know that?"

"No, I didn't know that," Elin said, but she could have been answering anything. She was tracking the knife and its proximity to Amelia, and she'd brought one knee up like a sprinter on the block.

"They posted a video, and I wasn't supposed to watch it, but what sixteen-year-old kid ever does as he's told?" He touched the tip of the blade to Elin's throat and then pushed it in, drawing a bead of blood onto the metal. "They started cutting him here."

Elin froze. Grace couldn't even see her breathing.

"Kieran, *stop.*" Grace put as much authority as she could into the command, and it worked, insofar as he withdrew the knife a fraction. She couldn't maintain it, though. "Please, you need to stop this now. We can all walk out of here. Please, just stop it."

He laughed at her. "I don't think so, Doc. Wake the kid up."

"No!" Elin yelled. "Grace, don't." The knife went back, cutting deeper, making her moan. "Please don't," she said, oblivious to the blade, her attention entirely on Grace. "Grace, *please.*"

Grace held up her hands. "I'm not doing anything unless you move that knife."

He glared at her like a wild animal, his nostrils flaring and his pupils so dilated that they blacked out his irises. "Fucking do it," he said, but he lowered the knife, allowing Elin to gulp rapidly for air.

"Fine." Grace unzipped the holdall. "I need to get her on the floor. I can't manage her breathing from that position." She took out an oxygen cylinder and a ventilation bag and placed a needle-topped syringe beside them.

"Don't fucking touch her," Elin snarled. She was trying to get up, but Kieran kicked her in the small of her back and strode over to the sofa.

"Put her right here," Grace told him.

He lifted Amelia within her nest of blankets, as if unwilling to acknowledge there was a child wrapped up in them, and laid her where Grace indicated.

"Thank you." Grace put a hand on Amelia's forehead. She was cool and clammy, her breaths fitful shallow rasps. "What have you been giving her?"

He shrugged, interested enough in the process to stay in a crouch beside them. "Diazies, mainly. Some morphine I nicked off my mam. That going to wake her up?"

"Yes, it should." Grace took the cap from the needle, and he leaned closer, the knife held loosely in his left hand, the gun in his right.

Gun, Grace decided, and stabbed the needle through the back of his right hand.

He howled in shock and pain, his wrist flexing, and she dived over Amelia to grapple for the gun he'd lost his grip on. Her fingertips grazed the metal, but he recovered far more quickly than she'd anticipated, punching and lashing out at her. The skin above her eye split, raining blood across her vision, and then he was gone, smashed aside by Elin hurling herself bodily at him, catching him full force with her shoulder and taking them both to the floor. Grace lunged for the gun again, getting hold of it in both hands, the metal instantly slick with her blood. In the corner, Kieran was back on his feet, and she saw a flash of silver and crimson as he raised the knife above Elin's prone form. She reeled around and pulled the trigger hard, knocked off balance by the blast and the recoil and the pure terror of what would happen if she missed. He staggered, a dark patch blossoming on his thigh, but he didn't go down. He lurched forward, coming for Amelia, his knife swinging in another high arch. Grace fired without thinking, aiming for his chest but striking lower to blow a hole in his guts. His mouth fell open, and the knife clattered to the floor as he clutched at his belly. He sank to his knees and then tipped onto all fours, his eyes never leaving Elin.

"I hate you, you bitch. I hope you fucking die too," he muttered through reddened teeth, but his arms couldn't hold him, and he dropped, his chin bouncing off the floor. Knocked senseless, he grunted and fell still.

"Oh God." Grace crawled across to Elin, who hadn't reacted to the gunshots and wasn't moving. "Elin?" Grace shook her, putting an ear close to her mouth. She was breathing, but her lung had obviously collapsed again, and blood foamed at her lips. *"Elin!"*

Elin's eyelids flickered, and she coughed, spraying blood onto the carpet. "Mouse?" she whispered.

Grace cried out in relief. "I've got her. Don't try to get up, okay? I'll be right back." She sprinted to the front door, knocked its bolts aside, and kicked it wide open.

"We need help in here!" she screamed into the void, and numerous black-clad shapes, closer than she'd dared hope, responded at once, swarming from the tree line to converge on the cottage. Spotting Safia and Suds amongst them, she lifted her hand in a vague wave and realised she was still holding the gun. She launched it onto the path, as far from the cottage as she could get it. "It's all right. It's safe," she said, but the words caught in her throat, and she couldn't raise her voice to make herself heard.

The police, moving in a tight formation, had almost reached the garden gate. She left them to it and ran back inside.

SAFIA. MONDAY, 8:14 A.M.

The stillness in the cottage sent a chill through Safia. The kitchen was deserted, the smears of blood on the wall and hearth rug the only indication that something terrible had happened here.

"It's clear, Sarge," the ART lead told her, coming through from the next room. "And he took both bullets. Apparently, the doc's a damn good shot. ETA on medics?"

"Five," she said. "The choppers are responding as well." Though her tone betrayed nothing, she felt like sitting down and rocking for a while. From her vantage point in the woods, two gunshots had been plainly audible, and seeing Grace at the cottage door had only partially eased the dread that had made her walk away from her colleagues and dry-heave into the leaf litter.

"Tell them to put their foot down," the ART lead said. When he stepped away from the door, she hurried into an adjoining room that stank like a slaughterhouse. It took her a moment to fully comprehend the carnage in the comfortably furnished space, and she heard Suds swear beneath his breath, too appalled to put any real vehemence into it.

No one had opened the curtains, and officers were using torches to supplement the lamplight. She played her own across Kieran, unconscious and handcuffed, and surrounded by ART officers and a pool of clotted blood. She found Elin collapsed close by, but all she could see of Grace was the top of her head. Safia knew she should be standing back and organising the scene, requesting CSI, and removing surplus personnel. Instead, she looked up at Suds, who nodded gravely at her.

"Stay with Elin," she told him. "I've got Grace."

Half-hidden by a sofa and wholly focused on the limp child in front of her, Grace didn't react to Safia's approach. Two empty syringes lay by Amelia's thigh, and Grace was using a ventilation bag to force oxygen into her lungs.

"Hey." Safia kept her voice low. "What do you need?"

Grace looked up then, one eye stuck together with blood that was still trickling from an ugly wound splitting her brow. "I need her to breathe," she whispered. She pumped the bag again. "Where are the paramedics?"

"They'll be here any minute. Suds is with Elin."

Grace nodded, a sob hiccupping out of her. "Can you ask him to untie her hands? Kieran, he forced me to tie her, and I couldn't—I didn't have time. I had to leave her."

Safia squeezed her shoulder. "Don't worry, I'm sure Suds will sort that out. How's she doing?"

"I can't tell." Grace touched Amelia's cheek. "The drugs I've given her could take a while to kick in, but there's a chance she might not respond at all. She's been like this for at least twenty-four hours, and she's so tiny."

"Bet she takes after her mum, though."

Grace's smile was weary but genuine. "Stubborn as hell?"

"That's the one." Safia listened to her comms for a few seconds. "The Manchester chopper is landing just outside, and the paramedics are on the lane."

"Thank goodness," Grace said, and then froze, her fingers tense on the bag but not exerting any pressure. "Come on, that's it. That's it. Good girl." She placed a hand on Amelia's chest, and Safia watched it gently rise and fall.

"Is she doing that?" Safia asked.

"Yes." When Grace tickled Amelia's palm, the fingers twitched in response. "It's definitely her," she said.

ELIN. MONDAY, 8:26 A.M.

The man in the orange flight suit had a kind face and a friendly manner, but he wasn't Grace, and he wasn't telling Elin what she wanted to know.

"We're going to take you to Manchester Royal on the helicopter," he said. "But I think it'd be safer to put you to sleep first."

"No." Pushing at his hand sent pain lancing through her chest, but it stopped him injecting the anaesthetic he'd just drawn up.

"I need to speak to Grace," she said. "Please...*please* let me speak to her."

There was noise all around her: footsteps, furniture being shoved aside, shouted questions and responses; and she was cold and scared and drowning all over again, and she had lost sight of Grace and Amelia amidst the press of green and black and orange uniforms.

"Elin." Grace's voice bore that strange combination of sternness and tenderness that had become her trademark. She took Elin's flailing hands and nodded to someone beyond Elin's limited field of vision.

"Careful," she said. "That's perfect. Thanks, Suds."

A shuffle of movement, and Suds was gone again, leaving behind a bundle of blankets. When Grace rearranged it slightly, Elin caught a glimpse of tatty brown curls and a freckled nose obscured by a plastic mask. She felt Grace guide her hand to Amelia's forehead, and she wept as she touched her daughter for the first time in five days.

"Hey, sweetheart." She stroked a finger down Amelia's discoloured cheek, watching her eyelashes flutter. "Is she okay?" she asked Grace.

"She will be," Grace said. "She's poorly, but she's breathing for herself. She's going to Manchester Children's, so she'll be right next door to you at the Royal, and I'm going to stay with her. You've done all you can." Grace took the syringe from the HEMS doctor. "You can go to sleep for a while now."

That was good enough for Elin. "Tell her I love her," she said.

"Of course I will." Grace turned Elin's wrist to access her IV line. "Am I okay to give you this?"

"Mm." Elin found Amelia's hand and wrapped her own around it. There was a sting in her wrist, followed by warmth tracking up her arm, and Grace's murmurs of reassurance suddenly vanished, along with everything else.

SAFIA. MONDAY, 5:58 P.M.

The insistent clicking of fingers drew Safia's attention from her phone call. She turned to see Suds holding up his laptop at the far end of the room, its screen dominated by a Word doc reading, *Sit your arse down*.

She stuck two fingers up at him but abandoned her pacing to sink into the closest armchair. The surgical staff at Manchester Royal were letting her and Suds wait in one of the rooms set aside for relatives, and so far an endless stream of calls and things she needed to organise and authorise had been keeping her distracted. She dreaded to think what she would do when she finally got on top of it all.

"No, sir," she said, resting her head back as her face started to throb in synch with it. "I doubt anyone besides Grace will be able to give us a statement for the next twenty-four hours at least, and she's got enough on her plate, so I think it would be unwise to push her for one."

"I agree," Chevs said. "She's the closest thing we have to an independent witness, and I'd prefer to keep her on side if possible."

Safia bit her sore lip. The notion that Grace was somehow detached from all of this was a logical conclusion for him to have drawn, but if he'd seen her with Elin he certainly wouldn't be thinking of her as impartial.

"I'm sure that won't be a problem," Safia said. "She's over at the children's hospital with Amelia. I'm going across there as soon as we hear anything from the team working on Elin."

There was a squeak she recognised as Chevs's desk chair. He was leaning back as well, probably as tired and tense as she was.

"What's the latest on her condition?" he said, sounding genuinely concerned. Safia's preliminary overview of the scene at the cottage had not made for pleasant reading, and he had phoned her within minutes of its submission.

"She's still in surgery. Grace said the vest she was wearing mitigated some of the bullet's impact, but there was plenty of internal damage. The X-rays and CT scan in A&E also showed facial fractures, multiple rib fractures, and bruising around one of her kidneys from the first time Kieran beat her."

"Bloody hell." The chair squeaked again, its sound more pronounced as he shoved forward. "What's *his* prognosis?"

"He'll live." She hadn't really pursued updates beyond that. "Jo Shaw went to Leeds with him. She's going to let us know when he's out of theatre, but that won't be for hours yet. CSI are still at the cottage, and we're running his van through ANPR to build a picture of his movements. Grace gave us the address that she and Elin were sent to in Birmingham, so we have a team there as well."

"Is that where they smacked Lowry with the car?"

"Apparently so." Safia failed to keep the admiration from her voice, although she hadn't tried very hard. "CSI have retrieved a bullet from the local brickwork, which will no doubt match his gun, and we also have the bullet Grace took out of Elin. Everything, including the gun Elin lifted from the body on the Heath, is on its way to Ballistics. If it all pans out the way I expect, Lowry will be looking at multiple charges."

"Excellent," Chevs said. "He's still playing the infirmity card, but he's not going anywhere, so he can piss around as long as he likes. We have more than enough to be getting on with." He chortled. "Or rather, *you* have."

"Yes, sir." She used her free hand to massage the back of her neck. While she lacked Kami's talent with knotted muscles, the tension eased enough for her to check the wall clock without wincing.

"Safia?" Chevs's firm prompt brought her back to the call. It probably wasn't the first time he had said her name.

"Sir?"

"Good work on this one. If I'm honest, I thought it would go to complete rat shit, but you've managed to drag it out of the fire, so well done to you both. Rest assured you still have a job, and come back down here to tidy everything up when you're ready."

She blinked her vision clear and felt tears slide down her cheeks. She was too knackered to appreciate the sense of relief. "Thank you, sir."

"Yes, well." He coughed. He was far more comfortable delivering a bollocking than praise. "Keep in touch."

She kept hold of her phone after he ended the call, doing her usual review of its notifications: three emails, one missed call from a CSI, and a WhatsApp from Kami.

"We still have a job," she told Suds, who beamed at her over his screen. "He actually sounded quite chipper about it all."

"I think that calls for a cuppa." Suds came over to collect her mug. "Anything else on there?" he asked, nodding at her phone and overlooking her tear-streaked face.

She flicked through the emails. "Not really. Jo says the owner of the cottage has been brought in for questioning, and local teams are speaking to Kieran's close family and friends. They're also working on identifying the dead bloke from the Heath."

Suds switched the kettle on. "We're getting there, Saf. Slowly but surely."

"Yep." She knew this would seem strange to a layperson: the amount of legwork still to be done, even though one suspect had been caught red-handed and a mass of forensic evidence and witness testimony was stacked against the other. Confirming Kieran had only been working with one accomplice was paramount, though, and it was the main reason armed officers were currently keeping their own vigil outside theatre two, just down the corridor, and the paediatric High Dependency Unit.

She sipped the tea Suds handed her and opened Kami's WhatsApp message. It was a selfie of Kami and Bolly, its perimeter liberally decorated with bouquet and firework emojis. *We are very proud of you,* Kami had written. *Please come home before Bolly eats all your socks.*

Safia laughed and then started to cry in earnest. Without saying a word, Suds knelt in front of her and pulled her into his arms. She tensed, but she couldn't pretend she didn't need this. Clinging onto his sweater, she buried her face in his chest and for once let herself have a good bawl.

Grace. Tuesday, 2:45 a.m.

The nurse made a note on Amelia's chart and dimmed the light over her bed.

"Need anything?" she asked Grace.

Grace started to shake her head, but the nagging ache behind her left eye cut short the gesture. If the A&E doctor had had his way, she would have been admitted for neuro obs after he'd stitched her eyebrow back together and clucked his tongue at the mess she'd made of her arm, but that was never going to be a viable option.

"No, thank you," she said.

"You know where I am if you change your mind."

The nurse closed the door behind her, the frosted glass blurring the outline of the armed officer tasked to safeguard the HDU's newest arrival. Grace settled back in her chair and stroked Amelia's fingertips where they poked from the bandage that secured an IV. Once Amelia had stabilised, a bed bath and clean pyjamas had removed the reek of vomit and stale urine, and a warming blanket was slowly putting some colour back into her cheeks. Her fingers were still dusty with talc, and Grace smiled as the smell of Johnson's Baby Powder drifted up to her. It was such an archetypal childhood scent, synonymous with Sunday night bath times and stories told snuggled under the duvet.

A quiet knock broke into her chain of thought. The officer waited a beat and then opened the door a crack.

"DS Faris to see you," he said. For a big bruiser, he was very formal, and it took Grace a second or two to realise her visitor was

Safia. She stood abruptly, sending her chair screeching across the tiles, and felt the room dim even further as a wave of dizziness almost floored her.

"Elin?" She caught Safia's arm and used it to steady herself. "Is she okay?"

"Bloody hell, Grace." With more luck than judgement, Safia managed to manoeuvre her back to her chair. "Haven't we all had enough drama for one day? Stick your head between your knees or something."

It was sound advice, and from her stooped position Grace heard Safia pull up a chair and sit in it.

"Elin looks better than you," Safia said, her voice carrying past the high-pitched whine of Grace's tinnitus. "Or at the very least, she's being sensible enough to get some sleep."

"I'm guessing the anaesthetic has a lot to do with that," Grace muttered. She turned to face Safia, resting her head on her folded arms. "Is she really all right?"

"Her surgeon seemed to think so." Safia ripped a page from a notepad. "I wrote it all down and made him spell the hard stuff."

"Thank you." Grace scanned the summary for ominous findings, and then reread it once her pulse rate had returned to near-normal.

"What's the verdict?" Safia asked. "I came straight here, so I didn't have time to google."

Grace sat up properly, feeling brighter than she had in hours. "It's pretty good, all things considered. He's cleaned out the debris and repaired the damage from the bullet's track. There's extensive bruising to her lung, but that's to be expected, and he located and fixed the bleed that was making her lung collapse. She's anaemic and there's obvious infection, but her bloods aren't suggestive of sepsis."

"That sounds encouraging," Safia said.

Grace put the notes into her pocket. "Is anyone sitting with her?" She tried not to sound too plaintive, but she couldn't bear the thought of Elin being alone.

"Suds is there at the moment, and her parents left about an hour ago."

Grace retook Amelia's hand, smiling at her instinctive attempt to grip. "Elin doesn't need her parents, she needs this little dot."

Safia shuffled lower in her chair and stretched her legs out, reminding Grace that she wasn't the only one who'd declined medical attention of late. "Has she woken up yet?"

"Not properly," Grace said. "Her sats are improving, though, and all her injuries were minor. She was dry as a bone—we don't think she was given anything to drink for the last forty-eight hours or so—but her urine output is picking up now, which is a really good sign."

"And how are you?"

Grace stared at Safia, blindsided. "I have a headache," she admitted, but that was the tip of the iceberg, and Safia wasn't stupid. "And whenever I stop doing stuff and everything goes quiet"— she swallowed, tasting acid—"whenever that happens, I see him bringing that knife up, and I hear the gun fire, and it makes my wrists ache and my ears ring, and I wish I felt sorry for shooting him but I don't." The latter part came out in a rush of shame. Though she had admitted this to herself, the only other person who would truly understand was unconscious in the neighbouring hospital.

"I'm sure you don't need me to tell you that you did what you had to do," Safia said. "And that you saved two lives today, not to mention your own, and that you have bigger balls than the ballsiest thing ever."

If she'd intended to shock a laugh from Grace, she succeeded. "I don't know how I feel about that."

"Consider it a compliment." Safia groaned and hauled herself to her feet.

"We did okay in the end, didn't we?" Grace said.

"We did better than okay. And all the rest of it? I don't think you have a single thing to feel sorry about."

"Thanks, Safia." One thing Grace would never regret was making that call to the police.

Safia zipped up her jacket. Beyond the room's large window, heavy rain was blurring the lights of the city. "My pleasure," she said. "I won the coin toss, so I'm off to bed. Suds will keep you updated, but you can always phone me if you need me."

"I will."

The door clicked as it closed, the sound innocuous but enough to disturb Amelia, whose eyes flew open as she fought against the sheets.

"Hey, hey." Grace kept her voice to a murmur, but Amelia kicked harder, her back hitting the bedrail as the monitors registered her terror, and still she didn't make a sound. She raised a bandaged fist to her mouth and bit on her knuckles, her teeth working hard on the skin.

"Mouse?"

The nickname caught Amelia's attention, and for the first time she seemed to see Grace when she looked at her.

"You don't need to be quiet anymore," Grace said. "You've been so brave, sweetheart, but you and your mum are safe now, and you can cry if you want to."

Amelia's bottom lip quivered, and she clambered to her knees, taking in the room and the equipment before coming back to stare at Grace. Grace didn't move a muscle under the scrutiny. She was hardly daring to breathe.

"My name is Grace, and I'm a friend of your mum's. She asked me to stay with you because she's poorly as well." Grace wasn't sure what she should say or whether Amelia was awake enough to understand, but Amelia had swapped to sucking on her fist, and she seemed less likely to bolt over the side rail, so Grace persevered. "Your mum told me loads about you. She said she loves you very much, and that you like chocolate biscuits, and fish and chips, and driving really fast, and she says you're not naughty at all."

A faltering smile twitched at Amelia's lips, but it vanished as quickly as it had appeared, and she started to shiver.

"Where's my mummy?" she whispered. "I want my mummy."

"I know you do." Grace stood, half a plan formed and the rest taking shape. "I'll sort it. I'll get you to your mum, I promise."

Amelia held out her little finger. "Pinky promise?"

Grace nodded solemnly and shook on it. "Pinky promise."

❖

The ART officer probably hadn't expected to add "porter" to his job description, but he was game enough, and he stayed well behind the wheelchair and out of Amelia's sight until she was settled on Grace's lap.

The Central Manchester hospitals, although separate entities, comprised one massive interconnected building, allowing passage from one speciality to the next. This early in the morning, the corridors were largely empty, with only the odd medic wandering past, too bleary-eyed to question at what point they had started to heavily arm their auxiliary staff.

The ITU team had agreed to Amelia's transfer far more readily than Grace had anticipated, and Elin's nurse escorted them past the curtained bays to a cubicle at the far end of the unit. Its door was already open, the lighting bright above the bed at its centre, and Grace shook her head in disbelief as Elin smiled at them and managed a weak wave.

"Morning," she said. Her raspy voice told Grace she hadn't been off the ventilator for long, but she held out her arms to Amelia, who almost lost her IV in her haste to get to the bed.

"God, she's nippy," Grace said, amazed, as ever, by the resilience of sick children. She hung the drip from Elin's stand and watched Amelia curl into the crook of Elin's good arm. Amelia didn't need telling to be careful; she rested her palm against Elin's cheek and left it there for Elin to kiss.

"I missed you, love," Elin said, and rocked her gently as she whimpered.

Feeling like an intruder, Grace retreated toward the door. She was on the threshold when Elin called her name.

"Will you stay?" Elin asked, as Grace turned back. Amelia was humming softly, already half-asleep, her fingers twined in Elin's hair.

Grace nodded, unsure exactly what she was feeling but certain she didn't want to be anywhere else. She pulled a chair close to the bedside. She had countless questions to ask, and Elin's chart was right there at the foot of the bed, and she hadn't checked the monitors properly—

"Grace?"

When Grace raised her head, the room seemed to be melting around her.

"Mm. What?"

"That chair reclines."

"It does?"

"Just lean back. Suds almost ejected himself earlier."

Grace chuckled and then groaned at the sheer indulgence of comfortable leather and a clean pillow.

Elin touched the tip of Amelia's nose. "We take a lot of the little things for granted, don't we?" she said. She was bruised and pale and still obviously unwell, but she was holding Amelia tightly, and her smile was so contented that it erased every worry line from her face.

"I think everyone does that." Grace wondered whether she ever would again, though, and she saw the same question reflected in Elin's expression. She wished she could click her fingers and get them through the worst of it, but it didn't work like that. "It's going to take some time," she said.

"I know."

Grace turned out the lights, leaving them in the red-amber glow of the monitors.

"Go to sleep," she said. "It'll keep till tomorrow."

Safia. Friday, 1:35 p.m.

The rain timed its downpour to perfection, half-drowning Safia and Suds as they ran from the car, and then ceding to bright sunshine the instant they arrived at the hospital entrance.

"I won't miss the bloody weather," she told Jo, who cackled at her from the other end of the call. "I'm sure I've shrunk while I've been up here."

"I hope not," Jo said. "You were only titchy to start with."

Safia shook off her coat and led the way to the stairs. "I'm going to lose you in a minute, Jo. Cheers for the update. You've made my day, despite the drenching."

"Any time. I hope Suds's headache isn't too nasty."

Safia laughed. Jo had kept her promise of a pint the previous evening and promptly drunk Suds under the table.

"He'll live," she said. "I treated him to a Maccie's, and we've just called at Costa on the way in."

"You southerners are such lightweights. Give them all my best, won't you? And have a safe trip home."

"We will. I think I'll drive, though." Safia paused by the stairwell. "Be careful out there."

"You too, Saf. I'll speak to you soon."

The nurse on the ITU desk waved them through, rightly assuming they knew their way to Elin's cubicle.

"Hey, check you out," Safia said, pausing by the door to watch Elin take halting steps to a chair. She had been back in surgery on

Wednesday, having a pocket of infection drained from her lung, but she had improved in leaps and bounds since then.

"They're kicking us down to the HDU tomorrow," Grace said, arranging Elin's various attachments. "I think the Spanish might have something to do with it."

Safia was about to ask which Spaniards in particular were to blame, when she caught the tinny sound of singing coming from the blanket fort built over Amelia's camp bed. As an auntie numerous times over, she was well acquainted with *Dora the Explorer*.

"Hey, Mouse," she called. "Do you want a present?"

"Sí," Amelia said, and stuck her head out of the fort. She sidled over to Safia, confident enough in her company, though still wary with Suds.

Safia crouched and gave her a bag. "This is barfi, and it'll help you get good and plump. It's like fudge, only miles nicer. I got you mango, chocolate, and milk. Suds helped me choose them."

Amelia nodded, taking that latter point on board. "Thank you," she said, catching his eye briefly, and then scampered back to the fort.

Elin watched her go, waiting until the cartoon restarted. "She's still waking up screaming, but she got through last night without wetting the bed."

Safia sat in the chair that Suds brought over for her. "Poor little mite. I've woken up in a cold sweat a few times as well, and I was only there for a fraction of it."

"I think we've all been doing that," Grace said with marked understatement.

Elin's relapse had left Grace with deep purple circles beneath her eyes. Safia doubted she'd managed anywhere near enough sleep to suffer nightmares; she certainly hadn't been to the hotel room they'd booked for her. As Suds distributed the drinks they'd bought, Safia opened another bag of barfi, glad to push the calories onto the adult patients as well. "I got us some slightly more adventurous flavours: cardamom, rosewater, and pistachio. Help yourselves."

Lids popped off coffees, filling the room with the scent of hot milk, and Safia tutted her disapproval as she watched Grace dunk a piece of barfi. "You can take the girl out of the north..."

Grace shrugged, unabashed, and bit into the sweet. "So, where are we up to?"

Safia had an entire list to get through, but Jo had just bumped one development to the top of it. "Shall we start with some good news? The Crown Prosecution Service have reviewed both of your statements and examined the related evidence. They're satisfied the shooting was in self-defence, so you can stop worrying about any charges being brought, because it won't be happening."

Grace dropped the remaining chunk of barfi into her cup. It splashed coffee onto her fingers, but she didn't seem to notice. "Are you sure?"

"One hundred and ten percent positive," Safia said. "You did nothing wrong." She wondered whether Grace had subconsciously wanted the law to punish her for her lack of remorse, but it didn't base its decisions on such things, and that conversation Safia had had with her was one she'd take to her grave.

"What about Elin?" Grace asked.

"I'm getting to that. Due to the extreme nature of the circumstances that led to her actions, and her physical and mental condition at the time, the CPS will not be pursuing charges against her either, unless you have any objections."

Right on cue, Amelia clapped her hands as a song ended, and Grace smiled, as if reminded of whose life she had really been defending. She put her coffee down and reached for Elin's hand.

"No, I don't have any objections," she said, almost as an afterthought while she checked Elin's heart rate. "Breathe, Elin."

Elin sucked in a tremulous breath. "Have you charged Lowry?" she asked once she'd recovered enough to speak. Her statement had been painful for Safia to take, the details teased out over hours on the sole good day she'd had before the infection had really hit her, and one of the most difficult aspects had been getting her to talk about Lowry's involvement. The mention of his name had triggered so many monitor alarms that her nurse had eventually given up and muted them.

"As of this morning, he's been charged with one count of murder and two counts of attempted murder, amongst numerous other things."

"I hope assaulting you was one of them," Elin said.

"It was. You already know Ballistics matched his gun to the bullet found on the Heath. They also matched it to the one removed from you, and to one found embedded in a garden wall in Birmingham. He's been refused bail and transferred to Belmarsh Prison to await trial."

"I thought I'd be happy with that," Elin said, rubbing the skin around the split in her forehead. "That it'd draw a line under all this shit, but I still want to ask him what the hell he was thinking, and then wring his damn neck. What am I supposed to tell Mouse at Christmas when he doesn't show up for supper? 'He probably still loves you, but he also tried to murder you by default, because he was too proud to admit he needed help?'" Glancing at Amelia's bed, she unclenched her fist a finger at a time and sighed. "Will he get treatment for his drinking in there?"

"To some extent, yes," Safia said. "It's by no means a perfect program, but there is one." She closed her notes. "Shall we finish this another time?"

"No," Elin said. She looked at Grace, who nodded her accord. "We want to get it done."

Suds, who had an almost eidetic memory, didn't need a prompt. "Kieran Elson is still in the ITU," he said. "He's listed as critical but stable, so that's unchanged. We identified his accomplice as Darren Medway. Medway was local to these parts, and an old schoolmate of Kieran's, with no previous convictions. His late granddad owned the caravan Kieran sent you to, and his only recent connection to Kieran seems to have been a short stint working security at a Moorside club. Perhaps he needed the money, or Kieran had something to hold over him. We might never get to the bottom of that, unless Kieran feels chatty when he wakes up, which seems improbable. At any rate, we're certain Medway was the only other person involved." Suds took a couple of black-and-white photos from his bag and gave them to Elin. "We reviewed the CCTV footage you pulled the night Amelia was kidnapped. That's Kieran's van about three hundred yards from your Airbnb, and traces of his DNA and Medway's DNA were found on the clothing you bagged. If you ever decide to give up installing security for a living, you should consider a career in the police."

Elin turned the photos face down and coughed, sounding like an eighty-year-old bronchitic. "I'll pass, thanks."

"Don't blame you," Safia said. She spent a moment putting the photos away, aware that the next point might be distressing, but she didn't procrastinate for long. "Jo interviewed the owner of the cottage that Kieran rented. We initially thought he'd chosen it for its remote location, but the owner knew him of old. Apparently, Kieran and his dad would stay there when Kieran was younger. His sister wasn't interested, but Thomas would take Kieran at least twice a year to shoot and fish. The owner remembered them when Kieran phoned her to book. He said he was going back there to mark his dad's anniversary."

Safia stooped and dropped her notepad into her bag. She wanted to stay hidden down there and let Suds deal with this last part, but she knew the responsibility was hers. She sat back up and leaned forward. "The cases against Kieran and Lowry are very likely to go to trial, which means we will need you both to testify twice." She opened her hands, abandoning the standard script. "I'm so sorry. I wish there was another way, but there isn't, unless they plead guilty."

As with most things, Elin and Grace took the news stoically, no doubt resigned to sacrificing the next few months in pursuit of resolution.

"Amelia won't be involved, will she?" Elin asked.

"No, she's far too young." Safia could still hear her chattering along to the cartoon. "And we'll try our best to minimise the disruption for you all."

The music and the commentary stopped abruptly, and Amelia came wandering over to Elin, barefoot and with her thumb in her mouth.

Elin ruffled her hair. "Nap time?"

Amelia nodded and held out her arms to Grace, who scooped her up. She squirmed into a comfy spot like a cat bedding down for the night and fell asleep just as suddenly, her mouth falling open around her thumb. Grace took her arm and gently lowered it.

"I'm the stand-in while Elin heals," she said.

"Are you now?" Safia didn't need her skills as a detective to interpret these clues. This wasn't the same Grace Kendal who had lived in that sterile London flat. Despite her weariness, she seemed to have found a sort of peace, and there was a spark of mischief in the innocent look she gave Safia.

"I'm thinking about spending more time up here," she said. She sipped her coffee, the very portrait of nonchalance. "Elin and I have been discussing the benefits."

"We compiled a list," Elin said, and began to count the items off on her fingers. "The air's cleaner, the cost of living is much cheaper, and you get proper snow in winter."

Grace took up the mantle. "They serve chips with gravy, and no one looks at you funny if you ask for barm cakes."

"These are all very important things," Safia said.

Suds sniffed. "What's a barm cake?"

"I rest my case," Grace said.

Safia dragged Suds to his feet. "On that note, we should make a move so we can beat the traffic. I'll phone you in a couple of days, unless something crops up in the meantime."

"Give my love to London," Grace said.

Safia laughed. "I will, but don't hurry back." Surveying the three of them, she nodded in satisfaction. "The north definitely suits you."

GRACE. 24TH SEPTEMBER, 1:30 P.M.

That's the one." Grace pointed to a mid-terrace Victorian with a pale green exterior wash and large bay windows. "She said it was pea green. That's not bloody pea green."

"It's more of a sage," Elin said, performing a neat parallel park into the only available space. "And it's very pretty."

Stiff from the long journey, she got out of the car in stages and took the arm Grace offered her, as Amelia skipped off into the front garden. Stopping just shy of the gate, she ran her fingers through her fringe. Although she'd had the new hairstyle for over a month, she was still dubious about it.

"Can you see it?" she asked.

Grace cupped Elin's face and kissed her forehead, her lips touching the raised edge of the scar. "No, I can't see it."

Elin smiled fondly. "You never see it, though."

"They won't either," Grace said, and opened the gate.

Their knock on the front door prompted frenetic barking and hurried footsteps heading in multiple directions. It was Safia who greeted them, gathering them for hugs and then peering around for the missing party.

"She's on your lawn, picking you some flowers." Elin held out a ribbon-bound bouquet. "She said ours were rubbish."

Safia laughed as Kami—wiping what looked like soot from her face—came to collect their overnight bags.

"Welcome to our new home," Safia said. "Come in and drink lots of wine."

A high-pitched cry of "Saf! Saf!" made her turn back, and she crouched, cooing at the handful of daisies and dandelions Amelia presented to her. "Thank you, Mouse. Those are beautiful. Do you remember Kami?"

Amelia's thumb went into her mouth, and she wrapped an arm around Grace's leg. She had only met Kami a couple of times, and she was still suspicious of strangers. Grace picked her up.

"Shall we go and find out what smells so good?" she said, handing Safia a Tupperware tub as they walked into the hallway. "I'd like to say it's from an old family recipe passed down through generations, but that'd be a filthy lie. I cheated and used a jar of sauce."

"Fabulous," Safia said. "You can't go wrong with a good dollop of Dolmio." The BYOB housewarming had been her idea, where the B stood for bolognaise in their culture-clash potluck. "Spag's on the boil. We also have biryani, chicken karahi, all the trimmings including garlic bread, and some seekh kebabs to chuck on the barbecue."

She showed them through to the back garden, where an unseasonably warm autumn was dappling the long lawn with sunshine. She and Kami had only moved in a month ago, but the path was already lined with terracotta pots brimming with herbs, reminding Grace of the ones she'd rescued from her old house. Even now, Elin's car bore a vague scent of rosemary and lemon thyme, and occasional eight-legged passengers were still revealing themselves at inopportune moments, much to Amelia's amusement.

A hydrangea at the bottom of the garden suddenly parted, and a blur of dog, all tail and tongue, made a beeline for them. Amelia yelped with delight, half-throttling Grace in her eagerness to get down. When Grace lowered her to the path, she threw her arms around the dog's neck and shrieked through an enthusiastic face-licking. Seconds later, they'd chased each other back into the bushes.

"Meet Bolly," Safia said.

Elin was tracking the sound of giggles and snuffling mutt. "I guess we're getting a dog, then." She didn't sound at all bothered by the idea, and she relaxed onto the garden bench, stretching out her legs and putting an arm around Grace, who leaned into her warmth.

"It's lovely here," Grace said.

"We were lucky to find it," Safia said, pouring wine for Grace and Elin, and juice for herself and Kami. "We're still fixing bits of it up, but things have generally stopped leaking and falling apart." She raised her glass. "Cheers."

"Cheers," Elin said. "Here's to the end of it all."

The last time they had seen Safia, the jury foreman had just delivered its verdict on Kieran Elson. Elin's testimony at that trial had taken three days, double what she had spent testifying against Lowry. Both men had received life sentences, with minimum terms in excess of twenty years. With the case out of the headlines, the phone calls from the media had gradually tapered off and then ceased altogether, and a move to a cottage in a small village had returned Elin, Grace, and Amelia to relative anonymity. People did tend to recognise them, but the community was down-to-earth and largely focused on farming, so the novelty of quasi-celebrities in their midst was short-lived.

"How's the new job, Grace?" Kami asked from somewhere within a plume of grill smoke.

"Smashing." Grace kicked off her sandals and played her toes through the grass. "Manchester Royal is a regional trauma centre, so there's plenty to keep me busy, and I've picked up some shifts for their HEMS as well, on the actual chopper this time, not just the car."

"She hates flying," Elin said, a distinct note of pride in her voice, "but she does it anyway."

"I think I rediscovered my mettle sometime around February." Grace sipped her wine and nudged Elin's foot. "It's been quite the year for new experiences."

Safia cocked her head as the oven timer pinged. "On that note, who's up for Pakistani, Bengali, and English-slash-Italian fusion cuisine?"

They ate on a picnic rug, lighting candles in lanterns and lazing back on beanbag cushions as the sun set and bats started to flit through the trees. Amelia dipped parathas into everything, sharing them with Bolly, and then fell asleep on Elin's knee. Grace, her cheeks hot with good food and wine, plaited a daisy chain crown and set it on Elin's head.

"Are you drunk, missus?" Elin said.

"I might not be totally sober," Grace admitted. She thumped a hollow into their beanbag and curled up beside Elin, resting her head on Elin's chest. Above them, a clear sky showed countless constellations, some of which she could name, most of which she had yet to learn. She heard Amelia fuss as a night terror gripped her and then quieten again as Elin murmured a song Amelia had been trying to teach them. When Elin faltered, Kami took over, singing in Bengali, the gentle lilt to her voice enough to soothe Amelia completely.

Grace found Elin's hand and pressed it to her chest. "You make my heart happy," she whispered. "Both of you." It was true, and she'd known it for months, but she'd never quite found the right time to say it.

Elin didn't reply. She didn't need to. Her eyes shone in the candlelight, and she kissed Grace slowly. Grace caught her breath, seeing stars surrounded by more stars as she swayed against the cushion.

"Oh," she said. If she hadn't been drunk before, she certainly felt it now. "Well, that's made every bit of me happy."

Elin lay back with her, one hand resting over Amelia's, her other clasped around Grace's. They were quiet for a long while, long enough for Safia to assume they'd fallen asleep. She covered them with a blanket and tiptoed inside with Kami.

Grace yawned and turned to face Elin. "I could stay here all night."

"You say that now, but you'd regret it in the morning."

"Mm, probably."

"How about we have five more minutes?"

"Ten," Grace countered, snuggling closer, "and you have a deal."

Elin arched an eyebrow. "Did Mouse teach you that?"

"Yes. She said you always fall for it."

"Jesus wept." Elin's shoulders shook as she laughed. "What have I done?"

"Hey, you started this." Grace poked her in the ribs, an unsubtle but effective reminder. "And you're bloody stuck with me now."

"Oh, I am, am I?" Elin kissed her again with that sweet familiar urgency, and then brushed her lips across Grace's cheek. "I think I can live with that. There's no one in the world I'd rather be stuck with."

The End

About the Author

Cari Hunter lives in the northwest of England with her wife, their cats, and a field full of sheep. She works full-time as a paramedic and dreams up stories in her spare time.

Cari enjoys long, windswept, muddy walks in her beloved Peak District. In the summer she can usually be found sitting in the garden with her feet up, scribbling in her writing pad. Although she doesn't like to boast, she will admit that she makes a very fine Bakewell tart.

No Good Reason, the first in the Dark Peak series, won a 2015 Rainbow Award for Best Mystery and was a finalist in the 2016 Lambda and Goldie Awards. Its sequel, *Cold to the Touch*, won a Goldie and a Rainbow Award for Best Mystery. *A Quiet Death*, the final book in the series, was a finalist in the 2018 Lambda and Goldie Awards, and won the 2017 Rainbow Award for Best Mystery. She has since won Goldies for *Alias* and *Breathe*, with *Alias* also winning best Lesbian Mystery and Best Lesbian Book at the 2019 Rainbow Awards.

Cari can be contacted at: carihunter@rocketmail.com

Books Available from Bold Strokes Books

Bury Me in Shadows by Greg Herren. College student Jake Chapman is forced to spend the summer at his dying grandmother's home and soon finds danger from long-buried family secrets. (978-1-63555-993-4)

Can't Leave Love by Kimberly Cooper Griffin. Sophia and Pru have no intention of falling in love, but sometimes love happens when and where you least expect it. (978-1-636790041-1)

Free Fall at Angel Creek by Julie Tizard. Detective Dee Rawlings and aircraft accident investigator Dr. River Dawson use conflicting methods to find answers when a plane goes missing, while overcoming surprising threats, and discovering an unlikely chance at love. (978-1-63555-884-5)

Love's Compromise by Cass Sellars. For Piper Holthaus and Brook Myers, will professional dreams and past baggage stop two hearts from realizing they are meant for each other? (978-1-63555-942-2)

Not All a Dream by Sophia Kell Hagin. Hester has lost the woman she loved and the world has descended into relentless dark and cold. But giving up will have to wait when she stumbles upon people who help her survive. (978-1-63679-067-1)

Protecting the Lady by Amanda Radley. If Eve Webb had known she'd be protecting royalty, she'd never have taken the job as bodyguard, but as the threat to Lady Katherine's life draws closer, she'll do whatever it takes to save her, and may just lose her heart in the process. (978-1-63679-003-9)

The Secrets of Willowra by Kadyan. A family saga of three women, their homestead called Willowra in the Australian outback, and the secrets that link them all. (978-1-63679-064-0)

Trial by Fire by Carsen Taite. When prosecutor Lennox Roy and public defender Wren Bishop become fierce adversaries in a headline-grabbing arson case, their attraction ignites a passion that leads them both to question their assumptions about the law, the truth, and each other. (978-1-63555-860-9)

Turbulent Waves by Ali Vali. Kai Merlin and Vivien Palmer plan their future together as hostile forces make their own plans to destroy what they have, as well as all those they love. (978-1-63679-011-4)

Unbreakable by Cari Hunter. When Dr. Grace Kendal is forced at gunpoint to help an injured woman, she is dragged into a nightmare where nothing is quite as it seems, and their lives aren't the only ones on the line. (978-1-63555-961-3)

Veterinary Surgeon by Nancy Wheelton. When dangerous drugs are stolen from the veterinary clinic, Mitch investigates and Kay becomes a suspect. As pride and professions clash, love seems impossible. (978-1-63679-043-5)

A Different Man by Andrew L. Huerta. This diverse collection of stories chronicling the challenges of gay life at various ages shines a light on the progress made and the progress still to come. (978-1-63555-977-4)

All That Remains by Sheri Lewis Wohl. Johnnie and Shantel might have to risk their lives—and their love—to stop a werewolf intent on killing. (978-1-63555-949-1)

Beginner's Bet by Fiona Riley. Phenom luxury Realtor Ellison Gamble has everything, except a family to share it with, so when a mix-up brings youthful Katie Crawford into her life, she bets the house on love. (978-1-63555-733-6)

Dangerous Without You by Lexus Grey. Throughout their senior year in high school, Aspen, Remington, Denna, and Raleigh face challenges in life and romance that they never expect. (978-1-63555-947-7)

Desiring More by Raven Sky. In this collection of steamy stories, a rich variety of lovers find themselves desiring more, more from a lover, more from themselves, and more from life. (978-1-63679-037-4)

Jordan's Kiss by Nanisi Barrett D'Arnuck. After losing everything in a fire Jordan Phelps joins a small lounge band and meets pianist Morgan Sparks, who lights another blaze, this time in Jordan's heart. (978-1-63555-980-4)

Late City Summer by Jeanette Bears. Forced together for her wedding, Emily Stanton and Kate Alessi navigate their lingering passion for one another against the backdrop of New York City and World War II, and a summer romance they left behind. (978-1-63555-968-2)

Love and Lotus Blossoms by Anne Shade. On her path to self-acceptance and true passion, Janesse will risk everything—and possibly everyone—she loves. (978-1-63555-985-9)

Love in the Limelight by Ashley Moore. Marion Hargreaves, the finest actress of her generation, and Jessica Carmichael, the world's biggest pop star, rediscover each other twenty years after an ill-fated affair. (978-1-63679-051-0)

Suspecting Her by Mary P. Burns. Complications ensue when Erin O'Connor falls for top real estate saleswoman Catherine Williams while investigating racism in the real estate industry; the fallout could end their chance at happiness. (978-1-63555-960-6)

Two Winters by Lauren Emily Whalen. A modern YA retelling of Shakespeare's *The Winter's Tale* about birth, death, Catholic school, improv comedy, and the healing nature of time. (978-1-63679-019-0)

Busy Ain't the Half of It by Frederick Smith and Chaz Lamar Cruz. Elijah and Justin seek happily-ever-afters in LA, but are they too busy to notice happiness when it's there? (978-1-63555-944-6)

Calumet by Ali Vali. Jaxon Lavigne and Iris Long had a forbidden small-town romance that didn't last, and the consequences of that love will be uncovered fifteen years later at their high school reunion. (978-1-63555-900-2)

Her Countess to Cherish by Jane Walsh. London Society's material girl realizes there is more to life than diamonds when she falls in love with a nonbinary bluestocking. (978-1-63555-902-6)

Hot Days, Heated Nights by Renee Roman. When Cole and Lee meet, instant attraction quickly flares into uncontrollable passion, but their connection might be short lived as Lee's identity is tied to her life in the city. (978-1-63555-888-3)

Never Be the Same by MA Binfield. Casey meets Olivia and sparks fly in this opposites attract romance that proves love can be found in the unlikeliest places. (978-1-63555-938-5)

Quiet Village by Eden Darry. Something not quite human is stalking Collie and her niece, and she'll be forced to work with undercover reporter Emily Lassiter if they want to get out of Hyam alive. (978-1-63555-898-2)

Shaken or Stirred by Georgia Beers. Bar owner Julia Martini and home health aide Savannah McNally attempt to weather the storms brought on by a mysterious blogger trashing the bar, family feuds they knew nothing about, and way too much advice from way too many relatives. (978-1-63555-928-6)

The Fiend in the Fog by Jess Faraday. Can four people on different trajectories work together to save the vulnerable residents of East London from the terrifying fiend in the fog before it's too late? (978-1-63555-514-1)

The Marriage Masquerade by Toni Logan. A no strings attached marriage scheme to inherit a Maui B&B uncovers unexpected attractions and a dark family secret. (978-1-63555-914-9)

Flight SQA016 by Amanda Radley. Fastidious airline passenger Olivia Lewis is used to things being a certain way. When her routine is changed by a new, attractive member of the staff, sparks fly. (978-1-63679-045-9)

Home Is Where the Heart Is by Jenny Frame. Can Archie make the countryside her home and give Ash the fairytale romance she desires? Or will the countryside and small village life all be too much for her? (978-1-63555-922-4)

Moving Forward by PJ Trebelhorn. The last person Shelby Ryan expects to be attracted to is Iris Calhoun, the sister of the man who killed her wife four years and three thousand miles ago. (978-1-63555-953-8)

Poison Pen by Jean Copeland. Debut author Kendra Blake is finally living her best life until a nasty book review and exposed secrets threaten her promising new romance with aspiring journalist Alison Chatterley. (978-1-63555-849-4)

Seasons for Change by KC Richardson. Love, laughter, and trust develop for Shawn and Morgan throughout the changing seasons of Lake Tahoe. (978-1-63555-882-1)

Summer Lovin' by Julie Cannon. Three different women, three exotic locations, one unforgettable summer. What do you think will happen? (978-1-63555-920-0)

Unbridled by D. Jackson Leigh. A visit to a local stable turns into more than riding lessons between a novel writer and an equestrian with a taste for power play. (978-1-63555-847-0)

VIP by Jackie D. In a town where relationships are forged and shattered by perception, sometimes even love can't change who you really are. (978-1-63555-908-8)

Yearning by Gun Brooke. The sleepy town of Dennamore has an irresistible pull on those who've moved away. The mystery Darian Benson and Samantha Pike uncover will change them forever, but the love they find along the way just might be the key to saving themselves. (978-1-63555-757-2)

A Turn of Fate by Ronica Black. Will Nev and Kinsley finally face their painful past and relent to their powerful, forbidden attraction? Or will facing their past be too much to fight through? (978-1-63555-930-9)

Desires After Dark by MJ Williamz. When her human lover falls deathly ill, Alex, a vampire, must decide which is worse, letting her go or condemning her to everlasting life. (978-1-63555-940-8)

Her Consigliere by Carsen Taite. FBI agent Royal Scott swore an oath to uphold the law, and criminal defense attorney Siobhan Collins pledged her loyalty to the only family she's ever known, but will their love be stronger than the bonds they've vowed to others, or will their competing allegiances tear them apart? (978-1-63555-924-8)

In Our Words: Queer Stories from Black, Indigenous, and People of Color Writers. Stories selected by Anne Shade and edited by Victoria Villaseñor. Comprising both the renowned and emerging voices of Black, Indigenous, and People of Color authors, this thoughtfully curated collection of short stories explores the intersection of racial and queer identity. (978-1-63555-936-1)

Measure of Devotion by CF Frizzell. Disguised as her late twin brother, Catherine Samson enters the Civil War to defend the Constitution as a Union soldier, never expecting her life to be altered by a Gettysburg farmer's daughter. (978-1-63555-951-4)

Not Guilty by Brit Ryder. Claire Weaver and Emery Pearson's day jobs clash, even as their desire for each other burns, and a discreet sex-only arrangement is the only option. (978-1-63555-896-8)

Opposites Attract: Butch/Femme Romances by Meghan O'Brien, Aurora Rey, Angie Williams. Sometimes opposites really do attract. Fall in love with these butch/femme romance novellas. (978-1-63555-784-8)

Swift Vengeance by Jean Copeland, Jackie D, Erin Zak. A journalist becomes the subject of her own investigation when sudden strange, violent visions summon her to a summer retreat and into the arms of a killer's possible next victim. (978-1-63555-880-7)

Under Her Influence by Amanda Radley. On their path to #truelove, will Beth and Jemma discover that reality is even better than illusion? (978-1-63555-963-7)

Wasteland by Kristin Keppler & Allisa Bahney. Danielle Clark is fighting against the National Armed Forces and finds peace as a scavenger, until the NAF general's daughter, Katelyn Turner, shows up on her doorstep and brings the fight right back to her. (978-1-63555-935-4)

When in Doubt by VK Powell. Police officer Jeri Wylder thinks she committed a crime in the line of duty but can't remember, until details emerge pointing to a cover-up by those close to her. (978-1-63555-955-2)

Lightning Source UK Ltd.
Milton Keynes UK
UKHW040650050922
408358UK00001B/217